Children of the Sun

Book One of
The First People

HERU PTAH

SUNRASON BOOKS

NEW YORK CHARLOTTE KINGSTON

To Sunshine

Thank you Queen

I appreciate you

_4/25/23_

Published by
SUNRASON BOOKS

instagram: @eyeofheru
herumind@gmail.com

Copyright 2022 Henry Heru Ptah Richards
Design and Layout by Henry Heru Ptah Richards
Cover Painted by: Mshindo I. Kuumba

Book ISBN: 978-0-9852881-2-9

Published 2022
Printed in the United States of America

For Ena

ACT ONE
THE LIGHTNING
STORM

1

He rose from every ocean in every time. He was the size as far as the eye could see or imagine. His eyes were islands, the light of yellow moons. His teeth were mountains. His nostrils were chasms. His mouth was a black hole. His breath was in one moment a vacuum and the other a whirlwind. His spittle was torrential rain. His tongue was forked and forged of fire. His skin was scales made of meteors. He was a serpent coiled around all creation. He was chaos, he was corruption, he was rage—he was fear.

She stood on the mountaintop as the waters crashed against its exterior. The snout of the serpent was a light-year away and yet felt immediate. She could feel all of creation tremble below and above her. She was afraid but she held fast. She held the staff firmly in both hands. She chanted her name, and the staff became alive—bright as the noon sun—and the light stung the serpent's eyes. He roared, he reared, he raged forward and de-voured her.

2

Sochima was amazed and afraid at the same time. He could feel the goosebumps rising on his brown skin. During the story, his six-year-old eyes never blinked. "Did you know he would eat you?" he asked.

"He swallowed me, but he did not eat me. And yes, I knew he would," Nana answered.

"Then why did you go there? Why did you let him eat you, swallow you?" Sochima asked.

"Because he had something I needed, and it was inside of him, deep inside of him, and it was the only way I would be able to find it."

"Did you find it?" Sochima asked.

Nana smiled. "Yes."

"Woooow. And how did you get out?"

She looked at him, then looked up and whispered, "I'll tell you another time."

Sochi, short for Sochima, sat beside his grandmother, legs crossed, on her hospital bed. He turned and looked back at his mother, Gabrielle, a sienna-complexioned woman in her late thirties who stood in the doorway. A doctor in a white coat stood beside her. They spoke in hushed tones, and their faces were very somber. The joy and wonder previously in the room from Nana's story went away.

Nana was sixty-nine, old enough to have lived a full life but young enough to still have a lot of life in her. For most of her life, she was healthy and full of energy. Until last year when she sleep-walked, which she had never done before, and left home and didn't come back, and she didn't answer her phone. She was lost for three days, and the family filed a missing person's report. A police officer found her, sitting in her coat, nightgown, and slippers, peacefully on a bench, holding her walking stick, in Meridian Park in Washington, DC, for they lived in the District of Columbia.

Physically she seemed fine despite being dirty from being outside and unwashed for three-plus days. Mentally she was out of sorts and couldn't explain where she had been for the three days and made a fuss about everyone making a fuss about her. She didn't calm down until Sochima hugged her. Since he was born, they had a special bond. She named him in fact. She named his sister Aminata as well. Aminata and Nana used to be very close. However, Ami was twelve and now preferred to spend her days more with her friends than her nan.

They took Nana to the hospital, and she was diagnosed with FTD, Frontotemporal Dementia. It was not unusual for older people to develop dementia, but FTD was more common among the young—those under sixty. It was significant for its virulence. A few months later, Nana went to bed and didn't wake up, and for a whole month she was in a coma. When Nana finally came out of her coma, she was unable to speak fluently or feed herself because she had forgotten how.

She wouldn't eat from anyone, only Sochima. He attentively sat at her bedside spoon-feeding her porridge and wiping away the dribble that would fall from her mouth. Their bond grew even stronger. They would spend hours having great conversations. However, Sochi seemed more like he was talking to himself. Nana soon lost the power of speech, or so it appeared. Sochima and her still communicated, and he often acted as her translator. Yet, despite everyone's best efforts, Nana was not getting better. Nana was dying.

3

Aminata sat in the principal's office. The principal sighed disappointedly. They were looking over Ami's latest report card. Ami had anticipated she would receive poor marks this grading period, but even she was surprised at how badly she had done. Ami went to a very prestigious private school. The children of senators, celebrities, and CEOs went there. Ami got in based on her exceptional academic achievement. She had been so exceptional that at age twelve, she was already a junior in high school and was taking a few college-level courses.

"Is there something wrong at home?" the principal asked her. Aminata could have told him that her father was a marine and that he had died in combat a year ago. She could have also told him that her grandmother, who lived with her, who she was very close with, had fallen into a near vegetative state within the last few months. "No," she replied.

The principal could sense that Aminata was holding back. There was sadness in her shoulders. "Aminata, you are one of our best students. And we're happy to have you here. So, I am going to look at this report card as an anomaly rather than a new pattern. But I need you to get back to being the student you've always been."

"Okay," Ami replied.

"Also, if you ever need to talk, our counselors are here for you."

"Okay," Ami replied.

"And finally, I'll need you to have your report card signed by your mom and let her know that I'll need to have a meeting with her."

Ami sighed. "Okay."

4

"Hey Amy," a girl called to Aminata.

Aminata's nickname was Ami (pronounced *Ah-me*), but everyone called her Amy at school. The desire to be liked can be a powerful thing. It can become so strong it can feel like a need. "There is no such thing as peer pressure," Nana always told Aminata. "It is all self-pressure. It is the pressure you put on yourself to fit in with others instead of following your spirit." What Nana said sounded wise, but Nana had not been twelve in a very long time, and not in the time Aminata lived in, where there were literally apps to gauge your popularity. How does a teenager with no noteworthy accomplishments have over one hundred thousand followers? It helped to already look like a supermodel. Aminata was twelve, and she looked twelve in a land of giants. The other high schoolers looked so big, especially the girls. They looked and dressed like grown women. Aminata felt out of place, awkward, and unattractive.

Nana was Ami's first teacher, and she had taught her well. Aminata read over a hundred books by age five and was leagues ahead of everyone in her age group. There was a competitive thrill that came from wanting to be the best. Then she would notice how the other children would groan and murmur whenever she answered a question. Even at this school, where she was among the best and brightest, even in a classroom of children four years older than her, she felt like a mutant. After a while, all the sighs and the murmurs weighed on her, and she kept her hand down when she knew the answer.

One day a girl called to her, "Hey Amy." Ami was so surprised she was talking to her; she didn't bother correcting her on the pronunciation of her name. Ami rarely said her name in full. Aminata sounded too formal. The only person who ever called her Aminata was Nana, and mistaking Amy for Ami wasn't an egregious offense. The sixteen-year-old needed help with a chemistry problem. Aminata was happy to help her—the first time, and the second, and the third. The girl was very popular, and she invited Aminata into her circle of friends. She wasn't one of them. She was more like their little mascot. Aminata knew they were using her, but at least they were talking to her, and she didn't feel so out of place.

5

Aminata got on the metro at the Tenleytown station. She was the only one of her friends who took the metro to and from school. Most of them were either picked up by their parents or their driver. Now and again, they'd offer to give her a ride home, and Ami would politely refuse. She would say the metro was only a few blocks away and it was a short ride. This wasn't the truth. The ride could be anywhere from thirty to forty minutes. The truth was she didn't want them seeing where she lived. Brightwood was a good middle-income neighborhood, but it wasn't Tenleytown where their school was located, or Adams Morgan or Dupont Circle, where many of her friends lived. Children can't help but see you as different when they see how different from them you live. And it wasn't that she believed they would make fun of her, but they might pity her, which she felt was worse.

Aminata didn't mind the long ride as it gave her a chance to start on her homework. At least that's what she used to do. Recently she found herself just listening to her headphones, saving her homework until she got home, and sometimes not doing it at all.

She heard a great deal of noise coming from the other end of the car. Six girls her age had gotten on at the last stop. They were being very loud and very profane. They were so loud Aminata heard them over her headphones with the volume cranked to the highest. They may have been part of a gang. It was best to look away and pay them no mind; otherwise, she might draw their attention. However, they were cursing and being so loud, Aminata could not help but look—and looked longer than she intended because one of the girls looked very familiar.

6

Amaris and her friends got on the Red Line metro at Dupont Circle. They made their presence known to everyone; laughing and cursing; talking about girls they did not like and boys they did. They were teenage girls, but they spoke like drunk sailors. They knew people were watching them, and they did not care. Amaris was thirteen with a cinnamon complexion and straight black hair, which she wore in cornrows and two long braids. All the girls were her friends, but Marisol was her best friend. Amaris and Marisol—they were the two Maris. Amaris was Mari-1 and Marisol was Mari-2. Mari-2 saw something and brought it to Mari-1's attention. "Yo, why that girl looking at you?" she said.

"Who?" Amaris asked.

"That girl over there," Marisol jutted her chin in Aminata's direction.

Amaris turned and saw the chocolate-complexioned girl at the other end of the car with her mop of woolly hair, her earbuds on and her head in her phone. It had been six years since she last saw her, they had both changed a good deal since then, but Amaris recognized her right away. That was Ami. They used to be friends, best friends in fact—but that was a long time ago.

"She nobody, forget her," Amaris said.

"Well, if she keep looking over here I'ma go punch her in her face," Marisol said.

Their stop came, and as the girls were loudly getting off, Amaris did not look at Aminata, but she violently bumped into her shoulder as she walked by. Aminata was surprised and hurt by this, but she did not say or do anything. Amaris was quite different from the girl she once knew. It was obvious she and her friends were fishing for a fight, and Ami had no desire to get jumped and stomped on. Hopefully, she would not run into these girls again. Aminata and Amaris used to be friends, but whoever Amaris had become, Aminata didn't like at all.

7

Amaris lived in Barry Farm, which depending on the year was either the number one or number two worst neighborhood in Washington, DC. Her family moved here two years ago when her mother could no longer afford their apartment in Navy Yard.

Navy Yard was far from the best neighborhood in the city, but it was better than Barry Farm.

You don't live in bad neighborhoods, you survive them, and no one survives alone. There was a strong gang presence in Barry Farm. Amaris saw it as soon as she moved in—and as she saw it, she was either going to get jumped into a gang or jumped on every day. She figured one beating was better than several, and hopefully her sacrifice would keep her mother, and brother and sister safe.

Three years ago, her father, Javier went to El Salvador for the funeral of his cousin Manuel. Customs detained Javier at the airport on his way home. He was born in El Salvador and came to America when he was nine. At eighteen, he drove a car and picked Manuel up from a party, not knowing his cousin had just beaten a man almost to death. Days later, his cousin was arrested and eventually deported. Javier was also charged as an accomplice. Javier was unaware of this, and a warrant was issued for his arrest but never executed. Javier had no idea about the warrant. He got into no further legal trouble, so the warrant sat there, for twenty years, until a customs agent decided to do a very thorough check. After being detained for a year, Javier pled guilty to the charge and received no additional jail time. Nevertheless, it was a felony conviction. Immigration revoked his residency, and he was sent back to El Salvador.

Losing her father upended Amaris's entire family. The burden of supporting a family of three children and paying for Javier's legal expenses now fell squarely on her mother. Amaris had a brother and sister, Dieu and Alta, who were four-year-old twins. Her mother could no longer afford to pay for their daycare and was forced to send the twins away to live with Amaris's grandmother in Virginia, for which she paid her a weekly stipend. Now it was just Amaris and her mother living in their house.

Amaris's home was modest, but it was clean, and always had the smell of good cooking. Her mother, Samantha, an almond-complexioned Cuban woman in her late thirties, was in a hurry to get to work. She worked two jobs, taking care of an elderly couple during the day and working as a hostess at a restaurant at night. It was exhausting but doable. She was on her way to the restaurant and was peeved that Amaris was just getting home. "Mari why are you just getting in?" she asked.

"Sorry," Mari said.

"Don't say sorry. You know I only ask you one thing, which is to come home right after school."

Her mother looked at her, expecting Amaris to say something. "What? You told me not to say sorry."

"Don't get smart, mija. I know what you were doing. Hanging out with those girls."

"My friends."

"They're not your friends."

"Whatever," Amaris said dismissively.

"Don't whatever me."

"I don't mean to, but you stay getting on me about my friends."

"Because they are not your friends, Mari. They're not good for you, and they're going to bring you down."

"Well, you moved me here. You didn't expect me to make friends? Well, these are the girls that are here, so I made friends," Mari argued.

At that moment, the weight of working two jobs and raising three children felt unbearably heavy. Samantha felt it in her shoulders and her neck. She clasped her hands together as if making a prayer and sighed. "Do you think I wanted to move us here? You don't think I wish we still lived in our old apartment, or somewhere better, and we were all still together? Do you think this is the plan me and your father had? Believe me, it's not. But I'm trying my best, Mari. And I wish Papi was here," her mother said.

"Yeah, I wish Papi was here too because this sucks," Amaris said, and it was a needle prick to her mother's heart.

Samantha was going to be late for work and she didn't have the energy to argue with her daughter. There was a small altar in the corner of the dining room. Samantha walked over to it and lit a candle. She said a prayer and made the sign of the cross.

Amaris had seen her mother do this thousands of times, and though it had been explained to her, she never truly understood it. "The rice is done. The chicken is in the oven. Take it out in ten minutes," her mother said. She walked by Amaris, took her coat from the rack, and got her bag to leave.

Amaris saw that what she said hurt her mother, and it made her feel terrible. As her mother was about to go out the door, she hugged her and said, "I'm sorry Mommy."

Samantha hugged her back and kissed her on the forehead. "Me too."

8

"Konbanwa Aminata. Anata no tsuitachi wa dōdeshita," Sochima greeted Aminata in Japanese and bowed as she came through the door.

Ami sighed with annoyance. "Stop showing off, Sochi."

"I'm not showing off. I'm just practicing. C'mon, practice with me."

Ami took off her jacket and placed it on the coat rack. "You know I'm not as good with languages as you are."

"Yes, you are. You speak Spanish, and you're working on French."

"Yeah, because those are Romance languages. They're not that far off from English. Chinese, Japanese, Arabic, those make my head hurt."

"Okay, do you want to practice in Spanish?"

"No," Aminata said emphatically with an accent. "Now, I'm done practicing."

"I see what you just did," Sochima giggled.

"Great. It's good to know that big head of yours is working."

Sochima was a gifted child. They both were. But if Aminata would be placed in the top five percentile, Sochima would be in the top one. They both excelled at learning; however, there was still a challenge for Aminata that she enjoyed. There didn't seem to be any challenge for Sochima. He had a near-photographic memory. He was reading at age one. He had memorized every country and its capital and could identify them by shape at age two. He was teaching himself Japanese simply by watching anime.

Their Mom posted a video of Sochima doing algebra at three years old, and it went viral. It got millions of views. News stations came calling and wanted to do stories on their family. The decorated soldier, the teacher, and the grandmother raising two gifted children. They said two but they meant one and a half, as Aminata was mainly an afterthought in their coverage. She was four grade levels ahead, but people had seen that before. Sochima was a rarer breed.

Their family was getting a lot of attention. Nana felt it was best to stop doing interviews and posting videos of the amazing things Sochima was doing. She feared too much outside influence might corrupt the children. Their parents agreed, and that it was best for the children to have as normal a childhood as possible.

They also agreed that Nana would continue homeschooling Sochi, as she had done with Aminata. It was difficult for Sochima to socialize. He was too advanced for children his age, and it would be unsafe to put him in an environment with students at his level.

Sochima said something insulting to Aminata in Japanese.

"Hey, I don't know what you just said, but I know what you meant. Okay."

Sochima giggled and hugged his sister. "I love you, Ami."

"Ewww. Get off," she said, pushing him away.

"And how many times do I have to tell you, call me Amy?"

"Why?" Sochima asked.

"Because that's what I like."

"Why?"

"Because that's what my friends call me."

"I like Ami better," Sochima said.

"Well, it doesn't matter what you like. It's what I like. Now respect my wishes."

"Okay Ami, I will," he said out of reflex and not intending to be cheeky.

Aminata ground her teeth.

"Ami, come here please," her mother called from the kitchen.

Ami turned to Sochi in anger.

"What? I didn't do anything," Sochi said.

"I know. But I can't get mad with Mom." Aminata left the living room and met her mother in the kitchen. "Mom, can you call me Amy, please," Aminata sheepishly requested.

"What? Why would I do that?"

"Because that's what I prefer to be called. So, can you respect my wishes?"

"There's like a billion Amys in the world. We gave you your name for a reason. It's either Aminata or Ami. You choose."

"Okay," Aminata conceded.

"Now, your principal left a message saying he needs to set up a meeting with me. Do you want to tell me what this is about?"

Aminata took out her report card and handed it to her mother. Gabrielle looked it over and was immediately taken aback. "Ami, there are mostly Cs and only two Bs here."

"Yeah."

"Ami, you have never gotten lower than a B-plus in your life, and you cried when it happened."

"Maybe I'm maturing. I mean, grades aren't everything," Aminata said.

"Don't give me that. It says here that you've been missing homework, and you haven't turned in assignments or you turn them in late." Aminata was silent. "I haven't been checking to make sure you've been doing your work because I've never had to. You've always been so conscientious."

"Well, maybe I'm just not as smart as we all thought, and things are catching up to me."

Gabrielle took a step back and exhaled. "Maybe we have been pushing you too hard. Do you feel that way? Do you feel pressured?" her mother asked.

"I don't know. Sometimes," Ami said.

"I know it has been hard for you in the last year. First Dad dies, and now everything that's happened to Nana. It's understandable that it would affect you. So, if you need to take a step back and figure things out and just be a regular kid, I understand."

"Thank you," Ami said.

"But do you like the school you go to?"

"Yes."

"You should. It's a very nice school. It's also very expensive. In fact, after taxes, it costs just a little less than what I make for the entire year. Do you know what that means?"

"It means we can't afford it," Aminata said.

"Fortunately, it's completely paid for through scholarships. But Ami, you won't keep your scholarships with grades like this." Aminata took in everything her mother just said.

"I can help Ami. I mean Amy. I can help you with your schoolwork," Sochima said.

Aminata looked at Sochima and ground her teeth, holding back from screaming at him, then walked away to her room.

"What did I do?" Sochima asked.

Gabrielle sighed. "Go to your room Sochi. I'll call you when it's time for dinner."

9

Everyone dreams—every night—sometimes three or four times a night. Most dreams aren't remembered. The ones that are often don't feel like dreams. They feel real and yet not real. You can hear and you can see, but you can't taste or smell. You don't feel physically but you do feel emotionally—like fear, or joy or sadness.

Sochima had the feeling of being swung around. He was in a playground, and his father held him by the forearms swinging him in a circle. He knew it was his father though he could not see his face. It didn't yet occur to him that his father was dead and so he should not be seeing him. Sochi could not see his expression, yet he sensed that his father was in a crazed, semi-sadistic state of joy. Sochi wanted to stop swinging, and he said, "Stop," but his father didn't listen and swung Sochi around even faster. Then Sochi was not being swung by his father anymore. He felt like he was wrestling with an invisible force, until Sochi found his voice and yelled, "Stop."

Sochima woke up and found himself in a very awkward position. His head was hanging down over the side of his bed, his blanket had been tossed off his body, and his right hand was extended straight up in the air. Why was his hand in the air? Sochima lifted his head and saw someone above him holding his hand. It was a boy, like himself, but older, nine or ten, hanging down as if his knees were bent behind an invisible jungle gym, hanging the way monkeys would, with his hand extended, holding onto Sochima's right hand. The boy grinned at Sochi—an odd grin—more mischievous than malevolent, though there is a thin line between the two.

Sochima quickly pulled his hand away. His heart rate spiked, his breathing quickened and the hairs on his head stood on end like being slightly electrocuted. The hanging boy remained the same, grin and all, frozen in place until he steadily faded away, leaving Sochima to wonder if he had truly seen what he saw or was this still a dream. Sochima quickly recovered himself, grabbed his blanket, and wrapped it around him like a shield, when he noticed his room door, which was ajar, slowly close on its own. Did he just see what he saw? How could that be? Could it have been the wind? However, the windows were all firmly closed. There was no wind in the house. Sochima's thoughts raced with the beating of his young heart. He kept asking how and why the door closed when he saw the knob turn and the door slowly open again on its own. The only thing behind the door was the blue-blackness of the night.

Sochima felt a presence like heat in the room. It gave him goosebumps. He felt it in his hair. He felt it in his teeth. He couldn't see it, but he knew it was there. It rushed over him in waves. His breathing quickened, and his heart felt like it wanted to tear through his chest. He was the most afraid he had ever been in his young life. For a moment, his thoughts were in complete disarray. But then he remembered something Nana had told him. "We all feel fear, in whatever form it takes, from the biggest to the smallest of us. Courage is not the absence of fear. Courage is being afraid, evenly deathly afraid, and nevertheless confronting it. Do not run from Fear. Stand your ground, chant your name, and tell Fear to go away." Sochima marshaled his resolve, found his voice, slowed his breathing, and began chanting his name, the special name Nana had given him. He told the presence in the room to leave, and he watched as the door closed on its own. What Nana told him to do worked.

Sochima had conflicting emotions. He was terrified that there was a spirit in his room. Yet he felt empowered that he had stood up to it, told it to leave, and it obeyed. Or did it? The door slowly opened on its own again, and the presence reentered his room stronger than before. Sochima sat up in a monk's pose, regulated his breathing, and repeatedly chanted his name while saying, "Go away. Go away. Go away."

10

Aminata felt loved. She felt protected and needed at the same time. A great feeling of warmth came over her while she slept, and she slept better than she had in months. She woke up feeling rested and peaceful but also heavier than she should. She tried moving but felt confined. She looked behind her and saw that Sochima held onto her tightly. When did he get into her room? This was what she got for not locking her door.

"Sochi, what are you doing in here? Get off." Dead asleep Sochima didn't answer. "Get off Sochi. Get off." Sochima could have been comatose he was so knocked out. Aminata wasn't having it. She violently pushed him off, knocking him off the bed. Sochima woke up with a loud thud. "Ow."

11

They sat at the kitchen table. Aminata, Sochima, and their mother, who was soothing Sochima with a zip-locked bag of ice as a small bump had developed on his forehead from where he landed. "Really, Ami. You had to push him off the bed," Gabrielle said.

"He's lucky he's not bleeding," Ami replied.

"Ami, that's not nice," her mother said.

"Okay, I'm sorry he fell, but that's what he gets. What was he doing in my bed?"

"I was scared last night," Sochima said.

"Sochi, you're big enough to sleep on your own now," his mother said.

"I know, but there was a ghost in my room, and I got scared."

"Yeah right, whatever. You're just scared of the dark," Ami replied callously.

"No, I'm not scared of the dark. Well, I am, but there really was a ghost," Sochi argued.

Gabrielle was unnerved by Sochima's story. She wasn't sure she believed it wholeheartedly, but she didn't dismiss it either. Nana often spoke about spirits, and Sochi and Nana were very close. Had he become more spiritually aware, or had his imagination just run wild?

"There wasn't a ghost, Sochi. You just have a big head, and you like making things up, and sometimes those things scare you," Aminata said.

"No, you have to believe me. It threw me around while I was sleeping. It was a boy but older than me. Then the door closed and opened by itself," Sochi said.

"The door closed and opened by itself?" Ami repeated incredulously. "Yeah, I don't believe any of that."

"Ami, you have to believe me," Sochi said pleadingly.

Her mobile phone rang, and Gabrielle walked to the kitchen counter and answered it while the children continued to bicker. The call wasn't long, and Gabrielle looked very serious after she hung up. "Ami, Sochi, I have something to tell you."

The seriousness in their mother's voice immediately drew their attention. "Mom, what is it?" Aminata asked.

"Nana has been moved into a hospice," Gabrielle said.

"I thought she was already in the hospital," Sochima said.

"She was. But now she's been moved into a hospice. It's a place where they make sure she doesn't feel any pain, and she's as comfortable as possible," Gabrielle explained to her children.

"Okay, so when is she coming home?" Sochi asked.

"She's not coming home. She's never coming home," Ami said on the verge of crying.

"Why not?" Sochi asked, still confused.

"Nana is not getting any better, Sochi. The doctors have tried their best, but she's dying," Gabrielle said.

"No she's not," Sochi said combatively.

"She's stopped talking, Sochi. She hasn't spoken in weeks," Gabrielle said.

"She does talk. She talks to me all the time," Sochi argued back.

"She isn't Sochi. And she's stopped eating."

"Yes, she does eat. When I feed her, she eats," Sochi said.

"She used to. And I thank you so much for being there for her, but she won't even eat from you anymore. Her mind is gone Sochi and she's suffering. And we don't want her to suffer anymore."

Sochima seethed with anger and sadness and slammed his closed fists on top of the table yelling, "She's not dying," then left the room in a huff. Aminata quietly sat at the table, holding in her emotions. Since Nana got sick, she knew that her death was the most likely outcome. Now the reality was hitting her, and losing two of the people she loved most in the world in the span of a year was a bit too much.

12

Aminata loved her father. She loved him so much, when she was six years old, and she and Amaris were playing grown-ups, and they would talk about who they wanted to marry: Amaris would choose a celebrity and Aminata would always choose her father. "You can't marry your father," Amaris would say to her.

"Why not?" Ami asked.

"Because he's your father," Mari said.

"I don't care," Ami said. Her father was the strongest, bravest, most handsome man in the world. When he told her she was beautiful she believed it, more so than from anyone else. He made her feel safe and protected. When he held her, she felt like nothing in the world could hurt her. He was a soldier. He protected his family and his country—until the day men in army suits came to the door.

If a nuclear bomb could go off inside just one person that was how her father's death affected Aminata. She felt shattered, and what the bomb didn't destroy at first, the radioactivity slowly ate away. She could barely move, barely eat. She cried every night. Her mother had to remind her to shower as she would forget. She would get upset with Sochima when he came to her wanting to play. She would snap and take her anger out on him. Why was he acting normal? Why wasn't he as devastated as she was? Nana had to explain that Sochima was five, and for most of his life, his father had been away serving in the military. He didn't have the connection with their father she did, and as brilliant as his brain was, death was something Sochima was still coming to grips with.

Aminata felt like she was losing her grip on reality. She began seeing her father everywhere. She saw him in her dreams. They would be at family gatherings, and he would be there smiling, and she would forget that he had died, and she would wake up smiling as well, but then remember that he was gone, and she would cry. She would see him in the grocery store, in the park, and riding the metro. But was it him, or was it just some man that made her think of him? She would sometimes wake up to him sitting at the side of her bed before slowly fading away. As much as she loved her father, seeing him all the time was beginning to drive her insane, and she told him to go away—and eventually, he did. She didn't dream him or see him anymore.

13

Aaron Gates was in the United States Marines for over seven years. This was all of Sochima's life and most of Aminata's. During the financial crisis eight years prior, he'd lost his job as a carpenter. It was a union job and finding another was difficult. He found himself doing day labor; standing on street corners in the cold with two dozen plus men hoping for someone to come by and pick him up that day. If he was lucky enough to get picked, it was harder work for less pay with no healthcare. He had a wife and a daughter to provide for. He needed stability. He saw an ad for the marines one day, and something clicked, and he enlisted.

14

Lance Corporal Davis kicked in the door of the Syrian apartment, which triggered a tripwire—which triggered a bomb. It was a two-second hurricane compacted into a fist. It knocked everyone off their feet and blew off most of Davis's face. It easily could have been Aaron who had been the first through the door with the skin of his face seared off. There are no atheists in foxholes. Every soldier believes in God. Every soldier knows that it's only through God's favor he sees another day.

After Davis had been tended to and taken away the rest of the unit was able to examine the apartment. This was the home of a high-value insurgent. A confidential informant had led them here. It seemed he had led them into a trap. The sprinkler system had gone off, and the apartment was a wet charred mess. Their target was gone, and they were unlikely to find any salvageable intelligence, but they looked anyway. That's when Aaron saw a simple walking stick leaning against the wall in a distant corner. Everything else around it was charred and covered in soot. It looked unaffected by the explosion.

Aaron walked over to it. It was sixty-three inches in height and an inch and a half wide. Sculpted from a wood he did not know, it looked like something made from a different era. It was not much to look at; a bit crooked in the middle but straightened out at the top. Aaron picked it up. He could feel something emanating from it. If he were to use it as a cudgel, it could do great harm and as a walking stick it would always hold you up.

Aaron felt connected to it and decided he would keep it. "Whatchu got there, Gates?" A fellow Marine asked. "Walking stick," Aaron answered. "My mom has trouble walking sometimes. I think she'll like it." The stick wasn't intel, and it wasn't valuable. No one objected to Aaron claiming it.

From that day forward, Aaron and that stick were inseparable. He took it with him everywhere he went. He even slept with it and had the most fantastic dreams. Aaron carried the stick with him so much that his fellow Marines started calling him stick-man, though they said it in good fun. Aaron carried the stick with him on missions. He created three diagonal straps for it on the back of his rucksack. On his first mission, while he sat in the back of a Humvee with the stick held in front of him, a fellow Marine asked, "Gates, why you always carry that stick? I mean, I don't ever see you without it."

Aaron answered simply, "It's my lucky stick."

"Yeah. Well, I can use some luck. Mine if I rub it?"

Aaron did not object. "Nah, go ahead."

"Hell, I can use some luck too," another marine said, and Aaron allowed him to give it a rub as well. And before they left base, all seven men in their squad had given the stick a rub. And at the end of the day, all seven men returned unharmed. And so it was, on mission after mission, for months. They once drove over an IED that failed to explode. They had skirmishes with insurgents involving multiple regiments, and their unit had no injuries. No man in the unit could say for certain that the stick was the cause of their good fortune, but none of them neglected to rub the staff before leaving base.

Their success rate started drawing attention from on high. Their unit was given a commendation. Their Commanding Officer was promoted, and they were given a new Staff Sergeant. He was a younger man with ambitions of being a general one day. On their first assignment under his charge, he noticed Aaron about to enter the Humvee with his stick, and he called to him. "Sergeant, what is that?"

"Oh, this. It's just my lucky stick, sir."

"Your lucky what?"

"My lucky stick."

"Yeah, we always take it with us on missions," Daniels said.

"And we always come back," Jones seconded.

"Is that so," the Staff Sergeant said. "So, you mean to tell me that the great success this unit has had is all attributed to that stick? That it had nothing to do with your discipline, due diligence, and training. Perhaps we should take back your commendations and give them all to the stick? Sounds ridiculous, doesn't it?"

No one in the unit answered.

"Sergeant, return the stick to your barracks and go do your job."

"But sir," Aaron mildly protested.

"You don't but me, Sergeant. Now leave the stick behind and go do your job."

"Yes sir."

The other members of his unit watched disheartened as Aaron walked away with the stick. Some murmured, 'bullshit,' but no one protested aloud. When Aaron returned and got on the Humvee, he felt as if he had left part of his soul behind. He felt exposed and unprotected. They all felt a bit down driving off base that day not doing what they considered an important ritual. They told jokes and laughed louder than they should to take their minds off it.

Seven men drove off base that day, and not a single man returned. An insurgent fired upon their escort helicopter, and it crashed into their Humvee. A fire broke out, gases ignited, and there was a terrible explosion. When their fellow Marines came upon the aftermath, everyone and everything was burnt. When they placed Aaron's body in his coffin, preparing to send him home, knowing how much the stick had meant to him, they placed it on top of his body and put his hands over it.

When the body returned home and the funeral parlor was preparing it for Aaron's service, the attendant mentioned to Nana that they were having difficulty dressing the body because they couldn't remove the stick. Rigor mortis had set in, and Aaron's hands had a death grip on the staff. They feared they would have to break Aaron's hands to remove it. Nana told them not to desecrate her son's body more than it had been, and she would remove the stick herself or, if need be, she would stitch the suit he would wear around it.

The explosion that took Aaron's life had left his body disfigured. Strangely when Nana looked at the body, she saw her son whole and handsome as he had always been. She touched his hand, and suddenly his eyes opened. It gave her a jolt. He looked at her for a second. Then his eyes closed. The grip of his hands loosened, and Nana was able to remove the stick. It was hers now.

15

"What do you see?"
Ena inhaled, squinted her eyes (though she was told not to), bit her lip, ground her teeth, and finally surrendered. "I can't see it, but I know it's the big E," she said.

Ena, Nana, was eighteen years old, living on the island, and she was going blind. For the first seventeen years of her life, she had perfect vision. A little after Ena turned eighteen she noticed that a street sign she used to be able to read from a block away was blurry, and reading license plates on moving cars was becoming a strain. She went with her mother to see an optometrist and got a prescription for a pair of glasses. The prescription was light, and the lenses were thin. They made her see perfectly again. The problem appeared to have been solved. However, six months later, her vision had deteriorated to the point where the glasses no longer helped; in fact, it was far worse than before she had gotten the glasses. Three months after that, she was back at the optometrist, unable to see the big E on the eye test. "You'll need to see a specialist," the doctor said.

She saw a specialist the next day, and in the following weeks, she saw dozens more. Many flew in from other countries, and none of them could explain why she was losing her vision. There was nothing structurally wrong with her eyes, she hadn't gotten hit in the head, and she had no family history of vision loss. Nana's vision deteriorated to the point she could no longer read or write.

Everything in the world became blurred, like a camera out of focus. It was no longer safe for her to leave the house alone. Emotionally Nana handled all this well enough. She cared more for the toll this was putting on her mother than herself. Her mother had been with her to every doctor's appointment and through every grueling test. It's difficult for a parent to see their child suffer and have no way to help them.

As there seemed to be no natural causes for Ena's vision loss, her mother turned to the supernatural. There were no shortages of spiritualists on the island. Mainly they functioned to tell you if someone had put a curse on you, usually done out of spite, envy, or some perceived slight you had done them. Nana soon learned that most spiritualists were bunk.

They'll never tell you they don't know or can't see something, and what they see is usually very vague and gathered from information that you tell them. Their cures usually involved killing a chicken and being doused with its blood. Nana was against killing animals ritualistically for her benefit. She despised the idea of blood sacrifice of any kind.

Still, she believed what was happening to her was supernatural. She began to see things that she had never seen before and that no one else saw, like transparent strings floating in the air, like wavelengths to an unknown frequency. She saw these all around her, all the time, but these were just the start. She began seeing people walking around who shouldn't be there. They just wandered about, looking lost and confused. At times they looked disheveled, beaten, even bludgeoned, and missing parts of their skulls. She soon realized she was seeing ghosts. She never told anyone the things she saw, and she never stared at the ghosts, lest she let it be known that she could see them, and they decide to see her.

She began having dreams about flying, where she would start levitating out of bed, and through the ceiling, and above her house, then flying over her entire island. These were wonderful dreams, the kind of dreams you never want to end. She woke up from one of these dreams to a little boy sitting beside her bed. He looked at her, and he was very sad and sullen, then he slowly faded away.

One day, returning home from the doctor, Nana's mother left Nana sitting at a bus stop while she went to the market across the street. Her mother told her to stay put as it had become un- safe for her to walk about outside alone. Nana watched the blur of people and traffic going by.

She watched as spirits weaved through them, passing through moving cars without being hit. While sitting there, a man in his seventies, dressed in a black church suit and a black hat sat next to her. He sat there silently for a few minutes before saying, "Can you see them?"

Though he was a stranger, Nana felt immediately at peace with him. "See who?" she asked.

"The lost souls," he said. "You see that one walking there?"

"You can see them too?" she asked.

"Hmm, mm."

"Who are they?"

"When someone dies, sometimes it happens too sudden, or it's too painful, or they're too in love, or too in hate, and their soul can't completely let go of their body, and they hold on to a trace of it. And that trace has weight, and the soul cannot be weighed down, it must be free in order to move on. So, they are trapped here, lost. Until they can find a way to let go of the weight they carry."

"That's sad," she said.

"Yes, it is," he replied.

"Since I can see them, am I going to be like them?" she asked.

He put his hand on top of hers. "No, Nana, you're going to be alright," he said.

Nana felt so at peace with him she didn't even question how he knew her name. "I'm going blind," she said.

"No. You're going through a change."

"A change to what?" she asked.

"Something greater," he said.

"I don't feel greater."

"You have a mind greater than the prime minister and all the politicians on this island put together."

"Am I supposed to become prime minister?" Nana asked.

He laughed. "Your path is much greater than that. You are supposed to become a teacher."

"A teacher?" Nana repeated. And though it was never a career Nana had considered before, once he said it, it felt right.

"But first, you must learn," he said.

"What should I learn?" she asked.

"Learn everything," he replied. "But start with history."

"Why history?" she asked.

"Because everything has a history. So, when you learn history, you learn everything." Nana absorbed all he said more than anything anyone had ever said to her. "You're going to be alright," he said again, getting to his feet. Nana noticed for the first time that he carried a wooden walking stick. Everything Nana saw was a blur, except for this stick, which she saw so clearly. She reached out to touch it, and the man pulled it away from her. "Not yet," he said, then he walked away. Soon after, her mother returned and found Nana in good spirits.

The next day for the first time in months, Nana's vision did not worsen. It stabilized, and in the coming weeks, it began to improve. Her vision never came all the way back, but within a year, it improved to the point where she could read and write again, and she could wear glasses. And though the glasses didn't fully correct her vision, they allowed her to see most things and navigate the world safely.

Once Nana could read again, she didn't stop reading. She read and studied voraciously. As the man in the church suit had told her, she became a teacher. Though Nana would gain the education of multiple PHDs, she never went to university and never became accredited. A high school diploma was her highest honor.

She rarely taught adults unless they sought her out. She primarily taught children between the ages of six and thirteen, believing those were the most crucial years. She taught hundreds of children throughout her career, on the Island and when she migrated to the United States, first in New York City and then Washington, DC.

All great teachers are always looking for that great student to complete them. Nana met and fell in love with Michael Gates, an electrician who also migrated from the island. They had five children. They raised two doctors, an engineer, a lawyer, and a carpenter—who became a soldier. She found her great students in the children of the soldier; first with Aminata and then again with Sochima. Once Sochima was born, she retired and put all her attention towards him and Aminata's studies. She was truly fulfilling her purpose. She believed the children were special. What role they were to play in the world, she did not know, but she would do her best to prepare them for it.

When Nana saw the staff in her son's coffin, she immediately recognized it. It was the very same staff the man in black carried so many years ago. She was sure of it. How did Aaron come to possess this? And now, after all these years, it was hers.

16

Like her son, after Nana held the stick, it never left her side.
She walked with it to her son's funeral, and it held her up when
they lowered his body into the earth. When Aminata and Gabrielle both broke down, it gave Nana the stability to comfort them.

One night, months later, she slept with it and had a dream
beyond anything she had ever experienced. She was on a ship
at sea. Like grains of salt spread on a blackboard, stars littered
the sky. There were people around, possibly dozens, perhaps
hundreds, she couldn't tell. They were like silhouettes behind a
screen talking gibberish. She looked in her hand, and she was
holding the walking stick. However, it had changed. It looked
like solid light. It was a staff with an ankh on top and what the
Egyptians called a Djet just below it. While she marveled at the
beauty of the staff, she felt water on her feet. She looked down
and saw that the water was ankle-deep.

She felt the boat begin to sink, going deeper and deeper
down. The water pulled away and rose. She looked towards the
horizon, and there was none. There was only water, rising up,
blotting out the sky. The ocean became a wall as far and wide
as the eye could see. The other passengers saw it and screamed
in terror. Nana was too afraid to scream. Terror took her by the
throat as the wall rushed towards them. She closed her eyes.

When she opened her eyes, she was somewhere else. Where?
She did not know. It was light and yet dark. It had form and yet
was formless. It was here she saw them. They were male and
female, but they were not man or woman. Who they were, Nana
could not comprehend. They spoke intimately. Did they see her?
If they did, they behaved as if they did not.

"Why have you done this?" the female presence asked.

"I did it for love," the male presence answered.

"He loved you."

"And I love you . . . Why can't you love me?"

"I do love you, brother."

"No, not like that. Love me more. Love me the way you loved him. That's all I ever wanted."

"I cannot," she said.

"Then I cannot let you go."

The male presence left, and only the female remained. She turned her attention in Nana's direction. "You can come out," she said.

Nana was surprised she addressed her. Nana thought she had been invisible. "It's okay," she said. Though she did not know who this presence was, Nana could sense the immense power in her. Her presence felt so warm and nurturing. Nana felt at peace and safe. "I need your help," she said. Nana was thoroughly confused.

"How could I help you?"

"He has bound me here. He cannot hold me forever, but for as long as he can, he can do immeasurable harm. So much destruction. So many will die. And in order to stop it, we need to bring him back. We need to put him back together."

"Who?"

"My brother. My husband. Ausar."

"You are Auset?"

"I am."

"You are real?"

"You doubted me?"

"I believed. But it feels better to know you."

"It is an honor to know you as well, Ena. And now I need your help," Auset said.

"Why me?" Nana asked.

"Why not you?"

"But how could I be of help to you? Look at me. I am an old woman. I am too small to give aid to a God."

"No, Nana. You are grand. You are grander than you know.

And you and those from you will accomplish great things."

Nana laughed. "You sound like someone I met a long time ago. Have we met before?"

"No. You met another," Auset replied.

Auset's words heartened Nana. "I will do what you ask," Nana accepted though she did not know what she was agreeing to. But how does one refuse a God? And even after Auset had explained to Nana what she was asking of her, and though it was so daunting, it seemed impossible, Nana steadied herself and asked, "Where should I start?"

"Start at the heart. It will be the hardest to get. Everything will fall into place after that."

"How will I get there?"

"The staff of Ptah will take you."

Nana looked at the staff in her hand. It has a name, and she was now a part of its legacy.

17

Nana stood on the mountaintop and faced the serpent. With the staff in hand, shining brilliantly, she held her breath as the serpent swallowed her. Inside the beast she closed her eyes, sat as a monk holding the staff firmly in front of her, and meditated. The staff created a bubble of light and safety around her.

She was in the belly of chaos. It was like being in the epicenter of a tornado, an earthquake, and a tsunami all at once. All around her was violence and destruction. She heard pain and felt wailing. It wanted to invade her and suffocate her. It was intoxicating and enticing. She had to fight an overwhelming urge to give into rage. It was not just anger. It was pure madness—and intense sadness. It was the desire to break and destroy, to scream, to bite, to fight, to riot, to kill, and to kill one's self. It took all her concentration not to be seduced by it. It tested her like the sweetest sleep.

Nana did not know how long she was inside the serpent; millenniums, millions of years, perhaps billions, or simply a millisecond. However long it was, it felt endless. There was no direction, no up, down, west, or east. She stayed in one place. If she tried to find the heart, she would be lost. Then she felt an incredible sense of calm and peace. The storms around her quieted, and she knew, at last, the heart had found her. She did not open her eyes. She opened her mouth instead and consumed it. In that instant, the staff transported her out of the beast.

When she reopened her eyes, Sochi was the first thing she saw; his big eyes, his bright smile. She had never been so happy to see someone and to be seen by them. Aminata was there as well, and she cried tears of joy. Sochi let everyone know she was awake, and before long her room was filled with family members.

She felt their love but could not express her love to them. She attempted to speak, and it came out jumbled. She felt as if she had been inside of the serpent forever. When Nana dreamed Auset, it caused her to sleepwalk for three days. Now she had been away from her body for over a month. The body, however, cannot function without the soul and had gone into a coma.

She had awakened from her coma, but it had taken a tremendous toll on her. She could barely speak. She had to marshal her energy to form a sentence. This was very distressing as her thoughts were clear, but she couldn't get them out of her mouth.

"My body is dying," Nana said to Auset.

"I know," she replied.

"When my body dies, I must let the heart go or my soul will be lost."

"You have to pass the heart on."

Nana knew intuitively to whom she was to pass this burden. "They're too young," Nana protested.

"They're older than you think," Auset said. "And you've prepared them. Believe in yourself."

18

Gabrielle had taken time off work to help care for Nana in the last two weeks as her health deteriorated. Nana was her mother-in-law, but Gabby loved her as genuinely as she loved her own mother. In many respects, they had a closer relationship. They had worked together at the same middle school for over ten years.

Nana taught history, and Gabrielle taught math. When Gabrielle arrived, Nana had already been at the school for twenty years and was the most respected teacher by the students and faculty. The principal and vice principal often sought her advice, and it was Nana who commanded the children when the principal called them to the auditorium. She was also a great mentor for younger teachers, guiding them through the difficulties of their first year. Nana mentored Gabrielle, and they became good friends. Nana introduced Gabrielle to her son, Aaron. She felt they'd make a good match, and two years later, they were married.

They were currently living in Nana's house. When Aaron lost his job and enlisted in the Marines, Nana insisted Gabrielle and Aminata move in with her. Aaron, at first, didn't like the idea of moving back home, but because he'd be away so often, he knew Gabrielle would need help raising Aminata and soon Sochima as well. Nana enjoyed the company as she had been living alone. All her other children had long ago moved away, and her husband, Michael, had died of a stroke five years prior.

Nana was the strongest person Gabrielle had ever met, and it had been heartbreaking seeing her decline in the last year. She received another call from the hospice. The doctor told her Nana wouldn't survive the night. Gabrielle relayed the message to Nana's children, but now for the hardest part, she had to tell

Sochima. Nana was so much more than a grandmother to him; she was his teacher in all subjects and his best friend.

Sochima sat on the sofa with headphones on listening to Japanese while working on a sequential math problem on his tablet. Gabrielle got his attention and told him she would call a babysitter to stay with him.

"Why?" he asked.

"I'm going to the hospice to say goodbye to Nana," she said.

Sochima was silent for an extended moment as he absorbed what his mother told him. But then he said, "I want to go. I want to say goodbye to Nana."

"I don't think you should go Sochi. I don't think you should see her like that."

Sochima was insistent. "I want to go. Please, mommy. Please let me go," he said.

19

It was three in the afternoon and Aminata was on the met-ro headed home. Today was a particularly hard day in school. Ami didn't remember a thing that happened. It had all been a long blur, class after class, bell after bell. She tried her best to appear present because she knew she needed to get her grades back up if she wanted to remain in that school, but her mind was miles away. Nana was dying, and Newtonian physics didn't seem all that important. Aminata put in her earbuds and tried to drown the world out. Ten minutes into her ride, the world came crashing in.

Amaris and her friends got on the metro. They were as loud and profane as they had been the day before. Aminata wanted to ignore them, but they were so loud it was impossible to concentrate on anything else. She had to look. She saw Amaris and then she saw her friend Marisol. Marisol looked at her as well, and then Aminata looked away.

"Yo, it's that same girl from last time," Marisol said to Amaris.

Amaris turned and saw Aminata. "Yeah, so?" Amaris said.

"Well, I don't like the way she looking at me. Let's jump her," Marisol said to the others.

The other girls were down. Amaris said, "Nah, she ain't worth it."

"Nah, I don't like how she looked at me. And you see that bag she wearing?" They all looked at Aminata's book bag. It was in the distinctive colors of her school. "She go to that rich school. She think she better than people. And I said I was gonna smack the shit out of her if she kept looking at me."

"Let's do it," another of the girls said.

Amaris was looking for a way to change their minds when another friend said, "Hold up. You see that man standing in the back?" They all glanced at him. "He's undercover."

"How do you know?" Amaris asked.

"Cops always be standing up even when they got seats. They're not allowed to sit down. Plus, I seen him pull Yonnel off the train a couple weeks ago," she said.

"Okay, we wait till he gets off. Or we get off when she does and do it then," Marisol said, and they were all in agreement. Marisol wanted to stream the beatdown live as well.

The girls had gotten a lot quieter in the last ten minutes. They spoke to each other in hushed tones. Aminata didn't know what to make of this. Then she noticed they didn't get off at the stop they had gotten off the previous day, and now and again, she could sense one of them staring at her. Something felt very strange. Her stop was coming up next, and the girls moved towards the doors she would exit. Aminata felt uneasy and didn't want to get off at the same stop as these girls, when suddenly Amaris bumped into her and said, "You not gon' say sorry?"

"Excuse me," taken back Aminata replied while taking off her earbuds.

"You not gon' say sorry?" Amaris said again.

"Sorry . . . for what?" Aminata asked.

"You just stepped on my foot," Amaris said.

"No, I didn't," Aminata replied, utterly confused.

Amaris's friends were confused as well. This was obviously the buildup before they jumped her, but they had already agreed to wait until they got off the train to do it. *Whatchu doin' Mari?* Marisol thought.

"Yes, you did," Amaris said.

"No, I did—" Aminata began saying when Amaris slapped her across the face.

Ami's face lit up with electric heat. She was shocked literally and figuratively. She had never been hit like that before. She had never been in a fight before. She didn't know what to do. Mari paused for a moment, thinking Ami would hit her back, but Ami didn't. So, Mari hit her again and grabbed her hair, and the two girls began tussling back and forth. It was a terrible scene on the metro. Adults looked on aghast but did nothing. Marisol and the other girls thought about jumping in, but then they saw the undercover officer approaching and decided one of them going to jail was enough.

The plainclothes officer grabbed Amaris and Aminata and separated them. Two other plainclothes officers revealed themselves. One of them looked disappointedly at the other girls, hoping they would have done something to give them a reason to arrest them. When the next stop came, the three officers gruffly pulled Aminata and Amaris off the train.

20

Hospices looked like hospitals just smaller and more private. Sochima couldn't tell much difference between them, other than there were different nurses and doctors here, and he had grown attached to Nana's previous nurses. This place also felt heavier. There was no hope in this place, just sadness. As they walked by each private room, they heard cries and whimpers.

Nana had five children. Aaron had been her second of three sons and the third born overall. Her two other sons and two daughters had all left DC and made lives for themselves in other parts of the country. They had cycled through visiting their mother while she battled her illness. When Gabby called and told them they had moved Nana into a hospice, they all came with their families, knowing this was the last time they would see her alive. The Gates family filled the room and the hall outside. There were over thirty of them.

Sochima was the youngest person in the room who was able to walk. He saw the older people hovering around Nana, holding her hand, touching her brow, and commenting on how much weight she had lost. Nana looked worse since the last time Sochima saw her. She was sixty-nine but she looked like she was in her eighties. Her eyes were sunken, her face was drawn, and her sienna skin was pale. Her chest heaved as every breath was a struggle, and you could hear her straining. "Do you want to say goodbye?" Gabrielle asked him.

"No," Sochima angrily replied. *She's already dead,* he thought to himself. Sochima walked away and sat on one of the chairs outside of the room. His face was sour, and his fists were clenched. He felt angry though he didn't know why or at whom. He saw some of his teenage cousins off to the side, using their phones and laughing, and he became even angrier. *Why are they here? They didn't even know Nana. They don't care.*

Gabrielle never wanted Sochima to see Nana like this. She feared it might traumatize him. But he had begged to come, and he had always been extremely mature for his age. Now she saw that she should have listened to her instincts. She would have to speak to him, but she was dealing with so much now. Namely, she had been texting and calling Aminata, and she hadn't answered. Her phone had been going straight to voicemail. "Ami, what's going on? I've been calling and texting. We're all at the hospice. I've sent you the address. Come straight here."

Sochima sat by himself swinging his legs under the chair,

when he saw something in the corner of his eye. It was a strange light. It radiated but did not brighten the room. Sochima turned in its direction and saw Nana standing at the end of the hall. She looked at him and smiled. She looked younger and more vital than he had ever seen her. She wore a long flowing robe that fell to her ankles, no shoes, no glasses, and an ankh around her neck. Her hair was a brilliant grey afro, and there were strange glowing symbols inlaid in her robe,

She called to Sochima with her hand. He walked over to her, and as he was about to say her name, she put her finger to her mouth. Sochima understood. "Nana, I'm so happy to see you," he said.

"I'm happy to see you too," she replied, though neither of their mouths moved. "Now, I need you to do something for me. I need you to go into the room and bring me, my staff. But don't let anyone see you do it."

"Okay, Nana," Sochi replied. He then walked back down the hall into the room, weaving his way through the legs of all the older people, who were all very distracted, tending to Nana's body. It was striking how different Nana's soul looked from how her body now appeared. He felt like saying, *You guys, that's not Nana. Nana's outside.* But he did not because they wouldn't believe him and because Nana had told him not to tip them off. The staff was in the corner in the back of the room. Sochi got to it, and as it was taller than he was, he had to hold it with both hands. He began walking out of the room when Gabby saw him. "Sochi, where are you going with Grandma's stick?" she asked.

Sochi had to think fast. "Nowhere. I just want to hold it."

Gabrielle thought for a moment before saying, "Okay. Just sit outside with it." She asked his two teenage cousins if they'd keep an eye on Sochima.

They said they would, and after two minutes, they turned back to their phones and forgot about him. Seeing his opportunity, Sochi walked away and brought the staff to Nana at the end of the hall. Nana took Sochi by the hand and led him away.

21

"What an asshole," Amaris said to herself, cursing the undercover cop, who not only stopped the fight and pulled her and Aminata off the train but also handcuffed them, put them in the back of a squad car, brought them to the nearest police station, processed them and now had them in a holding cell. They were supposed to get a phone call. He told them they would get one soon. Soon was over an hour ago. Not that Amaris wanted to make that call. She would have to call her mother, and God knows she didn't want to do that. She could hear her mouth already, and she would never hear the end of it.

Aminata dreaded calling her mother as well. She was going to be so upset; first, the bad report card, and now this. Nevertheless, Ami would rather bear her mother's disappointment than be here another second. They were in a large holding cell with girls much older than them and grown women, all of whom looked as if they had been here before. Some of them looked hard and walked around simmering as if they could explode into violence at any moment.

Aminata sat on a bench by the front of the cell close to the bars. She tried to make herself look as small and invisible as possible. She kept her eyes down and away, doing her best not to look at anyone, in hopes no one would look at her. It didn't work. Both Amaris and Aminata stood out because of their age. It was not unheard of, but it was uncommon to see girls that young here. Amaris tried her best to look hard, while Aminata looked terrified, as if she could break into tears at any moment. Her fragility made her attractive. "Yo, who you wit'?" One of the older teenage girls approached Ami and asked her.

"Excuse me?" Ami replied, fearful and confused.

"Who you wit'?" The girl asked again.

Ami had no idea why she was asking this question and how to answer it.

"She not wit' nobody," Amaris answered for her.

The girl turned to Amaris, who sat on the other side of the cell. The girl's eyes hardened. "Am I talkin' to you?" she asked Amaris.

"Yeah, you are now," Amaris smartly replied.

The girl smirked and walked towards Amaris, for which Ami was grateful. "And who you wit'?" she asked Amaris.

"I ain't wit' nobody either," Amaris answered.

This girl was part of a gang. Mari couldn't be sure which one or what conflicts they may have with any other gangs in the city. The gang Amaris was a part of was small and local to her neighborhood, but she didn't know how far the name stretched and who they may have upset. To keep the peace, it was best not to claim any gang. This was, of course, true for Aminata. With Amaris, the girl smelled bullshit. "Hmm mmm," the girl remarked. "Where you live?" she asked.

Amaris was thinking of a good lie when a uniformed female police officer walked by the holding cell and banged the bars with her baton to draw everyone's attention. "Hey, you two, get away from each other." The girl did as the officer said while continuing to stare Amaris down.

The officer had walked to the cell because Aminata and Amaris caught her eye—Aminata especially. She looked so young, lost, and scared. The officer could tell Amaris was the same, but she was putting up a good front. To her eyes, these girls shouldn't be here. She approached Aminata. "Hey," she said to her.

"Hi," Ami quietly replied.

"What's your name?" she asked her.

"Aminata," Ami said.

"Aminata. That's a pretty name."

"Thank you."

"What school do you go to, Aminata?" Aminata told her, speaking lower as she did not want the other girls in the cell to know. "That's a very good school," the officer said. "You must be very rich," she joked.

"No ma'am," Ami said.

"Then you must be very smart."

Aminata shrugged her shoulders.

"Why are you here, Aminata?"

"I don't know," Ami replied, on the verge of crying.

The Officer noticed Amaris paying attention to the conversation. "How about you? Why are you here?" she asked Amaris.

"Because your boy is an asshole, and he arrested us for no reason," Amaris said.

"My boy?" the officer asked.

Amaris pointed to the undercover officer who had arrested them at the other side of the station.

The female officer left the holding cell and approached the plainclothes officer. "Hey, Rogan. The two young girls in holding, you brought them in?" she asked him.

"Yeah," he replied.

"What did they do?"

"They were fighting on the Metro."

"How bad did it get? Anybody stabbed, anybody shot? Anybody in the hospital?" she asked.

"Nah, it didn't get that far. Just a slap and some hair-pulling."

"And you arrested them for that?" she asked.

"If we weren't there, it could have been worse. Fighting is getting out of hand on the metro. Trying to clean it up. Sending a message," he said.

"Okay. I think they got the message. Now let them go," she said.

"They can go, after they been arraigned and their guardians come," he said.

"Nah, they don't need to go through all of that. They're kids. Kids fight. Let them go now. Officer," she said, stressing the last word. And though it upset officer Rogan to do so, he had to respect her rank. "Whatever you say Sarge," he said.

A half-hour later, Aminata and Amaris were released.

22

It was five in the evening, but it was very dark out. Clouds had gathered, and it looked like a storm could break out at any moment. The bus stop was across the street from the Police station. There was a bus collecting passengers, and Aminata ran towards it. When she got on, the only available seats were in the back.

Aminata took a seat in the corner in the back row. She turned on her phone, already dreading the messages she would have gotten from her mother for coming home so late. As expected, her mother had left several texts, each growing increasingly frantic. None was more important than the first. *Doctors say Nana most likely will not survive the night. Come straight to the hospice to say Goodbye.*

Aminata's stomach dropped. Ami believed she had prepared herself for Nana's death. After all, it wasn't like when her father died. One day she spoke to him via video chat, and two days later, men in army suits came to the door. Knowing this was the last time she would see Nana left her with this awful feeling of emptiness. She texted her mother: *My phone battery died, and I was at school working on a group project. I just got a chance to charge it. I'm headed to the hospice now.* Ami didn't like lying to her mother, but now was not the time to tell her she had gotten arrested.

The bus was driving off when someone repeatedly banged on the front door. The driver reluctantly stopped and let them on. It was Amaris. Aminata sighed exhaustively when she saw her. She hoped, at the very least, Mari would stay up front. But no, she made her way to the back and took a seat in the back row, two empty seats away from Ami.

Ami cursed under her breath, folded her arms, and turned her body away.

After Mari settled in, she checked her phone. As she suspected, her mother had sent a dozen messages, cursing her for not coming home on time. *I'm in so much trouble,* Mari thought. She was dreading going home when she noticed Ami balled up in the corner, sad as a puppy, trying to keep her emotions in.

"What's wrong with you?" Amaris asked.

"We were just in jail," Aminata snapped back.

"Yeah, then they let us out, and nothing else happened. So that's a good thing."

"Except that we were in jail because you jumped me. And I didn't do anything to you," Ami said.

"Yes, you did."

"What? What did I do to you?"

"You know."

"No, I don't. Please, elucidate me."

"Yeah, see there it is. Using your big words. Acting like you better than people because you go to a fancy school. Looking down on me and my friends," Amaris argued.

"I was not looking down at you."

"I seen you. Yes, you did. You were looking at me with my friends, thinking that we're so loud, we're so ghetto."

"Oh my God. No, I wasn't. If I did look at you, it's because we used to be friends, and I didn't understand why you almost knocked me over like that on the train the other day."

"Yeah, we used to be friends, and then you left, and your people moved, and you went to your fancy school. And then the next time I see you, you look at me like I'm trash."

"Oh my God—I did—you know what. I didn't do that, but if you think I did, then I'm sorry."

"I don't care. You don't have to tell me, sorry. I know I'm not trash."

"You know what? Forget I said anything. Let's not talk to each other anymore. I won't take that train, and hopefully after today, we'll never see each other again," Ami said.

"Good, I don't want to see your stupid face anyway."

"Good." Ami turned away and looked out the window at the city going by. Involuntarily, she started crying as the weight of everything started breaking her down. Ami tried to conceal it, but Mari could hear her.

"Could you stop crying, please?" Mari asked callously.

"Please leave me alone."

"You're spoiled. I bet nothing bad ever happened to you before. You go to jail for a little bit and start crying."

"My grandmother is dying, okay," Ami burst out. "My grandmother is dying. Now please leave me alone."

"Nana is dying?" Mari asked.

It surprised Aminata that Amaris knew Nana. Then she remembered that Amaris knew Nana when they were younger, and they were neighbors. There were times when Nana took care of them together. "Yes," Ami said and turned away.

Mari had fond memories of Nana, and it broke her heart to know she was dying. She felt bad for what she said. She respected Ami's wishes and remained quiet.

The bus drove on, and Ami looked out the window while wiping her eyes when she saw a little boy, no more than five or six, walking with his hand up, as if someone was holding it, while he carried a grown person's walking stick, dragging on the ground. This was very odd. She looked closer, and, for a second, she thought that boy looked like Sochima. She looked again and realized, "Oh my God. Sochi. Sochi," she shouted as if he could hear her from the bus. She got up and began ringing the bell frantically. "Stop the bus. Stop the bus," she repeated. "Please stop the bus. I have to get off."

Though it was against regulations to stop the bus away from an established bus stop, the driver seeing how scared and desperate Aminata was, made an exception. He stopped the bus, and she ran off in the direction her brother was walking. Ami got off in front of Meridian Park. Sochi had already walked inside. Looking at all this, Amaris could only think, *What the hell?*

23

Nana's spirit walked Sochi to the center of the park. It was about to rain, and no one else was around. "We're here," Nana said to Sochi.

"Why did you bring me here, Nana?" Sochi asked.

"Do you remember everything I told you about Kemet? About Ausar and his brother Set, about Ra and the serpent Apep?" Nana asked.

"Yes, Nana," Sochi said.

"Well, it's all true."

"I know it is. I know you wouldn't lie to me."

"Good. Now you remember I told you how I got the heart from Apep?"

"Yes. You let him swallow you, and you were inside of him for a very long time until the heart found you," Sochima answered.

"Yes. But now my body is dying. And when my body dies, my soul will go away."

"Where will your soul go?"

Nana silently pointed to the sky. "And I've lived my last life Sochi, and I can't take the heart with me. So, I'm passing the heart to you, and when you're grown and ready, it will be your responsibility to find the thirteen other pieces of Ausar and put him back together. Do you understand?" she asked.

"I think so," he said.

"I know it's a lot. I know it's a lot. And you're so young. But I wouldn't pass this burden to you if I didn't believe you could carry it. And it is not just me who believes in you. There are powerful forces out there that believe in you and your—"

"Ami," Sochi blurted happily as his sister ran to him.

Seeing Ami there at that moment, Nana smiled. No matter how many incredible things she had already seen, creation never ceased to amaze her.

"Sochi," Ami said, a bit out of breath, having run through the park looking for him.

"Ami. I'm so happy you're here." He hugged her.

"Sochi, what are you doing here by yourself? Did you run away?" she asked.

"No. Why would I run away, silly? I'm here with Nana. She brought me here."

"Stop it, Sochi. Stop making up stories. Nana's at the hospice. She's dying, and Mom and everyone else are there. And Mom is probably worried sick that you're not there."

"No. Nana's not there. She's right here."

Beyond frustrated, Ami grabbed Sochi by the hand and started pulling him away when she heard, "Aminata, stop." Aminata knew the voice. It was a voice she hadn't heard in quite some time.

She turned around, and there was Nana, looking alive and resplendent, more beautiful than she had ever seen her. And like a prized possession, she held a glowing orb, the size of a softball, made of the most beautiful array of lights.

"Nana, is that you?" Aminata asked.

"Yes."

"How?"

"Look around you," Nana answered.

The world was the same, and yet not. The grass glowed, the trees shimmered, the wind sang, there was a slight vibration all around, and transparent strings floated in the air. When Aminata had come full circle, she found herself looking at herself. It was then she realized she had stepped out of her body.

"You're in the spirit world. It's a world you've known before but you've closed your eyes to."

Aminata noticed Nana's walking stick had become a staff of brilliant light. Sochima held it, and Aminata reached out to it.

"Why have you brought us here, Nana?" she asked.

"Because my body is dying. I don't have much time left, and I need to pass this on to you." She showed them the orb.

"What is that?" Aminata asked.

"It's the heart of Ausar," Nana said.

"Ausar? Like the Ausar?"

"Yes."

"Why do you have that?"

"It's a long story. Just know that our family, that you, both of you, have a great purpose. We must. You must find all the pieces of Ausar's soul and bring them together so that he can be born again and stop the God Apep from awakening and destroying creation."

"Nana—what?" Aminata said, feeling overwhelmed.

"I know it's a lot."   .

"You think."

"Isn't it cool?" Sochi said.

"No, no. Not cool—"

"Oh my God. Is that a dragon?"

Aminata was shocked to turn around and see Amaris standing behind her—but she was even more amazed by what Amaris was looking at in the sky. A dragon was moving through the clouds, and it seemed like it was manifesting the rain that began to fall.

"Storms are dragons in the spirit world," Nana said nonchalantly.

"Wow," Sochima said.

Aminata and Amaris were less enthused and more terrified.

"Who are you?" Sochima asked Amaris.

"Hello, Amaris. It is good to see you again. You have grown," Nana greeted her.

"Nana? Is that you?" Amaris asked, remembering the woman who used to take care of her when she was a little girl.

"Yes," Nana answered.

"You look great. I thought you said she was dying," Mari said to Ami.

"She is. Look behind you," Ami said to Mari.

Amaris looked behind her and saw her body three feet away, standing still, like a robot shutdown. "Oh my God. Oh my God. Am I dead?" she asked fearfully.

"No child," Nana answered her. "Whenever the soul of Ausar is exposed," Nana said, drawing their attention to the orb, "it creates a portal into the spirit world."

"What are you doing here? Did you follow me?" Aminata asked Amaris.

Amaris didn't immediately answer.

"It is amazing that you two are brought back together at this time after all these years. If she's here, it is because she serves some purpose in this," Nana said.

"Purpose. I ain't got no purpose. I was just walking through the park," Amaris said.

"Little do you know child? There is so much I'd like to tell you—all of you. But I'm running out of time. I can feel my body leaving. She turned to Ami and presented her the orb. "You have to take this now."

"I'm not taking that." Ami protested.

"Ami, we don't have time to argue."

"I'll take it," Sochi said. And though, given their ages, Nana would have preferred to pass it on to Ami, it was Sochima who she had intended to give it to when she brought him to the park. She took the staff from him and handed him the orb. He held it in both hands. "What am I supposed to do with it?" he asked.

"Open your mouth. It will do the rest," she said.

Sochi opened his mouth, and the orb went inside his soul, and they became one, and the portal closed, and they returned to their bodies. However, something had awakened in them, and Aminata and Amaris were still able to see Nana and the staff in their spirit form.

"You now have Ausar's heart," Nana said.

"That was a heart? Ewww," Mari commented.

"Seriously, why are you here?" Ami asked Mari again.

"Don't worry. I'm leaving."

"Wait. There is something else I must give you," Nana said.

When, "Who's that?" Aminata asked as she saw someone approaching.

24

There came a woman jogging through the park. She jogged in the pouring rain without an umbrella or a hat. They all stopped talking and just looked at her. She looked to be in her forties with blonde hair and rose-beige skin. There was something very odd about this woman. Nana immediately became on guard. Like getting goosebumps, she made Nana's spirit vibrate. What was it about her? All she was doing was jogging in the rain, minding her business. She appeared as if she might just jog by them, but as she was about to, she turned and looked their way, at Sochima specifically, and within a blink, she moved five meters, closing the distance between them, and grabbed Sochi by the arm. "You," she said.

Sochima and the girls were too stunned to scream. Nana was not. "Get away from him," she shouted and swung the staff at the woman creating a shockwave of blue energy. The stranger crossed her forearms in front of her and tiptoed as she was blown backwards a good twenty yards and brought to her knees.

"Whoa," the children said collectively.

The stranger's appearance changed when the energy created by Nana's blast subsided. She stepped out of her physical body and appeared much different from the body she had possessed. Her blonde hair was gone, replaced with a bald head. The spread of her nostrils was wide, the bridge of her nose was straight, and her lips were thick. Her complexion had gone from rose beige to deep chocolate brown, and she had transformed from a woman to a man.

He stood up and was now over six feet tall. He had a lean athletic build that looked hewn from obsidian. He wore a white sarong, no shoes, an ornate Egyptian necklace over his chest, and armlets on both arms. He lifted his eyes and sprouted wings from his back. They were blue-black like his skin and stretched nine feet in each direction. They breathed and gathered wind around them. He stretched his hand out and summoned the energy from the grass, turning the grass black, and fashioned it into a sword.

The children were amazed and terrified. What had Amaris walked into? There was a dragon in the sky, and she had just seen this strange woman transform into a dark angel. She wanted to run away, but Nana shouted, "Children keep behind me." Nana had no idea who or what this spirit was, but he was quite powerful. She feared him more for the safety of the children than herself. He streaked towards them. Nana stepped in front of the children and met his sword with her staff, causing a shockwave that shook the earth. The children screamed. Nana and the stranger clashed again, volleying back and forth, Nana parrying all his blows until she found an opening and was able to push him back.

The dark angel halted for a moment and began to pace back and forth. He looked at Nana. He looked at the children. "It's you. You are the ones," he said.

Nana looked confused. "I don't know what you're talking about."

He looked at the staff in her hand. "That staff. Mortals should not play with God's things."

"No, they shouldn't," Nana replied.

"How did you come by it?" he asked.

Nana did not answer.

"No matter. Give it to me and the boy, and I'll spare your souls."

"I don't know who you are or what you are, but you will not have this staff, and you will not hurt these children."

"I am God's Guardian."

"Which God?"

"There is only one."

He flew straight at them. Nana swung at him with the staff. He dodged and smacked her away with his left wing. "Nana," Ami and Sochi shouted. He reached for Sochima, but Aminata stood in his way. "Stay away from my brother," she said and was stunned as the dark angel's hand went through her and grabbed hold of Sochima. And though he was holding Sochima's hand, it felt like he held his soul. Amaris instinctively threw a punch at the dark angel, and it went through his face. He turned and looked at her coldly and it scared her to the bone.

Nana had been knocked a few meters back. She recovered and ran towards the dark angel. She held the staff high, and the transparent strings floating around drew to it, filling the staff with energy, which she unleashed in a vertical shockwave as she roared, "Let him go." The shockwave raced across the ground, knocking the dark angel into the sky. He gathered himself in front of the moon, with the rain coming down and a storm dragon flying above him. He looked up at the dragon, and the dragon reared back and breathed out lightning. He grabbed the lightning by the hand, controlled it, twirled it overhead, fashioned it into a bow and three arrows, pulled back, and unleashed in the direction of the children. Nana got to them just in time, slammed the staff into the earth, and said, "Geb, help me." The earth moved and formed a cocoon around them. Inside, lit only by the staff, they could hear the lightning arrows hitting the outside like battering rams. Nana began to chant. "Run out, thou who comest in darkness. Comest thou to kiss these children? I will not let thee kiss them. Comest thou to soothe them? I will not let thee soothe them. Comest thou to harm them? I will not let thee harm them. Comest thou to take them away? I will not let thee take them away. I have made this protection against thee," she said, and the children were imbued with a light that faded away just as a lightning arrow broke through, and the cocoon fell. The dark angel raced towards them from the other side of the field, throwing lightning-like curve balls. Nana swatted them away, but they were too many, and one got through, and then another, and the force knocked her to her knees. And at that moment, on the other side of town, Nana's body flatlined. She had run out of time, and he was too strong and would not stop coming. He forged the energy of the lightning into a spear and raced toward them. Nana turned to the children. Though they were young and unprepared, Nana had no choice. She looked at Aminata. "Take this," she said and handed her the staff, and Ami reached out for it but could not hold it. "Now, hold onto each other and never let go," Nana said, looking at Mari as well. Mari listened, and they all held each other just as the dark angel's spear pierced Nana from behind. The staff turned from brilliant light to wood, and Ami held it in her hand as Nana's soul shattered into a million pieces.

ACT TWO
THE GREAT GAME

25

"Nana noooo," Sochima shouted into the dark, as in an instant the world went from being filled with light to pitch-black. How did this happen? Sochima thought maybe the darkness was due to him closing his eyes. However, to the best of his knowledge, his eyes were open. Nevertheless, to be certain, he closed them, and when he opened his eyes again, the world was still dark and deathly quiet, save for his heart beating loudly like a mallet wanting to break through his chest. His eyes began to adjust to the lack of light, and slowly the world transformed from blackness to where slivers of moonlight were visible.

"Sochi," he heard.

"Ami? Where are you?" he replied.

Sensing the nearness in his voice, "I'm here," she said.

"What the hell?" Aminata heard and knew that it was Amaris. "What the hell just happened? Why is everything so dark?" she asked.

"I don't know. Nana . . . Nana," Aminata called out. There was no answer. Aminata recognized she was lying down. She tried to sit up, but a force held her in place. She wanted to cry out, but the force gripped her by the throat, and she couldn't speak. Her eyes began adjusting to the darkness, and a face slowly appeared. It was a young woman's face. It was translucent and angry, yet all the anger was shown in her eyes as her mouth was shut. Ami tried to call the others for help, but she couldn't speak. As she listened, it sounded as if they were struggling as well. Then she heard Sochima yell out, "Go away," and as if on command, the force holding Aminata down slackened, and the translucent face moved away while keeping the same expression. Sochima yelled, "Run," and Aminata and Amaris, without delay, did as he said, and all three got to their feet and ran forward into the darkness, Aminata holding onto the staff Nana had given her.

Fairly soon, they collided into a wall and followed the slivers of light, feeling their way around until they found an opening and ran out. The darkness gave way to moonlight. It was still very dark, but the moon was a blessing, and they were happy to be able to see each other. They looked behind from where they came. It was a small hut built on an earthen mound with a thatched roof. Suddenly the roof caved in, and the hut collapsed. Three ghostly figures, a man and two women, were looking at the fallen hut. They turned and, with malice in their eyes, looked at the children. Ami recognized one of the women as the face that held her down. Mari and Sochi recognized their own as well. Instinctively the children ran forward into a jungle—too frightened to question how they came to be in a jungle. When Mari looked behind her, she saw the spirits following. The children kept running until Sochi remembered something, and he stopped and sat down in a monk's pose.

Aminata shouted, "Sochi, what are you doing? Get up. Get up."

The spirits began to circle him. The male bent down to be at Sochima's level face to face. The women moved toward Ami and Mari. Mari was confused about why they had stopped running. Sochi began chanting his name and controlling his breathing. The male spirit screamed silently and attempted to grab Sochi, but it seemed like there was an invisible field around him the spirit couldn't penetrate as Sochi repeatedly chanted his name and said, "Go away, leave us in peace, and go in peace." When Sochima reopened his eyes, the male spirit was gone. Ami and Mari watched the female spirits steadily fade away as well.

"What the fuh-dge just happened?" Amaris said.

Aminata wanted to know that as well—and "How did you know to do that?" she asked Sochima.

"Remember, I told you that night a ghost was in my room?"

"Yeah," Aminata said, having a vague recollection. Mostly she remembered not believing him.

"Well, I told him to go away by saying my name. So, when I saw that they were ghosts, I just did the same thing."

"So those were really ghosts?" Mari asked, while a bit out of breath.

"Yeah . . . I guess so," Ami said.

Mari took all of that in and looked around their environment. They were surrounded by trees she had never seen before, and the air was hot and humid. "Where the hell are we?"

"I don't know. But let's keep going forward. I want to be far away from those things," Aminata said.

"Go forward? Forward where? Do you even know where we are and how we got here?" Amaris asked.

"No."

"Like seriously, how did we end up in the middle of a jungle?"

"I don't know. Nana gave me the staff before she," Ami couldn't bring herself to say it. "I held onto it, and then everything was black."

"It was the staff. The staff brought us here," Sochima said.

"How do you know that?" Aminata asked him.

"It's magic. You saw how Nana used it."

In all this craziness that made sense to Amaris. "Well, then use it to send us back," she said to Aminata.

"How?" Aminata asked.

"The same way you sent us here."

"I didn't send us here."

"Look, I am sorry Nana is dead. I liked her. I liked her a lot. But she was a little bat-shit, and now we are in some crazy place, and I need to get back home, otherwise, my mother's going to kill me," Amaris yelled.

"Why are you yelling at me? I don't even know why you're here," Aminata shouted at her.

"Me either," Amaris yelled back.

"Then why did you follow me?" Aminata asked.

Amaris didn't say anything.

"Well?"

"I don't know, maybe it's because you tell me your abuela is dying and I feel sorry for you, then you run off the bus calling for your brother. My bad. Sorry, I felt sorry for you."

"You felt sorry for me? Really? After you jumped me on the train and got me thrown in jail."

"Well, you don't have to worry because I'm never feeling sorry for you again," Amaris said.

"That would be nice."

"Ami, you were in jail?" Sochima asked.

Aminata didn't answer. She simply grunted in frustration.

26

Amaris heard the rush of running water. She turned around and saw a stream nearby. Living in a big city all her life, she had never been this close to a large body of fresh water. Curiosity and thirst drew her to it. She bent over by the bank and caught the water in her hands. She took it to her lips. It was amazing. She didn't think she had tasted water that had been so clean and refreshing. An electric charge shot through her body. She drank and washed the sweat and humidity from her hair and face. Rubbing the cold from her eyes, she glimpsed something in the water. Confused by what she saw, she opened her eyes fully to get a better look. She fell onto her ass and hurriedly crawled backward.

Taken aback by Amaris's reaction, "What? What is it?" Aminata asked.

"The water. There's something in the water. Look," Amaris said, sounding frightened.

"No. If it has you that scared, I don't wanna look."

"Just look, so I know I'm not crazy."

"Everything is already crazy. I don't want it to get any more crazy."

"Will you just look? Please," Amaris pressed.

"I'll look," Sochima said and walked over to the stream and bent over. "Oh wow."

"What is it?" Aminata said.

"Do you see it?" Amaris asked.

"This is so cool."

"What is it, Sochi?" Aminata asked.

"Come look," Sochima ushered her over.

Aminata tentatively walked over, bent down, and looked in the stream. At first, all she saw was running water and a fish here and there. Then something started to take shape. It was her reflection—but it was not her reflection. It was the reflection of a woman in her early twenties. Their complexions were similar, but this woman had longer, straighter hair than Ami should, and her eyes were more almond-shaped. Ami shuddered and jumped back. "I told you," Amaris said. "What is that?"

"I think it's your reflection," Sochima said.

"Hell no. That's not me," Aminata said, outright rejecting the idea.

Both Aminata and Amaris slowly walked over and looked into the river again. All three of them could see their reflections. They were all grown up, especially Sochima, who had become a full-grown full-bodied man. "This is so awesome. I'm so big." There was something familiar about their reflections. They looked like the spirits that attacked them. "I think we're in their bodies," Sochima said.

"That's why they attacked us," Aminata said.

"Ewww. How did we get into their bodies?" Amaris asked.

"It's obvious the staff sent us here to find another piece of Ausar. And we were put into their bodies because our spirits can't affect the physical world without a body. Duh," Sochima said.

"What? How do you know that?" Aminata asked, feeling uncomfortable with her little brother knowing more than she did.

"Well, I guess I was the only one paying attention when Nana was telling us stories," Sochima said.

"I'm older than you. Nana was telling me stories long before you were born, and she never mentioned anything about jumping into other people's bodies," Aminata said.

"Whoa," Sochima said, suddenly noticing something about Aminata and Amaris and quickly putting his hand over his eyes.

"What? What's wrong? What happened? Why are you covering your eyes?" Amaris asked frantically.

With his left hand covering his eyes, Sochima pointed at them with his right hand and said, "Boobies."

That seemed like such an odd thing for him to say. Amaris was confused until she looked down and realized she was topless; both she and Aminata were. They quickly covered themselves with their hands. "Thanks, Sochi," Amaris said angrily.

With his eyes still covered, "Why are you mad at me for? I didn't do anything," Sochima said.

"Yeah, well, just make sure you keep your eyes closed. And turn around," Amaris said.

"Fine. I don't want to see you. Girls are gross," Sochima said while turning around.

Aminata and Amaris looked at each other. They were both angry and frustrated, trying to figure out how to cover themselves. Aminata being very modest, felt incredibly uncomfortable. She didn't even like being undressed in front of her mother. Amaris saw a nearby tree with large, broad leaves. She pulled a leaf off and attempted to make a bra out of it, but the branch wasn't flexible enough to tie around her. Aminata pulled out a thin, flexible branch from the foliage on the ground. She used it as a hook to hold the large leaf in place, then tied the branch behind Amaris's back.

"Thanks," Amaris said begrudgingly. She then did the same for Aminata. They were now covered as best as they could be without real clothes.

"You can turn around," Aminata said to Sochima.

Sochima turned around and giggled. "You guys look stupid."

"Have you seen yourself, buddy? You're only wearing a rag and a belt," Amaris said.

"Yeah, but I'm a dude," Sochima replied calmly.

"We're obviously in the bodies of people from an Indigenous culture, and this is how they dress," Aminata said.

"This is so gross. And if we're in their bodies, are they in our bodies?" Amaris asked.

"No, silly. We just saw their spirits. They are here. Well, hopefully not here now. They're around," Sochima said.

"And where are our bodies?" Amaris asked.

"Our bodies are back home. Well not home, but probably in the park where we left them," Sochima said.

"Doing what?"

"Sleeping, I guess."

"You guess?"

"What do you want me to say? I'm only six. I don't know everything."

Amaris tried to control herself and not take all her frustration out on Sochima. "If the staff sent us here. Why didn't it send us in our own bodies?" she asked.

"I think, I remember Nana saying once that spirits can travel through space and time, but our physical bodies can't," Aminata said.

All of this was beginning to give Amaris a headache. "You know what, I don't understand any of this, and I don't care. I just want to go home and get back in my own body."

"We can go home when we find all the pieces of Ausar," Sochima said.

Amaris didn't understand anything this six-year-old in a grown man's body was saying. "Okay, well, you guys can do that. Just use your stick and send me home."

"No. We can't leave here until we get the next piece," Sochima objected.

"That's great. Then you guys can stay and go on your adventure. I want to go home. So, give me the stick so that I can go."

"It's not a stick. It's the staff of Ptah," Sochima said.

"I don't care what you want to call it. Give it to me so I can go home," Amaris said.

"We're not giving you the staff, then we'd be trapped here," Sochima said.

"Well then, let's all go home. You guys can drop me off, and then you can come back here and go on your little adventure," Amaris argued.

"It's not a little adventure. We're trying to stop Apep before he wakes up and destroys all of creation."

That did Amaris's head in. "Yeeeaah. Look, I don't care about—whatever. I want my Mommy. I want my own body. I wanna go home."

"She's right. I think we should try to go home," Aminata said.

"Ami," Sochima said, feeling betrayed.

"We don't know what we're doing, Sochi. We don't know where we are. We don't know what's happening to our real bodies. And Mommy is probably worried sick."

"Yes, that's why the quicker we do this, the quicker we can get back home," Sochi said.

"No, Sochi, we should go home now," Ami said.

"Ami, Nana lost her soul to send us here. She did it for a reason."

"I know, Sochi, but we're just kids. This is too big for us."

"No, it's not. We're big now," Sochima said and moved his arms in a circle to illustrate the bodies they were in.

Aminata wasn't sold. "We're going home, Sochi."

"Good," Amaris said.

Aminata held the staff but had no clue what to do with it. "Home," she said. "Take us home." Nothing happened. "Washington, DC. Take us there." Nothing happened. "I have no idea how this is supposed to work."

"Maybe you have to meditate with it," Amaris said.

"I've never been good at meditating. But I guess it's worth a shot."

Aminata sat in a monk's pose with the staff held erect in front of her, closed her eyes, and attempted to meditate. She attempted for thirty minutes.

"Are you in a trance yet?" Amaris asked.

"No. And if I was, you would have just broken me out of it," she exhaled exhaustively. "This is no use."

"I told you. We can't leave until we find the other pieces of Ausar." They seemed unconvinced. "You guys should listen to me."

"Why should we listen to you?" Amaris asked.

"Because I'm the man," Sochima said.

"What? Whatever," Amaris said dismissively.

"Yeah, shut up, Sochi," Aminata said.

"Okay, forget that. I have the heart of Ausar inside of me, and it's telling me we need to go that way."

"Telling you how?" Aminata asked.

"I don't know. I just feel it. And I just feel like we need to go in that direction."

"Fine," Amaris gave up. She didn't care about who this Ausar was, but using the staff to go home wasn't working, and she was tired of staying in this one place, not knowing if those spirits would return.

27

As they continued walking through the forest, night turned to dawn, and rays of sunlight began to light their way. They had run out of the darkness so fast Amaris didn't realize they weren't wearing shoes. Amaris never liked walking barefoot. At home, she always wore flip-flops or socks. When she wasn't, she was stepping on a rug or some form of carpeting. Now she was walking barefoot with her boobs barely covered by a large green leaf and a knotted piece of cloth for a skirt. Insects and worms were crawling through the ground, and she was tiptoeing through them.

"You look ridiculous," Aminata said to her.

"I don't care. I don't like walking on dirt," Amaris said.

"It's not dirt. It's soil; it's the earth. It's natural."

"Does it get your feet dirty?" Amaris asked. Aminata didn't answer. "Exactly. Because it's dirt."

"So, who are you again?" Sochima asked Amaris.

"Mari," Amaris replied flatly.

"And you guys are friennndss?" Sochima asked with his hands open as if weighing two invisible objects.

To which Aminata quickly answered, "No."

And Amaris answered, "Used to be. We used to live next door to each other."

"I don't remember you. And I remember everything." Sochima said.

"That's because you weren't born yet. You were just a belly," Amaris said.

"You saw me in my mom's belly?"

"Yup. And it was a big belly too. And I knew you would have a big head. And I was right."

Aminata smiled at that.

"Ha ha," Sochima remarked sarcastically. "You don't know me well enough to make fun of my head. And it's because I'm smart."

"Good for you," Mari said sarcastically.

"So, why were you guys arrested?" Sochima asked.

"Because she's a bully," Ami said, still upset about everything that had happened.

"You don't know what you're talking about," Amaris replied.

"I don't? You're in a gang, and you go around picking on and beating up other kids."

"You don't know what you're talking about—and I saved you," Amaris replied.

Aminata couldn't believe what she was hearing. "You saved me? Are you insane? You jumped me on the train for no reason and got us arrested."

"Yeah, and that was saving you," Amaris said flatly. Aminata was gobsmacked. "Those other girls were planning to follow you off the train, and then we were all supposed to jump you, and they were going to live stream it," Amaris explained.

"And why would they choose to jump me? Did you tell them to pick me?" Aminata asked.

"No. But, my friend Marisol, you cut your eye at her, and that made her mad. So, she was like, let's mess that prep schoolgirl up."

"What? I didn't do that," Ami said.

"Yes, you did. When we got on the train. You looked at me, then you looked at her, and cut your eye away," Mari said.

Ami searched her thoughts, trying to remember if she had done that. She couldn't remember exactly but had to admit that she may have. She remembered seeing the girl with Amaris, and thinking she didn't like the look of her and that she was kind of scary. But that was a fleeting thought. Could her thoughts have come through in her eyes that quickly? "And that was it? Because I looked at her for like, less than a second," Ami asked.

"Yup. It was enough because she seen it and she ain't like it."

"And so, you were all going to jump me because of that?"

"Yeah. When we're together, we know we acting loud. And we know people be thinking we ain't shit. So, if you look at us and we see you, we gonna come at you. So, she said to everyone let's get this chick. But then I said, nah, I got this. So, I came at you by myself. And I did it on the train because it would be harder for the rest of them to jump in, and I knew transit was in the train undercover and would break the fight up. So yeah, when I jumped you, I saved you."

In some twisted way, Aminata had to admit that made sense. "Do you do that a lot?" she asked Amaris.

"Do what?"

"Just pick out a random kid and jump them?"

"I told you why they were going to jump you."

"Yeah, because you thought I was looking down on you, which I wasn't."

"Yes, you were."

"So, that's what you guys do, you just make up a reason to not like someone and then you beat them up?" Aminata asked.

"No. Most times we're fighting other girls who messed with us," Amaris said.

"And sometimes you just pick on some innocent kid you don't know." Amaris shrugged her shoulders, finding it difficult to defend some of the things she had done with her friends. "What happened to you, Mari, you were never like this before?" Aminata asked her.

"I was seven when you left. You don't know what I was like."

"Yes, I do."

"Well, some of us didn't get to live in nice neighborhoods and go to fancy schools," Amaris said.

"So, you became a bully?"

"Listen, you're either going to be the one getting beat up or the one doing the beating. Who do you want to be?" Amaris asked.

"I don't want to be either," Ami said.

"Well, sometimes you don't have a choice."

28

The sun had fully risen, and they had been walking for half an hour when they came across a series of thin cylindrical trees. In the middle, they were all dripping what looked like a thick white liquid from an incision in the stem. The liquid flowed through a makeshift funnel, which emptied into an open container made of dried clay, held sturdy by two prongs beneath it.

Sochima was the first one to notice it. It was a strange thing being in these foreign bodies. In one instant, Aminata could see Sochima in the body of the grown man he occupied, and in another, she could see his spirit and the six-year-old boy he was.

Before Aminata could tell him not to touch it, Sochima was already examining the white liquid between his thumb and forefinger.

"It's sticky," Sochima said.

"Please don't put it in your mouth," Aminata said.

"I wasn't going to put it in my mouth. I don't eat everything."

"Yes, you do."

"No, I don't. Plus, it smells."

Aminata crept closer to one of the clay bowls. The stench repelled her. "Yeah. It's really strong."

Amaris gave it a whiff as well. It smelled like those workout bands her mom would always buy and then put down after two weeks, only it was so much stronger. As she looked around, she noticed that there were dozens of trees being tapped. Collecting this liquid meant something to someone. "Let's leave it alone and keep going," Amaris said, and the others agreed.

As they continued walking, the forest gave way, and they entered a large cornfield. Sochima pulled an ear of corn from its stalk and peeled it open. He was surprised to find that it was reddish brown and not yellow. "Why's the corn red?"

"I think that's how it is naturally," Aminata said.

"I wonder how it tastes."

"Please don't eat—" Aminata began saying, but it was too late. Sochima had already peeled and bitten into it.

"It's kinda sweet," Sochima said.

"Yeah, and it might have worms or bugs in it."

"I'll live," Sochima said, shrugging his shoulders.

They walked through the cornfields for another ten minutes. When they came to the end of the fields, they were amazed at what they found. There was a valley below them. There was a great pyramid over one hundred feet tall. It was a step pyramid with seven large steps leading to the top. It gleamed in the early morning sun. It stood at the head of a complex about a mile long. It was like a plaza with various stone structures and monuments all placed symmetrically. "Whoa," all three said at once. Given the presence of the pyramid and how they were dressed,

Aminata surmised they were in either Mexico or Central or South America. Then she saw something that narrowed the choices down to one.

"Do you see that?" Sochima asked, pointing to an enormous stone sculpture.

"Yeah, I see it," Aminata said.

Even at a distance Amaris could see the colossal stone head carved in the image of a man.

"I think I know where we are," Aminata said.

"Where?" Amaris asked.

"We're in Mexico," Sochima said.

"Yeah," Aminata agreed with him.

"How do you guys know that? You've been here before?" Amaris asked.

"No. But I've seen pictures," Aminata said.

"But Ami, it doesn't look like this in the pictures. Everything is all messed up. It's all grass and the pyramid just looks like a big hill," Sochima said.

"Yeah, I know, Sochi. That's why I don't think we're in our own time," Aminata said soberly.

"What does that mean, not in our time?" Amaris asked.

"I think we're in the past. Like way in the past," Aminata said.

"How far in the past?" Amaris asked, growing increasingly anxious.

"I don't know exactly. But this looks like the Olmec civilization. That means it could be," Aminata was trying to remember the dates when,

"Anywhere between 1500 BCE and 400 BCE," Sochima answered for her.

Amaris was freaking out. "Wait wait wait wait wait. What does BCE mean?" she asked.

"Before the common era, before year one," Aminata answered. "It means we could be anywhere from 2400 to 3500 years in the past."

Amaris's eyes opened wider than they had ever been.

"We're time travelers. This is awesome," Sochima said gleefully.

Which annoyed Amaris to no end. "Shut up, Sochi. This is not awesome. This is the complete opposite of awesome."

"Don't tell my brother to shut up," Aminata said.

"I'll tell him to shut up all I want. I'll tell you to shut up. And why am I the only one freaking out about this?" Amaris said.

"I'm freaking out. I'm freaking out. I'm just too freaked out to freak out," Aminata said.

"Guys, arguing is not going to get us anywhere. The next piece is down there," Sochima said.

"Are you sure?" Aminata asked.

"Yeah. I can feel it pretty strong," Sochima said.

"Good, then let's get it and get out of here," Amaris said.

29

Four colossal stone heads pointed outward at the head of the complex. Like gargoyles, it was as if they were there to stand guard and ward off evil. They were quite large. Each appeared over seven feet tall and could have easily weighed twenty tons. They were carved from massive blocks of basalt stone, in the image of men with broad faces, broad noses, and thick lips, wearing some form of a crown or protective headgear, who looked to be of a similar people but also quite distinct from each other. The artistry was astounding, and the pictures Aminata and Sochima had seen of these monuments in their time did not do them justice.

This complex was apparently the center of this civilization, and people began coming in to start their day. The people looked like them—like the bodies the children occupied. They had a complexion that ranged from mahogany to copper. Their hair texture ranged between woolly and straight. They had a variety of hairstyles. Many of them shaved the sides of their heads. They were comparatively short as most of the women were below five feet, and the men were just above it. They were fashionable as well. Beyond the loin cloth skirts for women and briefs with belts for men, they wore large necklaces, armlets, and bracelets intricately made with exotic stones. A few of them looked at Aminata and Amaris oddly for wearing the leaf coverings, as many women their age naturally went topless. Many people wore tattoos and various forms of elaborate keloid scars that dotted their bodies and faces. It was both enthralling and jarring for the children. It was very difficult for them not to stare.

"Where is this thing we're looking for?" Amaris asked Sochima.

"I think it's further down. It might be closer to the pyramid," Sochima said.

"Alright, let's hurry up and get there," Amaris said.

"Let's hope no one asks us anything," Aminata said.

"Why are you worried about that?" Amaris asked.

"Because we won't be able to talk to them," Aminata said.

"I got you. I speak Spanish—*ish*," Amaris said.

"So do I, but they don't speak Spanish."

"Wait, I thought you said we were in Mexico."

"We are. But this is Mesoamerica. It's pre-Columbian," Aminata said.

"What does that mean?"

"It means it's before Columbus came, before the Spanish colonized them, so they don't speak Spanish."

"Okay," Amaris said, then noticed Sochima had walked off and was conversing with a merchant. "Then how is your brother talking to that guy?" she asked.

Aminata was shocked by what she was seeing. "I don't know. He's good at learning languages, but there's no way he could learn it that fast." Then a woman walked by Amaris and said good morning, and reflexively Amaris answered her in the native language. "How did you do that?" Aminata asked her.

"I don't know. I just did it," Amaris said in their language.

And Aminata understood her. "I guess because we're in these bodies, we naturally know how to speak their language. It makes sense since language is a function of the brain."

"I don't care how it works. I'm just glad it does," Mari said.

Sochima returned to them carrying three flat cakes made of maize. "Maize cake?" he said, offering it to them.

"Can you not think about food for one second," Aminata said to him.

"You guys don't want it? Because I'll eat all three," he replied.

"Let me try it," Amaris said, realizing that the body she was in was feeling hungry. She took a cake from Sochima and bit off a piece. After a few bites, she nodded and said, "Not bad."

"Fine, I'll take one," Aminata said, admitting she was also hungry.

They continued walking as they ate the cakes, trying their best to blend in with everyone, when Amaris noticed something. There were people who wandered about aimlessly. They often walked with their heads down. They looked lost and distressed. Amaris saw one of them walk through someone else. They were both completely unaware. "Did you guys see that?" Amaris asked.

"Yeah. I saw it. I think that guy is a ghost," Aminata said. Amaris began to stare at him. "Don't stare. I don't want them to know that we can see them. I don't want them chasing us like before."

"Yeah, you're right," Amaris said, trying her best to look away. "So, we can see ghosts all the time now?" she asked.

"I think so. The same way we saw that angel last night," Ami said.

"I don't know what that was, but that was no angel. Angels are good," Amaris said.

"I just called it an angel because it had wings," Aminata said.

"Nana said she used to be able to see ghosts all the time when she was young," Sochima said.

"After he died, I used to be able to see dad," Ami said.

"You did?" Sochi asked.

"Yeah. But then it got to be too much, and I told him to go away. And I didn't see him anymore."

"Why didn't you tell me?" Sochima asked.

"I don't know. I guess I didn't want to believe any of it was real," she said.

"Yeah, well, it's real. And we're here," Amaris said. They arrived at the base of the pyramid. The pyramid was far more massive and magnificent up close. Standing at the base and looking up, it filled their entire field of vision. There were stairs leading up to an entrance.

There were four men with spears guarding it. As the children approached, they blocked their path. "What are you doing?" one of the men asked.

"Just heading inside," Ami said to him.

"You know better. Unless Po Ngbe brings you inside, you are not permitted," he said. "Step back. Now."

They stepped away out of earshot of the guards. "Who's Po Ngbe," Amaris asked.

"I don't know," Aminata said. "Sochi?" she asked.

"I don't know either."

But as they thought of the name, an image came into their heads quite vividly. "I think he's a religious leader. Like a shaman," Aminata said.

"Yeah, he is. I just saw him in my head. Freaky," Amaris said.

"So, what do we do now?" Sochima asked.

"I say we just run past them and go inside," Amaris said.

"It's four of them, with spears. We're not getting by them."

"You guys suck. I wish my girls were here. We'd take 'em," Amaris said.

"Well, I'm sorry we're not in a gang like you and your friends, and go around beating up people all the time," Aminata said.

"Shut up," Amaris said.

"Make me. You don't have your girls with you, remember? It's not six-on-one anymore," Ami said.

"Oh, please. Don't act tough. You don't know how to fight.

I slapped you, and you didn't do anything. I can take you by myself," Mari said.

"Guys, all this fighting is not helping," Sochima said.

"Yeah, well, maybe when we get the next piece, me and Sochi will take it and go and leave you here," Ami said.

This terrified Amaris. "You can do that?" she asked fretfully. Ami smirked. "Tell me you won't do that. That's messed up. Don't joke like that," Mari said.

"Maybe I will, maybe I won't. Keep acting tough and see what happens," Ami said.

As they bickered, five men began walking towards them, calling the name "Kele." They were calling Sochima; however, he did not recognize the name.

"Kele, why do you not answer when we call you?" Bu, one of the men, asked Sochima when they arrived.

"Um ... I don't know," Sochima said, unable to come up with a lie.

"Nakawe, Inda Jani," he addressed Aminata and Amaris, respectively. "It is good to see you are all well. We visited your home and saw that it had fallen."

Aminata remembered that the hut they ran out of collapsed after leaving. "Yes. Yes. Fortunately, we ran out before it fell."

"And you are all unharmed. Good. Good."

Another of the men spoke to Sochima. His name was Ki. "Kele, we found your bow and your blade under the wreckage of your home." He handed them to Sochima. "I am surprised you would leave without them."

Sochima took them. "Um—thank you," he said, not knowing what else to say.

"It was very dark when we left. We were not able to find anything," Amaris answered for Sochima.

That answer seemed to satisfy the men.

"Well, you will stay with us for as many nights as it takes while we rebuild your home," he said.

"Thank you," Aminata said.

"Now we will leave you women to your day. Come Kele."

"Come . . . Where?" Sochima asked nervously.

This was an odd question. "To the hunt," the man answered.

"Hunt? Like hunting animals? Nooooo. I'm sorry, he can't go," Aminata answered for Sochima.

"He must. He's our best hunter," Bu said.

"I am? Cool," Sochima said.

Aminata looked at Sochima as if she wanted to smack him.

"Yeah, but he's not feeling well. He got hit on his big head when the house fell," Amaris said.

"He seems well," Bu said.

"Trust me. He's not himself. So, he can't go hunting," Aminata said.

"Kele, why do your women speak for you?" Bu asked.

This came as a shock to the children. "My what?" Sochima said and then couldn't help giggling. "Oh my God," he pointed at Aminata and Amaris, "You're my women."

Aminata and Amaris began saying, "Shut up," but caught themselves before saying Sochi and said, "Kele." And Sochima broke out into a fit of laughter.

This entire display was extremely odd to the other men. Just then, there was a great stir in the crowd. Aminata turned around to see what it was. People were walking through the plaza—over two dozen of them. They looked quite different from the others. Their clothes were multi-colored and much more elaborate. The women wore capes made of feathers. The men wore capes made of animal skins. Their jewelry was richer and more artistic. However, what made them so striking were their heads. Their skulls were elongated and shaped like a cone. "They are so beautiful," a woman nearby said of them. Beautiful was not the word Amaris would use; nevertheless, she played along. "Yeah. Beautiful."

A woman carried a baby, not yet two years old. The baby had padded planks of wood on both sides of his head, bound together with a white cloth.

So that's how they do it. But why would they do that to a baby? Amaris wondered.

Aminata had only seen pictures of cranial deformation in books. She found it off-putting but knew this was because she wasn't born into the culture. She knew there were tribes of people who still maintained the practice.

The woman with the baby turned and looked at Aminata and Amaris for an extended moment. The baby looked at them intently, almost as if it could see through them, before the mother turned and walked away with the others. The look the baby gave them raised the hairs on their head.

The group of nobles approached the entrance to the pyramid. They nodded to the guards. The guards slightly bowed their heads, and the nobles proceeded inside.

"Why do they get to go in?" Amaris asked.

"They must be special. Like celebrities or royalty," Aminata said.

"Yeah, well, they're super weird," Amaris said.

"Yeah, they are," Aminata replied.

"And that baby. Whoa. And you thought your brother's head was big," Amaris said.

Aminata smiled and looked to see Sochima's reaction, but Sochima was not there, and neither were the other men.

"Sochima. Sochima," Aminata called to her brother.

The people around them found that name to be odd.

"Kele. Remember, his name is Kele," Amaris whispered to her.

"Yeah. Kele. Kele," Aminata called for him again. He was nowhere to be seen, and it began to worry her.

"You look for Kele?" one of the women asked Aminata.

"Yes. Have you seen him?" Aminata asked.

"Yes. He has gone with Ki and Bu and the others," she said.

"Where have they gone?" Aminata asked, growing more frantic.

"Where they always go. Into the forest," the woman said.

Aminata and Amaris ran from the pyramid complex to the forest outskirts. Aminata was about to enter the forest when Amaris stopped her. "Where are you going?" Amaris asked her.

"I'm going after Sochi," Ami said as if it wasn't obvious.

"Do you know which way he went?"

"No."

"Do you know how to track him? Can the stick track him?"

"Um. I don't think so."

"Then how are we going to find him in that?" Amaris asked, pointing to the vast and dense forest.

"I don't know. We just go in there and keep yelling his name until he answers," Aminata said.

"I don't know about that. That's a big jungle. We could get lost."

"He's lost. And we have to find him."

"He's not lost. He's with those guys, and they know the jungle way better than we do. And Sochi was the one who led us here."

"What are you saying? We don't go after him?"

"Not unless you wanna get lost."

"He's not your brother, so you don't care. And he might be in a grown man's body, but he's only six."

"You're right. I don't care about your stupid brother. But I care about getting out of here and getting home. And that won't happen if we all get lost." Aminata looked unconvinced. "Look, when I was a kid, I got lost in the mall, and I spent over an hour walking all over trying to find my mom. But if I had just stayed where she last saw me, she would have found me in like five minutes. That's all I'm saying." Amaris was beginning to make sense to Aminata. "I know how you feel. I have a little brother and sister too, you know. And if they were lost, I'd be freaking out. But us getting lost, too, won't help."

"Fine. We'll wait here," Aminata said, surrendering. She then looked deep into the forest. *Dammit Sochi. Where are you?*

30

When you're six just about everyone and everything is big-ger than you are. You feel like an ant, like you're two-dimensional, as if an entire world is happening above you that you can't see. You spend most of your life hoping someone puts you on their shoulders so you can see the world without getting a crick neck. When you're six people don't pick you up as much as they used to. The cuteness of that wore out after age three. They prefer to hold your hand while they trot along, ignorant to the fact that it takes you three steps to keep pace with their one. Everyone tells you you're a big boy, but you don't feel big. Your feet hurt, and your neck hurts, and the days are long, and you can't help counting them off because when you're six, all you care about is getting bigger.

Yesterday Sochima was a little boy just over three feet tall. Today he was a full-grown man, five and a half feet tall, which made him the tallest of the men he was walking with. He also appeared to be the strongest. He had never been the biggest or strongest person ever. These men looked up to him. Sochima liked the idea of that. He liked being big. He liked being in this body. He liked being in this world. Unlike the girls, he didn't want to go home—at least not right away.

Within the blink of an eye, they had traveled thousands of miles and years in the past. They were seeing things he could only read about in books. He wanted to soak up this experience. So, he did not object when the other men led him away into the forest. The girls were probably upset with him. Then again, when were they not upset with him? It was bad enough with one sister. Now with Amaris, it was as if he had two constantly telling him to shut up.

Sochima was so preoccupied with his new body he was unaware that he was the one leading these men into the forest. "Kele, where do you walk? The deer run deeper this way," Bu said.

"Oh, sorry," Sochima said and began walking in the direction Bu was pointing. *Bu.* That was his name. How did Sochima know it? It just naturally came to him. Memories of Kele's life came to him as well. Bu was his friend. All these men were his friends.

The forest was his home. He had walked this path many times. Being in this body was like riding a bicycle after not riding one for a long time. At first, you feel awkward and unbalanced, but as you continue riding, something magical happens; muscle memory takes over, and you start riding without thinking.

"Kele, you are not yourself today. How hard did you hit your head when you ran from the house?" Bu asked.

"Um—hard," Sochima said.

"And what was it that caused your house to fall?"

"Um—don't know."

"I think it was Nakawe and Inda Jani," Ki said.

Nakawe and Inda Jani. They were talking about Aminata and Amaris.

"It is hard to keep two women happy under one house," Ki said.

"It requires a great deal of stamina," Bu said, and the others laughed.

Sochima did not get the joke but laughed louder and more dramatically than the others. Then Bu saw something and hushed them. "Look there," he said, guiding their eyes through the forest forty yards ahead. A young deer was eating from the forest floor. All the men crouched low and became very still. Following them, Sochima did the same. "Let us get closer," Bu said. Following Bu's lead, everyone crept closer to their prey until they were thirty yards away. "Now, Kele," Bu said.

"Um—now what?" Sochima asked.

"Use your bow. Shoot it."

Sochima turned to Ki and handed him the bow. "Why don't you do it?" he said.

"Do not be silly. You have the strongest bow arm and the steadiest aim," Ki said.

There was no getting around this without having to answer questions Sochima did not know how to answer. He awkwardly took the bow and nocked an arrow, going by things he had seen on television. He aimed, released, and missed terribly, going way above the fawn and into the air.

"What are you doing?" Bu asked with quiet intensity. Fortunately, Sochima had missed so badly that he had not frightened the deer away. "Give me the bow," Bu said. However, his competitive nature took over, and Sochima wanted to prove that he could do it.

"No. Let me try again," he said. This time Sochima did not think beforehand. He let his body guide him. He nocked the arrow, steadied his breathing, aimed at the deer, then let loose.

The arrow went through the deer's neck and brought it down. Bu patted him on the shoulder. "Great shot." Ki and the others patted him on the shoulder as well. Sochima was proud of himself.

They walked over and found the fawn whimpering in the brush, holding onto its last bit of life. Its doe eye looked directly at Sochima, and he watched as it closed, and its soul levitated briefly above its body, then slowly faded away. Sochima no longer felt happy about what he had done as he realized, *they have souls too.*

The others had not seen what he saw and were quite pleased with how clean the kill had been. This fawn would fetch a good price. They would prefer to keep the venison for themselves and their families, but it would be more valuable selling it to the nobles, especially on the day of the great game. They may even pay double for it today.

They began to make fun of the nobles for their perceived frailty and their 'maize heads', as they called it, and how they bred within themselves, as they believed their bloodline descended from the Maize God. Again, Sochima laughed at jokes he did not understand—but then, strangely, they all stopped laughing until Sochima was the only one. He turned around and saw in the brush twenty feet away two green orbs with dark pools in their center. What was that? he wondered as the pools came forward and the beast revealed itself.

With a dead peccary dangling in its mouth and blood dripping down its spotted yellow coat, it sauntered with its barrel belly, giving it the appearance of either being pregnant or well-fed. They all stood frozen in place with equal parts fear and reverence. In the forest, the Jaguar was King. The Jaguar was God—and the only way to appease a God was through sacrifice. In this encounter, they calculated at least one of them would die. They had all been a part of many hunting parties. In every instance when they encountered the God, one of them would not return. Who would it be? Who would the God choose?

It gave no indication. It was calm and conserved. It dropped the peccary. It licked the blood from its mouth. It yawned, baring its teeth and tongue, and scratched its ear. Though outnumbered, it felt in absolute control. It took its time. And just as it had lulled them into a moment of complacency, it chose—and it chose Sochima.

There was a millisecond between when it looked in Sochi's direction and before it attacked with silent ferocity. Two trots, and it was airborne, mouth open. Sochi had no time to think. Instinct took over, and as fast as the cat moved, somehow Sochi moved faster. He dodged its advance, and it knocked Ki, who had been behind him, over. Its three hundred pounds hit him with two thousand pounds of force. His head hit a branch knocking him out.

The jaguar was upon Ki, ready to finish him, when Sochima, without thinking, grabbed it from behind and wrestled it away, holding onto its neck with his forearm, and holding on for dear life. It was like trying to corral a hurricane. It was wild, unpredictable, and incredibly strong. He could feel its muscles flex.

He could feel its heartbeat, and its pulse, and the blood flowing through it. Its fur was coarse and scraped his skin. Its roar was deafening.

Bu and the others stepped back as Sochima and the jaguar tumbled on the ground. They were all in shock at what Kele was doing. They had never seen anyone brave, or fool enough, to wrestle a jaguar before. Though this wasn't an act of bravery, it was purely instinct. Sochima didn't know what he was doing either. He had jumped on the jaguar's back and now didn't know how to get off. Bu and the others couldn't help because the jaguar moved too fast, and they feared they'd hit Sochima with their blade or an arrow by mistake. The jaguar roared and thrashed, yet no matter how much it fought, Sochima found the heart and wherewithal to hold on. Sochima had his dagger on his hip, and Bu shouted at him to stab it, but he didn't. After seeing the soul of the deer leave its body, *they have souls too,* he remembered. *They have souls too.*

Sochima whispered his name in the jaguar's ear, and steadily the beast began to calm down, and Sochima felt safe enough to dismount it. Both on all fours, Sochima, and the jaguar stared at each other. Its green eyes looked intently at Sochima until it broke contact, picked up the peccary it had dropped earlier, and retreated into the forest.

31

It had been over an hour. Amaris and Aminata stood in the same spot, looking into the forest, waiting for Sochima to return. "When he comes back, if he's not dead, I'm gonna kill him," Aminata said.

"You sound like my mom," Amaris said.

"I sound like my mom."

"Difference is my mom is literally gonna kill me when we get back. I can see her face. She's so mad right now."

"And my mom will kill me if I get Sochi killed."

"So, I guess you can't kill him," Amaris joked.

"No, I guess I can't." Aminata sighed. "I didn't know you had a brother and sister," Aminata said to Amaris.

"There's a lot of things about me you don't know."

"There's a lot of things about me you don't know. How old are they?" Ami asked.

"They're four. They're twins," Mari said.

"Twins. Wow. Is that cool, or is it weird?"

Mari thought for a bit. "More cool than weird. They get on my nerves, but I love 'em, and I miss 'em."

"Why do you miss them?" Ami asked.

"Don't worry about it," Mari replied.

Aminata was going to question her further when, "What are you doing?" a woman called to them. Startled, Aminata and Amaris turned to their left and saw Abha, a woman much like themselves but a bit older. "Why do you stare into the forest?" she asked.

"Um—we're waiting for—Kele to return," Amaris said.

"Why?" she asked.

"Because he's gone hunting," Amaris said.

"He goes hunting every day, and you do not stare into the forest, waiting like lost cubs."

"He hit his head when our house fell. And we're worried he's not well," Aminata said.

"Kele hits his head often. He is strong, and his head is hard. He will be fine. Come, we have work to do," she said, walking away while ushering them with her hand.

"Um—work?" Amaris asked, wondering what on earth that could be.

32

As the day grew more people came into the complex; artisans, butchers, and fishermen, all trading one good for another. There were hundreds, maybe thousands, of people. It was difficult for the girls to get a count. It was like being in a marketplace and a carnival in one. It was a festive occasion, and they often heard people mention something called the great game.

They followed Abha to a tent held up by bamboo. There were large pots of boiling hot water outside. Women stirred the pots with large wooden sticks. Some pots had banana peels in them to produce lilac dye, others had saffron and safflower to create yellow, and others boiled indigo for blue.

Inside the tent, several women were working. A woman meticulously picked the seeds from a large pile of cotton plants, which looked very similar to cotton balls in their raw form. Another woman laid the seeded batches of cotton down and beat them repeatedly with a stick until they flattened into a thin sheet. Another pulled threads from the cotton, twirling them around a small stick. Another had a ball of already prepared thread which she warped around the poles of a wooden board.

When the women saw Aminata and Amaris, they looked at them strangely. "Why are you wearing leaves?" one of the women asked them.

"Our house fell, and it was dark, and we couldn't find anything," Aminata answered.

"Oh—I'm sorry. But why wear leaves? Nothing would be better," she said.

The girls didn't know how to answer. Abha found two pieces of cloth and handed it to them. "If you want to wear something, wear these," she said. The girls were grateful for the fabric.

They took off the leaves, wrapped the cloth around their breasts, and knotted them in the back.

Abha, like all these women, was a weaver. Nakawe and Inda Jani were weavers as well. Abha sat down on a stone stool and put on a backstrap loom, which was an apparatus of interlocking wooden sticks used for weaving threads into fabric. There was a rope tied to the center pole in the tent, and a strap worn around the waist. Abha controlled the tension on the warp by leaning back and forth while constantly slipping the wooden planks in and out, weaving the threads into fabric. She was incredibly skilled. Aminata was amazed watching her.

"Why do you stare? Sit down. Put on the loom. Work," she said to them. Amaris and Aminata gave each other the same confused look as they sat on stone stools beside her and placed the straps of the loom behind them. Abha could not ignore the awkwardness with which they did this. "You two are very strange today. Did you hit your heads as well?" she asked.

"Yes. Yes, we did," Amaris was quick to answer. She then asked Aminata, "How are we supposed to do this?"

"I don't know. Watch her, and try to do the same," Aminata said.

Abha worked the loom like a machine, her brain and hands completely in-sync. And as she watched Abha something within Aminata clicked and her hands began working on their own. Within minutes she was weaving threads into fabric as efficiently as Abha was. She didn't have to consciously think about doing it. It was better not to. Her body was doing something it had done thousands of times. She looked at Amaris and saw that she had caught on as well. They looked at each other and smiled.

They were soon indistinguishable from the other women. Being with these women was not unlike being with women in their own time. They spoke about their lives, and their husbands and children. They spoke about ballplayers and the great game that was taking place tonight. And they were often crass, the way Amaris and her friends could be.

Though she had acclimated to it, Amaris couldn't deny just

how arduous and tedious this work was. It would take hours just to weave one square foot of fabric. "So, we stay here working our fingers to the bone all day while the men go hunting," Amaris said.

The other women found that an odd thing to say.

"Do you want to go hunting instead?" Abha asked her.

Amaris thought about running through the hot jungle, waiting for something to jump out and try to eat her, then replied, "No, I'm good." The other women laughed. Soon after Amaris and Aminata laughed as well.

Young children were playing nearby. A little girl was playing with a sculpted clay elephant. Another girl played with a figurine of a man lying on his stomach with his legs bent all the way around to touch the back of his head. There were boys playing with a black ball, bouncing it off their hips. It was the size of a soccer ball, but unlike a soccer ball, there was nothing soft about it. The ball got away from the boys and bounced on Aminata's foot. It hurt terribly, and Ami had to make sure nothing was broken as her toes throbbed in pain. Amaris could see the pain on her face. "Are you alright?" she asked, holding back her laughter.

"Barely. What the hell is that ball made of?" Ami asked while gritting her teeth.

Amaris pointed to a craftsman working under a tent across from them. "Remember those trees with all that white stuff leaking out," she said.

The craftsman had several clay bowls filled with the gluey white substance. He poured them into a larger bowl, squeezed the juice from the vines of a blue plant into it, and then stirred them together. He had several rubber balls already formed behind him. Aminata remembered something about the Olmecs. They were called the rubber people.

Suddenly there was a great deal of noise and a flurry of activity. Two men were ushering people out of the way while two other men carried another on a stretcher made of bamboo sticks and several large leaves wrapped around them. Aminata recognized one of the men. He was one of the hunters Sochima left with. Aminata had not seen Sochima and feared he was the man lying on the stretcher. She looked at Amaris, and they both feared the worst.

They stepped out of their looms and ran towards the hunters, trying to get a look at the man on the stretcher, when they ran into Sochima. He was carrying the stretcher from behind.

"Sochi, are you okay?" Ami asked.

"Yeah, I'm fine. Gotta go," he said, carrying the stretcher with the injured man through the crowd.

"Where are you going?" she asked.

"To see Po Ngbe," he said and continued running.

33

Bu and Sochima carried Ki on the stretcher to the base of the pyramid. A crowd had gathered around them. People had been calling for the shaman. Po Ngbe came through the entrance and stepped past the guards. He was a striking figure. He had deep mahogany skin with inky black straight hair. He wore an elaborate headdress over his elongated skull with the head of a large serpent adorned with plumes of falcon feathers, which carried down his back like a tail. He wore a large necklace made of jade and bones.

He walked down the steps and approached Ki on the stretcher. He placed his hand on Ki's chest above the heart. "His heart beats slow," he said. He pulled back his eyelids. Ki's eyes were pools of red. "He bleeds on the inside. He will not live long. Carry him in." He then nodded to the guards, and they stepped aside and allowed Bu and Sochima to enter the pyramid.

Ami and Mari attempted to follow, but the guards quickly turned them away. Po Ngbe looked at them as if they should know better before walking inside. Ami and Mari looked on, distressed, as Sochi faded into the shadows.

34

The walls on the inside were lined with hieroglyphic stone carvings. However, they moved too fast for Sochima to make them out. Once they passed through the inner corridor, they entered an enormous chamber. It was much cooler here than outside, and the air was less humid. There was an altar in the very center. Placed in a semicircle behind it were six large stone slabs, three feet wide and over seven feet tall. Each slab had an image carved into it of a monstrous figure. There was a feathered serpent, a jaguar-man, a shark full of teeth, a child with a gruesome face, a man with a maize head, and a dragon rising from a shaman.

A shaft of light shined down on the altar from an opening in the roof. This was the primary light in the room, leaving everywhere else in blue and grey shadows. In the four corners were four giant statues of dwarves, with their hands held high as if they were holding up the ceiling. As they approached the altar, Sochima could feel the presence of the next piece of Ausar growing stronger. It was here.

The altar was carved from a large block of pure stone and stood four feet off the ground. The top of the altar was a flat smooth surface six feet long. Beneath the surface was the sculpture of a shaman seated in front of a small alcove, wearing a headdress with the mouth of a jaguar.

Po Ngbe instructed them to place Ki on top of the stone altar. He was barely conscious. To their right, there was a fountain of running spring water. "Clean your hands," he said to them. Bu and Sochima followed Po to the fountain, where all three washed their hands clean. Po Ngbe also filled a large clay basin with water.

When they returned to the altar, Po Ngbe handed Bu a black

dagger made of obsidian. "Remove all of his hair," he said.

Bu began cutting the hair from Ki's head. He quickly cut off large handfuls in clumps. When he got it to a low buzzcut, he wet the blade and cleaned Ki's scalp carefully. The blade was quite sharp and effectively removed the hair. While he did this, Po used a stone mixer and crushed the leaves of a blue plant into a small clay bowl. He then poured water into the bowl and mixed it into a paste. "Lift his head and open his mouth," he said. Sochima lifted Ki from behind, and Bu opened his mouth. Po Ngbe carefully poured the solution into Ki's mouth and worked it down his throat so that he swallowed.

"How was he injured?" Po Ngbe asked them.

"We were hunting when a jaguar attacked us. He knocked Ki to the ground, where Ki hit his head on a branch," Bu said.

"He was the only one injured you were able to save?" Po asked.

"No one else was injured," Bu said.

"No one? Jaguars do not so easily abandon their prey," Po said.

"No, they do not. Kele wrestled him away, and the Jaguar fled," Bu said.

Po Ngbe looked astonished. He turned to Sochima. "You wrestled a jaguar?" he asked.

Before Sochima could answer, Bu answered for him. "Yes, he did. It was—something I had never seen before. Then he stared the jaguar in the eye, and the jaguar backed away and retreated into the forest."

Po Ngbe was very impressed by this story. "The spirit of the Hero Twins flows through you," he said. Sochima did not know what that meant or what to say, so he smiled awkwardly. "And do you play the game?" Po asked.

"Yes. Of course. We have played all our lives," Bu said.

Agreeing with Bu, Sochima said, "Yes," as well.

"Good. Good. Unfortunate that your friend has been injured, but destiny smiles on us that you were brought to me today."

Five minutes later, Po Ngbe took a blade and gently pierced

the bottom of Ki's foot. Ki did not react. "He is ready. Still, hold him down, lest he wakes up," Po said. Bu stood on his right side and held Ki down by the hand and the shoulder. Following Bu's example, Sochima did the same on his left side. Po used a smaller obsidian blade that was fashioned into a scalpel and made a vertical cut down the skin. He pulled the skin apart, exposing the skull, and used two pieces of sharp bone as anchors to hold the skin apart.

He created a small circle at the back of Ki's head. He cut around the circle repeatedly until he had created a grove in the skull. He used another tool made of bone and gently hammered it into the center, after which he pulled the circular fragment of the skull away, revealing the dura mater of the brain. Blood immediately flowed out. Sochima had never seen a living brain nor so much blood before. A part of him thought it was cool; another fought hard not to pass out. All this while the presence of the next piece vibrated beneath his feet. If only he could get to it. The guards would not allow Amaris and Aminata inside the pyramid. They needed to find another way in. Sochima saw the light from the sun shining around them and looked up at the opening in the ceiling.

35

Amaris and Aminata waited outside anxiously for Sochi-ma to return.

"What's taking so long?" Ami asked.

"Do you think he got the next piece?" Mari asked.

"I hope so. Maybe if it's right out in the open," Ami said.

The guards parted the way, and Po Ngbe, Sochima, and Bu walked out. Many people were waiting to hear what Po Ngbe had to say. "He rests. If the Gods permit, he will live." The people applauded the good news. "And tonight, we will play the great game. And I, Po Ngbe, have chosen Bu and Kele to play for us."

Po Ngbe announcing their names for the great game sent two shockwaves through the crowd. The first was a wave of surprise, and the second was a wave of applause. Po Ngbe placed his hands on Bu and Sochima's shoulders, and the people cheered even more.

Sochima had no idea what the great game was and did not know what to make of all this attention. Bu was surprised and humbled. He turned to Po Ngbe. "Great Po Ngbe. You honor me. You honor my family. Thank you. Thank you," he said repeatedly.

"I do not choose hastily. I see something great in you," Po Ngbe said to Sochima. "The both of you," he said, including Bu as well. "And I know you will bring great honor to us."

Sochima did not understand what any of this meant, but he said, "Thank you," because it seemed appropriate.

"Now make your preparations," Po Ngbe said and went back inside the pyramid.

"Can you believe it, brother? We will play in the great game together. Something we have dreamed about since we were children, but we never believed possible," Bu said to Sochima and hugged him tightly.

"Awesome," Sochima said, faking enthusiasm.

"Now, I will go speak to my family. I know they will be very excited."

"Great, and I'll go speak to my . . . women," Sochima said as he saw Amaris and Aminata walking up the steps towards him.

The people surrounded Bu as he descended the steps, congratulating him on being chosen to play in the game. They began to crowd Sochima as well, but Aminata and Amaris pushed their way through and pulled him away to the side, out of earshot of anyone else.

"Sochi, what is going on? Why are you playing in some game?" Ami asked.

"I don't know. I didn't choose it. Po Ngbe just said I was in the game, and that was it. I don't even know what the game is," he said.

"I think it's that game we saw the kids playing with the ball when they bounced it off their hips," Mari said.

"The one with that really hard ball?" Ami asked.

"Yeah, I think so," Mari said.

All three began to visualize the game in their mind as memories of it came to them.

"Oh, it's the ball game," Sochi said. "Ami, Nana showed us stories about it."

"Yeah. I remember. I think the Olmecs invented it," Ami said.

"Okay, cool. I'll play the game," Sochi said.

"No, bro, you're not playing any stupid game. Because we're getting out of here, like now. Did you get the next piece?" Mari asked.

"Ummm—no," Sochi said.

Mari sighed with disappointment.

"Then what happened in there?" Ami asked him.

"It was crazy. There was this big room with like huge statues of dwarves. And then there was this altar made of stone with a statue of Po Ngbe sitting under it. And there is this hole in the ceiling, where the light comes through. Then Po Ngbe cut Ki's head open. And I saw his brain, and there was a lot of blood."

"Okay, that sounds cool—and gross. But what about the next piece? Why didn't you get it?" Amaris asked.

"I couldn't get it. I think it's inside the altar," Sochi said.

"So, it's inside a big rock?" Mari said in frustration.

Ami was frustrated as well, but she was also relieved. "But you're okay?" she asked Sochima.

"Yeah, I'm okay," he said.

"Good," Ami said, then thumped him in the head with the butt of her palm.

"Ow. Why did you do that?" Sochi asked.

"Why did I do that? What's wrong with you? Why did you run away?"

"I didn't run away. Those guys pulled me away to go hunt with them."

"Yeah, but you didn't have to go. We were covering for you," Amaris said.

"Yeah, yeah. But, but . . . I didn't want them to think that I was a little boy," he said sheepishly.

Ami and Mari couldn't believe what they were hearing.

"You are a little boy," Aminata yelled as loud as she could whisper.

"No. I'm big now. I'm Kele. And Kele would go hunting with his friends."

"They're not your friends," Ami said.

"Yes, they are. Back home, you have friends. They're weird because they call you Amy when your name is Ami, but they're your friends." He turned to Amaris. "And you have friends. They're bad because they make you beat up people. But they're still your friends. Back home, I don't have friends. Nana was my only friend. And now she's gone. And now I'm Kele, and these are my friends," he said.

"Dude, we're not here to make friends or play some stupid game. We're here to find a piece of a dead guy, so you can eat it, and we can get out of here and get home. And you had your chance to get it, and you didn't," Amaris said.

"I couldn't get it. Po Ngbe was there," he said.

"Then how are we supposed to get it now? They won't even let us inside." Amaris said.

"I think I have an idea," Aminata said.

"What?" Amaris asked.

"Sochi, you said there's a hole in the ceiling, right?"

"Yeah," he said.

"How big is it? Is it big enough for us to fit through?" she asked.

Sochima thought for a moment, recalling the sunroof's dimensions. "Yeah," he said.

"Then, I think we wait till night, then when no one is looking, we climb up the pyramid from the back. There are no guards there. Then we sneak in from the hole in the top of the roof."

"And how are we supposed to get down from the top of the pyramid?" Amaris asked.

"We go back to the tent and tie together all the fabric they have and make a rope out of it and use it to climb down," Aminata said.

"That's awesome. Great idea, Ami," Sochima said.

Amaris, however, wasn't sold on the plan. "So, we just stay pretending we're these people and hope nobody figures it out. Then when night comes, we're gonna sneak away and climb up a hundred-foot pyramid and drop down from the roof and hope we don't die from falling."

"Yeeaaah," Ami said, feeling less confident about the plan.

36

As the day progressed people continuously approached Sochima and congratulated him on playing in the great game. One word from Po Ngbe and he had become one of the most famous people in the city. Even the nobles came and bowed their heads to him. Later Sochima and Bu were given their outfits for the game. It consisted of a great red belt made of leather and lined with rubber with a strip that hung over their loincloths to protect their privates. They also wore protective padding on their elbows and shins and a protective helmet made of rubber that fit tightly over their heads. It reminded Aminata of the helmets babies wore. Sochima wore one when he was a newborn when they feared he was developing a flat head.

Two artists approached Kele and Bu. "Great champions," they said in greeting. "Po Ngbe sent us. We are to capture your likenesses before the great game." They instructed Sochima and Bu to sit. They had mounds of clay and began to sculpt it into their image. While they did this, looking at Sochima, it occurred to Aminata just how much Kele looked like one of the colossal heads.

37

As the sun set, almost everyone in the village walked through the forest about half of a mile from the pyramid complex to another complex where the great game would be played. It had a long narrow alley flanked by two walls with sloping sides, with what resembled bleachers, or some form of viewing area, running along the top. The alley was forty meters long and ten meters wide.

In the center of the court, on both walls, there was a ring made of stone placed ten feet up, with a hole in the center the size of a basketball. The ground of the alley was made of soft, compacted earth, while the walls were hard stone. There was a walled-off endzone at both ends of the alley, with two colossal stone heads looking outward. At the front of the alley, there was a dais. It looked like a small temple. Po Ngbe stood before it. He saw Bu and Sochima among the crowd and beckoned them forward. Bu left his wife and three children, and Sochima left Amaris and Aminata and approached Po Ngbe on the dais.

As they approached, two other men were addressing him. They both had strong athletic builds and wore ball game helmets.

"You cannot do this," one of them said to Po Ngbe.

"I can. It is done," Po Ngbe replied.

"We have trained all our lives for this moment," he said.

"And I appreciate your commitment. But your sacrifice will no longer be required. Go forth. Live your lives."

"What life? A life of dishonor. Our destiny taken from us by peasant hunters."

"Your arrogance is your downfall. It is why you would lose.

The Hero Twins were peasants as you call them as well. It is my duty to choose who should best represent us, and I do not choose you. Now go."

They walked away angrily. Their faces soured, even more, when they saw Sochima and Bu behind them. While walking by, one of them purposefully ran his shoulder into Sochima's.

"Hey," Sochima said. However, they did not turn around and kept on walking. "What did we do to them?" Sochima asked.

"We did nothing, but we have taken their place, and I understand their pain. They have worked their entire lives for one purpose, and then it is taken from them at the very last moment."

"Bu, it's just a game," Sochima said.

Bu looked at him and said, "You say very strange things today, Kele."

At that point, Sochima imagined it was better he didn't say much to prevent him from saying something he shouldn't.

As they climbed the dais to Po Ngbe, two other men climbed up as well. They were dressed in game helmets and pads as Bu and Sochima were. They were their opponents. Bu knew them. They were great ball players. Along with the two men Bu and Sochima had replaced, they were the best players in the city.

Games were played all the time, but the great game was played once every hundred years. To be alive and chosen to play in a great game was every boy's dream. These men had worked their entire lives for this moment. Standing next to them, Bu felt a bit unworthy.

Po Ngbe turned the players around and addressed the crowd. The court was constructed in such a way that even at the far end, Po Ngbe's voice carried, and everyone could hear him. "We are all blessed to live in this time. Destiny chooses only a few of us to witness this moment. When the day is its shortest. When the moon and the seven earths are together. When the door between our world and the world of the dead is open, and we play the great game. When we choose the Hero Twins among us, so that the Maize God may be reborn, so that the sun and moon rise again for another hundred years, and our harvest be plentiful.

These four men honor us in this game. Two of them will honor us forever. Let the game begin," he said, and the crowd cheered.

Aminata and Amaris stood alongside Bu's family in the crowd. Bu had a wife, a one-year-old, a three-year-old, and a seven-year-old. Being the family of the players, they were placed in the front row. Aminata listened to Po Ngbe's speech. There was a seriousness to everything that she did not like. This game seemed too important to everyone. She couldn't wait for it to be over, so they could get Sochima and sneak away to the pyramid.

38

It was nightfall when the game began. The court and view-ing area were well lit by torches placed throughout. The game, in premise, was like volleyball. However, there wasn't a net. There was a marker placed in the center of the court delineating each side. Players were not permitted to cross it. You were forbidden to use your hands or your feet. Every other part of your body was in play, primarily your hips, thighs, knees, elbows, shoulders, and even the head. Using the head would not be advisable, as the ball was seven pounds of pure rubber.

Only at the beginning of each play was a player allowed to use their hands or feet to get the ball airborne. You were forbidden to hit the ball twice, but players could hit it as often between themselves before sending it to the other side. The slanted walls were also in play as players were allowed to bounce the ball off the walls. Points were scored whenever the ball fell on an opponent's side, or if the ball was knocked out of bounds. The first team to score seven points won the game. The first team to win two games won the match. Each game could be won immediately by putting the ball through one of the two stone rings in the center of the court. The ring was ten feet high and was only a few inches wider than the ball. It required a deft touch and a great deal of luck to score. Players could go their entire lives, never scoring a goal.

Every boy, since he could walk has played the game. Kele and Bu had played the game together often, but they were hunters by trade. The men they faced spent their entire lives playing and practicing—and it showed. Sochima had never played a sport in his young life. He was stunned by how fast everything was happening. The opposing team sent the ball at him, hitting his shoulder with such force that it knocked him down and went out of bounds before Bu could get to it.

It took Sochima time to get used to the weight of the ball and better cushion himself to its impact and redirect it. Sochima relied on Kele's memories to play the game, but his memories came too slowly. Bu and Sochima were completely out of sync, barely able to keep the ball up when they had it and leaving their opponents with easy scoring opportunities. Sochima also made two lame attempts at scoring the ball in the ring. "What are you doing?" Bu said to him. "Scoring a goal is almost impossible." Sochima listened to him and played conventionally on the next play, and they successfully got the ball over to the opposing side. Their opponents, however, quickly returned it to their side for a point. The score was six-love. The difference in the quality of the two teams was a lopsided embarrassment, and the people began to jeer.

One of the players, Bu and Sochima replaced, shouted, "Po Ngbe. Is this what you wanted? You replaced us for these peasants. They dishonor our gods."

Po Ngbe did not comment but turned to him, and he fell silent, and his teammate pulled him back. The crowd also fell silent, not wanting to jeer and provoke Po Ngbe's ire. However, the nobles in the crowd whispered to themselves. Po sat with his fingers interlocked and quietly seethed. He looked at Sochima, and his eyes said it all.

"Your brother sucks at this game," Amaris said to Aminata.

"I'd like to see how well you play a game you'd never played before," Aminata said.

"You're right. I'd probably suck too. Maybe not as bad. I just want him to hurry up and lose already, so we can get out of here."

Aminata wanted the game to end quickly as well, but she also didn't like seeing her brother embarrassed. Without thinking, she shouted, "C'mon Kele. C'mon Bu," which inspired Bu's wife to do the same.

Seeing his wife and children in the crowd, Bu said to Sochima, "Kele, my brother, we cannot lose—not like this. We would bring such shame to ourselves and our families. We cannot lose like this. Where are you? You know how to play the game better than this."

Sochima nodded and began having memory flashes of playing the game from when he was as little as four, up until last week. He took in a deep breath, determined to play better. Sochima put the ball in play, and he and Bu bounced it between each other until Bu found an angle and sent it over with his hip. Nevertheless, it was an easy ball to return, and the opposing team sent it back with force. The ball went off Bu's shoulder and was careening out of bounds. If it landed, that would be the end of the first game, and they would lose seven-love. Hearing the jeers from the crowd and seeing the disappointment on Po Ngbe's face, Sochima found the heart to chase the ball down, slide in the dirt and get under it, knocking it off his hip. The ball ricocheted off the wall, giving a surprised Bu an angle to get to it. He hit it off his thigh and back into the air, but the ball was low and would not reach the other side. Sochima ran to it, sliding in the dirt again, hitting the ball off his right hip at an angle too low for the opposing team to get to. The ball went right by them and scored.

The stadium erupted in applause. Aminata and Amaris also jumped up and cheered. That was a great rally, and the crowd was re-engaged. But their applause was short-lived as on the next play, the opposing team easily scored and won the first game. Nevertheless, something had changed with Bu and Sochima. That rally sparked something in them, and they became more connected.

In the second game, they played with great inspiration. Sochima did not have great skill or technique, but he had an unyielding will not to lose. He chased down every ball with abandon. Points their opponents and the crowd believed would certainly score, he kept in play and gave Bu the chance to return and score. The rallies in the second game were long, hard-fought, and filled with tension. Where the first game lasted less than ten minutes, the second game lasted almost half an hour. Their bodies were bruising from the constant pounding of the ball.

The score was six to five in the opposing team's favor. It was matchpoint. It had been a long rally, and the opposing team shot the ball with force, and it glanced off Bu's head, knocking Bu down, and ricocheted up off the wall. Bu was on the ground and in the way, and the only way for Sochima to get to the ball was to run on the wall. He did this without thinking or even knowing if he could do it. Everyone looked on in amazement. He got to the ball and was about to knock it over to the other side, but then he saw the stone ring . . . and he went for it. He hit the ball with his left thigh. It rode up the wall, entered the ring, and fell through. The simultaneous collective roar of the crowd was like a sonic boom that exploded outward. It shook the earth and shook your soul. Even the dead looked up and paid attention. Aminata and Amaris cheered so hard that they screamed and felt like they had the most intense brain freeze. Bu and Sochima had won the second game and tied the match, and most of the crowd was now firmly rooting them on.

While the crowd subsided from the explosion of Sochima's goal, Aminata looked at Bu's wife and children and noticed that Bu's seven-year-old daughter was crying, and his wife was trying to console her. Aminata couldn't understand why she would cry at such a joyous moment. Bu and Kele had a great chance to win the game. Surely that would be a good thing. "What's wrong? Why does she cry?" Ami asked Bu's wife.

"She doesn't want them to win. She doesn't yet understand what a great honor winning the game is. That our family will become nobles, that Bu and Kele will live on forever, and we will see them again in the afterlife."

It was then that everything began to make sense to Aminata. "We have to stop this game, and we have to get out of here," she said to Amaris.

"Why? It sucked at first, but now it's getting good. And Sochi might win," Amaris said.

"That's the problem. If he wins. He dies."

39

The final game had begun, and the score was two to one in Bu and Sochima's favor. Aminata and Amaris left the viewing area and made their way to the back of the court. Aminata was trying to figure out a way to get a message to Sochima. Thankfully, the ball rolled out of bounds, and she ran to recover it. She discretely called Sochima over to her to get the ball. Sochima ran to her. "Hey, Ami. This game is hard. Like, really hard. The ball hurts. But it's fun—and did you see the goal? It was so amazing," he said as he reached for the ball.

"Sochi, you can't win," she whispered to him.

"Yes, I can. We're up, and I'm really good at this game."

"That's why you can't win. If you win, you die," she said with as much seriousness as she could convey without letting anyone else hear what they were saying. Sochima looked confused. "They sacrifice the winners to their gods. So, you can't win."

"Are you sure?"

"Think about it," she said.

As soon as Sochi asked himself the question, Kele's memories gave him the answer. It hit him like a gut punch., and the six-year-old in him came out. "So, what am I supposed to do?" he asked on the verge of crying.

"I don't know. Find a way to sneak away. When you do, Mari and I will meet you in the forest, and we'll go back to the pyramid," Ami said.

"In the middle of the game. With everyone watching. How do I do that?" he asked.

"You're smart. Think of something."

Sochima walked back to the center of the court with the ball looking utterly perplexed. Bu asked Sochima if he was "okay," and Sochima did not answer. They put the ball back into play, and Bu set Sochima up to attempt a goal. Sochima froze, and the ball hit him directly in the head, knocking him to the ground. The point went to the opposing team, and the game was tied.

"What are you doing?" Bu asked.

Sochima got to his feet and said, "Time out," and made the letter T with his hands. Everyone was confused. They had no concept of a timeout. "I . . . I . . . need to pee," he said. Everyone looked utterly bewildered, as no one had ever halted the game for a bathroom break before. Sochima then ran off the court to murmurs and confusion, leaving Bu more perplexed than anyone.

40

Sochima met Aminata and Amaris in the forest and they ran the entire half mile back to the pyramid complex. Fortunately, no one was there. Most everyone was at the arena watching the ball game. They went to the tent where Aminata and Amaris had been weaving earlier and collected as much woven fabric as they could carry. They then made for the pyramid, hoping the guards would be at the game and they could enter from the front and not have to scale it. Unfortunately, the guards were still there.

They cut through the forest and headed to the back of the pyramid. They began tying all the fabric together into a rope. There weren't any steps at the back of the pyramid. To scale it, they'd have to climb each of the seven large steps individually. Sochima would climb up first, then reach down from the landing and pull Aminata and Amaris up. They did this for each of the seven large steps until they reached the top. Sochima and Aminata took a second to marvel at the view. The view from below was quite spectacular. The view from above was even better. They had never seen so many stars in the night sky. They could see hundreds of stars. They could also see the planets—and to Aminata, the planets seemed to be aligned.

"Wow," Sochima and Aminata said, and Amaris put her finger to her mouth for them to be quiet. She pointed down, and they all went prone and looked into the moonroof, their heads peeking over just enough for their eyes to see. There were people down there. They were noble, from the shape of their heads. There were sixteen men, wearing only their loincloths. They stood in a semicircle around the altar and the six standing pillars. There was also a noblewoman carrying a basket filled with something. They couldn't tell what was in it, but whatever it was, was moving. She then pulled one of them from the basket and placed it in the mouth of one of the men. He did not chew it, and he did not swallow it completely. He kept its body inside his mouth as its legs dangled and kicked. The children put their hands to their mouths to hold in their disgust.

The woman pulled another from the basket when another nobleman ran into the pyramid. "Stop," he shouted.

"How dare you interrupt," the woman said.

"The great game has been ruined," he said. This drew everyone's attention. "One of the players has run off before the game ended, and he cannot be found."

"No, this cannot be. We must find him. We cannot let this door close. All will be lost if the game is not completed." The woman ran out, and the men followed her. One of the men spat whatever was in his mouth out. Two other men helped keep him on his feet as he had become woozy. The children could see lit torches throughout the forest. Everyone was searching for them. "We cannot let them find us. We have to get out of here right now," Amaris said.

41

They tied the rope around the uppermost layer of the pyramid. Amaris double-knotted it and tested to make sure it was secure. After she was certain, she threw the long end down the moon roof. The moon cast a shaft of light that extended to the bottom. She handed the rope to Sochima. "Okay, Kele. You first," she said.

Sochima held onto the rope, went through the moonroof, and steadily guided himself down. Kele's body was strong and athletic, and Sochima could go down quickly.

Aminata was next, but she was not as confident. "I always sucked at this in gym class," she said.

"You're not Ami. You're Nakawe. You got this," Amaris said.

Ami appreciated the encouragement. "Thanks." She then took a deep breath, held tightly onto the rope, and guided herself down. Sochima stood below her, ready to catch her if she fell. She did not. She took three times as long as Sochima, but she safely made it down.

A minute later, Amaris was down as well. They stood in front of the altar and the six stone pillars with the monstrous carvings. Aminata studied them for a moment when they noticed a toad jumping on the ground.

"Whoa. Was that what was in that guy's mouth?" Amaris asked.

"I don't know. Maybe," Aminata said.

"Ewww. Nobles are so weird."

"Yes, they are."

"Guys, that doesn't matter now. The next piece is here," Sochima said.

"Where?" Amaris asked.

"Is it inside the altar?" Aminata asked.

"I don't think so. It feels like it's underneath it," Sochima said.

"Underneath it?" Amaris repeated with annoyance. "Dude, we don't have shovels. How are we supposed to get it if it's underground?"

"I don't know. This is just where it feels the strongest," Sochima said.

"Of course. It couldn't just be right there on top for us to take it," Aminata said in frustration and without thinking, tapped the staff on the ground. The ground trembled slightly, and a small hole appeared beneath where the staff fell.

"What the hell? The stick ever do that before?" Amaris asked Aminata.

"No," Aminata said.

Sochima had an idea. "Do it again, but, but, hold it there," he said.

Aminata did as Sochima suggested, and the ground trembled, and the hole grew deeper and deeper by many feet until the earth revealed a mummified object, which rose to the surface as the earth beneath it filled.

"Is that it?" Aminata asked.

It looked like the broken half of a tablet.

"Yeah, I think so," Sochima said.

"What the hell is it?" Amaris asked.

"It's a piece of Ausar," Sochima said.

"What piece?" Amaris asked.

"Well, I already have the heart," Sochima said.

"It looks like a lung. Like the right lung," Aminata said.

"Ewww," Amaris remarked, looking grossed out. She turned to Sochi, "Okay, go ahead, eat up."

"I'm not putting that in my mouth," Sochima objected.

"Why not? You did it before, and that's why we came here."

"What Nana gave me was like a ball of light. It wasn't like old, rotting meat."

Out of curiosity, Aminata poked the lung with the staff to get a sense of how heavy it was when the body of the lung turned to dust and seeped into the earth, revealing a beautiful orb of light, much like it was when Nana presented it to Sochima.

"Whoa," the children said collectively and looked around and saw that they had stepped out of the bodies they were in and were simply their spirits.

"We're out of their bodies," Amaris said.

"Good. We must be doing something right. Now go-ahead Sochi, eat it," Aminata said—when they heard "Children" coming from a voice in the air. They shuddered and looked around, but from where the voice came, they could not tell.

"Children," they heard again, but it wasn't calling to them. It was speaking to itself. "How many years? How many years has it been?" They kept looking around for where the voice came. The orb created a portal of light with a circumference of twenty yards. Beyond that were shadows through which they could barely see. "So many. Too many. So many I stopped counting. Don't count years anymore. I count lives. How many lives has it been? Ten? Twenty? One hundred? No, not a hundred. Somewhere between ten and twenty lives, I've spent waiting . . . for you." He scoffed. He chuckled. "For children."

They looked around furiously for where the voice came when Amaris noticed someone standing in the shadows, just outside of the circumference of the portal. "Look," she directed the others. They could see the shape of a woman holding something or someone. As she came closer, just to the edge of the light, they could see that it was the noblewoman carrying the noble baby.

"This is your post. Guard it with your soul. And I will give you everlasting existence." the baby said.

Seeing the baby speak so fluently sent shivers down their spines. "I knew there was something wrong with that baby," Amaris said.

"I watched this civilization grow. I watched it flourish. I

aborted it once in fear of your coming. Many, many, many lives ago. Took them from the mountains. Rebuilt it better. Stronger. All to protect against you . . . children."

"Um, sorry to disappoint you. So, we'll just be on our way," Aminata said.

"Humor. You use humor in the face of death." The noble-woman knelt and put the baby on the ground. The baby crawled into the circumference of the portal, and its soul left its body and transformed from a baby to a Jaguar-man—jaguar head, man chest, man arms, jaguar paws, jaguar legs, jaguar-tail—seven feet tall. "I knew there was something different about you three." His voice had changed as well. It was deeper and more resounding. "I know every living thing in this city, flesh, and soul. But today though the flesh was the same, the soul smelled different. Off. You deceived Po Ngbe to his folly and our down-fall. Boy, you do not know the grave tragedy you have commit-ted. How many lives will be lost because of it? But I will make it better. I'll make a quick meal of you," he said to Sochima.

"Stay away from my brother," Aminata said

"Aww, the protective sister. How sweet. And you?" he asked, turning to Amaris. "Sister too?"

"I just got off the wrong bus stop. And I just wanna go home," Amaris said with genuine fear.

"Awwww. Poor thing. So utterly lost. I pity you. But don't worry. I'll send you home." He got on all fours preparing to charge. Aminata turned to Sochima. "Sochi eat it. Now."

Sochima reached for the orb, but the Jaguar-man closed the distance between them, broke through Aminata and Amaris, pinned Sochima to the ground, and swallowed his head.

"Sochi," Aminata shouted and reflexively swung the staff, releasing a whorl of energy, knocking the jaguar-man away and freeing Sochima before his teeth could clench.

Sochima back-peddled away with his hands, happy to still have his head.

"You hurt me," the jaguar-man said. "How did you hurt me? He looked at the staff, glowing in Aminata's hand. "I see. So insulted I was by your presence I neglected the pretty stick. I will not make that error again."

He leaped into the air, clung to the ceiling, then pounced off, landing in front of Aminata. He grabbed hold of the staff with one hand and held Aminata by the throat with the other. "Now, let me have it," he said.

Though terrified, Aminata would not let go of the staff and found the courage to say, "No."

"Ami," Sochi shouted.

"Let her go," Amaris yelled as she ran towards him.

The Jaguar-man kicked Amaris in the chest and sent her flying backward out of the portal's light.

Sochima ran to help Aminata, but she turned to him and said, "Eat it."

Sochima ran to the orb but seeing what he was doing the jaguar-man roared, "Get away," with such ferocity, the force of his voice blew Sochima back. The jaguar-man returned his gaze to Aminata. "What were you thinking? That you would just come and steal from me? Poor child. Who told you to do this? Such cruelty to send children."

Amaris was kicked out of the circumference of the orb's portal onto her back. When she tried to stand, a force held her down. She looked up and saw the soul of Inda Jani, whose body she had occupied. She looked just as intimidating as when she held Amaris down early this morning.

"Get off of me. Get off. I don't want your body," Amaris shouted while fighting her off. Inda Jani released her. Amaris stood up, and there were the souls of Kele and Nakawe. They looked at Amaris and then to the portal and saw their bodies standing still in the light.

They walked into the portal, and they each attempted to re-enter their bodies, but while the portal was open, they could not. The jaguar-man saw them but paid them no mind.

"Poor lost souls," he said. Then he began to hear chanting and turned to find Sochima seated in a monk's pose chanting his name as he had done before.

"I am *Sochima Nebkheperure* . Let her go and go away."

"What is this?" the Jaguar-man said. While holding Aminata by the throat, he turned and walked towards Sochima, who continued to chant. "You take me for some pathetic lost soul that you can command. I am a hand of God. You insult me—boy."

At that moment, Inda Jani saw the orb and was drawn to its light—so brilliant, so beautiful. She was entranced. She stopped trying to enter her body and walked towards it. She reached down to touch it. Sochima saw her and shouted, "Noooo," The jaguar man turned and saw her as well. He became frantic. He tossed Aminata aside, releasing her and the staff. He leaped into the air and pounced on Inda Jani before she could touch the orb, and with his bare hands ripped her soul in two, shattering it. This angered the souls of Kele and Nakawe. They screamed into the night and attacked him. While they fought, Amaris got to Aminata, and Aminata looked at Sochima, and he knew what she wanted him to do. She then looked at Amaris. "Let's go," she said.

"Um, what are we doing?" she asked, following Aminata's lead as they ran towards the Jaguar-man as he tore the souls of Kele and Nakawe apart. Aminata swung the staff at his head, and Amaris kicked him, angering him, giving Sochima the opening he needed to sneak behind and get to the orb. The Jaguar-man saw Sochima and turned his attention away from the girls. Sochima held the orb with both hands and directed it into his mouth. The jaguar-man charged at him, but the portal closed and Sochima's soul disappeared as he returned to the body of Kele. Amaris and Aminata were also back in Inda Jani and Nakawe's bodies.

"Are you alright?" they asked each other. They all answered affirmatively. Then they heard crying. It began softly at first but grew in volume and intensity from crying to wailing to a full-on tantrum as the noble baby rolled around, pounding the ground.

"That is so freaky," Amaris said.

"Guys, let's get out of here," Sochima said.

"Okay, how do we do that?" Aminata asked.

"Like Nana said. We hold onto each other and don't let go," Sochima said.

"Okay," Aminata said. She held tightly onto the staff, and they held her, and then they were gone, and the bodies of Kele, Nakawe, and Inda Jani fell dead to the floor, and the baby's cries echoed through the chamber.

ACT THREE

THE LION KING'S LEGACY

42

Like before, there was light and then darkness. Only this time, the darkness did not persist. Amaris opened her eyes and saw streaks of light coming through the ceiling. The morning sun shined through the slits in the wood, stinging her eyes. She put her hand up to block it out and was taken aback by what she saw. She blinked three times to remove the cobwebs. *What the hell?* She wondered at seeing her hand. It was the color of dark chocolate. This was not what startled her. It was the size of her hand. It was large—unusually large. "Why is my hand so big?" she thought aloud. Startled at hearing her voice, "Why is my voice so deep?" she remarked. "Ami?" she called.

"Mari," an older man, sitting a foot away, sat up and answered.

"Ami, is that you?" Amaris asked.

"Yeah, it's me . . . Sochi?" Aminata called for her brother.

"I'm here," Sochima answered from behind. Amaris and Aminata turned around and saw him. He was an older man as well. They were all sitting under the canopy of a wooden boat, shaped like a large canoe, floating in the middle of a large body of water. There were five other men on the boat as well. Four of them wore turbans and gambesons and carried swords curved like a hook. There was also a boatman who stood at the top of the boat, with a long oar, which he pushed deep into the water to guide and propel the boat forward. All the men looked at the children oddly because of their sudden outbursts and the strange language they spoke. "Ministers are you well?" one of the men with swords asked. The children were attempting to come up with an explanation for their behavior when they heard a blaring honk, like the sound of a foghorn, before the boat was hit by something massive, as if blindsided by a truck. The boat turned over and everyone fell into the river.

Underwater, Aminata could see what had hit the boat. A bloat of hippos attacked them. The boat had unintentionally floated into the territory of the magnificent beasts. There were six of them, and they were ravaging the vessel and everything around it. As the other men swam to the surface, the hippos attacked them; their large mouths, their large teeth, biting into their legs, torsos, and head. Aminata could hear the men screaming as the water turned crimson.

She did not see Sochima or Amaris and feared for their safety. She also feared for herself, as the more pressing danger for Aminata was not the hippos but that she did not know how to swim. She was sinking, and she couldn't hold her breath much longer. Gravity held her like an anchor dragging her down into the abyss. Her chest hurt, and her lungs were on fire. The spirit of a man appeared before her. He looked at her intently, then began fading away when a hand came through his body and grabbed hers. It was Sochima. He pulled her up and swam towards the boat. Aminata wondered why he was taking her into the heart of the hippos. When they got to the boat, she found that they could breathe directly under it where the boat floated above the water. She found Amaris there as well.

"Mari," she said.

"Ami," Amaris replied, and they hugged each other, glad that they were all still alive, forgetting that they were not that kind of friends until they remembered and let each other go. They could hear the men screaming, fighting for their lives, and the large bodies of the hippopotamuses slamming into the boat.

"What are we gonna do you guys? Those hippos are gonna tear through this boat pretty soon," Amaris said.

"We have to swim deeper," Sochima said.

"Swim deeper?" The thought of going deeper underwater terrified Aminata. "No, no, I can't do that, I can't do that," Ami said.

"Ami, we have to. Hippos can't swim deep underwater. If we

swim deeper, we can get around them and get away," Sochima said.

"Yeah, that sounds like a plan," Amaris said.

"But I can't swim," Aminata said.

"I know, I know. I'll hold you, and I'll swim for you," Sochima said.

"Even if you did that, I wouldn't be able to hold my breath that long."

"Yeah, I'm not sure I can hold my breath that long either," Amaris said.

"It's okay. I can breathe for you guys," he said. They both looked at him as if he was crazy. The hippos were about to tear through the boat. "We don't have time. Just trust me."

"Okay," Aminata said.

"Now open your mouths."

"What? Why?"

"Just do it," Sochima yelled.

They both opened their mouths. Sochima went to Amaris first and blew air into her mouth. The air filled her lungs, and she felt she could hold her breath for minutes. Sochima then did the same for Aminata, and with the air in her lungs, a calmness came over her. She held onto the staff, and Sochima held onto her, and all three of them dived deeper underwater. They descended deep enough so as not to create any ripples the hippos might sense, and they swam away from the wreckage of the boat and the whirlpool of blood around it.

43

They came out of the water and crawled into the grass-lands surrounding the bank. They could see the hippos attacking the boat and the men in the middle of the river. One of the men with swords and the boatman survived the attack and made it to the other side.

The children collapsed in the bushes looking up at the sun.

"I didn't know hippos attacked people. I thought they were cute and playful," Aminata said.

"That was definitely not cute," Amaris said.

None of the children had ever seen someone die, especially in so gruesome a manner. They could still hear the screams of the men and the deafening honk of the hippos. They lay there physically and emotionally exhausted in the bush for what felt like an hour but was only ten minutes. When Aminata got the energy to raise her head, "How did you do that, Sochi? How did you hold your breath that long?" she asked.

"It was the lung from Ausar," he said. "It made me breathe longer. When I fell in the water, I felt like I could breathe for a really long time."

"Yeah, it was cool the way you did that. You saved our butts, big head," Amaris said.

"Don't call me that," Sochima said.

"Fine, you earned it," Amaris said and heard the deepness in her voice. It made her remember something. She crawled over to the river and looked at her reflection. "Oh my God. I'm a man."

Aminata and Sochima also went to the river and looked at their reflections.

"Yeah, I'm a man too," Aminata said.

They were all men, who looked to be in their mid-fifties. Their wooly hair and beards were half-gray. Amaris shook her head in dismay. "This is so gross. I didn't know we could be men," she said, sounding frantic.

"Me either," Aminata said, though she was more subdued.

This annoyed Amaris. "Why isn't this bothering you?" she asked Aminata.

"What are you talking about? It's bothering me," Ami said.

"Then why are you so calm? You're always so calm."

"I'm processing everything, okay? Yesterday, I didn't know I could come out of my body, and travel through time, and go into somebody else's body. So, the fact that I can also go into a man's body is just one of the things I'm processing," Ami said.

"Of course, you can go into a man's body, duh," Sochima said.

Sochima's glibness and sarcasm annoyed Amaris. "Hey, thanks again for saving me, but if you keep talking like that, I'm gonna smack you, okay," Amaris said.

"I'm big now. If you smack me, I'll smack you back," Sochima said.

"I don't care how big you are. I'll still kick your butt," Amaris said.

"I wrestled a jaguar. I'd like to see you try," Sochima said.

"That's when you were Kele. Now you're some old dude," Amaris said.

Aminata intervened between the two of them. "No one is kicking anyone's butt. And why are you always trying to fight people?" she said to Amaris.

"I'm not, but you're always so calm, and he's always acting like he knows everything, and it makes me mad," Amaris said.

"Look, that Man-Jaguar thing was in a baby's body. And back home, that angel Nana fought was in a woman's body," Sochima said.

"Yeah, you're right. I guess our souls can go into anyone's body. It doesn't matter their age or if they're a man or woman," Ami said.

"And where are their souls now?" Mari asked.

"Who's souls?" Sochima asked.

"The souls of the bodies we are in."

"Oh, they're gone," Sochima said.

"How do you know that?" Amaris asked him.

"I saw them fade away when we were underwater," he said.

"Yeah, me too," Aminata said.

"Where did they go?" Amaris asked.

Sochima shrugged his shoulders. "Wherever souls go after they die, I guess."

"But they didn't die; we're in their bodies," Aminata said.

"And Kele, Nakawe, and Inda Jani faded away too, but then

they showed up in the pyramid and tried to strangle me," Amaris said.

"Yeah, but they never really went away. They were always with us," Sochima said.

Both girls were shocked to hear this.

"Wait, wait, wait, you could see them that whole time? How comes we couldn't see them?" Aminata asked Sochi.

"I couldn't see them, but I could feel them," Sochi said.

"Feel them how?"

"I don't know. The same way I can feel where the next piece is. I just feel things," Sochi said.

"Then why didn't you tell us?" Amaris asked.

"Because . . ." he said and said nothing else.

"Are you gonna tell us, or what?" Amaris asked.

"Because, because, you guys were so freaked out about being in their bodies and you wanted to go home, and I didn't want to freak you out more. So, I didn't tell you," Sochi said.

Amaris ground her teeth. "Hey, buddy, how about you tell me everything that's going on, and then I'll know if I wanna freak out," she said.

"Yeah Sochi, that wasn't cool. You should let us know everything you're feeling," Ami said.

"Okay, fine." Sochima turned to Amaris. "Mari," he said.

"Yeah?" she answered cautiously.

"The guy whose body you're in is right behind you."

"What?" she shouted and jumped up and screamed like a thirteen-year-old girl in a fifty-year-old man's body and ran to Aminata. "Get him off me, get him off me," she shouted.

Aminata held her while looking around, wondering if her body's soul was behind her as well. "Sochi is mine on me too?" she asked.

To which Sochima held his stomach dying of laughter. "You should," laughter, "you should," crying laughter, "see your faces," more laughter, "you're so scared," Sochima said.

"Wait, so, there's nothing behind us?" Amaris asked.

More laughter, "No," he said. "Oh my God, you're a man, but you screamed like a girl."

"I'm so going to smack him," Amaris said and ran to strangle Sochima. He was able to dodge her, and she continued to chase him, and he kept Aminata in between them until Amaris came to a sudden stop as she felt a sharp pain in her leg. "Ow, ow, ow, ow," she said and held the back of her right thigh.

"What happened?" Aminata asked her.

"I don't know. I just felt a pain in my leg for no reason. I didn't even run long," Mari said.

"Yeah, can we stop? I think my back is beginning to hurt," Sochima said and held his back.

"Can you guys stop playing around and act your age, so we can try to find this next piece," Aminata said.

"Sure, it's that way," Sochima said, grimacing a bit, pointing beyond the grassy plains towards a sandy horizon.

"Great. Let's go," Aminata said.

"Wait. I'm gonna need a minute," Amaris said as she massaged the back of her thigh. "Being old sucks."

44

They waited another ten minutes by the riverbank for Amaris to recover and feel up to walking. The direction Sochima said they should be walking in looked barren and desolate. Aminata suggested they collect water from the river before leaving as they didn't know how long they would be walking in that dry region. Unfortunately, they had nothing to hold water in. They decided to drink as much water as they could, hoping their journey wasn't too long and it would carry them through.

Fifteen minutes into their walk, they realized they were not just walking into a desolate area but a vast desert. "Sochi, are you sure this is the right way?" Ami asked her brother.

"Yeah," Sochi answered.

"Can you tell how close we are?"

"No. Only that the more we go that way, the closer we get," he said.

Amaris looked out at the vast expanse, the ripples in the sand, and the massive dunes as far as the eye could see. "Guys, this is a desert. Like a real desert," she said. "Deserts are no joke. People die in deserts."

"Yeah, they do," Ami said, looking up at the sun and the vultures flying overhead.

Just then, they saw something coming from the south above the horizon. With the glare of the sun reflecting off the sand, it looked like a jagged silhouette. "What is that?" Amaris asked.

"I don't know, but it's getting closer," Aminata said.

They were soon able to make out that it was a camel and a man walking beside it. As he drew closer, they saw that it was in fact several men and several camels laden with heavy bags. As they came even closer, they saw dozens of men, a hundred or more, and dozens of camels in a caravan stretching a mile long. Like themselves, the men wore loose-fitting robes and sandals; some of them wore turbans. The children were amazed at what they saw. Many of the men walked by them with just a nod.

One of the travelers greeted them, "Hello friends," he said.

"Hello," Sochima replied.

"You look lost, my friends," he said.

"We are. We were in a boat, but it was attacked by hippos and capsized. We were able to get away and swim to the shore near here," Aminata said.

"I see. The Niger can be treacherous at times," the traveler said.

"Do you know where we are?" Amaris asked him.

He thought that was a strange question. "You are in the empire of Mali of the great Mansa Musa," he said. They were all startled to hear the name, Mansa Musa. It was a name even Amaris knew. "Your boat must have been a fine one," the traveler remarked.

"Why do you say that?" Aminata asked.

"Well, you are no fishermen," he said with a smile.

"How do you know that?"

"Fishermen do not wear such fine clothes," he remarked on their attire. For the first time, the children looked at what they were wearing. Though their clothes were disheveled from being in the water, they were made with fine linen and silk. They also wore gold chains, bracelets, and rings. "You are men of wealth and importance," he said.

"And who are you?" Amaris asked.

"I am a simple salt merchant, taking my goods from Taghaza to Timbuktu," he replied.

"How far is Timbuktu from here?" Amaris asked.

"Not far now. Well before the sun sets, we will be there. Is that where you mean to go?" the traveler asked them.

"Yes, it is," Sochima answered, seeing the caravan going in the direction the heart was leading him.

45

The children followed along with the caravan but just out of earshot of the traders.

"Okay, so we're in the Mali Empire during the time of Mansa Musa," Aminata said.

"Yeah, and he reigned from 1312 to 1337. So, we could be anywhere in between then," Sochima said.

"Okay, I know this. I've heard of Mansa Musa. I heard that he was like crazy rich . . . and that's it," Amaris said.

"And that he went to Mecca and gave away a lot of gold. But that's basically all I know too," Ami said. "Sochi, do you remember anything else?"

"Um, he went to Mecca in 1324, he took like sixty thousand people with him, he—"

"Yeah, I remember that, but are we in a time before or after 1324?" Ami asked.

Out of the blue, Amaris said, "It's after he went to Mecca."

"How do you know that?" Ami asked.

"Because we went with him," she said. Once she said that they all took a moment to recollect. "When you said Mecca, I had a vision of it in my head, and I saw us with him."

"Yeah, me too," Sochima said.

"Same. All these images just started flooding in my mind," Aminata said.

"Yeah, it feels so weird having memories of things I didn't do. I don't like being in other people's bodies," Amaris said.

"Me either," Aminata said.

They both looked at Sochi. He shrugged his shoulders. "I'm big. I'm cool," he said.

"Yeah, and you suck," Amaris said.

"No, I don't."

"Yes, you do. You're all like, I get to be in someone's body; this is so awesome."

"It is awesome," Sochima said.

"No, it's definitely not awesome," Amaris said while adjusting the garments under her robe. "And why does this thing keep moving," she said, and Sochima giggled.

"How about we keep moving? Which way Sochima?" Ami asked.

"Just follow them," he said, pointing to the camel caravan. "We're going the same way."

46

They walked alongside the caravan for another hour, speaking with a few of the merchants. They were a varied people, mainly of a very deep brown complexion, but a few were caramel-skinned with curly hair. They carried salt, copper, tea, tobacco, and animal skins to trade in Timbuktu.

Sochima was fascinated with the camels. He had never seen a camel in real life before. It was such a peaceful animal; quiet, humble, and strong. It bore its burden with such dignity. The merchants considered it their lifeline. They would not be able to transport their goods across the Sahara without it. "It is the camel," one of the merchants said, "that has made the Mansa so rich."

Since coming out of the river, they had been walking for two hours before approaching the city.

"My friend, do you know why they call the city Timbuktu?" the traveler asked Amaris.

"No, I don't," Amaris said.

"Many, many years ago, before the Keïta family created their empire. Before the Sosso kingdom and their King attempted to create their own, there was Ghana. Like Mali, they were a great empire and controlled all these lands. But this was not a city as you see now, with thousands of people living here. It was simply a stopping point where my people, the Sanhaja, would come and trade their goods and then move on. Part of their group was a slave woman called Buktu.

"One day, they tasked Buktu with looking after their belongings until they returned. While Buktu waited, she grew tired and thirsty. When they returned, they did not see her, and they were upset that she had abandoned their goods. But then she returned and told them that she had found this great well, and she took them to it. This well had the sweetest water they had ever tasted. The water had the essence of life itself. So great was their love for this well that my people decided to give up their nomadic ways and create a life for themselves here around it. In honor of Buktu's great discovery, they decided to name the well after her. As *tim* means well in my language, it became Timbuktu. And after many, many years the well of Buktu has grown into a great city," he said.

"That's a great story. Is it true?" Amaris asked.

"Of course, it is true. Why would I lie to you, my friend?" he said and smiled.

47

Timbuktu was indeed a great city. Like an artery, so much life flowed through it. People from the north, west, east, and south came to trade their goods. There was a multitude of ethnicities present and languages spoken; Mandé and Arabic were the most prevalent. The people were mainly of a burnt umber complexion, with broad noses, thick lips, and woolly hair. Most everyone wore loose-flowing clothes with leather sandals. Many men wore turbans, and most of the women veiled their faces, except for the enslaved women who sold fruits, vegetables, and baked goods. They did not look enslaved to the children; however, when they heard them referred to as such, the children were distressed by this.

The merchants from the caravan unloaded the solid blocks of rock salt from their camels, and within a short time, they were gone. Salt was always in high demand and was nearly as valuable as gold. People paid for their goods with gold dust and cowrie shells. Traders selling copper, tea, and animal skins sold quickly as well. This was why the caravans traversed the dangers and desolateness of the Sahara.

Like the Olmec pyramid complex, there were tents of women weaving cotton into fabric, using a process very similar to what the Olmecs used. Some merchants sold fabrics imported from the north and beyond. Others sold materials made from barkcloth; a cloth made from pounding the inner bark of a tree. There were also artisans selling tiny sculptures of warriors in uniforms, riding horses, and holding bows and arrows.

The children left the caravan and traversed the city on their own. Though this was a foreign land, they felt safe doing so.

The people were peaceful and polite, and the children witnessed no loud grievances between them. Some people walked about playing instruments.

Most of the houses in Timbuktu were huts covered in clay with thatched roofs, mostly in the shape of a cupola, like the hump of a camel. The buildings were made of mud bricks with wooden planks showing through the exterior. Their rounded contours looked organic as if the entire city were a living thing and the buildings naturally grew from the earth.

The children came to a well. They were quite thirsty after their trek through the desert. A woman watched over the well and gave them ladles of water from a bucket to drink. The water was naturally cool and very refreshing. There was something else very special about this well. "We're here," Sochima said to them.

"Here, where?" Aminata asked.

"Here, here. This is where the next piece is."

"Yeah?" Amaris said, sounding surprised that they had arrived. After joining the caravan and coming into the city, the children were so enthralled with everything they were seeing they had forgotten about looking for the next piece.

"It's down in the well," Sochima said.

"Okay, so how do we get it?" Aminata asked.

"I guess we have to go in the well," Sochima said.

All three of them looked down to see how deep it went. After six feet there was only darkness.

"That looks really deep," Amaris said, when, "What are you three doing?" someone called to them.

Startled, the children looked up and found a stern-looking man standing on the other side of the well. He was in his early seventies, but due to the tightness of his skin could be mistaken for ten years younger. He stood upright and had a lean body that was deceptively strong for his age. He wore a boubou, a garment made of three pieces: a long-sleeved shirt, a pair of loose trousers that narrowed at the ankles, and an overflowing wide, sleeveless gown worn over both. He was dressed richly;

however, he did not wear a turban or a beard and kept his grey hair low to the scalp. Once they saw him, all three children had a visual recollection of him.

"Balla," Sochima said.

"Moussa, Yambo, Oumou," Balla said, referring to Aminata, Amaris and Sochima in that order, and walked around the well to greet them. "You survived. Praise the ancestors," he said with a smile. "Your boatman told us hippopotamuses attacked the boat. Many of your guards died, and we feared we lost you in the Niger as well," he said.

"Yes," Aminata said. "We came out of the river and walked through the desert and followed a camel caravan into the city."

"Good. Good. I'm so happy you are all well. But why have you not gone straight to the palace?" Balla asked.

"We have not too long arrived in the city, and we were thirsty from our trek in the desert," Aminata said.

"Understood," Balla said.

A man approached Balla from behind. He was also in his seventies and wore a toga made of barkcloth. Weaved into the cloth were several symbols and patterns; similar to the symbols and patterns in the robe that Nana's spirit wore. One of the symbols looked like a goose pecking at its back, and another was of two circles touching each other, both filled with smaller overlapping circles creating a floral pattern. "This is Amu. The Hogon of his people," Balla introduced him to the children. The Hogan clasped his hands and bowed his head respectfully, and the children greeted him the same. Behind the Hogan came two dozen men wearing the most fantastic costumes the children had ever seen. They wore large wooden masks painted red, black, and white and carved to look like birds, cows, antelopes, lions, hyenas, and monkeys. They were topless, except for leather straps wrapped around their shoulders and back, which connected to the masks, and kept them in place.

Carrying a thin walking stick in their right hand, the men were silent and emotionless. Their masks did their talking for them. The children had to hold in their reaction, as being men their age, they shouldn't be looking at them with such amazement.

"Let us continue to the palace. The Mansa, the other ministers, and members of the Gbara are there," Balla said and prodded the children and the Hogan and his men to walk with him.

The children were in a dilemma. The next piece of Ausar was in the well, but it was deep in the well, and they did not know how to get to it. And Balla was a man of great authority. They did not know if they could refuse him. Amaris and Sochima were unsure what to do until Aminata decided to go along with Balla, and Amaris and Sochima followed her. It seemed to Aminata not going with him as the men in the bodies they occupied would do, would create a scene, which would make it even more difficult for them to get to the next piece. Hopefully, they could return later under the cover of night and retrieve it.

48

The Hogan walked alongside Balla, the children walked behind them, and the masked men of the Dogon followed. The Dogon delegation was a sight to behold walking through the city. People gawked at them as a relic of a bygone era.

"You are certain we are safe here?" the Hogan asked Balla.

"I am Belen-Tigui of the Mali Empire, and you are my guests. You are safe here," Balla said.

"But are we the guests of the Mansa as well? For many years now, the Mansas have been unkind to my people, demanding we abandon the gods of our ancestors, forcing us to take refuge in the mountains," the Hogan said.

"Today, the Mansa has us here to celebrate the completion of a new mosque in honor of his foreign God. You are here to remind the people of who we are and what we are losing. You are here to remind the Mansa as well. My forebears and I have long served the Keïta family. They would not dishonor me by dishonoring my guests."

Walking behind the two elders, the children quietly listened in. As they learned from Balla, and was confirmed by their memories, they were ministers in the Mali Empire. Ministers were the highest-ranking members of the Gbara. The Gbara was a thirty-two-member body, much like a parliament, established to advise the Mansa on critical issues of the state.

Of the thirty-two members of the Gbara, six were ministers. Sochima was the Minister of Coin, Aminata was the Minister of Trade, and Amaris was the Minister of Agriculture. There was also a Minister of Foreign Affairs, a Minister of Faith, and a Minister of Defense, who was the general of the army. Balla was the Belen Tigui, the chairman of the Gbara. He and the Minister of Defense were the second and third most powerful men in the empire.

49

The two-hundred-acre palace complex was closed off from the rest of the city by a twenty-foot mudbrick wall surrounding it. The palace gate was made of wood with gold and brass inlays. Seeing Balla, the palace guards opened the gates for them. As they passed, the guards bowed their heads to Balla and the children but not the Dogon.

Much of Timbuktu, having been built in the middle of a desert, was sand-colored. The palace, however, was like an oasis. The courtyard was filled with vibrant colors from lemon, orange, and mango trees that lined the perimeter and the numerous water fountains where exotic birds drank and flew about. There was a savannah behind the palace where zebra, giraffe, and gazelle grazed.

Though made of mudbrick, the palace itself was painted in a

brilliant, almost blinding white. With the sun directly above it, it shined like a beacon. It held over fifty rooms, five bathhouses, a grand hall, and a throne room. However, the emperor rarely used the throne room, as he preferred to handle matters of state in the courtyard.

As they entered the courtyard, they walked by the palace guards who were lined up on both sides, creating a pathway. There were a thousand of them, dressed in black turbans, gambesons, vambraces, and greaves. They carried wooden shields covered with elephant hides, spears, swords, and daggers. It was not common to have this many guards on hand—but today was a special occasion.

The people in the emperor's court were fashionable and wore bold colors; white, yellow, indigo, and scarlet, with all manner of jewelry; gold being ever abundant. Everyone wore some article of gold, whether they were Gbara or enslaved. There was so much gold it began to look cheap.

Much like outside, walking with the Dogon delegation, Balla and the children drew everyone's attention. Balla walked forward, passed the guards, to where the Gbara were assembled. News of the trouble the children experienced on the Niger river had gotten around, and the other members were happy to see they were safe. General Saghmanja, a stout man in his forties who was the minister of defense, was among them. "It is good to see you are all well, my brothers," he said.

"Thank you, brother," Amaris said for the three of them.

Court musicians began playing goblet drums announcing the arrival of the Mansa. The courtyard of more than a thousand people bowed, head to the ground, as if in prayer. The emperor emerged with a bow in his hand and a quiver of arrows over his shoulder. Mansa Musa was a man in his mid-forties; still youthful and vibrant though the gray showed noticeably in his beard. He had a pleasant face and a good figure. He wore a purple and white boubou made of imported Andalusian fabrics. His weapons—all made of gold—stood near his throne. He wore a gleaming white turban of the finest linen and a golden crown above it, adorned with precious stones. He wore crocodile leather shoes with the curled tip. He wore several gold chains; gold rings, and carried a scepter of pure gold. Mansa Musa sat on a wide ebony throne flanked by elephant tusks mounted on a dais under a lofty pavilion surmounted by a dome and a gold falcon. A Page stood on his left holding a silk umbrella. Once he was seated, everyone else rose.

Part of the Mansa's duties was to meet with dignitaries and address whatever issue they might have. The governor of one of the empire's vassal states had come to court to beseech the emperor concerning a land dispute. The man came wearing splendid robes. Though oddly, before approaching the emperor, he undressed until he was only wearing a loincloth brief. After which, he put on an old and tattered robe, the like a peasant would wear. Balla then gave him leave to approach. The man did so by hiking his robe above the knees and came forward in a very submissive and humble manner. When he was within twenty feet of the emperor, Balla gestured with his hand for the man to stop. He went down on his knees and kissed the ground, then took a ball of dirt and threw it over his shoulder. "Now you may speak," Balla said to him. The children were stunned by this display and had to keep their amazement in check.

The man spoke to Balla, who then spoke to the Page adjacent to Mansa Musa, who then relayed the message to the emperor. Mansa Musa then spoke to the Page, who then spoke to Balla, who addressed the kneeling man. The man was grateful for the outcome of Mansa Musa's verdict. He bowed and kissed the ground again, throwing more dirt over his shoulder. He got to his feet and walked backward, continuously bowing his head as he did.

Four other men came before the court to beseech the emperor, and each behaved the same as the first had done. Having concluded his adjudications for the day, the emperor left his throne and mounted a glorious white horse dressed in fine armor trimmed with gold. They opened the gates of the palace courtyard, and the soldiers began to march out. Mansa Musa rode out flanked in between them. The drummers marched behind him, announcing his arrival to the city.

50

As Mansa Musa rode through the city, thousands of people came to see him, bowing to the ground as he went by. It was hard for the children to determine if this was done purely out of love or a bit of fear, possibly a combination of both; nevertheless, the people did it enthusiastically. He was a sight to behold, and it was hard to take your eyes off him. Aminata saw Amaris looking at him in a way she believed she shouldn't, and spoke to her discretely so that no one else could hear them.

"Stop that," she said to her.

"Stop what?" Amaris asked.

"Stop looking at him like that."

"What? Like what?"

"Like how you're looking at him."

"I don't know what you're talking about."

"You're looking at him like how a girl would look at him," Ami said.

"What does that mean? And, no, I'm not," Mari said.

"Yes, you are, and you're in a man's body."

"Yeah, but I'm not a man."

"But you're in a man's body, and people are beginning to look at you like you're weird," Ami said.

Amaris glanced around and noticed that some of the other members of the Gbara were looking at her suspiciously. "Okay, I won't look at him at all," Amaris said and began looking down.

"No. Don't not look at him. Just don't look at him like a girl," Aminata said.

At this point, Amaris had gotten annoyed. "Ami, just leave me alone," she said.

Aminata saw her frustration and felt it was better for Amaris to look down rather than risk looking up at him as she did before.

Being Inda Jani had been difficult for Amaris, but at least she was also a girl not that much older than herself. To be a thirteen-year-old girl in the body of a man in his fifties was not something Amaris could get used to within a day—if ever. Being Yambo, she had to keep reminding herself of his name, was like wearing a suit that was grossly oversized, only the suit is your skin, and it feels loose and draped all over you. She never felt in sync with the body, and she couldn't wait for them to get the next piece and leave this place and this body as well.

The journey from the palace to the mosque was not a long one. The palace guards arrived before the emperor and lined up with swords and shields on both sides, creating a wide pathway. A great rug, intricately woven, leading from the street up the steps to the entrance of the building, had been laid out for his arrival. With the help of his Page, Mansa Musa dismounted his horse.

The Djingareyber Mosque was the size of a square block and roughly three stories tall. It was made entirely of mud brick, straw, and wood. It held three inner courts, twenty-five rows of spires aligned from east to west, and two minaret towers. To Sochima, it looked like a giant sandcastle. As the emperor approached, a man walked out. He had a caramel complexion and a curly beard. He was dressed in fine robes and a turban. His name was Abu Ishaq al Sahili. He was the architect of the mosque.

He bowed to the ground at the arrival of the emperor. Mansa Musa gestured with his hand for him to rise, and he did so and came forward, and the two men smiled at each other. At that time, a man appeared high above in one of the minarets and delivered the *adhan,* the call to prayer. He spoke Arabic in a clear, beautiful voice, almost as if he were singing. He delivered the adhan facing all four corners, north, south, east, and west before he concluded. When he finished, Mansa Musa alone entered the mosque. Everyone else, the thousands of people who surrounded the mosque went down on their knees facing east and recited the sunset prayer. The children followed everyone else, went down on their knees to pray, and found they could fluently recite the prayers in Arabic. While praying, Aminata noticed that Balla and the Dogon tribesmen were off to the side. They did not kneel, and they did not pray. When Balla saw Aminata, he gave her a subtle smile and a knowing look. Aminata did not know what that look meant and returned her focus to her prayers.

When the prayers had concluded, Mansa Musa left the mosque, and everyone rose to their feet. He then spoke to Abu Ishaq al Sahili, who addressed the crowd. "When I came to this city two years ago, I saw the greatness that it was and the greatness that it could be. With the opening of this madrasah and the rebuilding of Sankore, we make Timbuktu the center of the world. Where people from all parts of our great land and beyond come to trade not only in goods, but also in ideas. For our greatest trade asset is not copper, is not salt, is not gold, but books, because knowledge is the greatest and most precious asset in the world," al Sahili said, as the emperor said, and the people cheered.

51

That night everyone in the emperor's court returned to the palace for a feast. The children followed along, unable to pull themselves away and return to the well. Though admittedly, they felt safe for the moment and were also very hungry. They had the stomachs of grown men and had not eaten all day. They agreed with each other that they'd enjoy the feast and attempt to sneak away after they had eaten.

There were over a hundred people at the feast, each sitting at a table according to their station in the empire. The closer they sat to the emperor, the higher their station. They sat on richly made cushions at low tables, which stood only a foot off the ground. They ate from porcelain plates imported from China and drank from crystal glasses. Enslaved girls in their teens wearing golden anklets and bracelets and the flimsiest silk robes walked about serving them.

Being one of the six ministers in the empire, the children sat at a separate table from the other twenty-six members of the Gbara. Being the Belen-Tigui, Balla sat at their table as well. Mansa Musa and the empress, Inari Konaté, sat front and center. The empress was an elegant woman wearing a golden silk bou-bou dress, and a crown of jewels over her braided hair.

Abu Ishaq al Sahili sat closest to the emperor's table. The emperor gave him this great position because he was the architect of the mosque as well as the palace. He was a poet from al-Andalus who the emperor brought back from his pilgrimage to Mecca. The children remembered meeting al Sahili in Mecca and returning with him. However, they did not have pleasant feelings about him when they thought of him.

They served dinner in courses. It began with a bowl of kola nuts followed by vegetable soup. For the main course, they had *Tiguadege Na,* which was lamb stewed in a spicy peanut butter sauce served with jollof rice. For dessert, they had honey-flavored sesame seed biscuits. They drank fresh mango juice throughout, and ended the meal with three servings of a very strong tea.

After dinner, Balla sat on a cushion in the center of the hall with an instrument in front of him. It was called a balafon. It looked like a xylophone and was played much the same way by hitting keys with a mallet. With a clear voice that filled the room, Balla addressed everyone in attendance. "I am Balla Kouyaté. I am the grandson of Balla Faséké, who was the first Djeli of the Mali Empire. It is the duty of our clan to maintain the great history of our people so that this generation and many generations to come never forget who we are and how we became a great people. This is the *fasa* of the great Sundiata Keïta, the Lion

King, the first Mansa of Mali." Balla began playing the balafon and performing an epic poem: part spoken word, part song.

"King Nare Marghan of the Mandé people was considered the most handsome man in the land. He took for his queen, Sassouma Bereté, a most beautiful woman, and they had a son together, Dankaran Toumani Keïta. Now one day King Nare was visited by a soothsayer, who told the King that soon two hunters would come to him, and they would bring with them the ugliest woman the King had ever seen. The hunters said if the King were to marry this woman, she would bear him a son, and this son would grow up to be a great King, the greatest the land has ever known. King Nare meditated on this prophecy greatly, and when indeed two hunters came to the King's court as the soothsayer had prophesized. They brought with them, Sogolon, a woman so ugly she was called the buffalo woman, for she had a hump in her back. Heeding the prophecy, the King married her, to his wife Sassouma's dismay, and Sogolon bore the King a boy child, and he called him Sundiata.

Sundiata was born crippled and did not have the power to walk on his own. This dismayed the King, but still heeding the prophecy he intended to make Sundiata his heir, and he gave Sundiata his own Djeli, Balla Faséké, in order to teach Sundiata the history of the Mandinka people, and who would record the story of Sundiata as well. This angered Queen Sassouma very much, and she would bitterly tease Sundiata and his mother, Sogolon, for her ugliness and her son's disability, and the rest of the court did as well. Seeing how his mother suffered from their ridicule, Sundiata pledged to her that he would walk, and at ten years old, he made a crutch for himself from a stick made of the baobab tree and used it to stand on his feet and taught himself to walk. The King was very pleased by this. Seeing Sundiata get stronger every day, the Queen became envious and plotted to have Sundiata, and Sogolon killed. The king fell into ill health, and fearing for their lives, Sundiata, his mother, and his two younger sisters, fled from Mandé and took refuge in another village. King Nare died, and Sassouma's son Dankaran was named

King of the Mandé people. For many years Sundiata and Sogolon traveled the lands taking refuge in one kingdom after another, building lasting friendships on the way until they settled in the Mema kingdom. While living in Mema, Sundiata grew stronger and stronger and became a great hunter and warrior, especially adept with the bow and arrow. He fought and defeated the greatest general of the Mema people, Moussa Tounkara. Sundiata so impressed the King of Mema that he named Sundiata his heir.

At this time, darkness crept over the land as the great Ghana empire had fallen and fractured. Many Kingdoms sought to fill the void that Ghana had left, but none were as successful as the Sosso kingdom, led by their Sorcerer King Sumanguru. Sumanguru Kanté was a man of great power and great magic. He conquered kingdom after kingdom until he came to the people of Mandé. He entered the village wearing a hat made of human skin, a robe made of human skin and shoes made of human skin. He made a frightful sight. He and his warriors killed man, woman, and child until they came to King Dankaran who Sumanguru beheaded himself. Word of the attack rang out, and the Mandé people cried to Sundiata to return home and liberate his people. Sogolon, Sundiata's mother, told her son it was time to return and reclaim his throne. And with the army of the Mema and the surrounding kingdoms where Sundiata had lived during his exile, they amassed a great force to go against Sumanguru and the Sosso Kingdom, and they met in the great battle of Kirina, between Bowako and Kangaba, on the bank of the Niger. The battle was fierce, many warriors died on both sides, and the tide was not turned until Sundiata shot an arrow with an ostrich feather into the heart of Sumanguru. Sumanguru staggered into the forest, never to be seen again, leaving behind only the balafon, the instrument he had created.

With Sumanguru gone, Sundiata consolidated all the kingdoms into one, and he called it Mali, for it means the place where the emperor dwells. And he became the first Mansa of the Mali empire. But Sundiata, in his great wisdom, knew that no kingdom should ever be ruled by one man alone. So, he created the Gbara from the twenty-nine clans of the Mandinka, and he created the Kouroukan Fouga. So that we may live by laws and not only by the power of men. And so, we sing the name of the great Sundiata Keïta. *M'Fa Mansa,* king, my father. *Be Bara Mansa,* Emperor of all the people."

When Balla finished performing, he walked to Mansa Musa and placed his head on both sides of his shoulders. After which, he bowed to him. Mansa Musa nodded his head graciously, and everyone applauded.

"You honor my great uncle and our family as always," Mansa Musa said.

"Yes, as usual, a brilliant performance Balla," Inari Konaté, the wife of Mansa Musa, said.

"Thank you, your highness," Balla said.

"But we have heard the epic of Sundiata so many times; when will you do one for your current Mansa?" she asked.

"No, your highness. This is not done. It would be a bad omen to perform an epic of a Mansa while he is still living. His story is not finished. He has many more great things to do, then we will tell his story and sing his name," Balla said.

"Yes, he does have many more great things to do," the Empress said, though she seemed dissatisfied with Balla's answer.

"And now I have something even more special for your highness. Balla stepped back, walked to the center of the hall, and spoke in a loud voice so everyone could hear him. "I present to you, the Dogon," Balla said.

The Hogon and the masked men entered the hall. They all bowed before the emperor. Mansa Musa raised his hand giving them permission to rise. The Hogon stepped forward and spoke, "We are the Dogon. We are Mandé, we are Konyate, we are Traore, Koroma, Konde, Kamara. We are Keïta. We are Ghana; we are Mali. We are one. We were here when everything was but dust, and we will be here when everything is dust again. Our ancestors came from the sky, from the burning star and its dark sister to the land where the earth is black." At this point, a few of the men in masks began chanting, playing djembe drums and wooden clappers, while others started doing a ceremonial dance.

As the performance continued, Abu Ishaq al Sahili moved closer to the emperor and addressed him. "Great Mansa," he said. "Why do you entertain pagans in our palace, which God has built?"

"Do you desire to tell me who I can and cannot entertain in my palace?" Mansa Musa answered him.

"No great Mansa. I am but a humble servant. It is an observation only," al Sahili said.

"Your people, we're pagan too once, before the revelation came to the Prophet, peace be onto him. It took many years for them to convert heart and soul. For us, it has not yet been one hundred years, and our traditions are ancient. The people in our villages hold onto them fiercely. But as old generations die and new ones are born, they will see the light."

"Aye, great Mansa, you speak true, and with much wisdom," al Sahili said.

Mansa Musa returned his focus to the dance. And though he was quite devout in his beliefs, he found the dance, the drums, the chanting, and the costumes, all mesmerizing. It was as if they were in an ecstatic trance, and they were drawing him into a trance as well. The dance concluded with a thunder of drums. The Hogan walked in between the dancers and addressed the attendants. "We dance to honor our ancestors. We dance to honor the great Mansa Musa and his great mother, Nana Kankan." When the Hogon mentioned his mother's name, Mansa Musa's eyes narrowed, and his mood soured, though he did not outwardly show it. However, it was something Sochima could feel intensely. "We dance the *dama* to mark the end of mourning, so her soul may rest in the stars with her ancestors," The Hogan said.

The Hogan mentioning Nana Kankan changed the temperature in the room, and everyone waited to see how the Mansa would respond before they did. With a smile, Mansa Musa applauded, and then the entire room applauded. "I think we should leave now," Sochima turned to the girls and said.

The girls nodded in agreement. The children stood up during the applause for the Dogan and discretely made their way out of the hall.

They left the main hall and navigated through the many guards lining the passageways. No one questioned them, and they nodded respectfully to anyone who gave them a passing glance. They could see the exit to outside less than fifty feet away. They could see the moon shining. They continued their path when Balla came out of a passageway and surprised them. "Where are you going?" he asked.

Amaris had to think quickly. "We wanted to get some air," she said.

"That can wait. Come with me," Balla said.

52

Balla took them to a separate room in the palace and made sure they were alone. "We are close. We are very close. I have spoken to Ministers Mamadou and Adama. They are with us. Have any of you spoken to Saghmanja?" Balla asked.

"No," Amaris answered, though she did not know exactly what she was saying, 'No,' to.

Balla thought for a moment. "Our plans can move forward without him, but with him, they become so much easier," he said.

Plans? What plans? The children wondered. And just as they asked themselves the question, the answer came to them, and Sochima blurted out, "We're going to kill Mansa Musa."

"Keep your voice down, fool. Do you wish to let the entire palace know?" Balla said.

"Sorry," Sochima said, as he had surprised himself when he spoke aloud.

"If I did not know better, I'd think you were a child," Balla said.

"Forgive his outburst. He is—we are just excited," Aminata said, attempting to cover for Sochima.

"Passion is good. But passion alone will not get it done. If our plans are to succeed, we must have General Saghmanja, or risk civil war," Balla said. "I've called a meeting, just of the ministers and myself. We will present a united front and get him to join us. We may even offer him the throne if need be," Balla said.

"You want General Saghmanja to be emperor?" Amaris asked.

"No. He is a fool. But he is a powerful one. We offer him the throne to appease him. When the deed is done. We kill him as well," Balla said.

"What if he refuses and doesn't want to be emperor?" Aminata asked.

"Then we kill him then and there. He does not leave the room. Walk with your knives," he said to them. "I'll convene the others. We'll meet here in half an hour."

Balla left the room and left the children with a lot to think about.

"Holy—whoa," Amaris said. "Like what the hell?"

"We're going to kill Mansa Musa?" Sochima said as a question.

"No. We're not killing anybody," Aminata said.

"Yeah, and thanks for blurting that out," Amaris said.

"I'm sorry, I couldn't help it," Sochima said.

"It doesn't matter now. And I almost said the same thing," Ami said.

"See, I wasn't the only one thinking it," Sochi said.

"No, you're just the only one who said it."

"Stop it, you guys. We don't have time for this. I've been getting flashes of memories and it looks like we've been planning this with Balla for a while," Ami said.

"Yeah, I've been seeing memories too. We really don't like him," Mari said.

"So, we are going to kill Mansa Musa," Sochi said.

"Stop saying that," Mari snapped at him. "And we're not killing anybody. What we're doing is getting out of here, like right now."

"Yeah. Hopefully, we can get to the well and get the next piece before they realize we're gone," Ami said.

They left the room and walked down the steps to the palace hallway leading to the exit. The sooner they left the palace, the better. They were so anxious they considered running or even speed walking but thought better of it. They kept a steady pace and made the long walk down to the palace doors. There were guards posted. The head guard greeted them, *"As-salāmu ʿalaykum."*

"Wa ʿalaykumu s-salam," Ami replied.

"How may I help you, Ministers?" he asked.

"Just stepping out for some air," Ami said.

"Very well, Ministers. But do let us know if you plan to leave the palace grounds," he said.

"Certainly," Ami replied and stepped a foot outside when a member of the Gbara ran up to her.

Aminata was the Minister of Trade, and he worked under her. He was an ambassador to Morocco. After the emperor's pilgrimage, Morocco became a great trading partner. The empire imported cotton and oil as well as goods from Granada through there. He was leaving for Fez tomorrow to meet with the Marinid Sultanate to negotiate a preferential trade agreement. He was seeking Aminata's advice on how to proceed. Aminata did not hear a word he was saying. She smiled and nodded, and said, "Hmm . . . interesting . . . and what do you think?" repeatedly while praying for him to shut up so they could leave.

Sochima and Amaris stood by anxiously. Amaris had gotten so anxious she wanted to bash the ambassador over his head. And just as he was about to leave, "Oh, it seems the Belen Tigui is calling you," he said.

The children turned around and saw Balla up the hall. He was with the two other Ministers. Seeing the children at the doors, he gave them a hard look and beckoned them to him with his eyes.

"Dammit," Amaris mumbled. *Stupid idiot,* she thought of the ambassador.

They had no choice now. They had to go back. If Balla was bold enough to kill Mansa Musa and the general, he would undoubtedly kill them.

"This is not good," Sochima said as they walked back up the long hall. "What are we gonna do, guys?"

They kept their heads straight and spoke through their teeth to avoid drawing attention to what they were saying.

"Balla isn't going to let us out. I don't think we have a choice. If we were with the plan to kill Mansa Musa all along, I think we should go along with it, at least until we can get away from them and get to the well," Aminata said.

"No, we shouldn't do that," Amaris said.

"Why not?" Sochima asked.

"We should be quiet and wait and see what everybody else says. If they're all down with killing him, then we're down. If they're not, then we're not," Amaris said.

"But Balla said they were all down, except for Saghmanja," Sochima said.

"Yeah, and he controls the army. And a lot of people say they're down with something until the time comes, and then they back out. I've seen it," Amaris said.

"Okay, Mari. We'll do it your way," Aminata said.

When they arrived at Balla's position, he looked at them suspiciously. "Why were you at the doors?" he asked.

"We thought we had time before the meeting and wanted to get some air," Aminata said.

"No time for that. The time we've been waiting for is now."

53

Twenty minutes later Balla along with the six ministers, including General Saghmanja were back in the room. "Why have you called this meeting Balla?" Saghmanja asked.

"I have called this meeting because, after our great Mansa, we seven are the most powerful men in the empire—and the most important. And when our empire is in peril, we have an obligation to protect it and its people," Balla said.

"And what peril do you speak of?" Saghmanja asked.

"The greatest peril. The peril from within. Your name is Saghmanja Kamara," Balla said to the general then addressed each minister personally. "Your name is Mamadou Bérété, and yours is Adama Danhou." He turned to the children addressing Aminata, Amaris and Sochima in that order. "You are Moussa Sangaré, Yambo Konaté, Oumou Sidibé. I say your names because your names have a history that ties you to this land. In the future, the men in our positions will not have our names. They will have foreign names. And they will no longer understand our words because they will speak a foreign tongue. Because they will have given their souls over entirely to a foreign god," Balla said.

"Do you mean the one true God?" Saghmanja asked.

"Do not speak to me about God, Saghmanja Kamara. Do not insult our people. Our people knew God long before the foreigners came. And giving them honor above our own. Paying a poet 12,000 mithqals of gold to design a building in the same manner our people have done for centuries."

General Saghmanja took a moment to inhale everything Balla said. "I see what this is now. You calling only the seven of us here. You are conspiring to kill the emperor," Saghmanja said, though it was also a question.

"Yes," Balla answered straightly.

"You are mad," Saghmanja said.

"No general. I am quite sane. We are far removed from the days of Mansa Sundiata. The Keïta family has lost their way, ever since they gave themselves over to the foreigners and their god, they have gone mad. Mansa Abu Bakari II sends two hundred ships across the great ocean in search of the land on the other side. Only one ship returns. The captain tells us the others were lost in a great whirlwind in the ocean. So, what does our wise Mansa do? He commissions another expedition. This time with two thousand ships, he abdicates his throne and goes as well. Never to be seen again. That is madness," Balla said.

"Mansa Abu Bakari went in search of knowledge. It is by great pioneering men that we have progressed throughout time. Did not the Egyptians travel across the ocean centuries ago?"

"Yes, our ancestors traveled to the lands beyond the ocean many times, long before it became corrupted by foreign influence. But never once was pharaoh foolish enough to make the journey himself. Because he knew that his responsibility was primarily to his land and his people."

"That is why Mansa Abu Bakari left Mansa Musa to rule in his place. And he has ruled well. We are greater now than we have ever been. He has increased our empire three-fold and our coffers by ten."

"Conquering people smaller than you is not an accomplishment. Any fool can do that."

"Was Mansa Sundiata a fool? Did he not conquer people smaller than him?"

"Mansa Sundiata also won the battle of Kirina. He created our empire. Created the Gbara and the Kouroukan Fouga."

"And for all his greatness, Mali was still unknown. Our trade relationships through which our wealth comes were limited. Mansa Musa has connected us throughout the Maghreb to Mecca. He has built a great university. Now wise men and scholars from the world over come to Mali to study and share their knowledge so that we may become wiser. Mansa Musa has made Timbuktu the epicenter of knowledge and Mali the envy of the world."

"And when has envy ever been a good thing? He has shouted to the world that we have the most valuable resource in great abundance. And no, it is not books. It is gold. His pilgrimage to Mecca was the most wasteful and vainglorious exercise in all mankind. Over 60,000 people, over 12,000 slaves, over one hundred camels carrying their weight in gold, and by the end of it, he had given it all away. So many of us died of cold, starvation, and being constantly raided by bandits. How many of us died simply because they couldn't walk anymore, and others were left behind in a foreign land? Having run out of money, we were forced to beg for coin in order to return home and had to re-sell much of what we purchased while in Cairo. And the ingratitude of these people that they complained that the gold we gave out had devalued the gold in their country. And so, our great Mansa agrees to buy back the gold he gave away—with interest. But you did not see all of this because you had left before then."

"Yes, I did. And I conquered Gao and Timbuktu in his name. And I did not do this to betray him two years later," General Saghmanja said.

"You would think differently, if you had seen his greatest betrayal. While in Cairo, our great Mansa, a man who demands his people bathe themselves in dirt before speaking to him, debased himself before the Sultan of Cairo, a man who is a descendant of slaves, by kissing the ground at his feet. I have never been so ashamed for our people," Balla said.

"I have heard this story before. Our great Mansa made obeisance to God who created him, not to a man. But I grow tired of hearing you speak. There are five other ministers in this room, and I wish to hear from them," Saghmanja said.

"I speak for them."

"No. You've spoken enough. I know where your mind is. I want to hear them speak now. So, I know exactly who all the traitors are and how many heads I must cut off."

Saghmanja declared his threat with such conviction the children could feel the blade at their necks.

"If you defy us, the only traitor will be you. And yours will be the first head gone. But if you join us, we can make you and all your seed Mansa," Balla said.

"Oh, I see clearly now. Balla Kouyate, you are Sheitan in the flesh. You would so tempt me. And perhaps if I were a lesser man, you would succeed. But what you ask is not just a betrayal of a man but of God, and that I will never do," Saghmanja said, and his words moved the room—as everyone recognized that he could not be bargained with and as such must be dealt with.

Saghmanja turned to Sochima. "Oumou Sidibé. You are the minister of coin and oversee the wealth of our empire. Do you stand with your Mansa?" He asked Sochima. And because they had agreed with Amaris not to take sides until all was revealed, Sochima did not know what to say, and looked at Aminata and Amaris for an answer they did not know how to give him.

Balla looked at him with great confusion, disappointment, and anger. "Open your mouth and speak, fool," Balla said.

"Hmm. It seems he has nothing to say," Saghmanja said. He then turned to another minister. "Mamadou Bérété, you are the minister of foreign affairs; what say you?" he asked.

Minister Mamadou looked at Balla and then he looked at Sochima. Sochima had a recollection of Mamadou saying his support of the coup was contingent on Sochima's support, because Sochima controlled the coin. If Sochima would not support the coup, then Mamadou was left silent as well.

"What cowardly treachery is this?" Balla said.

"Hmm. So far, the only traitor is you," Saghmanja said. "He then proceeded to question Aminata and Amaris, and like Sochima and Mamadou, they were silent. "This is not looking good for you, Balla."

Finally, Saghmanja turned to minister Adama Danhou, and he answered, "I am no traitor. I have always been loyal to our great Mansa, as my fathers have loyally served the Keïta family. I listened to Balla's talk of treason, only to discover who all the traitors were so that I might deliver them to our great Mansa myself," he said.

"Yes, that was my aim as well when Balla came to me," Minister Mamadou said.

"Hmm. And you three?" Saghmanja asked of Sochima, Amaris and Aminata. Amaris gave them a subtle look, and they all agreed with the other two ministers. At which point Balla began to laugh. "You laugh, traitor?" Saghmanja said.

"Yes. Because no matter how long I have lived, the frailty of man never ceases to amaze me," he said and looked at Sochima with a deathly ominous stare. "You will regret your cowardice." He turned to the others. "All of you."

"No, Balla, you will regret your treachery. But not for long. Mansa Musa will have your head tomorrow." Saghmanja walked to the door, stepped outside then shouted for the guards in a loud voice. Within a minute, four guards had arrived. "Arrest the Belen Tigui and take him to the dungeon," he said. The guards did not know how to respond. They had never arrested someone so powerful before. "You heard me, arrest him. He is charged with treason and the attempted overthrow of your Mansa." Hearing this, the guards' eyes hardened, but they still made no move.

Balla smiled. "It is all true. Do as he says," Balla said.

The guards drew their swords, put them to Balla's back, and led him away.

General Saghmanja left the room as well and closed the door behind him,

54

The children's hope of leaving the palace and getting to the well was dashed for the night. After Saghmanja arrested Balla, he informed the emperor of the attempted coup. They placed the entire palace under lockdown and confined all five ministers to that room, with armed guards outside, as Saghmanja went about questioning every palace guard and member of the Gbara to discover who else may have been a part of the plot.

Ministers Mamadou and Adama banged on the doors and called to the guards protesting their treatment and professing their loyalty to the emperor. The children did not do this. It seemed pointless. Only General Saghmanja or Mansa Musa had the power to free them. And though they were together, they could not speak freely because of the other two ministers. Each of them, however, wondered if they had done the right thing by not supporting Balla. It was what the men in the bodies they occupied would have done. Perhaps if they had, Balla would have been able to sway Saghmanja to their side, and they would have been free from this room and able to get to the well.

It was a long sleepless night as they dreaded what might happen at any moment. At dawn, they heard the adhan ring out from the window of their room. Ministers Mamadou and Adama went down on their knees and prayed intensely. Neither of the children went down on their knees; nevertheless, they prayed in their own ways that they would get through this day.

An hour after prayers, they began to hear noises coming from outside. They looked through the small window in the room, but from their vantage point, they could not see what was happening. They could hear a large gathering of people. There was a lot of talking they couldn't make out, but now and again, they heard the word traitor. Within another hour, the guards opened the doors and led the ministers out of the room. Ministers Mamadou and Adama asked questions about where they were going and what was happening, but they received no answers. The guards silently yet respectfully ushered them down the long hall and out the palace doors.

The morning sun greeted them, high and bright. They were momentarily blinded as their eyes adjusted. Palace guards were lined up on both sides, creating a pathway leading through the courtyard and out the palace grounds. The guards ushered them forward. Even before leaving the grounds, they could hear the roar of the people outside. It was early morning, but the news had already gotten around, and there were hundreds of people gathered on both sides of the street, hungry for a beheading. The children heard chants of 'Traitor' and 'Kill them.'

The palace guards lined the streets, holding the crowds at bay. As they walked, they could hear sudden raucous outbursts further down. Ministers Mamadou and Adama were palpably afraid.

The children were also afraid, but Amaris walked between Aminata and Sochima and held their hands, and they were able to hold it together. It wasn't a long walk. In fact, it was a walk they had done before. Serendipitously, the guards were leading them back to the well. The well was in the city's center, where the executions took place. The guards formed a half circle creating a perimeter around the well.

The emperor's pavilion and throne had been transported here. Mansa Musa sat on his throne looking calm and unaffected. General Saghmanja stood beside him, as did Abu Ishaq al Sahili. Members of the court and the Gbara were also there. Gallows had been erected in front of the well. A large stone of pure granite was placed in front of it. It had wet blood running down its side, creating a pool of red mud at its base. An executioner stood behind the stone, his scimitar dripping with blood. Guards were dragging headless bodies away. The children saw the masks of the Dogon littered about, and they realized that the

Dogon delegation had been killed. They looked at each other, horrified.

The guards brought the children and the other two ministers forward and placed them beside the other members of the Gbara, who looked at them disdainfully and took two steps back to distance themselves as if they had a disease they could catch. Ministers Mamadou and Adama called to Mansa Musa, beseeching him, and professing their loyalty. He turned and gave them a cold eye, and they fell silent.

"Bring forth the traitor," General Saghmanja said.

The children looked up the street and saw Balla being led forward with large manacles on his wrists. The crowd of hundreds jeered him the loudest. "Infidel. Traitor. Defiler," they shouted. However, some were noticeably silent and looked distressed by what was happening. With his back straight and his head high, Balla walked forward unaffected, but when he entered the perimeter and saw the blood on the ground, the masks littered about, and the bodies piled off to the side, he fell to his knees in horror and sadness. On his knees, he saw the Hogan's toga, which had been rent from his body, with blood stains and footprints on its symbols. "My friends . . . my friends," Balla wailed. "Forgive me. Forgive me. I brought you here for this."

The guards brought him to his feet and led Balla to the gallows. Members of the court continued to jeer him. He turned to them with such a deathly cold stare that they fell silent. His coldest stare he saved for the children and the other two ministers. "Cowards," he said to them just above a whisper, sharp enough to slit a throat.

Once Balla was at the gallows, Mansa Musa stood up from his throne, and the city fell silent. Al Sahili approached the emperor to convey his message, but Mansa Musa chose to speak for himself this time. "This is a sad day, a very, very sad day. Balla Kouyate, you have served my family all your life," Mansa Musa said.

"Oh, I have served this land much more than that," Balla said.

"Your betrayal is as shocking as it is heartbreaking."

"No. You are the one who has betrayed us. Submitting to a foreign God and allowing foreigners to defile our land. I did what I have done to save the empire from the anarchy of a war of succession. Now I see there is no other way."

"You are an old man and too trapped in the past. Unwilling to see the future because you fear it so. The future will be a world of knowledge, of science, and of books—and they will tell our history. And there will be no place for you and your kind."

"And what future have we when we discard our past?" Balla asked. He turned to the dead bodies of the Dogon piled up against the wall. "You killed these men. They had no part in this and yet you killed them. They honored you, and you killed them. They honored your mother, the mother you killed, and you killed them," Balla said.

Those words poked at Mansa Musa's heart, and he gritted his teeth to hold in his rage. "I have entertained you enough. Take his head," he ordered.

"No. I think I'll take yours," Balla said.

The Guard put his hand on Balla's shoulder, pushing him towards the chopping stone. In an amazing feat of agility, Balla, a man in his seventies, put his foot on the stone, using it as a brace, and leaped in the air, doing a back flip, landing behind the Guard, with the chains of his manacles wrapped around the Guard's throat. This all happened within a second—and in the next, Balla tightened the chains, with such a sudden burst of strength he snapped his neck.

Everyone was stunned and horrified, none more so than the executioner. Balla kneeled and took the sword from the dead Guard's body. Before the Executioner could swing his sword, Balla eclipsed his airspace and stabbed his sword through the Executioner's stomach. The Executioner dropped his sword and clinging to life attempted to strangle Balla. Balla cut through the Executioner's side, ripping apart his innards and spilling his intestines on the floor.

"By Allah," Mansa Musa exclaimed.

With both hands still shackled, Balla pointed the bloody sword at Mansa Musa and shouted, "Kankan, you are next."

"Protect your Mansa," General Saghmanja declared to all the Guards. There were hundreds of them, and somehow it appeared insufficient. In the perimeter, they were too confined. Their archers couldn't fire for fear of hitting one of their own. Sumanguru was also wise not to take them all on at once. He moved through the crowd of screaming people, using them as cover. Guard after guard came at the seventy-year-old man, and one by one, he cut them down.

55

The children witnessed the men on the boat eaten by the hippos. That was a gruesome scene. Seeing someone killed by another human being right in front of them was even worse. They were as stunned by what Balla was doing as everyone else in the courtyard—and for betraying him, Balla had as much hatred for them as he did the emperor.

"We should go get the next piece now," Sochi said to the girls.

"Now?" Ami asked, surprised Sochi could even focus on the task at hand.

"Yes. While everyone is busy before they kill Balla."

"I'm not sure they can. He's killing everybody. I mean, what the hell do they feed old people in this place." Mari said.

"I don't know, but he's going to kill us too if we stay here," Sochi said.

"Yeah, especially since we turned on him," Ami said.

"So, let's go," Sochi said."

Mari watched as Balla danced through the emperor's guards, leaping over them, pirouetting in the air, landing and delivering quick, decisive strikes, leaving blood spewing and limbs hanging from joints. She turned to Mansa Musa, and though he tried to remain kingly and composed, she could tell he was terrified. "Should we try to protect him?" she asked.

"No," Sochi flatly declared.

"But what if he dies? And we caused this to happen. We could, like completely mess up history," Mari said.

"We won't," Sochima said.

"You don't know that. How is he supposed to die?" Mari asked.

"I don't know how he's supposed to die. I don't know if he dies here or of old age," Ami said.

"He dies ten years from now," Sochima said.

"But what if he was supposed to die ten years from now, and because of us he's going to die today?" Mari asked.

"Mari, we don't know that. The only thing we know is that we have to get the next piece, and we can't do it if we're dead," Ami said.

"We can't protect him any more than what his guards are doing," Sochi said.

"You're right. You're right," Mari said.

"Good. Let's go."

They began to make their way through the chaos, trying not to lose each other as people ran screaming in terror as Balla cut down anyone between him and Mansa Musa.

Six Guards surrounded Balla. These were the emperor's best guards. They came at him with both sword and spear. Still shackled, Balla parried and weaved through their attacks, and saw that Mansa Musa was being led away by Saghmanja and another dozen guards. "No—no," he said and took to the air, jumping over whoever was in his path, leaping off shoulders and heads.

The children got to the well. "Okay, what now? We never figured out how we were supposed to get this thing," Mari said.

"I guess one of us has to go in and get it," Ami said, looking at Mari.

"Why are you looking at me?" Mari said.

"Because you're the oldest—and the bravest," Ami said.

"No. I'm really not that brave. And don't kiss up to me."

"I'll do it," Sochi said.

"No, Sochi, I'm not letting you do that."

"Ami, I can do it. I can feel where it is, and I can breathe underwater."

"But how would you get out after you get it?" Mari asked.

They all looked perplexed until Sochi said, "We'll all go in. That way, we'll be together and just leave as soon as we have it."

"Um—okay. But you do know that if this doesn't work, we're going to die," Mari said.

"We won't die. I can feel it," Sochi said.

"You and your freakin' feelings."

While Balla was fighting his way to get to Mansa Musa, he spied the three ministers preparing to enter the well. *What are they doing?* He thought. Then something occurred to him. *No. It can't be.* Propelled by fear and rage, Balla broke off his attack on the Emperor's guards and, with the ferocity of a lion, tore through the crowd charging at the children.

The children turned around in time to miss the swing of his sword. Ami and Mari fell to the side, but Sochi was knocked off balance and stumbled backward into the well, falling fast and deep, the world getting narrower and darker until he was submerged in water.

"Sochi," Aminata shouted and attempted to dive in after him, but Balla grabbed her by the ankle and yanked her back. She fell flat on the ground, and the staff flew from her hand and fell into the well. "Sochi? Who is Sochi?" Balla asked. "You are not who you appear to be. Who are you?" He held the sword to Ami's neck. Mari took a sword from the ground and charged at Balla. He deftly blocked her advance and knocked the sword from her hand. Balla now held both Ami and Mari at sword point. "I'll ask again. Who are you?" Balla said.

Just then the dirt on the ground began jumping, and there was a great rumbling sound like thunder on the horizon. The earth shook, growing louder and more violent, and the walls of the well vibrated. A geyser shot out of the well ten feet into the air. Mari looked up and saw Sochi with the staff in one hand and the artifact in the other, seemingly floating on water. Seeing the artifact in Sochima's hand, Balla recognized that the moment he had spent lifetimes trying to prevent was happening.

The geyser came down, and Sochima came down with it, landing on his feet. Balla charged at Sochima but was hit by an arrow to his right shoulder by one of the emperor's guards. Balla staggered, and Sochima quickly put the staff to the next piece. The decomposed flesh turned to dust and seeped back into the earth. The soul of Ausar was exposed, and just like before, it created a portal, and everyone within its twenty-yard circumference stepped out of their bodies. Aminata, Amaris, and Sochima were just souls again. Likewise, the soul of Balla stepped out of his shell—however, he did not look like Balla.

"Sumanguru," they heard, and everyone turned and looked toward Mansa Musa.

The emperor looked on in amazement as he saw everyone around him walk out of their bodies, which stood motionless like automatons shut down. They all looked perplexed, not knowing if they had died and stepped into the afterlife. Some were surprised to discover that their bodies housed multiple souls; some had two souls, some as many as four; one active the others dormant.

Mansa Musa was in utter disbelief at what he was seeing. Three of his eldest ministers had turned into three very strange-looking children. And Balla had revealed himself to be the Empire's greatest enemy, wearing a hat made of human skin, a robe made of human skin, sandals made of human skin, and his front teeth sharpened to a point. He made a frightful sight. "Sumanguru," Mansa Musa said again.

"Hello, Kankan. We meet truly for the first time," Balla said, turning to face him.

"You have been Balla all this time," Musa said.

"And his father before him, and Balla Faséké before then."

"You are a Jinn."

"No, I am a guardian. I have protected this land for centuries. And I had the power to kill Sundiata, and end your lineage, or inhabit his flesh and rule in his stead. But he so impressed me that I let him live and taking the form of his djeli we became great friends. And I took pleasure in singing his praises. As I realized the best way to protect this land was not to lead it myself but to guide it."

"You have been guiding us into hell," Musa said.

"No. You have been guiding us into hell. And it was because of my vow to Sundiata to protect his family, why I have not stopped you sooner. But I will put an end to it now."

"Kill it," Musa ordered his guards, who were still bewildered being out of their bodies.

Sumanguru laughed. "You could not stop me as a seventy-year-old man. You will not stop me in my true form. But first." He turned to the children. "You," he said.

Amaris turned to Sochima. "Sochi. Eat."

Sochima reached for the orb. Sumanguru, in an instant, closed the distance between them and knocked Sochima away. Sumanguru grabbed the orb and held it in his spirit hand, but not for long, as like cinder, the orb burnt through his soul. His hand disintegrated into splinters fading away. Sumanguru dropped the orb, screaming before it could destroy more of his soul. Sochima attempted to get the orb again but with one hand and a sword made of soul energy, Sumanguru fought him off. Amaris and Aminata joined in, Aminata swinging at him with the staff and Amaris drawing his attention. Still, he held them off, keeping them away from the orb, until Mansa Musa and his guards joined the fight and Sumanguru became overwhelmed, giving Sochima the opening he needed. He put his hands over the orb and guided it into his mouth. Once it was inside Sochima everyone returned to their bodies, the children returned to the bodies of the ministers, and the portal closed.

Sumanguru was Balla again, and seeing the ministers and knowing they had the orb, knowing he had failed, he fell to his knees, breathless and bereft. He looked to the sky, "Father ... forgive—" he was about to say when Saghmanja swung his blade and took off his head.

Saghmanja then looked at the children in the ministers' bodies. "Who are you?" he asked, pointing his sword at them.

Aminata held the staff, and Sochima and Amaris held her. "We're gone," she said, and their bodies fell to the ground lifeless.

ACT FOUR
A BROTHER'S BETRAYAL

56

Sochima looked down at his bare feet submerged in water up to his shins. He was standing on a white piece of cloth, and the ground beneath him felt uneven. This was their third jump, and he had not gotten used to the suddenness of it all. It was the sensation of falling asleep, believing you had only closed your eyes for five minutes, only to discover that hours had gone by. There was a moment of darkness, a second of peace, and then the suddenness of waking up in a new environment and a new body.

He looked to his right and saw a girl in her mid-teens standing a yard away. She had a glassy look of confusion in her eyes. It was Amaris. They smiled at each other, happy that they had survived another jump. Sochima looked to his left and saw another girl who looked very similar to the body he had just seen Amaris in. Aminata smiled, and Sochima was happy to see his sister. They had all made it out of the madness Mali had become. Now, where had they jumped to?

It was a bright day. They could feel the sun on their shoulders. They were on the bank of a large body of water. There were dozens of people around. There were women washing clothes by stomping on them beneath the water. Aminata thought this was strange but seeing the clothes beneath her feet and piled behind her; it appeared that was what they had been doing as well. Farther down, there were women bathing young children, and women bathing together. Farther down from there, there were men bathing together. Farther into the horizon, there were fishermen in boats made of reeds.

Aminata was trying to piece it all together, but it was hard to tell where they were. For now, she was just grateful to have left

Mali alive. What a change from the horrors they were just seeing.

Aminata's smile faded as she saw two large eyes approaching Sochima in the water. They were the eyes of a crocodile—a massive crocodile. It was sixteen feet long from snout to tail and weighed upwards of two thousand pounds. Even for big crocodiles, this was a mammoth creature. It was the color of a dark day with skin like jagged gravel. It looked prehistoric. With its mouth closed, it let out a growl like a motorcycle gently revving.

Its size belied its speed. It was out of the water and upon Sochima in seconds. Sochima lost his balance and fell to the ground, his lower half submerged. The crocodile opened its maw of endless teeth and let out a hiss like the cry of steam. Amaris and Aminata thought about drawing the crocodile's attention to them, giving Sochima a chance to escape but then Sochima, without thinking, held his hand out and told the beast, "Stop," and to their surprise, the beast obeyed.

It stopped charging and slowly closed its maw. Its horrifying hiss fell silent. Sochima got to his feet, reached out to the beast, and touched it on its snout. Aminata was terrified for her brother but dared not speak, fearing she might break the connection Sochima and the creature had built. She had seen Sochima with the spirits in Mexico and was growing to trust him when he did these things.

Sochima petted the crocodile affectionately and said, "Go and don't come back. There is nothing for you here." The crocodile heard him and receded into the river. It was then that they saw two other crocodiles beside it. All three turned around and gently bumped a fisherman's raft before fully submerging and swimming away.

This scene had become a spectacle. People gathered around the children in awe. They shook them and held them by their shoulders. They heard names: Nebetta, Meryamun, Tumerisy. These were their names: Sochima, Amaris and Aminata, respectively. This was their village, and these were people they had known all their lives. It occurred to them that they were sisters: sixteen, fifteen, and thirteen-years-old, Aminata being the oldest and Sochima the youngest. A man in his forties put his hand on Sochima's shoulder. "Sobek blesses you on this day. I thought for certain I saw the crocodile drag you under. I thought I saw it, but then you stood tall, and you told the crocodile stop, and it obeyed you. I've never seen that before. You are a special child," he said.

"Thank you," Sochima said.

Though they seemed friendly, Aminata did not feel comfortable surrounded by so many people. "I think we should go," she said to the others.

"Go where?" Mari asked.

"I don't know. Just away from all these people."

"That way. We should go that way." Sochima pointed down the road.

As they walked through the crowd, a woman called them, "Where are you going?" They tried to come up with something to tell her when she said, "You are forgetting your clothes." They turned around and saw that they had left a batch of clothes on the stones of the riverbank. They were walking back to collect the clothes when the woman said, "Don't worry. I'll get them for you and bring them to your house later. Go home to your mother."

"Thank you," they said and continued walking forward.

57

As they walked, Aminata took in everything around them. Young children walked about naked, only wearing anklets and bracelets, with their heads shaved except for a single lock of woolly hair that grew on their right side. Pubescent boys wore a loincloth that covered their privates. Pubescent girls were topless but wore a papyrus skirt covering their privates as well. The children were dressed like pubescent girls; however, Amaris and Aminata did not feel the need to cover up as they did before. The women wore form-fitting linen dresses that fell to the ankles, with one or two shoulder straps covering the bosom. Some men wore a simple loincloth covering their privates. Others wore a kilt made of linen wrapped around the legs and waist, with a leather strap to hold it up.

Their skin was a deep dark brown, and their faces ranged from round to angular, with broad noses and full lips. A few had almond-shaped eyes. Others had the appearance of almond-shaped eyes with the thick black eyeliner they wore. Their hair was like curly wool. Their palms were close to the complexion of their skin. They looked appreciably no different than the people the children saw in Mali.

Now, where were they? Aminata was piecing it together when something stung the corner of her eye. They saw three brilliant white structures on the sandy horizon. Amaris couldn't believe what she was seeing. They looked like three triangular sons. "Oh shit. We're in—"

"Kemet," Sochima and Aminata said together.

Amaris was confused. "What? I thought we were in Egypt," she said.

"We are. Egypt is the name the Greeks called it. Kemet is the original name." Ami explained. She knelt and grabbed a handful of the soil. It was the color of dark chocolate. It felt moist and rich. "I can't believe we're actually here," she said.

"Then we must be way back in the past. Those pyramids look brand new. Whenever I see the pyramids on TV, they always look janky."

"They don't look janky," Ami objected.

"Yeah, they do. They look tore up."

"That's because, over the years, people stole the limestone that was on the outside."

"Well, it's messed up they did that because, wow, they look beautiful."

As they walked through the city, they were fascinated watching people go about their lives. They came to a market and saw merchants selling goods, as you would see in any time. There were farmers selling produce, other merchants sold wine, beer, bread and baked goods. Fishermen sold all the kinds of fish the Nile provided. Butchers sold fowl and cuts of pigs, sheep, and goats. They had a currency called the deben. Still, most people simply traded one good for another. As they walked through the marketplace, people stared at them and murmured. "That's them. That's the girl," they would hear.

Sochima looked down and noticed the small buds growing out of his chest. "Whoa, I'm a girl," Sochima said.

"You just noticed?" Aminata asked with a smile.

"Yeah. After the jump, that crocodile attacked us and then everyone came around us. I didn't have time to notice." He put his hands on his breasts. "I have boobies."

Aminata slapped his hand away. "Don't do that. That's not your body."

"Ow," Sochi reacted to being hit. "Okay." He moved his hands away. "Boobies are weird. They feel soft, but they're always moving."

"Hey, let's not talk about things that feel weird that are always moving," Amaris said.

"Okay. I mean, I don't mind it. It's just different," Sochima said.

"Yeah, well, you're a better man than me," Amaris said.

Just then, something occurred to Aminata. "Hey guys, have you noticed that the people whose bodies we've jumped into all seemed like they were about to die at the time we jumped in?"

"What do you mean?" Mari asked.

"I mean in Mexico after we ran out of the house. That house collapsed. They were sleeping inside. If we hadn't jumped into their bodies and woken them up, they would have still been inside the house when it fell."

"Hmmm," Sochima hummed, thinking it over.

"Then in Mali. Those ministers were going to drown or get

eaten by those hippos when the boat capsized. But Sochi could breathe longer underwater, and we were able to swim away."

"Yeah, that's true," Amaris said.

"And just now. I think these girls were going to get eaten by those crocodiles like that man said. But Sochi was able to stop them."

"So, what do you think? We're not just jumping into any-body's body?" Mari asked.

"I don't know. It feels random, but maybe not," Ami said.

"Or maybe, I'm just really awesome. Since I'm the one who told us to run out of the house and got the spirits to stop attacking us. I'm the one who saved us from the hippos, and I'm the one who stopped the crocodile. So maybe now you guys will just listen to me," Sochima said.

"Shut up, Sochi," Ami and Mari said simultaneously.

Sochima sighed and shook his head, and they all laughed.

They walked by a house, passing a woman in her mid-thirties standing outside. "Meryamun, Tumerisy, Nebetta, why do you walk by your house as if you do not know where you live?"

As soon as this woman addressed them, memories came flashing in their heads. This woman was their mother, and this was their house. "Oh my," Benerib, their mother, said. "You are you are in shock, almost dying from the crocodile."

"You heard about that?" Ami asked her.

"Everyone has heard. Aha, the fisherman ran and told me. Praise Sobek for sparing you. Praise Ptah for blessing you." She hugged all of them tightly. It felt good to be hugged, to feel a mother's love, even if it wasn't their real mother. She pulled away and held Sochima by the shoulders. "Nebetta, you told the crocodile stop, and it listened to you."

"Yes, *mut* (mother)," Sochima said.

"The Neteru speak through you. I knew you were a special child. No more washing clothes for you. You are meant to be a priestess." She hugged Sochima alone. While she hugged him, he looked at Aminata and Amaris and mouthed, "I'm awesome."

They smiled, shook their heads, and rolled their eyes.

Benerib stopped hugging Sochima and hugged and kissed the other girls. "My beautiful daughters. I am so happy you are alright. Come inside," she said.

Their home looked very similar to many of the other houses around. It was a rectangular box. It was the color of sand and made of dried mud brick. It had a four-foot fence with a wooden gate that encircled the perimeter. They walked up a small ramp leading to the wooden front door.

Inside were potted plants and bowls of fruit laid out to give the home color. The interior was like a studio with no separation between the living, dining room, and kitchen. There was a round wooden table with four chairs. The kitchen had a clay oven, with a window above it allowing the smoke to escape. The house smelled of fresh bread. There was an alcove in the far corner with a wooden stool with a small hole in its center and a small container filled with sand that sat beneath it. There were two bedrooms though they did not have doors separating them. There was one for the girls and one for the mother. They all slept on padded mats for beds.

"This is a great day. Ptah blesses my daughters and reveals Nebetta's purpose on the day of Pharoah's Heb Sed," Benerib said.

"What is Heb Sed?" Amaris asked, and Sochima and Aminata looked at her as if they were undercover agents and she was blowing their cover. Amaris had forgotten to ask herself the question before asking it aloud.

"Oh, Meryamun, you are not well. I'll have to take you to the healer."

Many times, the body they were in already knew the answer to whatever question they might have—and indeed, Meryamun did know the answer. It only took Amaris a second to recall it. "No, mother, I am fine. I know what Heb Sed is. Everyone does. It's a jubilee to celebrate thirty years of Pharoah's reign."

"Yes, this is Pharoah Pepi II's first Heb Sed," Aminata said.

"Good. You worried me, Meryamun. I thought maybe you were still in shock after being attacked by the crocodile."

Amaris hugged her. "No, mother. No need to worry. I was terrified by the crocodile attack, but I am not hurt. I am fine now."

"Good."

"Now, all of you get ready. Wear your best linens. It's a long walk to Djozer's complex, and the Heb Sed begins at Sunset."

58

The sun was setting. It bathed the world in orange. There was a sea of white linen offset against brown skin and black hair. There were thousands of people walking together in one direction. Everyone dressed in their best kilts and full-length dresses adorned with feathers and beads. Commoners who usually went barefoot wore sandals today, and those who wore sandals today wore ones made of leather and not papyrus.

Both men and women wore green and blue eyeshadow and lined their eyes in black kohl, to protect against the sun. They also wore scented hairpieces made from human hair arranged into careful plaits and strands. They wore armlets, amulets, and necklaces made of gold and silver, inlaid with precious stones: lapis lazuli, turquoise, carnelian, and amethyst. Their jewelry often displayed images of birds, scarabs, vultures, hawks, cobras, the ankh, and the Kemetic eye.

It was a joyous occasion. Everyone was in good spirits. As they walked, they were handed food: roasted fish on a stick, bread and beer, which the state provided. Sochima joked to the girls that he was drinking beer. Aminata did not object because Benerib did not object. It seemed drinking beer was the custom for everyone. Ami tried drinking beer once after she had begged her father for a sip of his when she was seven. One sip was all she needed. She never attempted drinking beer or any other form of alcohol again until now. This beer, however, tasted sweeter and not as strong. She didn't love it, but she could stomach it.

Amaris was amazed at all the trees she saw. There were palm, cedar and sycamore trees, and potted lotus blossoms. Kemet was green, and lush, and so different from how she imagined it would be. They passed magnificent temples, statues, and stone structures that reminded her of the Lincoln and Washington Monuments back home.

For the first time since Nana gave Aminata that stick, Amaris wasn't constantly thinking about going home. She liked the way she looked. She liked the way she dressed. She liked not being a man. Being a girl more or less her age felt natural, even when separated by over four thousand years in time. Benerib was not her mother, but she could tell she was a good mother. She had lost her husband fighting in the lands of Kush. What were they fighting for? They didn't honestly know. Your Pharaoh commands, and you follow. It seems no matter the time you lived, regular people were always dying for the ambitions of those who believed they were greater. It occurred to Amaris that Benerib's daughters were already dead, and when they left their bodies, Benerib would lose her three daughters in one instant, and she would be alone in this world. It was a heartbreaking thought. "Meryamun, why has your face turned so glum on such a beautiful day?" Benerib asked.

Amaris was surprised that her thoughts had betrayed her. "Nothing, mother. I thought of father for a moment and wished he was here."

"I as well. But we are here. And let us think only on good things today," Benerib said.

"Yes, mother."

Aha, the fisherman approached them.

"Good day, Benerib. And daughters," he said.

"Good day," Benerib replied.

"Have you met Nomarch Heqaib?" he asked.

"I've never had the pleasure or the misfortune to have met with the Nomarch," she replied.

"What Nebetta did is all anyone can talk about. Even on Heb Sed day. It's gotten the attention of the Nomarch, and he wants you to be his guest during the festival," Aha said.

Benerib was beside herself with joy.

59

Kemet was ruled by a Pharaoh, but like all governments, it was also broken into a bureaucracy. There were two Kemets, Upper and Lower, Lower being closer to the Mediterranean Sea and Upper being closer to the south. The Pharaoh was King of the two lands. The two Kemets were broken into forty-two Nomes, like cities, each governed by a Nomarch. Benerib and her daughters lived in Lower Kemet in Nome Men-Nefer. Heqaib was their Nomarch. Heqaib, like all important people of any time, walked with an entourage of family and guards. Aha introduced him to Benerib and her daughters. Heqaib was a man in his fifties with a slight build but a big smile and a baritone voice. He placed both hands on Sochima's shoulders. "So small and yet so powerful. Tomorrow, we bring you to the priests, and they will see which of the Gods speaks to you and who you should serve. Tonight, you walk with my family and me," he said.

"Thank you," Sochima said.

"And perhaps when you are a priestess, you will remember my patronage … and pray for me," he said.

Sochima did not know how to answer and simply replied, "Yeah … sure."

Amaris and Aminata couldn't help feeling left out by all the attention Sochima was getting. Amaris began to sigh and roll her eyes every time someone praised Sochima. Aminata was used to it. Since he was born, people have been amazed at what Sochima could do. Benerib noticed her daughter's expression had turned and addressed her. "Having a family member who is a priestess raises us all. Your husbands will come from great families," Benerib said to the girls.

"Oh, mother, we're too young to get married," Aminata said.

"Why would you say something so foolish? You are of the perfect age. And Tumerisy, you've always looked forward to getting married," Benerib said.

Aminata spoke, forgetting that she was in a much different time, where women routinely married in their teens. "Yes, of course, I want to get married," she said, correcting herself.

"And who knows? Maybe it will be to the Nomarch's son," Benerib said, drawing Aminata's attention to the young man who walked to the right of Heqaib, who had been eying her since they were presented to the Nomarch. It was clear he liked her. Ami had never had a boy look at her that way before. Then again, he was not really looking at her; he was looking at Tumerisy. She tried to imagine how Tumerisy would react to this. Would she be happy? Would she blush? Aminata decided that she should blush. The thing with blushing, however, is that it can't be faked. An awkward smile came across Aminata's face, and she appeared to be fighting the urge to use the bathroom. The Nomarch's son found this odd and turned away. Dealing with boys was complicated no matter the era or body you were in. Aminata felt embarrassed—and she didn't know why because she really didn't like boys at that age.

They walked with Nomarch Heqaib and his entourage to the Step Pyramid complex. It was an enormous complex covering nearly thirty-eight acres. When they arrived, there were thousands of people outside. Makeshift scaffolding and bleachers were built around the complex, allowing people to see over the thirty-four-foot limestone walls. If they had not been walking with Nomarch Heqaib, this would have been Benerib and the girls' vantage point.

They walked a good while before they got to the entrance. Every time Sochima felt they had come to it, it turned out to be wrong. There was only one true entrance with no door. They walked through a corridor with several stone columns like the stems of reed trees clustered together. When they came into the complex, there were already hundreds of people gathered to the right of the field around what they called the Heb Sed court. The Step Pyramid itself loomed large in the center. With all its limestone still intact, it was a magnificent structure, made of six successive steps, altogether over two hundred feet high.

"Wow," Amaris said. "They really did this pyramid dirty over all the years. Because it looks really messed up in our time."

"Yeah, I know," Aminata agreed with her.

"I can feel it. The next piece is inside of it," Sochima said.

"Good. But now how do we get in? Because there's no way we're scaling that thing," Amaris said.

Aminata could see the entrance. There were two men standing guard. However, with everything going on, they didn't seem that attentive. "Let's wait until dark. Wait until something big happens. Hopefully, the guards will be distracted, and we can sneak in," she said.

As they walked through the complex, a man grabbed Sochima by the hand. Sochima attempted to pull his hand away, but the man's hold was very strong. They all turned to him. "What are you doing? Let go of my daughter," Benerib said, at which point the man let go.

"Forgive me, mother," he said. "But are you the child who commanded the crocodile at the banks of the Hapi today?" he asked Sochima.

"Yes," Sochima answered cautiously.

"Well, then it is an honor to meet you. All of you."

"Thank you," Sochima replied.

They were all offput by this man and couldn't wait to get away from him.

"Let's go, girls," Benerib said to them while putting her arms protectively around Sochima. They walked away and rejoined the Nomarch's retinue.

The man watched them for a bit before turning and walking away as well.

60

Heqaib's retinue arrived where they would be stationed for the viewing of the Heb Sed. He greeted his fellow dignitaries. All forty-two Nomarchs from both Upper and Lower Kemet were present. They greeted each other warmly and spoke among themselves, as they drank wine and ate roasted gazelle. Mostly they spoke about Pepi II. Sochima listened in without making it obvious he was.

"A thirty-year reign is a tremendous accomplishment. Very few live to see a Heb Sed."

"Though a third of his reign should be credited to his mother, Queen Akhensenpepi II."

"Let us not besmirch our Pharoah's legacy. His family has been very good to us."

"That they have. We have never been better, as our seats can now pass to our sons," Heqaib said. "To pharaoh Neferkare and his first Heb Sed. May he see many more." They drank wine to that, and it was apropos as the royal retinue entered the complex at that moment, and everyone turned to the south toward the entrance.

Over one hundred guards and servants preceded the Pharoah. Two dozen drummers announced his arrival. Pepe II rode in on a palanquin; a golden carriage carried on the shoulders of four strong men. Behind him, riding a palanquin as well, was Queen Mother Akhensenpepi II. Behind her were the King's four wives, each riding their palanquins. The people cheered loudly at seeing their Pharoah.

The Pharoah's palanquin arrived at the Heb Sed court. The carriers lowered it to the ground and Pepi stepped out. He was a man in his mid-thirties. He looked youthful and strong. He wore a Nemes headcloth, a striped linen headdress that covered his head, front and back, with flaps that hung down the sides and over the shoulders. He wore a short white kilt, a gold-trimmed leather belt, a leopard-skinned shawl with the tail hanging down the back, and crocodile-skinned sandals with straps wrapped around the shins. He wore armlets made of gold, silver, rubies, and lapis lazuli.

When the Queen Mother's Palanquin arrived, he helped his mother to her feet. Akhensenpepi II was in her late sixties but appeared fifteen years younger. Her skin was rich, and her gait was strong. She wore an elegant white gown that covered her from the nape of her neck to her ankles, with a golden sash in the center. She wore a large necklace and armlets made of gold and silver and inlaid with precious stones. Her hair was black and braided in plaits that fell to her bosom. On her head, she wore a golden headdress with the wings of a falcon on both sides and the head of a vulture in the center. She was loved by her people. They cheered for her as loudly as they cheered for her son. She was a hero of Benerib's, and she was in awe to be so close to her. "She is so beautiful," she kept repeating.

All in attendance bowed before the Pharaoh, the Queen mother, and the four Queens. Pepi lifted his hand, giving everyone permission to rise. When he did, Heqaib and the other Nomarchs approached.

A very important foreign dignitary had traveled to Kemet to celebrate the Heb Sed. Harkhuf, a Nomarch from Upper Kemet, presented the King of Kush, Kemet's closest neighbor to the south. The King was a man in his forties with a strong build. He wore a linen kilt, crocodile skin sandals and a lion skin shawl wrapped around his left shoulder. He and Pepi greeted each other amicably and as equals.

"The river Hapi birthed our two great nations. We are one people. We are brothers. And like brothers, we have loved each other, and we have fought each other. Let us love each other more." the King of Kush said.

"Yes, we are one people. Yes, let us love each other more," Pepi said.

They hugged and held each other's hands high, and the people cheered.

"To celebrate your great reign, the people of Ta-Seti present you a gift," The King of Kush said, ushering his attendant to come forward. He brought forth a great wooden box. He opened it at the King's urging and inside was an exquisitely crafted bow and a set of arrows. "We are the land of the bow. And you will find no greater or more beautiful bow in all the world," he said.

Pepi held the bow in his hand, admiring its craftsmanship; the distinctive Kushite bend in the center, the elegant silk bowstring, the hieroglyphics etched all around the wood, and the ends inlaid with gold. "This is a great gift. The people of Ta-Meri graciously accept," Pepi said.

Following this, there was a procession of gifts from Nomarchs and dignitaries. The greatest gift was presented to both the Pharoah and the Queen Mother. It was a statue made of pure alabaster stone of Queen Akhensenpepi II sitting on a throne and Pepi II as a child sitting on her lap, evoking the image of, "Auset and Heru," Pepi said. He turned and presented the statue to his mother, as the statue honored her most of all, and the people cheered for they loved their queen.

After the gift giving there were performances by musicians and dancers and Kemetic martial artists. Hundreds of children filled the court and sang in praise of their Pharaoh. Pepi II was humbled and honored by their devotion. However, the Priests of Ptah put on the greatest show. There were two priests, and they had staffs that looked very similar to the staff Aminata had in its spiritual form. They stood on opposite sides of a large boulder. They slammed their staffs into the ground, creating a vibration. They whistled through the ankh at the top of their staffs at a frequency people were unable to hear. The vibration caused the boulder to levitate off the ground. The priests then moved the boulder back and forth between them by guiding the energy with their hands. Everyone looked on in amazement, the children especially.

Benerib held Sochima and said to him, "Nebetta, you're going to learn to do such wonderful things," and Sochima smiled.

The sun had set completely. The complex was lit with torches. It was time for the running of the Heb Sed. Two priests stripped Pepi down to just his loincloth and sandals. Another two priests led out a great black bull. In an open field between two rows of shrines, they had built a confined outer course where the bull would run and an inner course where Pepi would run. The outer course had barriers in place, along with priests and guards, to make certain the bull would not break through the borders into the inner course.

The high priest placed the red crown of Lower Kemet on Pepi's head. They prodded the bull to run, and Pepi ran as well. Pepi ran the course four times. When he had finished his fourth circuit, the high priest removed the red crown of Lower Kemet and placed the white crown of Upper Kemet on his head. The bull was released again, and Pepi chased it for another four circuits. After completing eight circuits in total, Pepi, though exhausted, stood tall, showing his vigor and vitality, proving he was still strong enough to rule. The people cheered. Watching Pepi run the Heb Sed, Ami had a strange feeling that she had seen this all before; only she saw it in first person.

Six guards strapped the bull down and held it in place. Pepi took the bow given to him by the Kushite King, nocked an arrow, and took aim. His arrow missed the bull and struck one of the guards in the shoulder. Pepi showed no reaction, and neither did the guard. The crowd as well knew better than to react. Pepi drew his bow and fired a second arrow. This one went just above the bull's head and into the leg of one of the priests who stood in the back. Again no one reacted out of turn. Adults held the mouth of children to keep them from saying something they should not.

Pepi was growing frustrated with his misses. He drew another arrow, took a deep breath, and let it fly. This arrow caught the bull in its right eye. The crowd of thousands erupted in joy. The bull raged, and the guards had to use all their strength to hold it in place. A priest presented Pepi with a sword. Pepi approached the raging bull and put the sword to its throat. The crowd cheered again. Priests with basins made of clay caught the blood of the dying bull as it flowed out.

The priests led Pepi out of the Heb Sed court into the main complex to the front of the Step Pyramid. A priest doused Pepi in the blood of the bull he had just slain. After which, he was washed clean with basins of water from the Hapi river. They then dressed him in a white kilt and shawl.

Pepi turned towards the step pyramid. There were ladders placed at each level. Pepi began his ascent. Two priests stood at each level to aid him up the six levels total. They had placed a throne at the very top. Pepi sat on the throne, and the High Priest gave him the royal crook and flail. He then called Pepi by his five names: Pharoah *Heru Netjerikhaw*–Heru Divine of Apparition. *Nebti Netjerikhaw*–The Two Ladies, Divine of Apparition. *Sekhem Bik-Nebu*–The Golden Falcon Is Powerful. *Neferkare*–Beautiful Is the Soul of Re, and *Sa Re Pepi*–Pepi Son of Re. The High Priest crowned him with the dual crown of Upper and Lower Kemet. The Pyramid gleaming with the full moon behind it looked like stairsteps going to heaven. Pepi sitting on top of the Pyramid looked like a living God.

Everyone looked on in awe. Aminata noticed that the Pyramid guards had moved from their posts and looked on as well. "I think we should go now," she said to Amaris and Sochima. The children took this opportunity to slip through the crowd and make their way down the walkway into the Pyramid. Amaris looked back at Benerib, who was still looking up at Pepi. She felt terrible that they were abandoning her, and she would never truly know what became of her daughters, but Amaris could not delay. They had a great mission to accomplish.

61

There was a torch held in a sconce on a wall as they walked inside. Aminata took the torch and walked behind Sochima as he led the way. The walls were etched with hieroglyphics and lined with limestone. The torchlight shimmered through the tunnels.

The inside of the pyramid was like a great maze with many twists and turns. It was easy to get lost, as they were being led by sense, and not sight or memory. They walked through the tunnels for over twenty minutes when they reached a dead end. "Okay, where to now?" Amaris asked.

"I don't know. The heart is just telling me to go down; it doesn't tell me which way to go to get there."

"Maybe, we should turn back and try again from the start," Aminata suggested.

"Yeah, but which way is it back to the start? We turned so much, I'm confused," Sochima said.

"You weren't keeping track?" Amaris asked.

"No. I was too busy trying to lead us to it. Why weren't you keeping track?"

"Why would I keep track when I thought you knew where you were going?"

"I don't know everything you know," Sochi replied.

"You don't? Cause you sure act like it."

"Guys, arguing isn't helping us. None of us really know what we're doing, and we all should have been keeping track. Now let's try to figure this out before we're trapped down here or caught by guards," Ami said.

"Wait, something is happening," Sochi said.

"What?" Mari asked.

"It's the next piece. It feels like we're getting closer to it."

"We didn't move. How's that happening?" Ami asked.

"I don't know. That's just how it feels." Sochima could feel its presence growing. "Yeah, it's definitely getting closer."

They heard footsteps coming through the darkness and saw an approaching torchlight down a tunnel. "Someone's coming," Ami said.

"We should go," Mari said.

"Go where? We're at a dead end. And whoever that is, is coming from the way we came," Ami said.

"I think we're okay, guys," Sochima said. "Whoever this is, I'm not getting a bad feeling from them. And they have the next piece."

"Wait? What? How can they be carrying it?" Ami asked.

"I don't know, but as they're getting closer, I can feel the piece getting closer."

A man, who looked to be in his forties, with a skull-shaped cap over his head, wearing a simple kilt and papyrus sandals, came out of the shadows. "Come children, this way," he said to them. He then turned and walked back the way he came.

"Um. Don't think so. My mother always told me not to follow strange men you meet in underground pyramids."

"Your mother is very wise. But you have nothing to fear, Amaris. I have what you came for." They were stunned that he knew Mari's name, and not the name of the body she was in, but her soul's name.

"Okay, that is scary," Aminata said.

"How do you know her name?" Sochima asked.

"I know all your names. Sochima. Aminata. He wore a necklace with a pendant. "He held the pendant in his hand. "The eye permits me to see many things. Now come. I have much to show you." He turned and walked back into the tunnel. With trepidation, the children walked behind him into the darkness.

62

They followed him down several tunnels going deeper and deeper until they came to a dead end. He gently touched the wall in front of him, an intricate pattern of overlapping circles lit up, the stone moved, and an entrance appeared. "You can put down your torch," he said as he put down his own. "You no longer need it."

Following him, they entered a chamber filled with light. However, there was no apparent source for the light. The light was coming through the walls. "Whoa," the children said collectively. If they didn't know better, they'd think the room was lit by electricity—but that could not be.

The chamber was two hundred and fifty square feet with a sixteen-foot ceiling. The walls were lined with hieroglyphics, telling a story they did not know how to read. There were hundreds of rolled manuscripts, written on papyrus, stacked in rows on shelves all throughout the chamber. There was a large stone tomb in the center. There was a wooden chair and table with bread, fruit, and wine.

"Is this Djoser's burial chamber?" Sochima asked.

"By Djozer you mean Pharaoh Netjerykhet. No, it is not. This is a chamber only I have access to," he answered.

"Who are you?" Sochima asked.

"I am the designer of this pyramid."

"Wait. Imhotep designed the Step Pyramid," Aminata said.

"Yes."

"Are you Imhotep?"

"I am."

"Holy shit," Aminata blurted.

"Wow, you're really Imhotep. That's so cool," Sochima said.

"Yeah . . . really awesome," Mari said. She then whispered to Ami, "Who's Imhotep?"

Ami was surprised by the question but reminded herself that Imhotep was not someone everyone knew. She and Sochima knew because Nana had taught them about him. "He was like the world's first multi-genius. Math, astronomy, architecture, and medicine. He built the first pyramid, which all future pyramids are based on."

"Okay. So, he's like a big deal. Got it."

"Wait," Sochima said. "If you're Imhotep and you designed the step pyramid, you did that during Djoser's reign, right?"

"More or less."

"But Pepi II is now Pharaoh. Aren't they like two hundred or more years apart?" Sochima asked.

"I've served the dual crowns of Kemet for over four hundred and fifty years."

"Whoa," Ami and Sochi said together.

"You look really good for your age," Mari commented.

"Thank you, Amaris."

"So, you're immortal? You really did become a God like they said," Ami asked.

"I am not a God. But I have been what you may call immortal. You have encountered other immortals on your journey thus far."

"Yeah. Two, I think," Ami said, thinking of the Jaguar-man and Sumanguru.

"Who were they? Do you know them?" Sochima asked.

"No. But I know of them. They are guardians. It's their duty to make certain no one recovers the pieces of Ausar," Imhotep said.

"Who told them to do that?" Aminata asked.

"Set."

"Are you saying Set is trying to stop us?" Aminata asked, sounding fearful.

"I'm sorry, but I'm lost. They know more than me, but I don't know who Set, Ausar, or even you are."

"That's quite alright, Amaris."

"We only know a little more than she does," Aminata said. "We really don't know what's going on or what we're supposed to be doing either."

"I understand. I see your frustration. I will try to help you as best as I can."

"Thank you," Ami said.

"Let's begin at the beginning."

63

Nun. Water. Everything. Nothing. Light. Darkness. Infini-tesimal. Infinite. Mound manifests. Primordial. Pyramidal. A thought—self-aware—reaches out and with each grasp takes form—hand, head, torso, leg—climbs the mound. Ra sits alone. Looks out and what Ra perceives expands around him. He looks deeper and it expands more. Endless emptiness. He looks down and sees Neith. Mother. Ra takes her hand. She sits beside him. The two together. But not to last. Inside Neith contrast, convulse. She retches and spits up. Serpent. Malformed. Chaos. Neith no more. Now Apep. He reaches out. "Brother." Ra rejects him. "Murderer." Apep laments. "No. You kill her. You make me. She exists as one. Two cannot be. One. Peace. Two. War. More than two. More war. Infinite more. Infinite war. Go back to one, go back to Nun, to mother." Apep reaches out. "No," Ra rejects and, in a burst, shoots out at the speed of thought—the speed of dark. Darkness expands. Apep follows bringing chaos. But Ra is too fast. At the other end of the expanse, exhausted, Ra stops. Ra exhales and from his breath come—Shu, dry air, and Tefnut, wet air. They are three and they are together. However, Tefnut, impulsive, goes into the dark and Shu follows. Ra fears for his children but is too spent to follow. His right eye becomes light and is sent to find them. To see his surroundings Ra gives light to his left eye. In the dark, Apep finds Shu and Tefnut. Apep entwines them, imbues them. In fear they combine. The right eye of Ra blinds Apep and frees the children. The right eye brings Shu and Tefnut back to Ra. They separate and are no longer two but four. Their children: Nut the sky and Geb the earth. Ra is grateful. But the right eye feels betrayed by the creation of the left. Ra makes his right eye the greater light, the sun, and his left the weaker, the moon.

Nut the sky and Geb the earth, conceived in fear but born in love, are inseparable. Shu intervenes pulling them apart with his feet on Geb, and Nut on his shoulders. Nut and Geb conceive children, two sets of twins: Ausar and Set, Auset and Nebhet. What was Nun is now nine and one—Apep. The more they divide the more Apep rages. His ire on the sun, the right eye of Ra. Ra and Shu and Tefnut, and Nut and Geb, and Ausar, Set, Auset and Nebhet fight Apep. Apep puts all to sleep except Set. Set alone fends off Apep until Ra awakens. Apep is defeated but not destroyed. Grateful for the victory and for his children Ra cries. Ra's tears fall through Tefnut and Shu, through Nut into Geb and form life. Knowing Apep rests but would return Ra creates more children to aid him in the battles ahead: Ma'at, balance and justice, Tehuti, knowledge and wisdom. He names his right eye Sekhmet and his left eye Khonsu.

With every battle with Apep life on Geb is nearly destroyed and Ra must create life again, and so creates more Gods to aid him in the battles to come. Ra creates Neith, but she is lesser than she was before, and the more Ra creates, the more Ra weakens, the older Ra becomes. Ra grows weary of the cycle. Calls all his children. Ra will pass on his lifeforce so that life on Geb may be everlasting. His remaining life force he will pass to Ausar. He appoints Ausar king to guide life in the path of Ma'at. All Ra's children accept his decision—all except Set.

64

"You are disappointed," Ra says to Set.

"Disappointed? That is a kind word. Betrayed is better."

"There is no betrayal. My blessing was never promised to you."

"Not promised but earned."

"Your brother earned it as well."

"I do not recall Ausar on the barge when all had fallen, you yourself, and I alone faced Apep."

"Yes, you saved us. You have saved us many times. But you also know what you have done and what you have caused."

"I did it to help."

"No. You did not."

"And for this, my brother gets the throne."

"The throne was not mine to give."

"Not yours? Who is above you?"

"Even I submit to Ma'at."

"You created Ma'at."

"No. I gave form to Ma'at. But Ma'at, like Izft has always been. Like Tehuti has always been. There must always be duality. There must always be balance. The power of the throne passes through your sister."

"Auset?"

"She chooses. She chose your brother."

At hearing this, Set felt doubly betrayed.

Set went to the primordial waters, to the abode of Apep.

"Hello Uncle."

Apep replied with a menacing growl. He slithered about circling Set, eyeing his prey, knowing he had the power to consume him at any moment. He opened his mouth, his tongue extended, wrapped around Set like a mummy, covering him up to his mouth. "I see you are happy to see me." His tongue pulled back and brought Set closer to his teeth. "I deserve this. The last time we were together, I was unkind." Apep inhaled and drew Set in closer. "I was mistaken. I ask for your forgiveness." Apep growled, contemplating his strange request. "Grant me an audience, so I may speak my truth. After which, devour me if I displease you." Apep unraveled his tongue and freed Set. "Thank you, Uncle."

"We have much in common. We are of the same kind. I wondered why it was you were able to entrance all the Gods but not I. Even Ra you put to sleep, but not I. You wondered this yourself. It was then I knew that we are the same. Your lifeforce flows through me. I am of you—more you than He. I am a child of chaos. Chaos that which is the true creator. Like you, I know what it is to always be second. I feel your pain and how you have suffered, how you have loved and not have that love returned. I understand your rage. Your ire. I say chaos, I submit to you. I worship you." Set knelt before Apep. Apep accepted his tribute and laid his tongue on Set's head, granting him his blessing. "Thank you, Father. Now I ask one thing. Give me a bit of your blood and your skin."

65

All Gods were present when Ra forfeit his lifeforce and passed his blessing onto Ausar. Ra was no more, and life on Geb became everlasting. Set raised a drink to Ausar's ascension. All the Gods drank, and all fell asleep. Set had poisoned them with the blood of Apep. With the others, he gave enough to put them to sleep. With Ausar, he gave enough to kill. Though Set knew this would not truly kill Ausar. Ausar would regenerate and resurrect. Set had to make certain this would not happen.

He made an axe out of Apep's skin, and with it he hacked off Ausar's arms, first the left and then the right, severing them whole from the shoulders. He did this so Ausar could never take up arms against him. He severed Ausar's legs, first the left, then the right, whole at the hip. Without legs, Ausar could never escape his imprisonment. Set severed his brother's waist and buttocks from his torso. Before casting it aside, he severed his brother's phallus. The phallus was the seed of life. Without it, Ausar could never seed children and, more importantly, reseed himself.

Set saw that Ausar's eyes were open, like a patient coming to during an operation. Perhaps his lifeforce was already resurrecting him. Set could hear his heartbeat, like the beat of a distant war drum growing in volume. Set had been too slow. Panicked, he worked more ravenously. He hacked into his brother's chest, tore it open, and ripped out the beating heart. Outside of the body, the beating slowed, but it did not stop. Set threw it to the side with the other body parts. Set could see Ausar's lungs breathing in rhythm. He hewed deeper, hacked out the lungs, the left and the right, and threw them to the side. The beating slowed to barely a whisper. Still, Ausar's eyes were open. And they looked at their brother with sadness, disappointment, and love—yes love. "Do not look at me. You do not love me. You loved being better than me. But I am the better now." Set swiftly hewed the head from the shoulders.

With that, he turned away believing his work was done. Though when he looked at the severed head, the eyes, the eyes were still open. They kept looking at him, staring at him—judging him. In his rage, Set plucked each eye from its socket. Set believed he heard laughter coming from the severed, eyeless head. "Are you laughing at me, brother?" For the final desecration, Set pried open Ausar's mouth and cut out the tongue. It is with the word that God creates, and now he could create no more. In the end, Set had hewed his brother into fourteen pieces: two arms, two legs, a waist, a phallus, a torso, two lungs, a heart, a head, two eyes, and a tongue. For a moment, he regretted what he had done, but this could not be undone, and yet it was unfinished.

Set stood on the mountaintop and called the serpent. Apep rose from the waters. "Great Father, I have something for you." Set threw up the fourteen pieces of Ausar, and Apep opened his mouth and swallowed. Set smiled. His brother would be lost in chaos forever. It was accomplished. However, the serpent roared in anguish as if he were being torn asunder. He churned and writhed and spat the pieces of Ausar out throughout space and time.

Set tracked one of the pieces down. It landed in the land of Khem in the reign of King Ka, ten years before Menes would unite Upper and Lower Kemet. It landed deep beneath the earth. Set attempted to retrieve it; his plan now was to pulverize all the pieces into dust and scatter them throughout time and space; however, the earth hardened and would not permit him. It hardened into a metal not even Set could break. "Father," he spoke to Geb. "You have taken sides, I see. I see now you have never truly loved me." He looked to the sky. "Mother, do you deny me as well?" The sky darkened, and a deluge fell. "Very well. Keep it. Keep all the pieces." Though aggrieved by Nut and Geb taking Ausar's side, he was relieved the pieces would remain where they had fallen.

66

Set made prisons from the skin of Apep for all the Gods. He gave them a choice. Accept him as they would have accepted Ausar or remain imprisoned. Some chose to accept. Others chose imprisonment. The God he cared for most was among them. "Love me," he said to Auset.

"That is not how love works," she replied. "And you have Nebhet. Love her."

"Do I have Nebhet? Is that why she had a child by my brother? Why did you not shun him for that?"

"He was deceived. Nebhet took my form, and he believed she was I."

"Then why have you not shunned her?"

"I did. And then she repented, and I forgave her. I would forgive you too if you would repent and work to undo what you have done."

"Somethings cannot be undone. And perhaps you are open to forgiving schemers as you yourself schemed to get Great Father's secret name." Auset said nothing. "You did not know I knew this. Perhaps that is why Ra granted the power of the throne through you."

"That was not the bargain," Auset said.

"So, there was a bargain. I see a bit of Apep lives in all of us."

"Some more than others. But not in Ausar. He is purely of Ra."

"He was. But no more."

"He will resurrect. You know this. And he will undo what you have done."

"Unlikely, in the many states he is in."

"What have you done Set?"

"Nothing. Only cut him to fourteen pieces. Then fed him to Apep."

"No."

"Yes. But Apep spat him out. Now he's lost throughout time. The belly of Apep would have been better. But lost in time just as good."

"You made a bargain with Apep."

"More like a covenant."

"Apep cannot be controlled. When he is released in full, he will destroy everything."

"He will destroy most things. And then I will contain him as I have done before and rebuild what is left in my own image."

"Your envy has blinded you."

"No. I see clearly. And I don't need the eyes of Ra for that.

Love me. Don't love me. stay in your cage. In time you'll beg to come out."

Set left. Alone in her cell, Auset called out for help and the staff of Ptah brought Ena Gates.

67

Amaris, Sochima and Aminata were astounded by what they just heard. Aminata looked at the wooden staff in her hand. "The staff brought Nana to Auset?" she asked Imhotep.

"Yes. As you have seen, the staff of Ra is very powerful. It was crafted from the primordial mound when Ra came into being," Imhotep said.

"Wait, you called it the staff of Ra. Nana always called it the staff of Ptah," Sochima said to him.

"That it is. Ptah is another name for Ra. Ra is another name for Ptah. Ra has many names. He is Khepra as the morning sun, Re at noon when the sun is at its highest, Amen when the sun sets and becomes hidden. He is Ptah; he is also Atum, as the Grand Architect and Creator," Imhotep said. Amaris looked utterly confused. "I sense your confusion, Amaris," Imhotep said to her.

"It's just that I've always been taught there is only one God," Amaris said.

"There is," Imhotep said.

"But you just mentioned Ra and all of his names, and Ausar and Set and Auset and Ma'at. I'm sorry I don't remember them all. There was a lot."

"What if I told you there was no God?"

"Wait. What?"

"One, many, none. All the same," Imhotep said.

"Now I'm really confused," Aminata said.

Imhotep took an apple from the bowl of fruit and placed it by the children directly in front of Sochima. "Here is an apple," he said, and before he could continue, Sochi took the apple and devoured it in two bites. "I did not mean for you to eat it, Sochima," Imhotep smiled.

"Sorry," Sochi said.

Ami shook her head. "God, I can't take you anywhere."

"I was hungry."

"You're always hungry."

Imhotep took another apple from the bowl and placed it on the table. "Do not eat this one … yet." He smiled at Sochima. "Now, how many apples are there?" He asked them.

Ami and Sochi replied together, "One."

He turned to Mari, "Amaris?"

"There's one apple," she said.

He handed a small knife to Ami. "Now, Aminata, would you do me a favor and cut the apple into two equal parts." Ami did as he asked, trying to make the halves as equal as possible. "Now, how many apples are there?"

Amaris quickly replied, "Two."

Aminata and Sochi replied, "One."

"Correct. There are two pieces, but it is still one apple. Now, Aminata, would you do me a favor and cut both pieces into two equal parts." Again, Ami did as he asked, making certain each piece was cut as evenly as she could. "Now, how many apples are there?" he asked.

All three answered, "One."

"Good. And now, you could cut this apple into as many pieces as you desire. In fact, with a knife small enough, you could cut it into infinite pieces, and you would still have one apple." His analogy made sense, yet Amaris still seemed confused. "Now think of your body as an apple," Imhotep continued.

"You're not going to cut us, are you?" Sochima asked.

"No, Sochima. But like an apple, you are one body, but that body can be dissected into many parts. You are made up of blood, bones, muscles, organs, and tissues, and you call them each by a different name." He snapped his fingers, and there was a flash of blinding light, and the children reacted and reached for their eyes. "Why are you rubbing your eyes?" he asked.

"Because you tried to blind us," Amaris said.

"Because they burn," Sochima said.

"Now, have you betrayed your body by giving your eyes a name and addressing them?" He posed this question to all of them, but it was primarily directed at Amaris. She did not know how to answer. "Creation is like your body. There is one creation made up of many parts. You can choose to see it as one or as many. You can choose to see it with a consciousness or without. You can choose to see the Creator as part of creation or separate. Neither is wrong. There is a disease growing inside of creation. Normally its immune system would keep the disease at bay, but the immune system has been broken, and the pieces have been hidden throughout the body, and it is your responsibility to find these broken pieces and put them all back together to fight off the disease," he said.

"Why is it our responsibility? Why were we chosen to do this?" Aminata asked.

"Why are any of us chosen to do anything? Did fate choose you, or did you choose fate? Sochima chose to follow his grandmother, you chose to follow Sochima, and you followed your friend." Both Ami and Amaris felt like saying we're not friends but didn't. "And now all three of you are here. And this is what you are here for." Imhotep touched the pendant around his neck. "The eye of Ra."

"So that's the eye?" Sochima asked.

"It is Ausar's right eye. And with it, I have seen you. And I am here to aid you as best I can."

"Aid us? You already know so much and what to do. Why can't you just do it, so we can go home?" Amaris asked.

"I understand your frustration, Amaris. I feel your burden. We all have our purpose to play. This is my purpose. The staff and the heart were passed to your family. This is your purpose and yours alone."

"I am not even a part of their family," Amaris argued. "How did I get pulled into this?"

"You got off the bus," Ami said, feeling Mari's frustration and feeling sorry for her.

"Family is bigger than how you currently perceive it," Imhotep said.

"But why were we chosen? I mean, we're just kids," Ami said.

"Aminata, you are not children. Your Ka, the spirit of the bodies you were born into, are children, but your souls have already lived many lives."

All three of the children were stunned to hear this.

"We can live more than one life?" Aminata asked.

"We all live nine lives," Imhotep said.

"Like cats?" Sochima asked.

"No. Like khats," Imhotep answered, and they looked utterly confused. "Let me explain. At the beginning of your soul's cycle, your Ka, your spirit, is born into a body, your Khat. Your Ka will look the way your body looks, and your personality will be a mixture of the essence of your soul and the experiences and memories that your body accumulates. When your body dies, your soul, your Ba, moves onto a new body, where it becomes Ka again to a new Khat; new personality, new appearance, new memories, as memories from your previous life are forgotten—but not erased. This cycle repeats itself, your Ba growing and evolving with each life until you have completed nine lives. Your ninth life is when your soul accomplishes its greatest purpose. When your Ba becomes your Akh and in the Duat, the afterlife, it is brought before the forty-two judges and the cumulative account of all your lives will be judged. If you have walked in the path of Ra, you become one of the justified dead and become like Ra, a sun, a star, in the heavens."

"We become stars?" Sochima asked.

Imhotep nodded yes.

"So, stars are people?"

"They are the souls of the justified dead."

"What happens if you're not judged to be righteous?" Amaris asked.

"Then your soul is devoured by Ammut."

"And then that's the end?" Aminata asked.

"Nothing truly ends. Nothing is created or destroyed. Your Ba is recycled into creation."

"You said we had already lived many lives. Do you know how many?" Aminata asked.

Imhotep turned to each one as he answered them. "Amaris, you are in your second life. Aminata, you are in your seventh life. Sochima, you are in your ninth."

They were all stunned to silence until Sochima turned to Aminata and said to her, "I'm older than you," and giggled. "I'm older than both of you." He giggled more, and his laughter broke through the seriousness of the mood. "So, will you guys listen to me now?"

Amaris and Aminata said, "No."

Sochima turned to Imhotep. "Can you tell them to listen to me?"

"I cannot help you there, Sochima," he said with a slight smile. "Now you must also understand that the order of your lives does not follow the chronology of the physical world."

"What does that mean?" Aminata asked.

"Your first life could have been a thousand years ago; your second life could have been three thousand years ago, your third a thousand years from now, your fourth, five hundred years ago; your sixth three thousand years from now. When and where you are reborn is random."

"So, if I'm in my second life, if I die, I can be reborn in the past?" Amaris asked.

"Yes."

"I don't want to be born in the past. The past sucks."

"If you were born in that time, you would not think so."

"There is so much we don't know," Aminata said.

"You now know more about creation than most beings who have ever existed. This knowledge has been passed to only the highest initiates. But it is necessary for you to know for you to complete your task." Imhotep removed the necklace and placed the eye on the tomb. "Aminata, if you would do the honor."

Aminata took the staff and touched the eye. The shell gave away and sunk into the earth. The soul was released, and all their souls left the bodies they were in. Imhotep's soul did not look so different from the body he had been in, but he radiated light.

Sochima moved towards the eye to take it inside of him as he had done before. However, Imhotep held him back. "No, Sochima. This one is for Aminata," he said.

"Really?" Sochima said, feeling a bit disappointed.

"Yes. It is unwise for one of you to carry all the pieces," he said.

"Um. I'm not sure I want it," Ami said.

"Would you let your brother carry this burden alone?" Imhotep asked her.

"Um. No."

"Trust me. Once you have taken it, your trepidation will go away, and you will see things more clearly," he said.

Still unsure, Aminata turned to Amaris. "Whatchu you looking at me for?" Amaris asked.

"I don't know, encouragement," Aminata said.

"Okay. Go ahead. Take it. I'll watch," Amaris said.

"Thanks," Ami said sarcastically.

"You will be fine, Aminata," Imhotep said.

"Yeah. It tastes like chicken," Sochima said. Ami gave him a cold eye. "I'm just joking. It doesn't taste like chicken. It doesn't taste like anything."

"Okay," Aminata said. She walked over to the table, took the orb in her hands, opened her mouth, and guided it inside of her. There was a second where her soul vibrated, but it soon passed. With the orb inside Aminata, they all returned to their bodies, and they were Nebetta, Meryamun, and Tumerisy again. "How do you feel?" Mari asked her.

"The same. I guess." Then Ami saw something. She saw Sochima hug Imhotep. Then a man came out of the shadows and grabbed Sochima by the arm. Only when she looked at Sochima and Imhotep nothing of the sort was happening.

Imhotep saw the puzzled look on her face. "Aminata, did you see something?" he asked.

"No. Um. I don't think so," she said.

Sensing the uneasiness in her. "I think it's time for you to go," he said to them.

"Yeah, I think so, too," Aminata agreed.

"Wait. Will we see you again?" Sochima asked Imhotep.

"I don't believe so," he said.

Sochima was sad to hear this, and he hugged Imhotep, just as Aminata had seen. "Sochima get over here now," she shouted at him.

"What?" Sochima turned to say just as the door to the chamber opened, and a hand reached out from the shadows and grabbed him by the arm.

Imhotep knocked the hand away, freeing Sochima, then pushed Sochima out of its reach. A man came out of the shadows. It was the strange man who had grabbed Sochima's hand during the Heb Sed. "What are you doing?" the man asked Imhotep.

"Go now," Imhotep shouted to the children.

"No," the man shouted and ran towards Sochima. It was then that Aminata saw him. She saw through his body and saw his soul. He was the dark angel they encountered in DC. The one who shattered Nana's soul. Though she was utterly terrified, "Grab my hand," she said to Amaris; then she reached out and grabbed Sochima just before the dark angel could get a hold of him. Their souls jumped in that instant.

The strange man held onto Nebetta's unconscious body. The unconscious bodies of Meryamun and Tumerisy fell to the ground. The strange man dropped Nebetta's body and turned to Imhotep. "Do you know how many millenniums I meditated through to find them here? And you allowed them to escape with the eye," he said.

"I gave it to them freely," Imhotep said.

"What? You betrayed us?" the strange man said.

"I betrayed nothing."

"You made a vow to Set."

"I made a vow long before that. What I said to Set were just words."

Enraged, the man took a blade from behind his kilt and lunged at Imhotep. With his forearm, Imhotep deflected his advance. The strange man swiped again, and again Imhotep blocked him and redirected his momentum. They fought a form of martial arts which was a mix of jujitsu and tai chi. There was grappling and counter-grappling, each fighting for the better position in an elegant dance. They were both great fighters, and neither man could get the better of the other.

To end the stalemate, the strange man left his body, and as the dark angel attacked Imhotep's soul. Imhotep's soul left his body to defend himself—but it was a ruse. The dark angel quickly reentered the strange man's body and slit Imhotep's throat. Imhotep smiled as the blood flowed and his body fell.

The strange man then slit the throats of all three girls, making certain they were dead. He slit the throat of the body he was in as well. In the spirit realm, Imhotep said to the dark angel, "That was unnecessary. I had no intention of jumping into their bodies. My purpose here is done." His soul vanished. The dark angel clenched his fists in anger before vanishing as well.

ACT FIVE
A CLASH OF FATES

68

Blink. Sleep. Wake. Repeat. Blink. Sleep. Wake. Repeat. New world. New body. However, your thoughts remain where you last were, on the last things you saw. Aminata's thoughts were on Imhotep and the dark angel. He was the same figure who shattered Nana's soul. He was in the body of the strange man. In Washington, DC, back in their time, he had been in the body of a woman. Was he like them, traveling through time, jumping from body to body? It appeared so. But how was he able to do this? For them, the staff was their conduit. How was he able to travel without it? Did he have one of his own—or some other artifact that acted as his vehicle? Had he been tracking them? How was he able to do that? He was obviously quite powerful. Imhotep was immortal, but was he powerful enough to fend off the dark angel? She feared for Imhotep. Though she had only known him briefly, she had grown to care for him. He had helped them so much.

"Great, I'm a man again," Aminata heard Amaris say from her new body, and Ami's thoughts returned to the present. The three of them were kneeling in a row together. Their legs were closed, and their hands were on their knees. They took stock of each other. They were all men in their thirties, with slim athletic builds and dark brown skin. They wore turbans and armor very similar to the kind the soldiers in Mali wore, which lead them to wonder, "Are we back in Mali?" Amaris asked.

It was a hot day. They were on the outskirts of a forest with tall trees and a river nearby. "I don't think so," Sochima said, as the area's topography seemed very different from Mali's. Aminata was feeling the same just before she suddenly shouted,

"Get down, now." She said it with such urgency, Sochi and Mari didn't hesitate for a moment. They did as she said, and seconds later a volley of arrows flew over their heads, landing in the ground and the trees around them. Aminata shouted, "Run," and they got to their feet and began running as fast as they could.

Arrows whizzed by as they ran into the forest to give themselves better cover. Aminata led the way. "Where are we running to?" Sochima asked as the heart was telling him they were running further away from the next piece.

"Anywhere they're not shooting at us," Ami said.

While trying to keep her head down, Mari looked behind her and caught glimpses of who was chasing them. They were men, like themselves, perhaps a dozen of them, some with bows, some with swords. They chased them fiercely. "What did we do to make them so mad?" she wondered.

The children kept running, trying not to trip over the ground vegetation and using their hands to cut through the branches and twigs in their way. Ami was struck with a vision of an arrow hitting Mari in the shoulder. She didn't have time to tell Mari to duck. She stepped in the arrow's path and knocked it away with the staff. Another arrow glanced off Ami's forehead, knocking off the turban she wore. It also knocked her off balance. Aminata lost her footing and tumbled down a ravine that led into the river.

Amaris and Sochima shouted, "Ami," and ran down the ravine after her. Aminata tumbled violently, and the staff flew from her hand as she fell into the water. Sochima and Amaris got to where the staff fell. Sochima picked the staff up, and Amaris prepared to dive into the river, but before she could, a large net was thrown over both her and Sochima, and they were dragged to the ground.

69

Aminata's father attempted to teach her to swim multiple times, but it never stuck. She could never float on her own and was only able to swim in bodies of water she could stand in. She did not know how deep the river was, but it was much greater than five feet. As she sank, the world felt like it was closing in on her, and she flailed her arms, reaching out for help. In Mali, it was Sochima who saved her from drowning. She kept looking for him or Amaris, but no help was coming. The world was closing in on her. Her chest was contracting. She would have to save herself. She calmed herself and muscle memory took over. Aminata did not know how to swim, but the body she was in did. She let go of control, and the body swam upward and broke the water's surface. She inhaled immediately. Breathing had never felt so sweet.

She saw the shore close by and swam to it. She came out of the river on all fours and sat on the bank, utterly spent. She looked ahead and saw Sochima and Amaris trapped in a net with a dozen men around them. They were on the other side of the river, about a hundred yards away. She searched her mind trying to figure out how to help them. In times of stress, she would clasp her hands tightly around the staff. It was then it occurred to her that she did not have the staff. It had fallen from her. Could it have fallen into the river? *No,* she feared. With the river's current, it could be anywhere by now, and they would be lost here.

HERU PTAH

70

The men surrounded Sochima and Amaris with their blades drawn. While lying on the wet earth of the riverbed, spitting gravel from his mouth, Sochima could see across the river to the other side. "Ami," he whispered, and Amaris heard him, and she looked across the river as well. They glimpsed Aminata hiding behind a tree. They knew Aminata couldn't swim and were relieved to see she had survived.

The leader of these men pulled the net away. "Chain them," he said. Two other men placed manacles on their hands. Amaris had handcuffs put on her when she and Aminata were arrested at the metro station back in DC. She recalled hating that feeling. She would take those handcuffs over these any day. These were made of rusted wrought iron and weighed five pounds, which felt like they added fifty pounds to your weight.

The leader approached them. "There were three of you. Where is the other?" he asked.

"He fell into the river," Sochima answered.

"And he does not swim?" the leader asked.

"No," Sochima said.

"Rare for an Andalusi." He then looked at the river and across to the other side. He saw nothing. "Hmmm. Beyond the river is Castile. I would not risk crossing its borders just for one man. No matter. You two will suffice."

One of the other men pulled out his dagger and put it to Amaris's throat.

"No," the leader said and held his hand.

"Tarik, why do you stay my hand?" he asked.

"Because I want them alive," Tarik answered.

"We were just trying to kill them," he said.

"That was because we were trying to stop them. Now that

214

we have them. I believe they are of more use to us alive. I think Sulayman would like to know what they know," Tarik said.

"Sulayman is in Cordoba."

"Yes. And we should make haste."

"But why not to *Ŷaīyyān*. Al-Nasir and the army are there, and it is closer."

"Al Nasir may be Caliph, but it is Sulayman who pays us, and that is where our loyalty lies. On your feet, apostate," Tarik said to Amaris and Sochima.

With his hands in fetters, Sochima picked the staff up, which was on the ground beside him. Tarik attempted to take it from him. Sochima held onto it tightly. Tarik pulled his hand back and gave Sochima a backhanded slap, which knocked Sochima to the ground. Amaris reflexively moved to strike back, but a dagger was put to her throat and held her in check.

Tarik moved to throw the staff into the river, but Amaris and Sochima shouted, "No," so urgently that Tarik stopped himself. *Why would they cry out for just a simple stick?* He wondered. This stick must hold some value beyond what he could see. And in truth, after holding it in his hand, he did not want to discard it. "Curious. I will hold onto this. Let's go," he said.

71

Aminata used the trees for cover and followed Amaris, So-chima, and their captors from the other side of the river. She did not know how far the river went, and she feared at some point their captors would take Sochima and Amaris deeper inland. To keep following them, she needed to cross the river to their side without being seen. She was so focused on not losing sight of them that she ignored her surroundings and the things creeping behind her.

"Turn around, Moor."

Aminata turned around slowly to find a sword and four arrows pointed at her. She was surrounded by five men. These men were much different from herself and the men that had chased them. They wore white cloth surcoats with red crosses emblazoned on the front. They wore chainmail underneath, which covered their head, neck, and arms, and fell to just above their knees. They were tan complexioned with straight brown hair, narrower noses, and thinner lips. They spoke an odd form of Spanish and Latin combined.

As she looked at them, something very strange happened. She began seeing double. In each of the men, she saw two of them, one hovering inside the other. It was like waking up and what your left eye and what your right eye sees are separate until they combine into one—only they do not combine. Previously, the children had been able to see the lost souls of the dead as they wandered around aimlessly. Now Ami could see the souls of the living while they still occupied their bodies. It made her feel off-kilter. She kept blinking, hoping the two images would combine.

Aminata looked quite strange, standing with her hands raised, blinking incessantly. "Something in your eye, Moor?" one of the men asked.

"Yes," Ami answered.

"I hate when that happens. Let me help get it out," he said, putting the tip of his blade an inch from Ami's eye.

Ami pulled back, and the man kept pushing the tip of the blade closer when another man on horseback rode up to them. "What are you doing?" he said to the others. "Put your swords down. This is one of the men we are here to meet." The other men lowered their weapons but continued to look at Ami with disdain. The man on horseback dismounted and hugged her like a great friend. Just then, she remembered him. This was Tomás. "Tahir, it is good to see you, brother," he said. Tomás was dressed like the others, but his surcoat had no red cross.

"And it is very good to see you," she replied, as she likely would have been killed without his intervention.

"You are alone. Where are Hassan and Bilal?"

He was speaking of the bodies Sochima and Amaris occupied.

"They were captured. They are across the river," Ami said.

Tomás looked across the river. He could see the dozen or so men who were walking away with Bilal and Hassan in fetters. "Dammit. The Almohads have them," he sighed. "We are too few. And they are in Almohad territory. I am afraid they are lost to us," Tomás said.

Aminata fought back her emotions and wanted to encourage Tomás to aid her in trying to rescue them, but he and especially the other men seemed disinclined to do so. "War is ugly. But let us meet with Alfonso in Toledo. Hopefully, we will soon put this war to an end." Tomás said.

Aminata had no choice but to go with Tomás. She had no doubt the other men would kill her if she did not. She looked at Sochi and Mari once more and then turned away. *Good luck, you guys. Please be safe.*

72

When your soul inhabits a body that's not your own, there are things the body knows that do not come to you as naturally as when you are in your true body. You must ask your new body the question and then search through a flood of memories to get the answer. *Where are we?* Sochima asked himself. After a few moments, "Al-Andalus," he heard Amaris say softly. They had both been asking the same question and came to the answer at the same time. Al-Andalus didn't mean anything to Amaris. However, Sochima remembered Nana telling him stories about medieval Spain, which was called Andalucía by the Christians and al-Andalus by the Muslim Moors, of which they were, as were their captors. These were their people, yet they believed they had betrayed them. They were taking them to the governor of Cordoba, a man called Sulayman. Sochima searched his thoughts but had no visual memory of this man. Nonetheless, he knew the name well, and it was a name his body feared.

The journey to Cordoba was the longest of Sochima's young life. It took almost two days, walking with the hot sun on their backs and the hot earth on their feet. Their manacles and chains made the heat ten times more oppressive. Their captors gave them dry bread to eat and water only if they rested by the river or a stream.

Fortunately, there were four rest periods throughout the day for prayers, as the day's journey began after morning prayers. Amaris and Sochima looked forward to these respites. In these bodies praying came as naturally to them as breathing. Tarik was unconvinced and opened their robes and bared their chests to ensure they were not secretly wearing crosses and attempting to deceive them into thinking they were still true believers.

During the first day, Sochima felt them getting closer to the next piece of Ausar's soul. At one point, it felt like it was only a mile away. They passed many soldiers on the road, as a great army had amassed in the nearby town. Sochima listened to the soldiers talk and overheard them call this town $\hat{Y}a\bar{\imath}yy\bar{a}n$. Once Sochima heard the name, he remembered it. It was also known as Jaén by the Christians. Hassan, the body Sochima was in, had been here before and was familiar with the terrain. Sochima wanted desperately to break away from their jailers, get the staff and go recover the next piece. Unfortunately, their shackles were quite strong, and a guard always kept an eye on them, even during the night when they slept.

Sochima tried to tell Amaris how close the next piece was, but a guard was always quick to strike them whenever they attempted to speak to each other. He and Amaris barely communicated on their journey. Whenever he looked at her, Amaris always appeared very deep in thought. He wondered if she was thinking about Aminata as he was. He was so happy to see Ami had made it out of the river and onto the other side, but he had not seen any sign of her since. He did not know if she was safe, but he believed strongly that she was alive—of this he was certain. However, he could feel the distance growing between them. It was like the sensation he felt with the next piece.

On the second night of their journey, Sochima awoke to a wolf staring at him. It did not snarl. It did not growl; it just looked at him calmly with its piercing green eyes. Instinctively Sochima said, "Hello," and was quite shocked to hear the wolf reply, "Hello." However, its mouth did not move. At this point Sochima was growing accustomed to supernatural things happening, so he was not as frightened as he previously would have been.

"How are you?" he asked the wolf cautiously.

The wolf replied, "Hungry."

Sochima swallowed whatever dry spit was in his mouth. "Do you want to eat me?" He asked the wolf.

"No. You smell different," the wolf replied.

Before Sochima could question the wolf further, one of his jailers awoke and threw a rock at the wolf, shooing it away.

73

Aminata had never ridden a horse before. Fortunately, the body of the man she possessed had. After the initial awkwardness of getting on, riding it came as naturally as riding a bicycle. They were riding to Toledo. These men spoke what Aminata gathered was an old form of Spanish. Like old English, it sounded awkward and stilted. Given their attire, she suspected they were in medieval Spain, in and around a time not too far from when they were in Mali. What the exact date was, she did not know. Then she thought, the body she was in should know. She asked herself, *what year is it?* And she got two answers: In the year of our lord twelve hundred and twelve, and six hundred and nine in the year of the Hijrah.

Knowing the year gave Aminata some sense of peace, like knowing the currency exchange when traveling to a new country. She could put things in order relative to her own time and the time periods they had already visited. They had been in Mexico during the time of the Olmecs, somewhere between 1000 and 400 BCE. Then they had been in Mali in 1327, then in Kemet during the reign of Pepi II around 2200 BCE. Now they were here in Spain, though it was not yet Spain. They were in the Kingdom of Castille, and Alfonso VIII was king.

Aminata kept thinking of herself as three though she was alone. She had been separated from Sochima and Amaris and didn't know whether they were alive or dead. Turning her back and walking away from them was one of the hardest things she had ever done. There was a feeling inside of her that made her believe they were still alive. Whether they were badly hurt or not, she did not know. What she knew for certain was that she was alone, and she was lost. She had no sense of direction or guidance. Whenever they jumped to a new place, the heart would guide Sochima to the next piece, and they would follow him. *What am I supposed to do?* she asked herself. Who does she follow?

Presently she was following this man Tomás because she had no choice. She was not in chains; nevertheless, she felt like a captive. If it were not for Tomás these other men would have killed her. Her name was Tahir, and she and Tomás were friends. They had fought together and had saved each other's lives on multiple occasions. From her body's experiences, she was in fact closer friends to Tomás than she was to even Hassan and Bilal, whose bodies Sochima and Amaris now occupied.

They rode side by side. Ami was becoming accustomed to her foresight and learning how to see their souls and their physical bodies separately. She did not blink as much as she had before. Tomás spoke of adventures they had been on and growing up in Valencia together. As he spoke, she recalled each memory; however, this made their conversations very stilted. She felt like she was speaking a foreign language and had to translate everything into her native tongue before responding. "You are not yourself, Tahir," Tomás said.

"I am sorry, my friend. But I am concerned for Bilal and Hassan," she said.

"Yes. My thoughts go to them as well. However, I do not like where my thoughts take me. I fear the Almohads have already killed them. They do not take well to those who they suspect of betrayal." Aminata looked at him sternly. That was the last thing she wanted to hear. "All we can do is honor their lives and make certain their deaths had meaning." Aminata didn't say anything, and Tomás understood he was hurt and felt it best to let him be and grieve in peace.

74

Hours before Sochi and Mari arrived, they could see Cordoba on the distant horizon. They could see a golden palace on a hill and the minarets of many mosques stretching into the clouds. They heard the *adhan,* the call to prayer, coming from the city. Everyone stopped and went down on their knees to pray.

It was another three hours before they entered the city. For a time, the city seemed forever out of reach. They did not know what awaited them in Cordoba, but they were tired of the road. Their hands felt like they might fall off from the weight of their chains, and the soles of their feet were chafed from their miles of walking.

Cordoba was a wonder of its time. It had paved streets with raised sidewalks. It had streetlights on every main avenue, and an abundance of fountains and gardens, made possible by an irrigation system run by waterwheels. Walking through the city, they saw many fine homes, mosques, universities, and bathhouses. The city was very clean, and the people were mostly courteous. Most people wore an *aljuba,* a flowing robe, of various colors, over a *sarwal,* which were baggy trousers. The men wore *imamas,* turbans made from wool or linen wrapped around the head with a tail in the back. Women wore a veil covering the lower half of their faces, mostly made from silk and sometimes embellished with gold. Both men and women wore leather shoes with a curved tip. The people were the most diverse of anywhere they had been, as they ranged in complexion from tan to very dark brown, and their hair varied from very thick woolly black hair to fine, straight blonde hair. They mainly spoke Arabic, but also an old form of Spanish.

Tarik and the others led them to the great Mosque. They walked through a courtyard of orange trees. The orange fruit and the green foliage were a great contrast of colors against the sandy walls of the Mosque's exterior, which looked very similar to a fortress. In the center of the courtyard was a great fountain with pink flamingoes fluttering about. There were other fountains used for ablutions, where people washed their hands and faces before entering the mosque.

The interior of the mosque was a remarkable sight. Dozens of columns, inlaid with gold and lapis lazuli, formed arches high above to the ceiling. The floor was paved with silver and mosaic inlays, and the mosque smelled sweet of incense and scented oils. They walked through a beautifully gilded horseshoe arch, leading into a rectangular room. They approached a man sitting in the back, wearing a white aljuba and sarwal, and an orange turban. The late afternoon sun shined through a window, and he read a book in its light.

"Sulayman," Tarik greeted him with a bow of the head. The other men did likewise, and Amaris and Sochima felt they should do the same. Sulayman closed the book, titled *Fasl al-Maqal* by Ibn Rushd, and rose to meet them. He had the athletic build of a man in his twenties, but the chiseled features and the eyes of a man in his fifties. He was clean shaved, and his skin was dark brown to the point of being purple. He looked up and admired the room he was in. "Beautiful, isn't it? I come here every day. I've seen it hundreds of times and never once has it failed to amaze me. I marvel at its beauty and its history. How it has grown through time, each Caliph continuing where his predecessor left off. One put the gold on the columns and the walls; another added the minaret; another built the mihrab pointing to Mecca; another built the arcades to hold the faithful. Amazing the things man can accomplish when guided by God."

"Sulayman, these are two of three men who we suspect of working for the Christians," Tarik said.

"And you know this because?" Sulayman asked.

"We caught another, and he revealed their identities to us," Tarik said.

"And where is the third?"

"When we chased them out of Ŷaīyyān, we lost the third in the Guadiana."

Sulayman turned to Amaris and Sochima. "Do you speak God's tongue or only vulgar Latin?" he asked.

"We speak God's tongue," Amaris answered in Arabic.

"And are you traitors, as he says?" Sulayman asked them.

"No. But we have been a part of the Christians' ranks. But only to gain information to help our cause," Amaris said.

"Hmmm? And who do you share this information with?" Sulayman asked.

"Ibn Jam`i," Amaris said.

"Ibn Jam`i? Al Nasir's vizier," Sulayman said.

During the two days they walked to Cordoba, Amaris had been contemplating what she would say when they arrived and were questioned. She knew their lives depended on it, so she thought of nothing else. She searched the memories of the body she was in and asked herself many questions. She heard them mention Caliph al-Nasir. Thinking of al-Nasir made her think of ibn Jam`i, his vizier. She imagined claiming they were working for the second most powerful man in al-Andalus would buy them some time at the very least. At least, she hoped.

"Ibn Jam`i is with the Caliph in Jaén. Convenient for you that he is not here to verify your claims. Or perhaps not," Sulayman said. "But I will get to the truth of it."

"They carried this with them." Tarik handed the staff to Sulayman.

Sulayman took it and looked it over. He was not impressed.

"A simple staff. What of it?" he asked.

"Perhaps nothing. But as I was about to cast it in the river, they shouted, no. And their eyes were filled with hurt and fear. It must mean something to them. Perhaps something unseen," Tarik explained.

"Interesting," Sulayman said, examining the staff more thoroughly. He turned to Sochima and Amaris. "Why does a young man need a walking stick?"

"It was my grandmother's," Sochima said.

"And she is with Allah?"

"Yes," Sochima answered.

"And you loved your Mama?"

"I did."

"So much that you, a mercenary, would carry it with you always, all because of sentiment," Sulayman said, then, with great force, brought the staff down over his knee to break it.

Sochima reflexively shouted, "No."

Amaris kept her reaction inside.

However, the staff did not break. Sulayman looked impressed. "It is light to hold. Yet quite solid." Sulayman swung the staff, striking the ground. Again, he examined it. "Not even a scratch," he proclaimed. It does not break. What wood is this made of?"

"I don't know," Sochima answered.

"Well. Let us see how it burns." Sulayman carried it to a nearby lantern and put the tip of it to the flame.

Sochima was about to scream out again, but Amaris held his hand.

Sulayman held it under the fire for quite some time, but it would not burn. He removed it and held it in his hand, and it was, "Cool to the touch," he said. "This is a most amazing staff. It was your grandmother's, you say?"

"Yes," Sochima said.

"And how did she come by it?"

"I do not know."

"Well, I see why you cherish it, as I will cherish it. Thank you for this gift you have given me." He held the staff at his side in a gesture of ownership. This angered Sochima. Amaris held his hand again to keep his emotions in check. "You two are more than simple mercenaries, aren't you?" He turned to Tarik. "Bathe them, give them clean clothes and have them join me for dinner," he said.

"You would dine with them?" Tarik asked, sounding confused.

"Yes. These men possess intelligence I wish to know. And I've found kindness with the threat of violence is more productive than pure violence. Also, they smell. You all do. And I do not do well with foul smells. Now all of you, go, bathe."

75

It took Aminata and the others a day and a half to get to Toledo. They could have made it sooner, but they did not want to overburden their horses, and they made camp and rested during the night. They ate rabbits they had killed earlier in the day and roasted them over a spit. It tasted undercooked and under seasoned, but the others ate it without complaint, so Ami did the same.

They passed through forests, open fields, and hamlets on the city's outskirts. Toledo was set on a hill above the plains, surrounded by a river on three sides. From the distance, they could see the tops of a massive square fortress and a great church. They entered the city from the east, crossing a great bridge that spanned a river the men called the Tagus. They passed through a great metal gate into the old quarter. The people here looked more like Tomás and the other men than Aminata. Still, there was a strong Moorish presence and a Jewish presence as well.

There were signs of what used to be many great homes and structures, though many of them looked run down and in disrepair. The city had an overbearing smell to it. It gave Aminata a headache, and she fought the urge to throw up more than once. It took her a great while to grow accustomed to it, but she didn't seem to notice it anymore after she did.

They rode through the city and headed towards the great church. The city was overflowing with soldiers. To Ami's eyes, there were more soldiers than citizens. "You see. All the kingdoms of Hispania are here," Tomás said. "Kingdoms that have fought each other have finally put their bickering aside for the greater good. This campaign will forever determine the fate of this land," he said. Ami respectfully smiled and nodded.

They came upon a great commotion. A hundred or so Jews had gathered and were angrily protesting. Armed knights held them at bay. Two Jewish men had been slaughtered in the street. The crowd cried for justice. Tomás asked one of the knights what happened. "The French," the knight replied.

Tomás sighed through his teeth. "It seems this barbary is the cost of inviting the French to war," he said to Aminata as they rode on. Aminata did not respond, but this entire display troubled her deeply.

They arrived at the church and dismounted their horses. Tomás left the other knights, and he and Aminata entered the church. They found King Alfonso VIII inside alone. He knelt and prayed beneath a figure mounted on a cross. The figure was of a man carved out of wood, dressed in a blue robe, with dark olive skin, short black hair, a broad nose, full lips, and a goatee. He looked worn and melancholy but not in anguish. He looked quite different from any other crucifix Aminata had ever seen. After taking a moment to examine it, she paid it no mind. Aminata and Tomás waited at the other end of the church for Alfonso to finish.

"Since the passing of his son Fernando, the King comes here every day," Tomás said.

Aminata nodded that she understood.

Having finished his prayer, Alfonso rose to his feet, turned about, and was happy to see his good friend Tomás at the other end of the church. "Tomás, you return to us," he greeted him.

"Your highness," Tomás said and bowed, "you know I will always be by your side."

"That I do. But in this world, when people leave you, it is always a blessing when they return."

"Very true," Tomás said.

"I see you bring a friend with you," Alfonso said regarding Aminata.

"Your highness, I present to you Tahir ibn Sa'd."

Aminata stepped forward. "Your Highness, she greeted him, following Tomás's lead. Aminata at first believed she had addressed him appropriately, but then Tomás and Alfonso looked at her waiting for her to do something. And it occurred to her she was in the presence of a King, and she had not bowed. She corrected herself, bent the knee, and rose when Alfonso gestured for her to do so. Aminata found this act of kneeling before royalty dispiriting. Fortunately, unlike Mansa Musa, Alfonso did not require her to throw dirt over her shoulder.

Alfonso was a man in his late fifties, old for this time but still a vital man. With his white hair and beard, he looked wizened. "Ibn Sa'd," Alfonso repeated to himself. "Was your father Sa'd ibn Umar."

"Yes," Aminata answered. When Alfonso asked the question, her memories told her it was true.

"I knew him. He was a good man. He fought alongside Ibn Mardanis."

"Yes, our fathers knew each other. We grew up together in Valencia. Our fathers fought with the Wolf King, and both died attempting to siege Granada," Tomás said.

"Aye, the Wolf King's great defeat, as Alarcos was for me. Though I, a Christian, and he a Moslem, ibn Mardanis and I shared much in common in our vision for this land on how our people could continue to live together, and our mutual hatred of the Almohad," Alfonso said. "Do you share in this vision?" Alfonso asked Aminata.

"Yes," Aminata answered—knowing there was no other answer to give.

"And you will fight with us, though it means fighting against people of your kind."

"Yes, your highness," she said.

"Good, because we have much fighting ahead of us, and we will need all the help we can get."

76

The Christian forces were stationed at the Alcazar. It was a massive square fortress sitting on a hill. King Alfonso mentioned that the Romans had built it as a palace, but the Moorish Caliph Abd al-Rahman III turned it into a fortress. For the time being, it served their purposes well, as the Pope had called a crusade against the Almohad Caliphate, and Christian knights from all over Hispania and France had answered the call, especially from the various orders; the Templars, Hospitallers and the Orders of Santiago and Calatrava.

Aminata overheard Tomás and King Alfonso mention there were over sixty thousand men altogether, made up mostly of farmers. The burden of providing for such a large force had mainly fallen on Castille. If they were to lose the coming battle Alfonso's kingdom would be bankrupt.

King Alfonso had been kind to Aminata, but many other soldiers looked at her distrustfully. "Pay them no mind," Tomás said. "For our cause, you are more valuable than a hundred of them, and the King knows this." Aminata was grateful to hear this, but she was nonetheless constantly on edge.

Tomás secured a private room for her. It was a small filthy room with a bucket for a toilet and a mattress stuffed with straw, but Ami was happy to have it, primarily because for the first time since coming out of the river, she was alone, and she wasn't terrified that a sword might strike her down if she said the wrong thing. She had been so on edge she never even wanted to think the wrong thing for fear her emotions might betray her. Now at least for a moment, her thoughts could wander to Sochi and Mari.

When last she saw them, they were being led away in chains. That was two days ago. Tomás believed they were dead. Something deep inside told her that they were alive. She couldn't explain it, but she felt quite certain they were alive. Were they unharmed or bruised and bloodied? She did not know. She prayed for their safety. She missed them terribly and felt so alone and afraid.

She wanted desperately to see Sochima and Amaris. She took a deep breath and closed her eyes, and suddenly there Sochima was, his soul sitting in a body, sitting in a small room, and there was Amaris as well, walking around pacing. Ami wondered if she was imagining this. She said, "Sochi," out of reflex, and was surprised when he looked up and said, "Ami."

"Sochi," she said again cautiously.

"Ami," he again replied.

"Can you hear me?" she asked him.

"Yes, I can," he answered.

"What? What's going on?" Amaris asked.

"It's Ami. I'm talking to Ami," Sochima said.

"How?" Amaris asked.

"I don't know. It's probably with the heart."

"So, you can hear her?" Amaris asked.

"Yes, I can hear her," Sochima said.

"Can you see me too?" Ami asked.

"No. Can you see me?" Sochima asked Aminata.

"Yes," Aminata answered. "I can see you and Mari."

"She can see the both of us. But I can't see her," Sochima told Amaris.

"Awesome. It must be because of the eye," Amaris said.

"Are you guys okay?" Aminata asked Sochima.

Sochima shrugged his shoulders. "We're alive. They haven't killed us yet."

"Yeah, same here," Aminata said.

"You were captured by the Moors too?" Sochi asked.

"No. Not the Moors. These guys are Christian. They caught me a little after I came out of the river," Ami said.

Feeling left out, Amaris sat next to Sochima and put her ear to his head. Sochima turned to her and said, "Mari, it's not a phone. You can't listen in."

It occurred to Amaris how silly what she was doing was, and they all began laughing. Given everything they had been through, it felt so good to laugh. Unfortunately, their laughter didn't last long. "What are we gonna do, guys?" Aminata asked. "We're miles apart, and I lost the staff. How are we gonna get out of here?"

"You didn't lose the staff. We found it after you fell into the river," Sochima said.

"You did? Oh, thank God," Aminata said, feeling immensely relieved.

"Well, we don't really have it. Not now. Sulayman took it."

"Who's Sulayman?" Aminata asked.

"He's the leader here in Cordoba."

"You guys are in Cordoba?"

"Yeah. Where are you?" Sochima asked.

"Toledo."

"She's in Toledo," Sochima said to Amaris.

"Great. How far is Toledo from here?" Amaris asked.

"I don't know," Sochima said. "It took us like two days to walk here from the river. How long did it take you to get to where you are?" he asked Aminata.

"Over a day, but I was on a horse. So, I guess we could be anywhere from three to four days walking distance apart," she said.

"We're like three to four days walk away from each other," Sochima said to Amaris.

"Okay. That's a long ass walk. But if we could get out of here, how would we even know how to find each other?" Amaris asked.

"The heart will lead me to her. Just like it leads me to all the other pieces," Sochima said.

"Are you guys close to the next piece?" Aminata asked.

"No. Not now. But yesterday, we were walking by an area where it felt really close. That's where we have to get back to."

"But first, we have to get back the staff and then find a way to get away from these guys," Amaris said.

"It's gonna be hard for me to get away. I think we were mercenaries or double agents, working both sides. I don't know if we were loyal to any side over the other. Either way, they don't really trust me over here," Aminata said.

"Yeah, they don't trust us either," Sochima said.

"There's this one guy, Tomás, who trusts me. I think we were all working with him."

"Tomás." Sochima thought for a second. "Yeah, I remember him. We were on our way to meet up with him."

"Yeah, I remember Tomás," Amaris said. "And I remember someone called El Rey Lobo," Amaris said.

"The Wolf King. Yes," Sochima said.

"We were all part of his camp," Aminata said. "At least our families were."

"But he's dead," Sochima said.

"But our fathers were loyal to him. And he hated the *al-Muwaḥḥidūn*," Amaris said.

The name sounded strangely familiar to Sochima. "Have you heard about the *al-Muwaḥḥidūn?*" Sochima asked Aminata.

"Yes, but over here, they call them the Almohads."

"Are we Almohad?" Sochima asked.

"No. They came recently. Our families have been here for a long time," Amaris said.

"And our families were loyal to the Wolf King, and they hated the Almohads. So do we hate the Almohads?" Sochima asked.

"I don't think that matters now," Aminata said. "Right now, we're just trying to stay alive until we can get away from both sides, get the next piece, and get out of here."

"Both sides are our enemy. The Almohads are holding us, and the Christians are holding Ami. And they don't trust us. And the only reason they haven't killed us is because they think that we can give them information to help them. So, we gotta be able to give them something," Amaris said.

"Okay. Ami, you tell us everything you learn from them, and we'll tell you everything we learn here," Sochima said.

"Got it," Ami said. "It's so great to talk to you guys."

"It's great to talk to you. I miss you. I love you," Sochima said.

"I love you too. Both of you," Ami said.

77

In Cordoba, Sulayman had an alcazar of his own. It was not too far from the Great Mosque. Tarik and his men led Amaris and Sochima to the *hammam,* bathhouse, inside the palace. It felt good to wash the two days of the road off. When they finished, they were given clean clothes; simple tunics and sarwals made of cotton.

After they dressed, they were brought to the great hall in the palace. When they arrived, Sulayman was already at the table. As they did in Mali, they sat on fine cushions at tables a foot off the ground. Tarik sat Amaris to Sulayman's left, and Sochima sat to her left. Tarik sat to Sulayman's right. Many of the other men sat throughout the hall and conversed amongst themselves. A musician was seated in the center of the hall playing an instrument. It looked similar to a guitar but smaller, with a pear-shaped base and a much shorter neck. The player was quite good, and the melody had a hypnotic quality.

"Do you like this song?" Sulayman asked.

"Yes," Amaris answered.

"It is a Ziryab original."

The name was unfamiliar to Amaris. Though the body she was in had some recollection of it. It was taking her a moment to access those memories when,

"Ziryab was a genius," Sochima said.

"Oh, the Blackbird was much more than that. Geniuses come and go from time to time. I am a genius," Sulayman said modestly. "Beyond being a court composer, Ziryab was a singer with the most beautiful voice. He added the fifth string to the oud," Sulayman said, gesturing to the instrument the musician was playing, "which greatly enriched its sound. He had knowledge of the stars, the earth, the weather. Since his time in the reign of al-Hakam II, much of Cordoba's culture we owe to him. He changed how we dress, how we eat, how we wear our hair. Even the Christians now follow him and eat their meals in courses. Have you witnessed this in your time with the Christians?"

"Yes, among the nobility," Sochima answered.

"And what else have you witnessed?"

"What do you want to know?" Sochima asked.

"Everything."

"The pope has declared a crusade against you—against us," Sochima said.

"This we know. Tell me more, or this may very well be the last meal you have."

"They have been granted papal indulgences."

"Aye. So, they can rape and pillage with a clean conscience. How many are they?" Sulayman asked.

"There are over sixty thousand. The Christian kingdoms of Castille, Navarre, and Aragon, along with the knights of the Hospitaller, Santiago, and Calatrava, and the French Templars have answered the call," Sochima said.

"And Alfonso of Castille leads them."

"Yes," Sochima said.

"Seems he has not learned from his defeat in Alarcos. Sixty

thousand, you say. We are over one hundred. We have the superior numbers," Sulayman said. "Still, it is the fool who underestimates his enemy. What else?" he asked.

"The kings of Leon and Portugal aren't there, though they have sent knights. Much of the cost of the campaign falls on Castile, and it is overburdening Alfonso," Sochima said.

"Leon, always playing both sides, so they can ally with whoever wins. I believe the King of Leon secretly wishes for Alfonso's defeat, so he might swoop in and conquer a weakened Castile. Pity he doesn't know we'll come for him next. What else?" he asked.

78

That night the highest-ranking men of the Christian forces dined in the great hall of Toledo's Alcazar. Among them were Alfonso VIII of Castile, King Sancho VII of Navarre, King Pedro II of Aragon, the Archbishop of Toledo Rodrigo Jiménez de Rada, Gomes Ramirez, Portuguese master of the Knights Templar, as well as the commanders of the other Hispanic orders. The Archbishop William of Bordeaux, along with several French knights of the Templar, were there as well. Along with Tomás de Vivar, a Knight of Castile, and Tahir ibn Sa'd, a Moor from Valencia.

They sat on chairs around tables that reached the abdomen. They ate lightly seasoned honey mutton with sweet dumplings and drank strong ale from iron goblets. Aminata stomached the food but did not enjoy it. It is hard to enjoy anything when you believe you are constantly under threat. She was seated in King Alfonso's inner circle next to Tomás.

"I tell you there is a land, a kingdom beyond Ifriqiya to the west. A land flowing in gold. A place so overabundant with gold the children play with it like they would common rocks," Tomás said.

"A fantasy," King Sancho VII of Navarre remarked.

"No. It is quite real, your highness."

"And what do they call this place?" King Sancho asked.

From Tomás's description, it sounded a lot like Mali to Aminata. "Ghana," Tomás said.

"Ghana?" the Portuguese bishop repeated.

"Yes. And Ghana means gold in their tongue. With such gold, we could not only conquer Hispania, but the world," Tomás said.

"But first, we would have to reconquer Hispania, which has been a centuries-long struggle. Then conquer the Almohads in Ifriqiya. Then conquer this kingdom of Ghana. And then the world," King Alfonso joked.

"Yes, and then the world on the other side of the world," Tomás said with a smile.

"A world on the other side of the world? You talk in tongues," the Portuguese bishop said.

"No, I do not." Tomás placed his hand on Aminata's soldier. "Our Moorish friends know a great deal. Knowledge that we have neglected for too long. Knowledge that we must master if we are to ascend in this world," Tomás said.

"You are a visionary, Tomás. And perhaps future kings will be like you and can see beyond our borders. I dream only of reclaiming the land of our ancestors," Alfonso said.

The French Archbishop William of Bordeaux saw Aminata in the body of Tahir and was troubled to see him sitting there. "Your highness, King Alfonso, may I ask why do you entertain the enemy at your table?" he asked.

"Tahir is not our enemy," Tomás said.

"He is Moor, is he not?" the Frenchman asked.

"You do not fully understand the history of this land. Christian and Moor have fought with and against each other many times when it has been advantageous," Alfonso said.

"Advantageous, you say. Then why call this crusade, if working with the Moors has been so advantageous? Why not keep things the same? Or did you call this crusade to keep the Kings of Leon and Portugal from attacking your lands while you seek to gain more, as I notice they are not present?" the archbishop said.

King Alfonso did not care for his insinuation or the archbishop's boldness but held back his tongue as he needed the Frenchman's forces.

"Tahir is Moor, but he is also Christian," Tomás said.

"Really? Have you been baptized?" William asked Aminata.

"I have," she answered.

"And you renounce Muhammad for the false prophet that he is?"

Knowing that when she jumped into this body, Tahir was engaged in one of his five daily prayers, she knew this was a lie. Nevertheless, she had no choice. "I have," she said.

"Then say it," Archbishop William pressed.

"I have renounced Muhammad for the false prophet that he is."

The French archbishop was still dubious. He leaned over to another Frenchman. "He can say what he will. I quicker trust a Jew before I trust a Moor. And I never trust a Jew," he said and he and the other Frenchman laughed discretely.

"And why don't you trust the Jews? Do we not all pray to the same God?" Aminata reflexively replied in French.

This came as a shock to the archbishop.

"You speak French," William said. "Aren't you a surprise?"

The Frenchman was not the only one surprised. "When did you learn to speak French?" Tomás asked Aminata.

It was then Aminata realized her error. Aminata knew how to speak French, but Tahir did not. They were all looking at her suspiciously. She had to think fast. "We Moors have been to many places and learned many things. While a part of the Almohad camp, a fellow Moorish traveler taught me," she said. Tomás took her answer at face value, though he wondered why his good friend had never told him this before.

"Yes, you Moors have *seeded* yourselves in many places," Archbishop William said. "And to your question, I do not trust the Jews because it was the Jews who invited the Moors to invade this land. Is that not right, your highness?" he addressed King Alfonso. Alfonso looked at him but did not reply. "They told them that this land was a fat pig ripe for the sticking, and then they led them through the back door. And after the Moors had taken over, they helped run their administration. If it weren't for the Jews, you Moors would not be here," William said.

His words lingered in the air for a moment, many of the other men nodded in agreement, before Alfonso responded. "We are all brethren, and believers in the one true God. Unfortunately, we have taken turns betraying each other. We have committed our sins against them as well. Hopefully, after this crusade, we will find a way to live peacefully together again, Christian, Jew and Moor." Alfonso looked at Aminata as he said the last word.

"Forgive me, your highness, but I do not share your optimism," William said and then turned to Aminata. "And you my friend, admit that you have been among the Almohads."

"Yes. While working with Tomás, to gain information to better help our cause," she said.

"Is that so? Well then, enlighten us. How great is their number?"

"Al Nasir has assembled an army over one hundred thousand strong," she said.

That number caused a great deal of grumbling in the room.

"How do you know this? Have you seen it for yourself?" Archbishop Rodrigo Jimenez asked.

"I have seen some of it, but I have not seen it entirely myself."

"Then how do you know the number is accurate?"

"I heard it from Sulayman himself," Aminata said.

"Sulayman is the governor of Cordoba. He fought with al-Nasir's father, al-Mansur in Alarcos. He is quite shrewd and is not known to embellish," King Alfonso said.

"Well, if that is true, we are but sixty percent of their number," the French archbishop said.

"You forget we have God with us," Rodrigo Jimenez, the archbishop of Toledo, said.

"As he was with you in Alarcos." A reminder of his defeat was an insult to King Alfonso. "Prayer alone does not win battles. We honor our lord by fighting wisely. We need an advantage over such numbers. Tell me—my friend—what more do you have to give? Or is your usefulness at an end?"

Aminata had to think of something. "Las Navas de Tolosa," she said.

"What of it?" King Alfonso asked.

"That is where al Nasir will meet you in battle."

79

The dinner began with a spiced vegetable soup, then an appetizer of roasted stuffed eggplant. For the entrée, they had a fish stew, and for dessert they had almond-crusted sweetbreads stuffed with cheese. Everything was well made, but it was difficult for Amaris and Sochima to enjoy it. Anxiety is not good for digestion. They had told Sulayman everything Aminata had told them. He seemed content, but he was a hard man to read.

A servant brought out a chessboard. It was a beautiful board made from rosewood, with pieces crafted in ivory, half of them painted black. The board looked more or less the same as chessboards Amaris and Sochima had seen before. The pieces, however, looked quite different, but when placed on the board, their positions were easily identifiable.

"*Shaterej,* my friends. Who of the two of you will play?" Sulayman asked Amaris and Sochima.

Amaris looked at Sochima, and he said to her, "I don't know how." Amaris found this surprising as she considered Sochi a genius and thought all geniuses played chess. "I told you I don't know everything."

"I will play," Amaris answered Sulayman. Her father had taught her how to play. Before he left, it was one of their favorite pastimes. Still, she had never beaten him. He would never let her. "But I don't play well," she said.

"It doesn't matter. Very few play as well as I do. And it is from losing how we learn."

"Okay," Amaris said.

"I give you the first move," Sulayman said. Amaris moved her pawn without much consideration. "So, you say you're not a traitor," he said.

"We're not," Sochima said.

"What are you then?"

"We are believers, like yourself," Amaris said.

"I believe you. The men told me when they found you, you were in the midst of prayer."

"We were," Sochima said.

"But do you believe in our vision and what we are trying to accomplish in this land?"

"Yes. I am a Moor. We are Moors," Amaris said.

"Yes, but what is a Moor?" he asked, and it seemed like a trick question. Fortunately, he continued without waiting for them to answer. "You ask ten men, you will get ten different answers. It is not even a name we gave ourselves."

"We are believers in the one true God, who seek the highest enlightenment," Amaris said. Amaris found herself becoming more in sync with the body she was in and speaking in the manner Bilal would speak.

"I like that. Unfortunately, we seek enlightenment in this most corruptible place," Sulayman said.

"What do you mean?" Amaris asked.

"Al-Andaluz is the gate of hell. It is beautiful. Yes. And as such, it tempts and corrupts even the most righteous men. First, the great Tarik ibn Ziyad came, crossing the Pillars of Hercules, which we now name for him. They were hard men, strong, rightly guided, that though they were but a few thousand, they swept through this land, stopping at the Pyrenees, only because they felt the rewards to continue were not worth the price in blood. Soon Abd al-Rahman, the last of the Umayyads, came, and his was a great emirate.

"But in our greatness, we became ensnared by the luxuries of the land. See, it is in our soul to create beautiful things. Where we saw barns, we built palaces. Simple churches, we turned into glorious mosques. Out of ignorance, we built universities. While the Christians bask in their ignorance, we embrace the knowledge and philosophy of the ancients. We have translated it and expounded on it. We love knowledge, we love language, we love poetry. Yet these things have also led us to ruin. Al-Hakam II was too seduced by poetry and beautiful things. And the caliphate eventually fell, and the Christians encroached. And for a hundred years, we were Taifas, separate principalities. Some barely worthy of recognition, all warring with each other. And while we bickered, our enemies strengthened and encroached, pushing us back farther and farther until we were paying infidels tribute to protect us from our own brothers."

"But were the Christians not just retaking their land," Sochima said.

This did not sit well with Sulayman. "By what right makes it their land?" he asked.

"They were here before us, and we took it from them."

"The Romans were here before the Visigoths and Vandals came from up north, and they took it from the Romans by conquest. And before the Romans, there were the Iberians, and the Romans took it from them by conquest. And the Iberians had conquered the people before them. And so on and so on. So, what gives any of these people more rights to the land over ours? Maybe you'll say how long a people have lived on a land gives them greater claim to it because time washes away all sins. We have been here now for five hundred years. Longer than the Goths, and the Romans, and the Iberians. I say we have the greater claim," he said.

"But if they were to add their years in control plus our years in control, they feel their claim is greater," Amaris said.

"Men can tell themselves whatever they want to feel righteous; it does not matter."

"Righteousness does not matter?" Amaris asked.

"No," he flatly answered.

"Shouldn't righteousness be our path? Is Allah not righteous?"

"No," he replied. Amaris found that shocking of him to say, as he seemed so devout. "Allah is most merciful and most wise. Of the two, most wise is most important. As only a fool is merciful all the time. There are times when the greater mercy is to show no mercy."

"I do not understand," Amaris said.

"I can see that you are simple men. You need to believe that what you are doing is good in order to do so."

"Shouldn't we all strive to be good?" she asked.

"For the greater good. But sometimes the greater good can look evil in the present," he said.

"I do not see how good can ever be evil," Sochima said.

"You are the chief of your tribe," Sulayman began. "There is another tribe across the river. You've gained knowledge that they plan to attack you. Should you wait for them to attack you and fight them off, or do you preemptively attack them while you have the advantage?" he asked.

"What is this knowledge? Where did it come from?" Sochima asked.

Sulayman sighed in annoyance that he would ask this question. "Men lead the other village, and it is man's nature to do so. That is all," Sulayman said.

"So, we should attack them because they are made up of men like we are made up of men?" Sochima said.

"That is the question," Sulayman said. "What will you do?"

"They have not attacked us. So, at this point, they are not our enemy. We should build our defenses to protect against any attack."

"Even if you do this, there is a great likelihood that you will lose many men in the assault, and you might still lose. Your greatest chance of success is to attack first. So, do you risk the slaughter and enslavement of your people when you could have prevented it?" he asked.

"So, to prevent the slaughter and enslavement of my people, I must slaughter and enslave another people. To prevent evil, I must become evil. This is the philosophy of tyrants," Amaris said.

"One man's tyrant is another man's emperor," he said.

"But where is the good in this?"

"Now you have come to it. There is no good or bad. There are only the conquered and the conquerors. Which do you choose to be?" he asked.

"I choose neither," she said.

"Oh, but you must choose. And if you do not choose, eventually someone will choose for you," Sulayman said.

"Inshallah, that will never come to be. Shah," Amaris said, having taken Sulayman's Queen and placed his King in check.

However, Amaris soon saw her folly as he had willingly sacrificed his wazir and, in one move, now had her in checkmate. Sulayman smiled, "Shah mat."

80

The following day over sixty-thousand Christian troops gathered outside the Alcazar preparing to leave Toledo. The bishops held a great mass and prayed over all the men. Standing beside Tomás, dressed in the same armor as the Christians, Aminata also prayed. She prayed that she would survive her journey with these men. She prayed she would be reunited safely with Sochima and Amaris. She prayed they would retrieve the next piece and be away from this place. She prayed for her mother, she prayed for her father, and she prayed for Nana.

King Pedro II of Aragon had brought a special gift to bless

their crusade. It was in a splendid carriage that opened from the back. Inside there was a statue of a woman sitting on a throne and a boy-child seated on her lap. They both faced forward, and wore gold robes and gold crowns. The robes covered everything except for their faces and hands, and the hair and feet of the child. Their features were that of any Castilian mother and child. Their skin was black and the child's hair was curly.

"La Moreneta," Alfonso exclaimed. He turned to Pedro II, "You bring the Virgin Mary herself to bless us," he said.

"Aragon could not bring as many men as we desired. Hopefully, the virgin come down from her mountain is recompense," Pedro II said.

Alfonso hugged him. "Her blessing is worth that of a hundred thousand men," he said.

Alfonso led the procession as all the Kings, and all the bishops, and all the knights, and all the squires, and all the infantrymen, and the farmers in the field, waited in line to kneel before the virgin and kiss her feet. Following behind Tomás, Aminata kissed her feet as well. The statue reminded Ami of the statue of Pepi II and his mother, Akhensenpepi II. The main difference being, in Pepi's statute, the child sat facing the side and in this statue the child faced forward.

The statue's presence lifted the morale of all the men, and King Alfonso VIII led them out to reclaim the land they believed was their own.

81

Sulayman led a caravan of over a hundred of his personal guard and attendants on horse and camelback from Cordoba to Jaén to join al-Nasir's forces. Sochima and Amaris traveled with them.

Sulayman was shrewd, and they could never get a true read on what he was thinking. He was no longer treating Sochima and Amaris like prisoners. They were unchained and well-fed, and they rode their own horses. Nevertheless, they felt like prisoners. One wrong word or a change in his mood, and he surely would have them beheaded.

Their heads may be safe for now, but once they arrived in Jaén, and met with al-Nasir and his vizier Uthman ibn Jam'i, they would surely lose them, when Amaris's lie about working for ibn Jam'i would be revealed. Amaris dreaded this moment incessantly.

Within a day they arrived at al-Nasir's camp. It was a tent city with over one hundred thousand men garrisoned. High-ranking soldiers and officials had full tents and makeshift beds. Infantrymen made do with the earth and the stars.

The Moors were a varied mix of Arabians, Tunisians, Algerians, Moroccans, Mauritanians, and Senegalese. The bulk were dark complexioned men much like Bilal and Hassan. The others were Arab and caramel skinned Andalusians. A small portion were the Saqaliba, enslaved men from northern lands, with light skin, light eyes, and straight hair, many of whom were Christian. They were Caliph al-Nasir's personal guard.

On arrival, Sulayman commanded his men to build his tent. He pointed to a great tent on the other side of the field. "That is the Caliph's tent. Mine should be just slightly smaller than his. Just slightly," he repeated with a smirk. "You two," he pointed to Sochima and Amaris, and Amaris believed he was calling them to go with him so that he could verify their story with ibn Jam'i. "Help them," he said, then he and Tarik walked off to the great tent on the other side of the field.

Amaris was relieved but still dreadfully afraid. She looked at Sochima, and he could do nothing but sigh and shrug his shoulders. They followed orders and aided the others in constructing Sulayman's tent, which, when it was complete, had a full bed, many throw rugs, a table, and two chairs. It took them over two hours to put it together, and Amaris dreaded every minute.

Whenever a group of men walked in their direction with a sense of purpose, she feared they had come to collect them. She almost wished, she and Sochima were imprisoned together, simply so they could talk freely. As it stood, they were constantly watched and could barely share a glance.

An hour later, Sulayman returned with Tarik and complimented the men on their efforts. He then looked at Sochima and Amaris—and said nothing.

82

Later that evening, Sulayman sat around a campfire, ate dinner with his men and told the story of Abd al-Rahman I, the last of the great Umayyad Dynasty, and how he survived the Banquet of Blood. Over eighty members of his family were invited to a grand feast by the Abbasids, and after dinner they were all bludgeoned to death. Abd al-Rahman I escaped and made his way across North Africa, and the straits of Gibraltar, and created a great emirate here in al-Andalus.

Hundreds of men gathered around to listen. Sulayman's influence on the men was very evident. They were entranced by him. Even the vizier Uthman ibn Jam'i stood and listened. Amaris heard the men mention that the aloof man standing off to the side was the vizier. Amaris looked at him, and for a moment, they locked eyes, then he looked away and moved on. When she turned back to Sulayman, she saw that he had been looking at her.

Later that night, Sulayman called Sochima and Amaris to his tent. He sat in his chair like a mini throne, holding the staff in his right hand. It angered Sochima every time he saw Sulayman with the staff. That was Nana's staff, that was Ra's staff, that staff had been around since the beginning of creation, and Sulayman was unworthy.

"I see your eyes. I see your thoughts. You wish to see ibn Jam'i," Sulayman said to them. "You wonder why I have not taken you to him." He spoke again before Amaris could answer. "The vizier believes I am too powerful. He believes I believe I control al-Andalus. This is true, of course. Al-Andalus is a little less than a third of the *al-Muwaḥḥidūn* empire. The bulk is in the Maghreb. The seat is in Marrakesh. This is where al-Nasir abodes most of the year. In his absence, the governance of this land falls to me. This enterprise is a son trying to outdo his much greater father. I served his father as well. Al-Nasir and ibn Jam'i feel I am part of the old guard and would like to see me diminished—or better dead. True, they do not know, I cannot die," he said with a smirk. Sochima and Amaris were unsure if he spoke literally or in jest. "Knowledge is the most powerful weapon in this world. So, I will keep you and your knowledge to myself. You work for me and only me now. Now go."

Amaris and Sochima bowed their heads before departing Sulayman's tent. As they walked away, they had a quiet moment to themselves. Amaris exhaled as if she had just let go of fifty pounds of weight. "Thank God, we don't have to worry about the vizier outing us," she said.

"Do you think he's the Guardian?" Sochima asked.

"Who? The vizier?" Amaris asked.

"No. Sulayman," he said. "Imhotep said that there is an immortal guarding each piece. And Sulayman just said he doesn't die. Do you think he's the guardian?" Sochima asked.

"I don't know. But I hope not. He's enough trouble as is," Amaris said.

83

The Christian forces surrounded a castle on a small hillock not too far from a large stretch of mountains. It used to be the home of the knights of the Order of Calatrava. Caliph al-Nasir took this castle from the Christians a year ago and ran the Order out.

After a two-day siege, the outer part of the castle had fallen and the governor forfeited so as to spare his people an inevitable slaughter. Hundreds of the inhabitants, mostly Moors, but Jews and Christians as well, streamed out. They walked by the Christian forces without being put in chains or harmed. Seeing this did not sit well with the French archbishop. He rode to the front to the side of King Alfonso. Aminata and Tomás were not too far off and were able to hear them.

"Your highness, may I ask what this is? Prisoners of war you allow to go free. Many of them able-bodied men," the Archbishop of Bordeaux asked.

"It is a bargain I made for the surrender of the castle," Alfonso said.

"But why make this bargain? We have the numbers to breach this castle. Their surrender was inevitable."

"We recovered a castle without a protracted siege or loss of men or any destruction to its exterior, so it returns to us as an asset. I call that a great outcome."

"Yes, but now that you've cleaned the rats from the kitchen, do not allow them to scurry into their holes. Kill them now while they flee."

Alfonso looked at him crossly. "I pledged my word that for the surrender of the castle everyone inside would be spared."

"War is deceit. We pledge our word to our Lord and Savior alone. Moslems do not keep their word; why should we?"

"If I do not keep my word and I slaughter these people, then the Moors would never surrender to me again, and every battle hence would be a protracted fight till the end, which will cost me more men in the future," Alfonso said, growing tired of this argument.

"I see," the archbishop said, seemingly swayed. He then took a rag and dabbed the sweat from his neck and brow. "This heat is insufferable," he said.

84

The following day King Alfonso, the other Christian Kings, and the commanders of the Orders were in the great hall of Calatrava castle. All men of importance were there except for the Archbishop of Bordeaux. They placed a great map of Hispania on a table and contemplated their next move. Tomás and Aminata ran into the hall. Tomás's urgency drew the attention of everyone. "Your Highnesses, forgive our intrusion," Tomás said as both he and Aminata bowed.

"What is it?" King Sancho VII of Navarre asked.

"The French abandon us," Tomás said.

Outside the Castle, Archbishop William and ten thousand Frenchmen were packed and ready to go. The Christian Kings and the heads of the Orders rushed out to meet them. "You would abandon us in our direst hour? You abandon Christendom?" King Sancho chastised the archbishop, who was already on his horse preparing to ride off.

"We abandon nothing," the archbishop said. "Over multiple crusades, we French have bled more than all the other kingdoms of Christ keeping the Mohammedans at bay. If not for the French, this land would be all Moslem, and you would not exist."

"And neither would you exist, and all of Christendom would be a black land," Archbishop Rodrigo Jimenez said.

"This is true, which is why we have always been ready to fight the Moslem scourge. But it has become apparent that you are not. And we will not bleed needlessly. It is too hot to fight. The men bake in their armor. Every day men fall from heatstroke. The Moors outnumber us, and we fight in weather they find preferable. And you have no stomach to fight. You spare Jews and Moors alike, so that they might return and stab us in the back another day. You have lived incestuously with the enemy for too long, you do not know how to rid yourself of them."

At this point, King Alfonso had grown exhausted of the archbishop's presence and incessant bickering. And though Alfonso could not afford to lose ten thousand men, he would not beg. Go then. "History will mark your cowardice," he said.

"History, your highness, is written by the living," the archbishop said and gave the order and the Frenchmen left.

85

Aminata desperately wanted to get away from these peo-ple, their politics, and their war. She did not study Spanish history. She had no knowledge of this battle that was supposed to happen or if it would even happen now that the French had left. The infantrymen grumbled that they should disband the crusade altogether because it was hopeless. Her knowledge of Moorish history was sparse, beyond knowing that they had occupied the Iberian Peninsula for almost eight hundred years. She knew that the Spanish expelled the Moors in 1492. This was the year 1212. 1492 was nearly three hundred years from now. By that equation, the Moors were destined to win this battle. Though no matter who won the battle, many men on both sides would die. She had to make certain that she, Sochima, and Amaris would survive.

Aminata had not showered in many days—no one had. Beyond washing their hands before and after eating, water barely touched them. Everyone smelled of days of sweat and wet wool. Eventually, the smell blended in, and she no longer noticed it. After the first three days, she itched from not bathing, but eventually, she grew accustomed to that as well, and the constant need to scratch herself went away.

Having Tomás was a blessing, and for her safety, she rarely left his side. He was a great friend, but he was not truly her friend; he was Tahir's. And though she had access to Tahir's memories, it was very difficult to be in someone else's body and pretend to be them for so long. Tomás could see that the person he was with was not truly his old friend. He kept on waiting for his friend to return to himself.

Tomás and Aminata sat in the back of the great hall. Alfonso and the other kings and the heads of the orders were upfront looking at the map, trying to find a way through the Sierra Morena mountains. It was a five-hundred-kilometer chain of mountains that ran west to east, forming a natural barrier between al-Andaluz in the south and the Christian Kingdoms in the north. The Almohad camp was in Las Navas de Tolosa, a stretch of plains just beyond the mountains. The Almohads held the pass through the mountains, and the Christians would be slaughtered trying to go through it.

At that moment, a knight walked into the hall. A peasant farmer walked with him. "Your highnesses," the knight introduced himself and bowed and tapped the farmer to bow as well.

King Sancho VII of Navarre raised his hand for them to rise. "What is it good sir?" Sancho asked.

"Forgive my intrusion your Highnesses, but I believe this man has information that you would like to hear." the knight said.

"Is that so? And what is your name?" King Sancho asked.

"Martin Alhaja your Highnesses," he said.

"And what do you have to tell us?"

"There is another passage through the mountains other than Puerto de Llosa, and the Moors don't know it. And if they know it, as of this morning, they weren't guarding it," he said.

This drew the attention of everyone in the room, King Alfonso especially. "And how do you know this passage?" Alfonso asked.

"I'm a shepherd; my family has worked the land for generations," he said.

"And where is this passage?" Alfonso asked.

"I'll take you to it."

86

The shepherd spoke true. There was a passage through the mountains that the Almohads were unaware of. King Alfonso sent Aminata and Tomás along with a dozen knights with the shepherd to scout it out. The shepherd had left a cow's skull nailed to a rock to mark the path.

While riding through the passage, seeing Aminata, the shepherd asked her why she was fighting for the Christians against her own people.

"Aren't you bold, sir," she replied.

"No bold. Just curious. Just making conversation," he said.

"Because I believe in King Alfonso, and I have no love for the Almohads," she answered. She believed this was something Tahir would say, and riding with Tomás and the other knights she knew she always had to prove herself to these people.

"Aye. I have no love for the Almohads either," the shepherd began. "Which is not to mean I have ill feelings towards all Moors. My family has worked on these lands for hundreds of years. Seen rulers come and go. The truth is, when the Moors first came, my people were happy. They treated us better than we were treated before. They showed us how to bring water to our fields and work the land better. As long as we paid a tax, and it was a fair tax, less harsh than it was before, they left us be to live our lives and worship how we chose. People didn't much complain. But then nothing lasts. One caliph comes in and then another. Some aren't as good as others. Things fall apart. Then the Almoravids came, and it wasn't like before. There were forcing people to become Moslem now, and if you didn't the taxes weren't fair anymore. People were getting killed. People left their lands and went up north to the Christian kingdoms. My people we stayed. The governors of Jaén always treated us fair. And after a time, the Almoravids weren't as harsh, and they let us live again. But then the Almohads came, and they were harsher than the Almoravids. And the governor of Jaén left for Cordoba. And it's all become too much. If he wins, I don't know how King Alfonso will rule. I'm praying it will be better," he said that last bit to Tomás.

"It will be. I promise you that," Tomás said.

"A promise is a comfort to a fool. But I'll take it anyway," the shepherd smiled.

87

They rode the entire passage and saw no sign of the Al-mohads. The passage's exit brought them to the rear of the Almohad camp. If the Christians attacked from here, the Moors would be caught completely off guard.

Sochima and Amaris were roughly two hundred yards away. Aminata seriously contemplated running away from Tomás and the others and making for the Almohad camp. However, she remembered how distrustful the Almohads had been of Sochima and Amaris. Also, wearing Christian armor, they would likely shoot her down before she reached them. With a heavy heart she turned away from Sochima and Amaris for a second time.

When Aminata and Tomás returned, the Christian kings were overjoyed to hear that the passage was real and passable. They quickly gathered their forces and led them to the pass. It would be a slow march as the path was narrow, and only a few men could go through at once.

While Aminata marched along with the Christians, she opened a connection with Sochima. She could see Sochi and Mari clearly. They were seated together under a tree. There were many other men around them. "Sochi, can you hear me?" Ami asked.

"Yes, Ami," he said, not showing any outward reaction. He discretely pinched Amaris on the hand, and she intuitively knew that he and Ami had a connection going. However, how would she listen in if Sochima couldn't speak aloud? Then an idea came to her.

She stood up and tapped Sochima to do the same. She began walking away, and Sochima followed her lead when one of the men asked, "Where are you going?"

"To pray," she said.

This was an answer the others could not question. The five daily prayers were one of the five essential pillars of Islam. The entire camp prayed at those five designated times. Nevertheless, one could pray any time they wanted. Mari and Sochi washed their hands and faces by one of the open barrels of water. They found a relatively secluded spot, then went on their knees and began praying. A few men looked at them oddly at first but soon looked away.

"Okay, Ami. What is it?" Sochima said.

"The Christians have found a secret passage through the mountains. It's a passage the Almohads aren't guarding. They'll be through it by the morning and catch you guys off guard," she said.

While Amaris continued praying aloud, Sochima quietly told her what Aminata had told him. "Okay, is this good or bad for us?" she asked and continued praying while Sochima relayed the message.

"If you guys are there when the Christians attack, you could get killed during everything. Can you guys get away?"

"No. Even though Sulayman says that we're working for him, we're always being watched."

"Can you get away?"

"No. Other than Tomás and Alfonso, everyone else pretty much wants to kill me."

"I think our best bet is to try to connect with each other when the fighting starts."

"If they catch you guys by surprise, these guys aren't trying to take prisoners. They want to kill all of you."

"So then maybe we should tell Sulayman."

"I think we should trade the information to Sulayman for the staff. We're very close to the next piece. Once we get the staff, getting it will be easy."

"Okay. That's the plan."

88

Amaris and Sochima approached Tarik a few yards away from the Caliph's tent. "We need to speak to Sulayman. We have important information for him," Amaris said.

"Do you now, apostate?" Tarik asked suspiciously.

"We are not apostates," Sochima said.

"So, you say. Yet for some reason, I do not believe you," Tarik said.

"And I don't care," Amaris said.

"You talk bold now. You were not so bold when I had you in chains by the river. I should have killed you then," Tarik said.

"*Alhamdulillah*, you didn't. Because we have important information for Sulayman," Amaris said.

"Then tell me, and I will tell him."

"No. We work for Sulayman, not you. And he needs to know at once," Sochima said.

Tarik looked at them both, wishing he had killed them. Nevertheless, he walked to the Caliph's tent to speak to Sulayman. A few minutes later, Sulayman walked out with the staff at his side. He gestured with his hand for Tarik to give them privacy. Tarik begrudgingly walked away. "You have information for me, so grave that you pull me from a conference with the Caliph," Sulayman said.

"Yes, we do," Sochima said.

"And you've held this information back from me all this time," he said. Amaris and Sochima did not respond, and he smiled. "Playing your board wisely I see . . . Well. Speak," Sulayman pressed.

"First, for this information we would like the return of my grandmother's staff," Sochima said.

"This staff means a great deal to you, doesn't it?"

"Yes, it does," Sochima said.

"Unfortunately, I've grown quite attached to it. As I am sure, you've grown attached to your heads. Now, what say you tell me this information, and I let you keep them," Sulayman said.

89

Sulayman re-entered the tent of the Caliph.

Al Nāṣir li-dīn Allāh Muḥammad ibn al-Manṣūr was a young man; only thirty years old at the time. He was almond-complexioned, with full lips, a straight nose, and a black and wooly beard. He was of an average height and build, and his demeanor inspired neither disdain nor admiration. If he were not Caliph, he would appear unexceptional. Being Caliph, he dressed richly, and his tent was even more lavish than Sulayman's. In the back, there was a great banner woven with Qur'anic verses and elaborate geometric patterns.

Al-Nasir, ibn Jam'i and two other generals stood over a table looking at a great map of al-Andalus and the northern Kingdoms. Sulayman walked towards the table. "My liege, it has come to my knowledge that the Christians will attack tomorrow."

This drew the immediate attention of all the men.

"Are you certain of this?" al-Nasir asked.

"Have you ever known me to speak when I am unsure?" Sulayman asked, then said, "My liege," to soften his response.

"No, I have not," al-Nasir said, choosing to dismiss the slight.

"If they attack tomorrow, then they walk into their own destruction. I see no way for them to get through the mountains. We have every access point guarded?" A general said.

"Not all," Sulayman said. He pointed to a spot on the map that had no markings on it. "Here. They will enter from here," he said.

"There is nothing there but mountains," ibn Jam'i said.

"Because it is not on our maps. It is not even on their maps. It is a small passage, known only to shepherds."

"Then how can you be certain that it is really there?" al-Nasir asked.

"Remember, I was governor of Ŷaīyyān before your father granted me governorship of Cordoba. Many years ago, I settled a land dispute between two shepherds, and the passage was brought to my attention then," Sulayman said.

"If you've known of this passage all along, why are you just now bringing it to our knowledge?" ibn Jam'i asked.

"I thought it inconsequential. It cannot support the mass movement of a large army at once. But if they move stealthily in small formations, it can be done," Sulayman said.

"And how did you come by this knowledge?" Al-Nasir asked.

"As I have said, I was governor of this land. Many people here are still loyal to me. They see things, they hear things, and they tell me. The Christians are slowly moving through the pass as we speak."

Al-Nasir, ibn Jam'i and the two generals took a moment to digest all Sulayman had said. "If this is so, then Allah blesses us, and we rout them as they come through the pass," a general said.

"Yes, if what Sulayman says is true, we will position our heavy infantry and our archers along the opening and tear them down," Ibn Jam'i said.

"My liege, may I offer a different approach," Sulayman said.

"And what is that?" al-Nasir asked.

"We let them through," Sulayman said flatly, and they all looked at him as if he was insane.

"Let them through are you mad?" al-Nasir said.

"If we attack them as they come through the pass, yes, we will kill a few, but the vast majority will see that the pass is blocked and they will retreat. If we pursue, then we go from being at an advantageous position to a disadvantageous one, and they can easily pick us apart as we traverse the passage. If we do not pursue, then we are at a stalemate with neither of us wanting to risk going through the mountains. Stalemates are not good. We are not well-provisioned for a long siege. It has already been quite costly bringing an army this large together to this point. We will ravage our food supplies. And when men are hungry and have no enemy to fight, they will fight each other. We fight under one standard, but we are not one people, and we do not all like each other. But now, if we let them through, they come into the battlefield that you have wisely selected. And this is a good field. Allah has blessed this land. We have the greater position and the greater numbers, and their only advantage, which would have been their element of surprise, will be gone, as they will find us ready. You will have the kings of Navarre, Aragon and Castille in your grasp, and will be able to deliver a defeat to the Christians greater than any Caliph has ever done." Sulayman said.

Al-Nasir and the two generals could do nothing but smile at the brilliance of the stratagem, and even ibn Jam'i was forced to say, "Sulayman, is most wise."

90

It was just before dawn when the Christians began com-ing through the passage. The Almohad camp was two hundred yards away, but it was hard to tell. The air was thick with smoke. It appeared as if the Almohads had a great feast the night before and lit many fires that had just recently gone out. The smoke still lingered in the air and obscured visibility. The Christians were stealthily making their way through when they heard a great boom. It was not an explosion. It was more like the sound of thunder. It shook the earth and your heart. Alfonso had heard that sound before, many years ago. It was the boom of a great drum made from a rhinoceros' hide. "They know we're here," Alfonso said as the boom came again.

The Christians drew their shields and stood on guard. However, no arrows were launched, and the Almohads did not charge.

"They do not attack us," Rodrigo said.

"They don't want us to escape through the pass. They want to fight us here," Alfonzo said.

"What should we do?" Rodrigo asked.

They had lost the element of surprise, but Alfonso believed God was on their side. "We came for a fight. Let's fight, Alfonso said. "Trumpets," he shouted, and the trumpeters that traveled with the army began playing, announcing the Christians' arrival, and guiding them to the field.

Within four hours, the Christians had all fifty thousand men in position. Alfonso led the vanguard in the center, along with the knights of the orders. Pedro II led the left flank, and king Sancho II led the right. Aminata was with Tomás in Alfonso's second line. Much of the smoke had cleared, and Ami could see across the field. She could not see Sochima and Amaris with her natural vision, but she could see them with her inner eye. They were in the Almohad frontline infantry. "Hey Sochi," she said.

"Hey Ami," he said.

Amaris heard him, and they all smiled. This was the closest they had been together since Ami fell into the river.

"Can you feel the next piece?" Ami asked him.

"Yes. It's very close," he said.

"I know. I can see it," Ami said.

"You can?" Sochi asked, sounding very surprised.

"Yes. I can see it underground."

"That's so cool," Sochima said. Aminata smiled to herself. She was also amazed at all the things the eye was allowing her to see.

Now, if only they had the staff, they could run out to the center of the field and retrieve the next piece. However, Sulayman still had the staff. Aminata saw him with her inner eye as he rode his horse up to the Caliph in the back, surrounded by his Saqaliba guards. Aminata saw Sulayman, and he terrified her because she could see his soul.

91

Al-Nasir was dressed magnificently in his cape and golden armor. With his jewel-encrusted blades, he looked better suited for a museum than a battlefield. Contrarily, Sulayman dressed simply in a black turban and gambeson, with vambraces and greaves. On his chest, he had the words *Allahu Akbar* woven in Arabic letters.

"My liege, let me honor you in single combat," Sulayman said to al-Nasir.

"Sulayman, they did not come all this way to have their fates decided by the sword of one man. Nor did I," al-Nasir answered.

"Do you doubt my abilities?"

"No. Far be it from me to doubt the great Sulayman. But it would be a fruitless exercise. They will not yield simply because you kill one man. Our numbers are greater, and we have the higher ground."

"I have fought many battles. I can tell you that hearts break before shields do. Take out their best warrior, and it breaks the spine of the others. Most of these men are farmers. They will be lambs to the slaughter afterward. And taking their best knights off the board early is fewer casualties on our side," Sulayman said.

Al-Nasir thought for a moment. "You make a reasoned argument. You have swayed me. Go then. Have your fun."

Sulayman crossed the line and rode down the small dirt ravine into the center of the battlefield. He dismounted his horse and with the staff and his clothes fluttering in the dry wind walked within the distance of the Christians' arrows. The Christian soldiers looked oddly at this display. "Who is that?" Gomes Ramirez master of the Knights of Templar asked, as very few of the Christians knew him by sight. Though they had all heard the name, "Sulayman," Alfonso said. Even from fifty yards away and seventeen years between them, he knew him.

"Alfonso," Sulayman called, speaking Castilian in a mocking accent, his voice carrying across the field. "Do you remember me?"

Alfonso was about to answer, but Rodrigo responded for him. "Kings do not bandy with those who are beneath them. Send your Caliph if you want to discuss terms of surrender."

Sulayman took the insult with good humor. "You're correct. I am not a king. I only make kings. I kill them too. Do you remember me, Alfonso? Do you remember Alarcos? Do you remember how close my dagger was to your throat before you ran from the field like a cowardly cur?"

The insult was a bitter memory for Alfonso and one that had haunted his dreams. Many nights, he had woken in fits of sweat recalling Sulayman's face. The man in him wanted to ride down to Sulayman and redress the insult. Rodrigo held the reins of

Alfonso's horse to keep him in place. Truthfully, it was not only Rodrigo that held him back.

Alfonso feared this man. His heart wanted to go, but his brain would not permit it. Fortunately, Rodrigo was there to speak for him. "You bore us, Moor. Tell al-Nasir kings do not speak to subordinates."

"I speak for my Caliph, and we have a proposition. Single Combat. I, an old man beyond fifty, against your best warrior, since Alfonso, is too much of a cur to face me. No one else needs die. And to the winner al-Andalus—all of it. From Gibraltar to the Pyrenees. We will even allow you to keep your lands and your titles, but you pay us tribute for this privilege." There was grumbling among both sides at Sulayman's proposition.

Ibn Jam`i spoke to al-Nasir. "Sulayman oversteps. We do not agree to this," he said.

"Do not trouble yourself. Whether they agree or not, whether Sulayman lives or dies, we will attack and rout them as my father did. This is merely the entertainment before the dance. Let Sulayman have his fun," al Nasir said.

Gomes Ramirez rode to Alfonso's side. "My lord, let me fight for you, I'll cut this Moor down, cut out his tongue, and bring it to you as a prize," he asked.

"No," Alfonso said quite definitively. "It is a ruse. Al-Nasir will attack. No need to entertain this farce."

Men, age, and time slows the body; it certainly had for Alfonso. Still, Sulayman was the best swordsman he had ever come across. He was seventeen years older, but he did not look it. Alfonso did not believe Gomes Ramirez could take him, and he could not risk losing one of his best fighters and the leader of the Knights of Templar so early in the battle.

"No?" Sulayman said. "There is not one among you who will face me. I am but an old man who spends his days reading and writing poetry. Are you Christians or cowards? Or is it to be Christian is to be a coward?" he goaded them. "Very well. Send two. Send three, send four, send six. Six men against just me."

"My lord, he insults God; this cannot go unchallenged," Gomes Ramirez argued.

"You are right. But not by you. Send six willing men," Alfonso said.

"Six?" Ramirez asked.

"Yes. If he wants to be slaughtered, let him be slaughtered," Alfonso said.

Gomes Ramirez looked to the other Bishops of the Orders and gave them a nod and all three sent two knights. The men broke the line and walked out to face Sulayman with their shields in hand and their swords drawn. The Christians clanged their swords against their shields. The Moors began to do the same, but with a simple gesture of his hand, Sulayman commanded them to stop. Al-Nasir did not like this display of power. It seemed Sulayman had more control over his troops than he did. Truthfully, he would not mourn if Sulayman died, and going up against six knights, very likely he would. *What game are you playing?* Al-Nasir wondered.

When the Christian knights were ten meters from him, Sulayman held his hand out. "Stop," he said. "This is unfair. I am an old man. Send six more. Make it an even dozen," he shouted.

The six Knights looked back to the line for instructions. Rodrigo turned to Alfonso. "What game does this demon play? We insult ourselves by engaging in this farce. There's nothing to be gained," he said.

"He will be dead. That is good enough. Send six more," Alfonso said to Ramirez.

Ramirez gave the command, and each order sent two more men. They walked to the center, joining the others. Seeing them, Sulayman was pleased and pulled two daggers, like small rapiers with nine-inch blades, from behind his back. They looked at him as if he were a lunatic. From what they could see, he wore little to no armor beyond vambraces on his arms and greaves on his shins. He carried no shield and held nothing else but a large wooden stick. They encircled him with their shields and swords on guard. When they were in position, Sulayman placed the staff on the ground, went down on both knees, put his daggers on the ground, and began to pray.

This stunned everyone on both sides. Was this an act of suicide? The Moslems loved martyrdom. Would the Christians strike Sulayman down unarmed as he prayed? This surely would enrage the Moors. They already outnumbered the Christians; would this act take away the Christians' only advantage being holy vengeance? The knights looked back to the line for direction on what to do. Ramirez looked to Alfonso, and Alfonso nodded for them to continue.

"He prays to a false prophet," Rodrigo said. "Let him die like a dog."

One of the Knights put his shield behind his back and two-handed his sword. He positioned himself to Sulayman's side, ready to take his head off. The others lowered their shields and relaxed their stance. The executioner raised his sword, and Sulayman looked at the knight directly in front of him—and smiled. The smile sent shivers down the knight's spine, but before he could react, Sulayman picked up his daggers, rolled on the ground from his kneeling position, lunged forward, and plunged his dagger, under the knight's chin, through his mail, through his mouth, and into his brain. Everyone was stunned. Sulayman pulled his dagger from the now dead Knight's chin, spun to his right, came to the back of another Knight, and put his blade through the back of his neck. The other Knights woke from their daze. The closest to Sulayman swung his broadsword. Sulayman grabbed the knight he had just stabbed in the neck, who was drowning in his own blood, used him as a shield, and the blow caught him, going through his clavicle into his breast. The knight was dismayed at striking his own man, and his sword snagged in the other knight's breastplate. Sulayman ran his dagger into the armpit of his sword hand, and another into his left eye. He cried out in pain, and Sulayman jabbed him again in the side of his neck. Three were down—nine remained.

They attempted to encircle him. Sulayman attacked with quick precise strikes where their armor was most vulnerable.

He would feint and cause them to swing, then swiftly move in, stab, then move away. It was an elegant dance. With barely any armor, he moved nimbly. He could roll. They could not. He would stab their feet and the back of their knees. Their chain-mail burdened them, and they couldn't swing freely for fear of striking their own. One by one they fell, "Too small . . . too slow . . . too weak . . . too easy," until there was none. "Allahu Akbar," Sulayman cried out, and the entire Muslim army of one hundred thousand chanted in unison, "Allahu Akbar."

"Allahu Akbar," he said again. "Allahu Akbar," they repeated, banging their swords against their shields and pounding their drums.

Al-Nasir looked on gleefully. From his vantage point, he could not see the fear in the eyes of the Christians, but he could feel it. He could taste the victory. He could do something his father had not done and destroy all the Christian Kingdoms in one stroke. Then the Moors began shouting, "Sulayman, Sulayman." Al-Nasir and Ibn Jam'i did not like this but they could do nothing about it. In a brilliant dance, Sulayman had defeated twelve of their best men, and most of them laid at his feet, bleeding badly, crying out, writhing in pain, dying but not yet dead. Seeing his men this way enraged Gomes Ramirez. "Give them a clean death, you bastard," he shouted.

Sulayman smiled. "No. I like them like this," he shouted back. "Let them suffer before they die. Let them pray for relief. And let them see that their prayers go unanswered. For they pray to a man and not God."

Gomes Ramirez was so enraged that before Alfonso could order him not to, he broke the line and rode down the field to meet Sulayman. As he approached, Ramirez considered running him down with his horse—but thought better of it. He feared Sulayman might injure the animal, and if he fell, he would be at a great disadvantage. He dismounted ten meters from Sulayman and approached with his sword and shield. Sulayman walked out of the circle of dying knights, walking with only the staff, slightly tapping the ground, causing a minor tremor with each step. Sulayman, Aminata, Sochima, and Amaris all noticed this. Sulayman was coming very close to where the next piece was buried.

Ramirez was the bigger man in both build and height. It did not matter. He feinted as if to do a vertical strike but, halfway through slashed horizontally. Sulayman evaded it regardless. Ramirez advanced again, slashing, feinting, thrusting. Sulayman dodged him calmly like a bullfighter, and like a bull, Ramirez grew angrier with every miss. He threw off his shield as it slowed him down, and with no weapons and only the walking stick, Sulayman had nothing that could pierce Ramirez's armor. Holding his sword with both hands, Ramirez advanced with a flurry of swings, each if they landed, would be a killing blow.

Sulayman continued to make him miss but backpaddled into the direction of one of the dying knights, who grabbed him by the ankle and caused him to slip. This was Ramirez's opening. Ramirez slashed downward with all his force. Sulayman held the walking stick up with both hands as a shield, and steel clashed against wood—and wood won. This astonished all the Kings and both camps. Sulayman pushed him away and got to his feet. He slammed the staff into the head of the knight who had tripped him killing him instantly. Ramirez came at Sulayman again. Sulayman deflected each slash with the staff. Ramirez did not understand how a thin piece of wood could hold up against steel. Sulayman parried and jabbed, punching Ramirez with the staff in the stomach and the chest. These blows did not pierce his armor, but they hurt tremendously. Sulayman jabbed him in the center of his chest directly at the heart with such force it caused an immediate cardiac arrest. Ramirez grabbed his chest and gasped for air. Sulayman jabbed him in the face, pushing in his nose guard and breaking his nose—the blood gushed—then the right eye, leaving him half blind, then one final crushing blow to the back of the head. Ramirez fell face down into the hot earth, with dirt in his eye, blood in his mouth, his heart constricting, and nothing he could do about it. Sulayman threw off his helmet and pulled down his hooded chain mail. He picked Ramirez's sword from the ground, held it with both hands, and slammed it into the back of Ramirez's neck, severing the head from the body. Alfonso felt the stab as if it was his own neck. Sulayman took Ramirez's head, held it high in the air then threw it across the field into the Christian forces.

"I've had enough of this," Alfonso said, giving the order, and the Christian front line of heavy cavalry charged onto the field. Al-Nasir gave the order, and his front line of infantry descended as well. Sulayman stood calmly in the center with the staff by his side as both forces rushed toward him.

92

War is a theater where men give their greatest performance. There is an intense anxiety a performer feels before they get on stage. For some, the anxiety goes away once the performance begins. For others, the anxiety turns to fear, and the fear can be crippling. They lose control of their bodily functions. They piss themselves, shit themselves. For some, after the embarrassment passes, they are relieved and fight freely. Some revel in the blood. Some become berserk and swing wildly, killing friend and foe alike. Maces, war hammers, and pickaxes may not cut through armor but they break bones and teeth and cause internal bleeding.

Aminata and Tomás were a part of Alfonso's second line consisting of heavy infantry. They remained in position, waiting on Alfonso's command. The cavalry had just charged in and had crashed into the Almohad first line. Amaris and Sochima were in that first line, and from Ami's vantage, it looked like they were being run over. Sulayman was also in the middle of that madness, and he still held the staff. Aminata kept looking at Alfonso to give the order for her line to charge, but he did not, and she couldn't wait any longer. If they wanted to get out of here, it would have to be now. She turned to Tomás and said, "thank you." He looked at her, confused, as she turned and ran towards the center of the battlefield.

"What are you doing?" Tomás shouted and contemplated following her but thought better of it. Medieval war is partial chaos. Some semblance of a battle plan is what saves it from falling into total anarchy. If Tomás broke formation as well, it might inspire others to do the same, believing the order had been given for them to charge, which would throw Alfonso's plan into disarray. Alfonso saw Aminata run into the heart of the fighting and wondered, *What the hell is that Moor doing?*

Aminata had her sword and shield but used neither. Her foresight was her best weapon. She saw every swing of a sword, slash of an axe, stab of a lance, bash of a hammer before they happened. There was a safe path, but she had to weave her way through it and be at the right spot at the right moment. She was a Moor in Christian armor. Christians saw her and believed she was with them until they saw her face and got confused, and when terrified men get confused, they strike without thinking. The Moors saw her armor and could care less what color her skin was. She was their enemy. Aminata needed to avoid both sides and navigate her way through the field of men and horses. Sulayman was her target, but he was thirty yards away, and hundreds of men, many on horseback, fought each other to the death between her and him. Seeing Sulayman's soul, she feared approaching him, but she had no choice. He had the staff. Amaris and Sochima were in the thick of this madness as well. It was difficult for Aminata to use her foresight to avoid getting hit and see how they were faring. She prayed they were doing well.

93

When al-Nasir gave the order for their line to charge, Ama-ris was set to run right at Sulayman. However, when she turned to Sochima, she saw that he was paralyzed with fear. "Sochi, let's go," she said.

"They're killing each other," he replied. Sochima knew all along they were preparing for a battle and that, eventually, these two sides would fight each other, but it had all seemed theoretical until now. Seeing the gruesome reality of it up close and knowing that he would have to participate was overwhelming.

"It's a war Sochi. We have to fight," Amaris said.

"I've never been in a fight before. I don't know how."

"I have. Follow me," she said. Sochima nodded and followed behind her as they ran toward the center of the field.

Amaris was a natural fighter, and Bilal was a skilled fighter. Her soul in his body made a good tandem. A sword weighs roughly three pounds. After thirty swings, the weight doubles, after another thirty swings, it triples, your muscles tighten, and your movement slows, and that momentary stagger is death. Amaris instinctually knew to conserve her energy and wait for her openings. In a world of madness, the calm man was king.

Amaris paid attention when Sulayman was fighting and how he exploited the weak spots in the Christians' armor. Most importantly, Amaris had no hesitation when it came to killing. In truth, she didn't think of it as killing. It was all happening so fast. She would stab someone, they would go down, and she would move on, not thinking twice about what became of them. This was war, and her only objective was for her and Sochima to survive.

Amaris pushed forward, and Sochima was behind her. They made a good team as she did most of the fighting, and he covered her back. Nevertheless, Sochima was forced to fight, often putting in the finishing stab on someone Amaris had put down. The brutality was not lost on him. His hands and face were smeared with blood. Men laid at his feet dying. At times he was forced to kick them off lest they take revenge from the ground. Bodies piled on top of each other, both Almohad and Christian. The stench of piss, shit, blood, and sweat was in the air. The sun shined high above. In this heat, sweat was the greatest impediment. Christian knights felt like they were cooking in their armor, and their sweat was the grease.

Amaris cut a path through, and they were within ten feet of Sulayman. They looked over and saw Aminata as well. It had been days since they had all been together. It was good to see her. There was no time for hugs. Sulayman had the staff, and they had to get it from him.

94

While Sulayman was distracted fighting other Christians, Aminata grabbed hold of the staff, hoping she could quickly wrestle it from him—but his grip was too firm. Sulayman turned to face her, and his face shook her soul. Sulayman looked her over, a Moor dressed in Christian armor. "Apostate. I think not," he said.

Aminata kept trying to pull the staff from him. He was too strong. He raised his dagger to stab her. Amaris attacked him, swinging her sword at his head. He caught her sword with the cross guard of his dagger.

"You," he said.

"Yup. Me," she replied.

"And me," Sochima said, jumping on his back from behind and putting him in a headlock.

Ibn Jam'i drew this altercation to al-Nasir's attention. "Our own men fight Sulayman? Is this your doing?" al-Nasir asked.

"No," he said.

"Interesting. Well then, let us see how this plays out," al-Nasir said.

Sulayman threw his head back into Sochima's nose. His nose broke, but he would not let go. Sulayman continued to deflect Amaris's attacks with his dagger. Aminata held her sword in her left hand. She could stab him. "Do it," Amaris shouted, but Aminata hesitated.

Suddenly Tomás, on horseback, charged at them with his sword drawn, ready to take off Sulayman's head. Sulayman kicked Ami away, knocked Mari backward, and threw Sochima over his shoulder onto the ground in front of him. Seeing Sochima, Tomás attempted to pull up so as not to run Sochima over.

Sulayman leaped off Sochima's back into the air, spun around, and with his dagger tore through Tomás's throat. Tomás's horse rode into the Almohad side of the field, with Tomás's body still astride, his head hanging off, horrifying everyone who saw it. Aminata had liked Tomás, and he was the only reason she had survived her stay with the Christians. However, she had no time to mourn him. The staff had fallen from Sulayman's hand. She ran to recover it. Sulayman saw her and raced to the staff as well. Aminata got to it first and slammed the staff into the ground with both hands.

Previously, whenever the staff had struck the ground, it had caused a minor tremor. However, here, directly above the next piece, it caused a minor earthquake. The ground Sulayman and the men around him were on rose and threw them into the air. In the air it finally occurred to Sulayman why this staff was so special and what a fool he had been. He had been arrogant, and his arrogance had made him blind. For centuries he had guarded the artifact, and he had become complacent. He had the thieves in his hands all this time. He could have killed them so many times already. No matter. They had not recovered it yet, and he would not let them have it.

He landed on the ground with his eyes so fixed on the children he neglected the Christian knights in front of him—and behind. The first blade pierced his side. The second came in his back. Four knights from the orders of Calatrava and Santiago surrounded and stabbed him repeatedly. "Die devil," one of them said.

Amaris saw Sulayman fall and was happy. Now Sochima only needed to take in the next piece, and they could finally leave this place. The ground had unearthed Ausar's mummified right hand. Aminata touched it with the staff, and the mummified flesh fell apart and seeped into the earth. The soul became a glowing orb, the world became a portal, and everyone within its twenty-yard circumference stepped out of their bodies. Both Moor and Christian stopped fighting and just looked around in a daze, wandering around trying to come to grips with being out of their bodies.

Alfonso and Rodrigo looked on from their position outside of the portal's circumference. "What in Heaven is this?" Alfonso asked. To their eyes, the men simply shut down and stood motionless.

"I do not know," Rodrigo said.

Ibn Jam'i and al-Nasir were likewise perplexed. Though they took heart in that outside of the portal's circumference, their forces were winning, as their cavalry stormed the field.

The children were souls again. They smiled at each other briefly. "Do it now," Aminata shouted to Sochima. "Do it fast," she pressed, fearing what would come. Sochima reached for the orb when they heard a booming voice say, "I will not fail." They looked up and beheld a giant, ten feet tall, made of smokeless fire, wearing a beaded necklace with a pendant with a six-sided star in the center. In the fire, they saw a face they knew too well. It was Sulayman. They had assumed before that Sulayman may be the Guardian. Now it was confirmed. He kicked Sochima and Aminata away from the orb and turned to Amaris. He saw the body of Bilal dormant beside her. "You, you are a child," he said.

"Yup. I'm a girl," Amaris answered, being glib while also deathly afraid.

He looked at how her soul was attired. "You are not of this time."

"No. And I just really wanna go home."

"I will send you home." He drew the energy from the souls of the dying Christians and forged a sword of fire.

"Whoa," Amaris said.

Sulayman was about to strike her when Aminata hit his leg from behind with the staff. He turned to her and saw the staff in its true form, of brilliant light. "Oh my. I knew it was special, but how short-sighted I was. Forged by Allah himself. Give it to me," he said.

"No. You're a bad man." Sochima said.

"I am God's chosen. And you are nothing but thieves," Sulayman shouted.

"Get the orb," Aminata said to Sochima. Sochima nodded and ran towards it.

Sulayman swiped down at the ground, just missing Sochima. "Insect," he said. "I will not be undone by insects." He raised his hand to swipe again, but Aminata blocked him with the staff, protecting herself and Sochima. He slashed again and again, and she blocked every blow. She could see his moves ahead of time; nevertheless, the force sent shockwaves through her soul. And though the staff would hold, she was not sure if she would.

Amaris was about to run to Sochima and Aminata to help, but then she saw the soul of one of the Christian knights reach for the orb. Amaris was terrified he would consume it, but it shattered his soul. And though they had just seen this, other souls, as if hypnotized, were drawn to the orb, and when they attempted to hold it, their souls shattered as well.

"Unworthy," Sulayman said of them.

Alfonso watched as dozens of his men dropped dead without anyone striking them. "What devilish work is this?" he asked.

"I do not know. This truly is the battle to decide the fate of men," Rodrigo said.

"Rodrigo, you and I are going to die here," Alfonso said fearfully.

"No . . . no. Here we will overcome our enemies."

This heartened Alfonso. He looked to his right, to King Sancho II, and nodded his head. The King of Navarre nodded in return, shouted the order, and led his men into the field.

Sulayman had Sochima and Aminata pinned, and they couldn't reach the orb. Amaris was right beside it. Sochima looked at her and nodded. *What was that nod? Did he mean for her to take the orb?* Sochima was the one who consumed the orbs. And Imhotep gave the eye to Aminata, not her. And the orb had destroyed all the men who had attempted to hold it because they were, as Sulayman said, unworthy. Would it not do the same to her? Amaris thought about all the bad things she had done in her life, all the fights she had been in, all the times she had lied to her mother. She could think of a hundred reasons why she wasn't worthy—but "Do it," Sochima shouted.

This drew Sulayman back to Amaris, who he had neglected. "No," he said as he rushed towards her. Amaris had no choice. She kneeled and stretched her arms to the orb. "Please don't kill me, please don't kill me," she repeated. The orb rose, came into her hands, and she guided it into her mouth. The portal closed, and all the souls returned to their bodies. But Amaris, Sochima, and Aminata remained as souls, as the bodies of Bilal, Tahir, and Hassan had died while their souls were absent.

Sulayman remained a soul as well. "Nooooo. I will rip your soul apart," he shouted.

He slashed at her with his sword of fire. Amaris dodged and rolled out of the way, until she could not, and Sulayman had her cornered. Aminata saw Sulayman's blade strike Amaris, and Aminata could do nothing about it. As the blade of soulfire came down, all Amaris could do was hold out her hand in defense—and to her surprise, she caught the blade in her right hand, and she did not shatter. In fact, she closed her grip and she shattered the blade, knocking Sulayman back. "Whoa," Amaris said. Sochima and Aminata were likewise amazed.

Seeing this angered Sulayman even more. He got to his feet as King Sancho of Navarre stormed onto the field, leading a charge of hundreds of fresh men. They passed through the souls of Sulayman and the children and ran over the bodies of the fallen. The Almohad soldiers who had just returned to their bodies were bewildered and unprepared. Sancho and his men tore through them, their line broke, and a clear path opened up straight to al-Nasir.

Ibn Jam'i alerted al-Nasir of the threat, as King Sancho and a thousand men stormed towards him. Al-Nasir was stunned at the sudden turn in a battle he was winning. He saw Sancho coming, and fear gripped his heart and his throat. He did not know what to do or say. His vizier spoke for him. "Protect your Caliph," ibn Jam'i shouted to the hundreds of Saqaliba surrounding them. The Saqaliba were al-Nasir's personal guard; however, they had no great love for him and would not needlessly die for him. When Sancho broke through their first line, they splintered. Seeing this, al-Nasir lost heart and called a retreat, and he and ibn Jam'i and a thousand men left the field. The Moors looked on in dismay as their Caliph abandoned them, and they turned from an army to anarchy, and what was once a battle became a rout.

Sulayman was heartbroken at this sudden turn of events. "Look what you have done. Look what you have caused," he said as he stood between Amaris and Aminata and Sochima, preventing them from getting to each other. "No. It will not end like this. I will not end like this," he said. He drained the soul energy from all the men around him. He formed two blades of fire. He flew into the air and then flew down with all his fury. The children ran to each other. Amaris held out her right hand, and Aminata held the staff and Sochima and thought of feeling safe.

ACT SIX
THE RETURN

95

They went from chaos to quiet. Their eyes closed, and a second later, there was no more blood, no more death, no cries of war—just quiet. It was their fifth jump, and they were still unaccustomed to its instantaneousness. It was to experience the speed of light the way light experiences the speed of light. One moment you were in one place, and the next another, vastly different. They were grateful to have escaped that theater of horrors, to be in a new place, and to even be in new bodies. Except, "Mari, you're you," Sochima remarked, shocked to see Amaris as herself.

"And you're you," Amaris said, equally surprised to see Sochima as himself. "Are we back in our bodies?" she wondered.

"No. We're not in a body. We're just souls." Sochima said.

"Are we dead?" Amaris wondered fretfully.

"We're not dead," Ami said.

"How do you know that? I think we're dead," Amaris said.

"We're not dead, okay? Now stop saying that," Ami said.

"But how do you know that we're not?" Amaris continued.

"If we were dead, if what Imhotep said was true, both of us would have moved onto our next lives, and Sochi would have moved onto the afterlife to be judged. The fact that we're all still together means that our bodies are still alive," Aminata explained.

"We're not dead," Sochima said. "We're just not in bodies."

"Why are we not in bodies? And where are we?" Amaris asked.

"I don't know?" Aminata said.

They were in a large open room, which looked like a well-constructed tent, with rows of bunk beds on both sides and an aisle down the center. There were no windows, but there was an opening in the back, and a small sunroof, which bathed the room in the morning light. It could have been a shelter or a hostel. It also looked like somewhere they would see in their own time. After being hundreds and, at times, thousands of years in the past, it felt good to be somewhere familiar. However, "I don't feel anything," Sochima said.

"What don't you feel?" Ami asked him.

"I don't feel the next piece. After every jump, I always get this feeling in my heart for the next piece, telling me where to go. But I don't feel it. Can you see it?" He asked Aminata.

"I wouldn't know where to look," she said.

"I don't think a piece is here," Sochima said.

"Then what are we doing here?" Mari asked.

A man appeared at the opening at the far end of the room. Standing behind the sunlight, all they could see of him was a shadow. He walked forward and remained a shadow until he came into the light. He wore fatigues of the kind the United States military wore in their time, with his helmet, rucksack, and rifle strapped over his shoulder. He also walked with a large wooden stick in his hand. His build and walk seemed very familiar to Aminata, and when he came further into the light, she could see that it was, "Dad?" she said with a bit of uncertainty. When he came fully into the light, all doubts were removed. This was their father. "Daddy," both Ami and Sochi said and ran to him and were dismayed as he walked right through them. *Were they ghosts, or was he? Was this a dream?*

Aaron Gates walked to his bed and left his staff on top. He sighed. Aminata looked at the staff on the bed and the staff in her hand. They were the same. Only on the bed, it was in its physical form, and she held its spiritual form. When Ami saw the expression on her father's face as he left the staff, she remembered a story she heard at his funeral. She remembered a fellow Marine speaking about Aaron always carrying the stick with him, that it was his lucky stick and had become a good luck charm for him and his entire squad. The day he was ordered to leave it behind was the day he died. Remembering this story chilled Aminata to her core. "Dad, pick up the staff," she said to him. "C'mon, Dad, pick it up." He turned and looked in her direction. For a moment, she thought he was looking at her, but he was seeing straight through her. Did he hear something? Did he feel something? He looked a few seconds longer as she kept calling to him, then he turned away and began walking out of the room, leaving the staff on the bed.

Ami looked at the wall over his bed. Along with pictures of Gabrielle, Ami, Sochi, and Nana, there was a calendar with dates crossed off. She saw today's date. It all came together. Today was the day he died. "Daddy, don't go. Daddy, come back."

"He can't hear you, Ami," Sochima said.

"Then we have to find a way to make him hear us. Today is the day he dies. That's why we're here. We're here to stop him from dying."

"I don't think we can do that, Ami," Sochi said.

"Yes, we can," Ami said combatively.

She looked at Mari. Amaris saw the desperation on Ami's face. She could tell how hurt she had been at losing her father. Amaris remembered when her father left and how that tore their family apart. If this was why they were sent here, "Then let's go save your dad," Amaris said.

96

Aminata, Sochima and Amaris followed Aaron out of the barracks and into the main base. The Syrian sun shined brightly. The base was teeming with military personnel and equipment. Military aircraft flew overhead. Aaron walked through the base to the MRAP (mine resistant ambush protected) vehicle waiting for him. A fellow Marine greeted him with a light tap on his helmet, and he and Aaron stepped into the vehicle. The children frantically followed behind, at first dodging people and objects in their way. However, no one could see or interact with them, and they soon started phasing through everything. For Amaris, this was very dispiriting. She felt like a ghost and had to keep telling herself she was alive.

The children followed the soldiers into the vehicle as it closed behind them. There were seven soldiers, a driver and another up front, and Aaron and four others in the back. They all took their seats and strapped in. The vehicle pulled off and left the base.

"You alright, Gates?" a fellow Marine asked Aaron.

"Yeah, I'm good," Aaron replied.

"Barret is an ass. Don't see how your stick was stopping us from doing anything."

"It is what it is," Aaron said.

"Yeah. Ours is not to question why. Ours is but to do and die, right?" Jones said.

"Yeah, but let's save the dying part for years from now," Aaron said.

"Hoorah," Jones replied, and he and Aaron fist-pumped.

At that moment, Aaron thought of his children and said, "Ami, Sochi," under his breath.

"Dad, Daddy, we're here. We're right here," Ami said.

"He can't hear us," Sochima said.

"Yes, he can. He just said our names. We just have to try harder."

Though Sochima loved his father, he felt that if this was the day he died, as much as they might want to, they shouldn't change it, as it may cause unintended consequences. Yet Ami was so determined Sochima didn't believe he could go against her.

Amaris stood beside them watching everything take place. As unnerved as she had been at being in someone else's body, she felt even more unnerved not being in a body at all. Were they in a dream? Were they dead? They were trying to stop Ami and Sochi's dead father from dying. This didn't make sense.

Then again, nothing that had happened since she got off that bus made sense.

Ami kept pleading with her father to turn back. It broke Sochima's heart to see her like this. Then something occurred to him. He put his hand on his father's chest by his heart, and Aaron reacted and looked up. "He felt you," Ami said. "Dad," Ami called to him again, and "Ami," Aaron replied, in his mind.

"Dad, you can hear me. You have to turn back. Please turn back. You're going to die if you don't turn back."

Aaron didn't understand how he was hearing his daughter's voice in his head and why she would give him such an ominous warning. He had dreamed of loved ones who had passed many times before. He believed he had seen ghosts under his bed when he was younger. He was a believer in things that could not be physically explained. His spirit had felt uneasy ever since leaving the staff behind. Now in his head, he heard his twelve-year-old daughter calling to him, warning him about his own death. He listened to her. Aaron knocked on the wall of the vehicle to get the driver's attention. He got the attention of all the Marines.

The driver, Daniels, shouted from the front, "What's up?"

"We need to turn back," Aaron said.

"Turn back, why? You got some new intel?"

"No intel. Just a feeling," Aaron said.

"A feeling? Like what?"

"Like if we keep going, we're all going to die today."

That raised the eye of every soldier.

"That's some messed up shit to say, Gates," Daniels said.

"I know. And I'm not saying it lightly. And I'll take whatever hit that comes from Barrett." Soldiers didn't like breaking orders, but they were also superstitious. They know that you can have the best training, equipment, plan, and preparation, and you can still die. They had never known Gates to waver about going on assignment before, the fact that he was so adamant that they should turn around gave them pause, and the driver stopped the vehicle. "Alright, Gates. Let's hear this out," the driver said.

A second later a huge explosion went off a few yards in front of them, just where they would have been if they had kept driving. Dirt and debris from the explosion rained down on the exterior of the MRAP. Fortunately, the vehicle was heavily armored. The explosion and debris made a lot of noise but no dents to the exterior.

"Let's get out of here," Jones shouted, and the driver began reversing. A dump truck pulled up a few meters behind them on the street, blocking their escape path. On the rooftops of the buildings on both sides of the street, four gunmen with automatic rifles came from cover and opened fire. On the inside, the gunfire sounded like a hurricane lashing a zinc roof. The children though they were in their spirit form and impervious to physical harm were terrified. The soldiers instinctually reverted to their training. "Jones, get on the turret and create a path for us out of here," Aaron said.

"On it," Jones said. There was a turret on the vehicle's roof with an armored canopy and view screen. Jones entered the turret and began firing on the dump truck behind them.

The ground began to shake violently. The sound reverberated through the vehicle. Sochima imagined he could feel it, even in his spirit form. Then he realized the heart inside of him was vibrating because of something else, infinitely more powerful. "Something is happening," he said to the girls. Then they all felt it.

"What the hell?" Aaron said, when the ground underneath them erupted, propelling the MRAP off the ground, into the air and on its back. Outside, a massive earthquake tore a fissure through the street. Windows shattered, fire hydrants exploded, car alarms went off, and buildings caved in. The shooters on the rooftops gave up their assault and ran for safety. The MRAP began falling between the cracks of the fissure. "We gotta get outta here," Aaron shouted to everyone. It would be better for them to take their chances with the shooters than stay inside and get dragged underground.

The earth was shaking violently as the soldiers pulled themselves out. Aaron looked out and saw buildings crashing down in the distance and people crying and running in terror. He had experienced earthquakes before, but they had been nothing like this. The children in their spirit form could see why this was happening. There was a massive dragon worm burrowing through the earth. "Are you seeing this?" Mari asked the others.

"Yeah," Ami and Sochi said together. The dragon worm then dove deeper underground and the quaking subsided. Everyone hoped it was over. Then they began to feel a heavy dry wind, and the dust around them rose, and in the distance, they saw a cloud of dust develop, and the cloud grew higher and denser until it became a tsunami of sand, and it rushed towards them. The sunny day became dark orange. The soldiers put their visors on, put rags over their mouths and took cover behind the fallen MRAP. The wind whipped the sand with such violence it could cut their skin. The storm morphed into a tornado. It tore trees from their roots, roofs off buildings, women from men, and children from women. The storm seemed sentient and acted with malicious intent. The children saw a dragon curled in the sky, spitting sand from its mouth. The children were unaffected and could only look on helplessly. Aminata wanted to help her father but how could she save him from this? She wondered for a moment if she was the cause of this. Was this creation correcting itself because she had prevented her father from dying when he was supposed to? Whatever the reason, this was the most violent storm she had ever witnessed. In the distance, a plane fell from the sky and crashed to the earth, and a US military helicopter was caught spinning in the whirlwind. Sochima began to shake and clutch his chest.

"What's wrong?" Mari asked.

"I feel it," Sochima said.

"Feel what? What are you feeling?"

"Him. I can feel him."

"Who are you feeling, Sochi?" Ami asked.

It was hard for Sochi to say the word. "Apep … Apep. He's here."

Aminata looked to the sky, and through the dark clouds she saw the faint light of a large yellow moon moving. The clouds and the wind had cosmic energy. The day became intensely dark. Aminata held the staff in front of them, and it became alive, and its light broke through the darkness. The yellow moon stopped and turned about and what was one yellow moon became two. And they saw it. They saw him. The face of a serpent as far as the eye could see. And he saw them. He saw the staff, and it enraged him. He opened his mouth and opened a black hole, sucking everything into it: cars, trees, buildings, people. It tore people apart, skin, flesh, sinew and bone. It ripped their bodies from their souls and then shattered their souls. The staff created a shield of light protecting Aminata and everyone around her. But the force was too strong, and she couldn't hold on. The MRAP flew away and tore apart. Then the soldiers, one by one, flew away and tore apart. Only Aaron remained, and they watched his body get torn asunder until there was only his soul. He saw his children. "Ami ... Sochi," he said, both confused and happy to see them.

"Dad," they replied. Then his soul shattered.

Aminata closed her eyes as she couldn't bear to see it.

They couldn't resist the pull of Apep any longer. They were being sucked into the black hole. Seeing her death before her eyes, Amaris screamed, "Mommeee."

97

Amaris woke up screaming in terror. Her mother jumped up from her seat at Amaris's bedside. "Mija, Mari, Mari. It's okay mija. I'm here. I'm here."

Amaris couldn't believe what she was seeing. "Mami. Mami? Is that you? Is it really you?"

"Si, mija, it's me. It's me."

Amaris hugged her mother tightly. "Mami, it's you. I'm home? I'm really back home?" Mari asked with such a sense of hope and joy.

"No Mari, you're not home."

"I'm not home," Mari said breaking into tears.

"No, Mari, you're in a hospital."

"Why am I in a hospital?"

"You got hit by lightning mija. You had a seizure and passed out. And you've been asleep these last two days." Amaris looked very confused. She pulled away from her mother and looked around. She was in a hospital, lying in bed, wearing a hospital gown. There was a TV mounted on the wall. Her mother's favorite show was on.

Mari began crying and laughing, such tears of joy. "I'm home, Mami. I'm home," Amaris said and hugged her mother so tightly.

98

Aminata and Sochima shared a room together. They sat in their beds eating jello pudding. A grateful Gabrielle was there speaking to their doctor. "So, the results from the cat scan are back, and neurologically they are fine—no signs of any damage from their seizures. And I checked their vitals, and they are perfect. They are healthy six and twelve-year-olds, as they should be."

"Oh, thank you," Gabrielle said.

"I want to keep them here one more night, just for observation. After being in a coma, sometimes the body takes a while to start working again as it should."

"Okay. But they're fine, right?" Gabrielle asked.

"Yeah. They're perfect," The doctor said to Gabrielle. He then turned to the children. "You guys are very lucky. If you had been any closer to the lightning strike when it hit, you would not have come out of it so well. What were you guys doing in the park alone during a lightning storm?"

Ami and Sochi didn't have an answer for him. Gabrielle intervened. "That's okay. I'll take it from here."

"Okay," the doctor said and left.

Gabrielle turned to her children.

"I know you guys have been through a lot, and you're probably still tired, even after being asleep for two days. But I have some questions, and they can't wait." Gabrielle said to them. Sochima and Aminata braced themselves for what was to come. Gabrielle turned to Sochima. "Sochi, why did you run away?" she asked.

"I was really sad that Nana was dying. And I got angry because cousins Suki and Karen were on their phones, and they were laughing and joking. So, I walked away from them. Then I walked down the stairs, and then I was outside, then I was lost, and I didn't know how to go back. So, I kept walking. Then I saw the park, and I wanted to sit down. Then I saw Ami, and I was happy, and then it started raining, really heavy, then I looked up and saw lightning, and then, and then I was here."

"And that's it? That's all you remember?" Gabrielle asked.

"Yes, Mommy," Sochi answered.

"Okay," Gabrielle said, then turned to Aminata. "Now you, Ami, tell me what happened? And don't lie. I already know you got arrested."

"You do?" Aminata asked, sounding surprised. And though it took place two days ago, Ami had experienced hundreds of years between then and had forgotten about it.

"Yes. It was the police who found all three of you in the park and brought you to the hospital. And when I got here and asked what happened, they mentioned that you and Amaris had been arrested for fighting on the subway."

"I'm sorry, Mommy," Ami said.

"That's so not important now. I don't care about it. I just want to know how you ended up meeting your brother in the park."

"I left the police station, and I got on the bus headed to the hospice. But then I looked out the window and I saw Sochi walking by himself outside of the park. So, I got off and chased after him. After I found him, it started raining, and then the lightning." Aminata wanted to unload everything that had happened, but she followed Sochima's lead and omitted everything else. "And then we woke up here."

"And that's all you remember?" Gabrielle asked, sensing they were leaving something out.

"Yes," Sochi and Ami answered together.

"Okay, I'm going to ask you something and I want you to be very honest." She took a breath. "Did either of you see Nana? Either while you were awake or while you were dreaming?"

"How could we see Nana? She was at the hospice," Ami asked.

"I mean, did you see her spirit?" Gabrielle said. "And don't worry, whatever you tell me I'll believe you." She turned to Sochima, as he had a special connection to Nana and had seen spirits before.

"I didn't see Nana," Sochima said.

Gabrielle turned to Aminata. "Ami?" she asked.

"No, Mommy. I didn't see Nana. I didn't dream her either."

"Okay," Gabrielle replied. She was both relieved and disappointed. She was disappointed because this added to her confusion. Gabrielle saw Nana's spirit just before Nana died. While Gabrielle held Nana's hand as her breathing slowed, Nana's spirit came out of her body and said to her, "The kids will be alright." Then she returned to her body and seconds later Nana was gone. Gabrielle wasn't quite sure she had seen what she had seen. However, it did make her think about the safety of her children. She checked for Sochi and realized that he was nowhere to be found, and Aminata still hadn't gotten there, even after finally sending a text saying she was on her way.

Gabrielle had just lost Nana, and now she couldn't find her children. She also noticed that Nana's stick was missing. She knew she had brought it to the hospice with Nana, but now it was gone, and every other family member swore they hadn't touched it. Then she remembered the last time she saw Sochima, he had it.

Fortunately, a few hours later, the children were found. Lightning had struck the ground nearby where they were standing. The shock jolted them unconscious. The police had brought them to the hospital. They had fallen into a coma, but they were alive, and despite being in a coma, physically, they were fine. Gabrielle had been by their side at the hospital the entire time, up until they woke up. They both woke up at the same time, which she was grateful for, but admittedly found odd. What was extremely odd was when she noticed Nana's stick under the sheets on Ami's bed. How on earth did it get there? It had not been there before. Gabrielle was very grateful to have her children back and awake but something supernaturally odd was going on. Unfortunately, the children were unable to or unwilling to answer the questions she had.

She would leave things be for now. "Okay," she said. Before leaving the room, she kissed Aminata and Sochima on the forehead, telling them both she loved them.

Aminata could see the strain this ordeal had caused their mother, making her feel worse for lying to her. "Why did you lie to Mommy?" Ami asked Sochi.

"Why did you lie to Mommy?" Sochima replied.

"Because you had already lied, and I didn't want to cause confusion."

"Good. Because she wouldn't understand," Sochima said.

"She said she would believe us."

"She wouldn't believe us. Not all of it. And she would think we were crazy."

Aminata had lived through it, and thinking it over to herself, she thought she was crazy. "Yeah, she wouldn't believe us," Ami said.

99

Gabrielle found Samantha at a table sipping coffee in the hospital cafeteria. They greeted each other with a hug, and Gabrielle sat at the table. "How is Amaris?" Gabrielle asked.

"She's good, you know. She's really good. The doctor says she's fine; nothing is wrong. Her brain is working the way it should. How are the kids?" Samantha asked.

"They're the same. Healthy. Which is the most important thing. But I think they're in shock, though."

"I know. Mari woke up screaming, screaming, screaming my name. Mommy. She was so scared, like she had the worst nightmare ever."

"Really? I wasn't in the room when the kids woke up. I was in the restroom, and when I came back in the room, they were both awake. But they were breathing heavy, and they did look scared."

"I figure Mari was calling out for me right before they got hit by lightning, and that's why she was still calling for me when she woke up," Samantha said. "It's the literal shock of it, you know."

"Yeah, that makes sense. But then all three of them woke up at the same time. You don't think that's strange?" Gabrielle asked.

"It might be. But to be honest, this whole thing is strange. I mean, Mari and Ami haven't seen each other in so many years, then they get into a fight on the metro, and they get arrested. And I wanna apologize to you for that."

"It's okay," Gabrielle said.

"No, it's not okay. And I know it's Mari who started it. She's going through some changes, and she's hanging out with these new girls, and they're so bad. And you know, I blame myself because of it. Because I moved her into that neighborhood, and those were the kids that were around, and she probably felt like she had to join up with them just to survive."

"I'm sorry you had to move into that neighborhood. I'm so sorry about Javier. I know it has been hard without him here."

"Oh, it has been. But at least he's still alive, and I can talk to him every night. I can't imagine what you've gone through losing Aaron."

"It's been a rough year. There's no other way to say it. And Nana was a rock holding us all together. Then Nana started getting sick and watching her deteriorate." Gabrielle sighed, trying to hold herself together. "And then she dies, and this happens to the kids." Gabrielle began crying, and Samantha hugged her, crying as well.

"I'm so sorry to hear about Nana. You know I loved her too. And me and Javi can never thank her enough for what she did. But it's all going to be alright. We're going to get through this. God doesn't give us more than we can handle, right?"

Gabrielle pulled away and dabbed the tears from her eyes. "I don't know about that. I think this is too much for me to handle all at once."

"You need rest. You've been up for the last two days. We both have. We should go home and get a good sleep. Then come back and pick the kids up and take them home."

"Sleeping in my own bed sounds good."

"Sounds good to me too."

"Then maybe after the kids are discharged. We all go out together. Hang out like we used to."

"That sounds great. Let's do that."

100

Aminata lay in the hospital bed using her phone. It felt so strange using her phone again after traveling to the past. She had just lived history, and now she held it in her hand. Anything she wanted to know, she could pull up at once. She simply needed to know the right questions to ask. She was researching the date her father died. She searched to see if there had been any earthquakes or sandstorms in Syria. There was a brief mention of a small sandstorm and a minor earthquake but nothing like the mass devastation they saw.

Gabrielle walked into the room. "Where is Sochi?" she asked.

"He's in the bathroom," Ami replied.

"I'm going to head home and get some rest, then come back and bring you guys a change of clothes, okay."

"Okay," Ami said. "Mom?"

"Yeah, Ami."

"How did Dad die?"

Gabrielle was taken aback by that question. "Why are you asking that? You know how your father died. He died serving in Syria."

"Yeah, I know that, but like, how did he die, exactly."

The last thing Gabrielle wanted to do at that moment was rehash the details of her husband's death, but this seemed important to Ami. "The vehicle he was in ran over a roadside bomb, and he and everyone in it died," she said.

"Was there an earthquake or a sandstorm when he died?"

"I don't know. There may have been. What's going on, Ami? Why are you asking about this now?"

"No reason. I've just been thinking about Dad lately."

"I know you miss him. Believe me, I do too. I could have

really used his help during all this. With Nana dying, then you guys being lost."

"I'm sorry Mommy," Ami said and hugged her mother.

"It's not your fault."

"You look tired, Mommy," Aminata said.

Gabrielle laughed. "Thanks."

"Go home and sleep. We'll be fine."

Gabrielle kissed Ami on her forehead. "I'll be back in a few hours."

101

Amaris sat in her bed, having a video chat with Marisol. "Girl, what happened to you? I've been texting and calling you for like two days straight. Did the cops take you to prison or something?" Marisol asked.

"Nah, girl, I've been in the hospital," Mari said.

"In the hospital? Did those Cops beat you up?"

"Nah, it wasn't like that. They let us go after like two hours. But then I got caught in the rain coming home, and I got hit by lightning, girl," Mari said.

"Are you for real? You got hit by lightning, and you're still alive?" Marisol asked.

"Well, it didn't hit me directly. It hit the ground close to me, and the shock knocked me out, and I been in the hospital the last two days."

"Oh my God. That is crazy."

"I know, right?" Mari said.

"But yo, when we was on the train, why did you jump that girl while the Cop was there?" Marisol asked.

"Yeah, that was a mistake. I shouldn't have did that."

"Yeah, I thought we said we would wait until the Cop left or jump her when she got off."

"Nah, we shouldn't have tried to jump her period. She's my friend, and that was wrong of me."

Marisol was shocked to hear that. "Mari, what are you talkin' about, she yo' friend? Since when?"

"Since forever. And that was wrong of me to do that."

Marisol looked stunned. "Girl, that lightning must have did something to you. Because you not talkin' like the Mari I know."

Amaris laughed. "Yeah, maybe it did. But thanks for reaching out and checking up on me. I'll talk to you later, alright." Amaris ended the conversation. She then went on TikTok and laughed at some silly videos and new challenges people posted. She appreciated being able to do something so trivial.

Aminata and Sochima walked into the room. "Ami, Sochi, how are you guys?"

"We're good. It's good to see you, in the flesh," Aminata said as she walked over and hugged Amaris.

"I know, right? It feels so nice to be me again and not be a man," she said.

They all laughed.

"Did your mom leave too?" Sochima asked her.

"Yeah, like ten minutes ago. She'll be back in a few hours though."

"Good, so we can get going now," Sochima said.

"Going? Go where?" Mari asked.

"What do you mean go where? Let's go get the next piece," Sochima said, bringing the focus back to something Ami and Mari were very happy not to think about.

"Oh, I'm not going anywhere. I'm done with that," Mari said, turning back to her phone.

"What are you talking about? You can't be done with it. We're not finished," Sochima said.

"I am. Since we started jumping all over the place, all I wanted was to get back home. And now I'm back home, back in my own body. And it feels so good to be me, and I'm not leaving." Sochima couldn't believe what he was hearing, and he turned to Ami for support, but Ami was silent. "All I wanna do now is chill, eat junk food, watch TV, go on IG, go on TikTok—"

"TikTok?" Sochima said, on the verge of losing it. "TikTok. You're going to let the world get destroyed because you wanna go on TikTok?"

"It's not just TikTok okay? It's not about TikTok. I'm just saying I just want to go back to being me. I just want to go back to being the Mari I was—when was it? Two days ago. Though it feels like ten thousand years ago. I just want to be a kid, living right here, right now."

Not getting anywhere with Amaris, Sochima turned to Aminata. "Can you help, please? Can you say something?"

"I'm tired, Sochi," Ami said listlessly.

"What does that have to do with anything?" Sochima asked.

"It means I'm tired. It means I haven't slept in what Mari says feels like ten thousand years. Since I got off the bus and chased after you, I watched Nana's soul shatter right in front of my eyes. And I haven't even gotten a chance to cry for her, because we jumped right into Mexico, where we almost got eaten by some jaguar-man. Then we went to Mali where we almost got killed by a man wearing human skin. Then we went to Kemet, and the same man who killed Nana somehow tracked us there thousands of years in the past. Then we're in medieval Spain literally fighting in a war, fighting a damn giant. And then … and then with Dad …" Aminata was exhausted and couldn't finish.

"Say it. Say it," Sochima said. "And then we saw Dad, and we saw him die. And we saw Apep. And we saw what is going to happen if we don't stop him."

"We don't know if that's true. We don't know what we saw. We don't know if that was just a dream," Mari said.

"It wasn't a dream," Sochi said.

"I don't know what it was," Ami said. "But I think it was my fault. I think I'm the reason why we went there."

"How?" Amaris asked.

"I don't know. But ever since I got the eye, I've been seeing things. And when we were in Spain, just before we jumped, I thought about my dad. Because everything was so crazy, and I just wanted to feel safe, and he always made me feel safe. And I just wanted to be with him. And then we were in that room."

"Okay. So, you're able to control where we go now?" Sochi asked.

"I don't know. I'm not sure. I wasn't thinking about it or trying to make it happen. It just happened." Then Aminata thought of something. "But maybe, because when Apep started destroying everything and pulling us in, all I wanted to do was go home, and I thought home, and then we woke up here."

"Well, I'm glad you did. Because I'm happy to be home," Mari said.

"But we're not done. We haven't finished," Sochima argued.

"But who says we have to finish it? Maybe our part is done," Mari said.

"We're supposed to find fourteen pieces. We only have five."

"Well maybe it's like a relay, and we did our part, and someone else will come and take up where we left off," Amaris said.

"It's not a relay. It's real. And it's our responsibility," Sochima said, growing increasingly frustrated.

"Why do we have to do it?" Ami asked.

"Because we're the only ones who can do it," Sochi said.

"Then why are we back here, in our own bodies?" Mari asked.

"Because … because there's a piece here for us to get. So, we're back in our bodies because we're here now, so we don't need to jump into other bodies. I can feel it. It's here," Sochi said.

"He's right. It's in Meridian Park," Ami said, and Mari hated Ami at that moment for saying that. "I saw it last night. I can see it now."

"Exactly. You see. That's why Nana brought me there. And that's why we found her there when Nana got lost that time."

They took a moment to absorb everything until Mari broke down. "I'm sorry you guys, but I can't do this anymore. I can't go through what we just did again. I'm too young for this."

"When are you going to get it? We're in kid's bodies now, but we're not kids," Sochima said.

"Maybe you guys aren't kids. But I feel like a kid. I'm in my second life. I don't know how long my first life was. Ami, you're on your seventh, and Sochi, this is your last life, so maybe you're ready to handle all of this and go save the world. But I'm not. I'm not ready for this," Mari said.

"I don't know what being in my seventh life means. I feel like a kid, and I don't feel ready either," Ami said.

"It doesn't matter if we're ready. We saw it. We saw what happens. We saw Apep," Sochi said.

"I know, Sochi. And I never want to see it again," Aminata said trying her best to keep from breaking down.

"You guys think you can just go back to how things were before. We can't. When we saw Dad, we weren't in the past, we were in the future," Sochi said.

"How can it be the future when it was a year ago?" Amaris asked.

"Because Apep is timeless," Sochi said.

That hit Amaris and Aminata like a nuclear bomb. They sighed heavily, feeling the literal weight of the world on their shoulders. "Okay Sochima," Ami said.

"Good. So can we go?" Sochima asked.

"No," Ami said.

"Why not?"

"Because I'm tired. And I just need a break. I need to just stop and breathe. And if the world gets destroyed while that happens, then that's just what happens."

"Same," Mari said.

Shaking his head in anger and frustration, Sochima stormed out of the room.

102

Aminata was sleeping for the first time in two days and ten thousand years. Fatigue affects the body. Exhaustion affects the soul. When the soul tires, it sucks away the very lifeforce, and simply getting out of bed feels like moving a mountain. Aminata needed this. She felt peaceful and rested. She opened her eyes and saw Sochima sleeping on the bed beside her. He had curled up under her arms. She kissed his head and held onto him tighter. She heard soft footsteps. She turned around and saw Amaris. "Can I sleep with you guys," she asked. Aminata smiled and nodded yes. Amaris got in the bed behind Aminata, and they all held each other tightly and went to sleep.

103

Hours later, the children went down to the cafeteria. It was sunset, but they wanted to have breakfast. The chef was kind enough to make pancakes and French toast just for them. They ate and smiled and laughed with each other. They took their minds off everything—even Sochima—and enjoyed being children and being themselves.

Aminata needed to use the restroom, and Amaris went with her. Aminata told Sochima they would be right back, and Amaris left him with her tablet and studio headphones.

The restroom closest to the cafeteria was out of order. The girls didn't want to return to their rooms and took the stairs to the restroom on the next floor. This restroom had a heavy door, and Aminata strained to push it open. After they had used the toilets and washed their hands, Amaris opened the door for them to leave. She opened it with great ease.

"You've really gotten strong," Ami said to her.

"Yeah. But just my right hand. And much stronger when I'm just a spirit," Mari said.

"I thought physical strength just had to do with the body and not the soul."

"I never thought about it before. But I guess the same way the eye makes you see things, and the heart makes Sochi feel things, the right hand makes me stronger."

"It's so weird all the things I can see now. I literally can see through people and see their souls. Sometimes their souls don't look like how their bodies look. And there are so many souls just walking around without bodies, just looking lost. Especially here."

"It's because they haven't completely let go of their bodies," Mari said.

Ami had never thought of it that way before but, "That makes sense," she said.

"Nana told me that a long time ago," Mari said.

Ami was surprised to hear that. "Nana? Really? When?"

"Do you remember back when we used to live next door to each other, and I was like six, and I got really sick?"

Ami thought for a moment. "Um. I'm not sure. I don't think so," Ami said.

"Well, there was a time I got really sick. Like really sick. Like people thought I was gonna die."

"Whoa," Ami remarked.

"Yeah, it was serious. It happened after mi abuelo, my mother's father died, and we went to Cuba for the funeral. The thing is mi abuelo, he was real close to me. Like super close. Because mi abuela, his wife, died the day before I was born, and he thought she was reborn as me."

"No way. That is crazy," Ami said.

"I know, right? But that's what he thought, and he was like a spiritualist. And when I went to his funeral, I think he put a spell on me or something."

"Why would he do that?" Ami asked.

"Because he thought I was his wife, and he didn't want to go to heaven without his wife. And when I got back, I got really sick. Like, I wouldn't eat. I could barely move, barely talk. I went to the hospital, but they just thought I had the flu. But mami, she knew it was something else. And when she took me home, she had other spiritualists up here come and visit me. They said there was a spell on me. And they prayed for me, and they sang, and danced, and did a lot of crazy stuff, and none of it worked. I was getting sicker and sicker. And I had dreams with my grandfather. And he would call me Maria, my grandmother's name. And he would say, 'Maria, just let go, let go Maria, and you'll be at peace, and we'll be together. And I would say, 'No papi, I don't want to go. I don't want to die.'" Aminata began tearing up when Amaris said this. Seeing Ami cry caused Mari to cry as well. "And one night, I don't know if I was dreaming or seeing things, but I was in bed, mi abuelo was there, and Nana was there, and she was talking to him. She said, 'She's not your Maria. I won't let you take her. Let her go. Let them both go. And rest in peace.' And he cried, and he said, 'Sorry Mari.' Then the next morning, I woke up, and Nana was wiping the sweat from my face. And Mami was there, and Papi was there. And they asked me how I felt, and I felt great. I felt so much better. And it was because of Nana."

"I never knew Nana did that. I never knew about any of that. I'm so sorry you went through that, Mari," Aminata said.

"Yeah, me too. Thank God Nana was there. She was special."

"Yes, she was," Ami said, regretting not speaking to Nana more as she got older.

"Do you think what we saw with your dad was real?" Mari asked.

"Um. I hope not. But it felt real," Ami said.

"We're never going to be able to go back to how we were before, are we?"

"I don't know. Hopefully, if we get all the pieces together, we can go back."

"How many more pieces do we need?"

"Nine."

"Nine sounds like a hundred," Mari said.

"We have to tell our mothers. We can't just leave our bodies like that again and not have them know what's going on. My Mom won't be able to take it," Ami said.

"Mine either. But how much do we tell them? Do you think they'll believe us or think we're crazy?" Mari asked.

"They'll have to believe us when we leave our bodies again. I just hope they understand," Ami said.

"Yeah. Me too," Mari said.

"Mari. I'm happy you came off the bus. I'm happy we became friends again. I don't think me and Sochi could have gotten through any of this without you," Aminata said to her.

Amaris shook her head and laughed. "Me too," she said.

Aminata smiled as well when suddenly, her expression became very grave. "What's wrong?" Amaris asked.

"We have to get back to Sochi right now."

104

Sochima sat in the cafeteria by himself playing a game on Aminata's tablet while he wore Amaris's studio headphones, which looked quite large on his small head. A flock of birds flew by outside and caught his attention. He walked to the window, which extended from the floor to the ceiling with a bar running across the center, to watch them. It was a murmuration of starlings. There were hundreds of small birds flying in a synchronized dance. They looked like inkblots, elegantly morphing from one shape to the next. It was beautiful and hypnotizing.

The cafeteria was nine stories up. From this height, Sochima could see much of Washington, DC spread out before him. He could see the Washington Monument and Meridian Park in the distance. The next piece was calling to him like hunger pains. It was as if the birds were forming an arrow directing him to where it was. If it were up to him, they would go get it now and carry on to the next piece after that, wherever that may be.

Suddenly the birds began dispersing, dozens of them going their own way. Sochima was sad to see them go when the lights in the cafeteria suddenly went out. Sochima pulled down his headphones and was about to turn around to find out why the lights went out when a firm hand fell on his shoulder—gentle yet unkind. It held him in place like an anchor. "Hello, Sochima," he heard. Sochima looked up, and his heart fell. It was the woman who killed Nana. Not the dark angel. She wasn't in her spirit form. She was the blonde-haired woman who jogged in the rain and grabbed hold of Sochima before Nana knocked her away, and she revealed herself. "Do you remember me?" she asked.

"Yes," Sochima replied, holding in his fear. "You killed Nana."

The woman smiled. "Oh, I did more than that. I shattered her soul. Do you know what happens to shattered souls?" Sochima shook his head no. "They come back as insects." Sochi looked visibly hurt and wondered if the woman was lying. "It's true. Could be a roach, an ant, a bee, a spider—a fly." She caught a small fly between her fingers. "Maybe this is grandma now." She crushed the fly. "Sorry, Nana. Onto your next insignificant life."

This made Sochima angry, and his chest and shoulders heaved. He thought about screaming for help but noticed everything had become eerily quiet. He looked around and saw that everyone in the cafeteria was sleeping; over two dozen people were knocked out. Those who had been eating had their heads on their tables. Those who had been walking were lying peacefully on the floor. The staff and the cooks in the back as well, while the pots on the fire continued burning. "Don't worry about them. A minor spell. They'll awaken after we're gone." Sochima's heart began racing. How powerful was this woman to put an entire room to sleep?

"I've been looking for you for a very long time. I meditated through so many centuries to find you in the Old Kingdom. Do you know how?" Sochima shook his head no. "When I touched you, it was as if your soul left an imprint on me. Now I can't get your stink out of my head." She smiled. "But it's for the better. I was so close before. But Imhotep betrayed us, and you and your sisters slipped away. When I came back to my body, I was so angry. It would be so difficult trying to track you through time again. But I realized the head was here, and you would eventually need to come for it. So, all I needed to do was guard my post as commanded, and you would come to me. And I awoke this morning, and I could smell you. You were so close, so pungent. I felt you in my teeth. I can smell the pieces of Ausar in you as well. Three pieces. You've been busy. Unfortunately, three times we've failed. I will correct this. Give them to me."

"No," Sochima said.

The woman abruptly slapped Sochima across the face. "That was not the right answer." Sochima had never been hit like that. And though it hurt, he kept telling himself that he was not a boy, he was a man. He had been to war and survived. He could take it. "Now I ask again. Give them to me," she said.

"No," Sochima said.

She slapped him again, even more forcefully. "Not the right answer."

Sochima's face was on fire, and he gritted his teeth, holding in the pain. "No," he replied, bracing for another hit that sent shivers through his six-year-old body. His eyes welled with tears, and he bit down on his lips to keep himself from breaking down and crying out but found the strength to shout, "No," before another slap came and knocked him off his feet and to his knees.

The woman grabbed him by his shirt and pulled him up. "Stand up, boy."

Sochima couldn't hold the pain in anymore and openly cried and wiped the snot away from his nose with the back of his hand.

"Such a brave little boy you are. Do you think I am unkind? Do you think I should be mild with you because you are a child? Do you think being a child makes you special? Do you think it means you should be protected? That bad things won't happen to you?" She smiled. "That is a fairytale. Your life isn't special. Young, old, fit, lame, it doesn't matter. The universe cares not. All life is valued the same. You live, you suffer, you die. What I offer you is kindness. I can rip them out of you by force and tear you apart, flesh and soul, in the process. But if you give them to me, I'll let you go to live your life—well, as much of it as you'll have left before our Lord comes."

Marshaling all his strength, Sochima again replied, "No."

The blonde woman smiled. "Good. I don't know who your Nana was, but she put a powerful spell on you, and I could not touch your bodies while your souls were away. But now that your soul is back in your body. You are mine." She then placed her right hand on Sochima's chest and began chanting a spell, pulling her hand upward, attempting to rip the heart out of Sochima. The pain was excruciating. Sochima felt as if he was being torn from the inside out. He cried out in pain.

Aminata and Amaris heard his cry outside just as they entered the cafeteria. Aminata saw the blonde woman hurting her brother. She saw her physically and could also see the dark angel, like a vampire kneeling over Sochima. "Get away from my brother," she shouted, running towards her with blind rage. The blonde woman turned and faced Aminata, releasing Sochima from her grip. Aminata swung the staff at her head. She deftly dodged it, caught Aminata by the wrist with one hand, and threw her across the room, crashing into the wall. Amaris threw a punch at the woman's head. She dodged it just in time but was surprised by its force.

It put a dent in the thick glass window and sent cracks like spider webs running down the floor. The blonde woman countered with an open-palm strike to Mari's sternum, sending her reeling backward over a table. "All three of you have the stink of Ausar in you," she said. "Good, I'll rip them out of you one at a time." Sochima jumped on her back and bit her on the shoulder. The pain barely registered. She pulled Sochima off and held him up by the throat with her left hand. She placed her right hand on Sochima's chest and began chanting again.

With his entire will to resist, "Let me go," Sochima shouted. And from within his soul came a burst of blinding energy. The blinding light caused the woman to flinch, and she dropped Sochima's body to the ground, but his soul stood up. Sochima's soul had separated from his body, and he looked the dark angel in the eye. The dark angel was more fearsome and powerful in his spirit form. Sochima didn't care. Not knowing how he was doing it, he manifested his anger, and the transparent floating strings in the spirit world, into balls of energy, which he threw at the dark angel, like punches.

"I see Heka in you," the dark angel said as he dodged and deflected Sochima's blows effortlessly.

Aminata could see Sochima fighting the dark angel. She saw that his female body stood still and defenseless. She took the opportunity to attack his body. She swung the staff at the blonde woman's head. To her surprise, the dark angel reentered the blonde woman in time to dodge her blow and knock her away. Amaris rejoined the fight, throwing haymakers at the blonde woman. She countered and hit back. Amaris blocked the impact of the blonde woman's blows with her right hand. Sochima used the distraction to attack the dark angel. However, the angel left his body and created a shield of energy to deflect Sochima and redirect it back at him, knocking Sochima away. Sochima came back to his feet and attacked again.

The fight went on. Sochima attacked his soul, while Aminata and Amaris attacked her physically, as the dark angel deftly transitioned in and out of his body handling all three of them at once. Aminata seized an opening, grabbing Sochima's body away from the blonde woman. Aminata realized if she took a moment and concentrated, she could see what the blonde woman would do before she did it.

She held Mari's hand and communicated telepathically to Sochi to do the same. She waited for the dark angel to make his move. When Aminata saw it moments before it happened, she told Mari, "Now." Amaris threw her right hand with all her strength. The blonde woman nevertheless caught her fist—but the dark angel was left open as Sochima unleashed on him. He deflected most of the energy with his wings, but Sochima was able to hurt him for the first time.

He had been playing with these children. He recognized now that the more this continued, the more attuned they would become with the souls within them and the more powerful they would be. "Enough," he said. "Let me show you what chaos can do." With his arms extended, he drew in all the lifeforce around him, sucking the soul energy from everything close by, living and non-living, animate and inanimate, and turning it into a massive vortex of energy, which he unleashed.

With the eye, Aminata could see it in time and communicated to the others. Sochima saw his body lying limp on the ground, and instinctually, he re-entered it and was able to get out of the way before the vortex unleashed, cutting through the floor and the ceiling to the other side of the building, destroying everything and everyone in its path.

The children were grateful to have survived the vortex but were saddened by all the people who hadn't. There was so much destruction all around them. People who had previously been sleeping were now dead, their bodies not only soulless but decomposed. Amaris couldn't help herself; she shouted, "What is wrong with you? You just killed all these people."

"When you have lived as long as I have, lives mean little."

"How long have you lived?" Aminata asked.

"Over three thousand years."

"Dude, you are really old," Amaris said.

"You'd be surprised how fast time goes after the first hundred," he said.

"Who are you?" Aminata asked.

"I am the first Guardian. I am the right hand of God. Amenhotep IV . . . Akhenaten . . . Akhenset."

None of those names meant anything to Amaris. However, Aminata and Sochima knew the name Akhenaten very well.

"What happened to you?" Sochima asked.

"I saw the light of the one true God—Set. It is my purpose to prepare the world for his coming. And he will bring chaos and fire and remake creation in his image."

"We will stop you," Sochima said.

"You will try. You will fail."

"Ausar will stop you," Aminata said.

"Ausar is dead, and so he will remain. Now give me his soul."

"We ain't giving you shit," Amaris said.

"You will. How much you will suffer before you do is the question."

The spell Akhenaten cast only put to sleep the people in the cafeteria. The noise of the battle and the vortex had carried throughout the hospital. Hospital security and police came to their location. They were astonished by the immense destruction and horrified by the bodies lying around. What could have caused all this? There was just a woman and three children. "What the hell happened here?" a police officer asked.

"Help us," Aminata turned and asked him.

The officer could see the fear in her eyes. "Put your hands up," the officer said to the blonde woman.

This did not go as Akhenset had intended. The more he killed, the more people would come and the more destruction he would cause. This was not the time for that. He would take what he came for. The girls would wait for another day. He chanted a spell and clapped his hands, and a blinding light filled the room. When the light cleared and they could see again the blonde woman stood by the window, holding Sochima by his chest with her forearm. The wind from the shattered window blew behind them.

Everyone was stunned except Aminata, who ran towards

Akhenset because she had already seen him fall backward out the window with Sochima. Aminata got to the edge of the window just after Akhenset had stepped off. Aminata followed them out the window. Her only concern was getting Sochima back, giving no thought to how they would survive the fall if she did. Holding the staff in her right hand she reached out to Sochima with her left. Sochima reached for her as well. The blonde woman held his body tightly—but not his soul. Sochima's soul reached out to Aminata, leaving his body. However, Ami couldn't grab his soul, and their hands phased through each other.

Aminata looked at the blonde woman. She smiled just before her eyes went blank. Akhenset left her body, grabbed Sochima's soul, and Aminata phased through the both of them. Aminata turned and saw Akhenset holding onto Sochi's soul, flying away. "Ami," Sochi shouted.

Ami had another more pressing problem. Both her and Sochima's bodies were falling fast to the ground and certain death. She grabbed Sochima from the limp body of the blonde woman and held him securely next to her. Her mind searched for a way to save them but couldn't come up with one. The blonde woman fell to the pavement with a resounding thud. All the bones in her body shattered. And just as Ami and Sochi were about to make impact, an invisible force held them in place, stopping their momentum ... then let them go. They landed with a thud but unharmed.

Aminata looked at Sochima. His body was fine, but his soul was gone. She looked up and saw Akhenset hovering in the sky, holding Sochima's soul with one hand, while the other was stretched out towards her and Sochima's body.

From the cafeteria window, Amaris saw him. "Mari," Sochi called to her. She reached out her hand to Sochima, and though she was not touching him she could feel her right hand pulling Sochima away from Akhenset's grasp.

Akhenset turned and faced her. "Too strong," he said, then he and Sochima's souls disappeared.

Both Amaris and Aminata screamed, "Noooo."

105

Gabrielle and Samantha returned to chaos. Fire engines, police cars, ambulances, and helicopters surrounded the hospital. There was a hole the size of an entire floor in the middle of the building. It looked like a bomb had gone off. There were news vans and dozens of reporters; to say nothing of the over a hundred onlookers live-streaming the chaos. The police created a barricade to keep people away. Gabrielle and Samantha had to fight their way through. At first, the police wouldn't let Gabrielle and Samantha pass the barricade, but they pointed to Amaris and Aminata who were surrounded by police and doctors. "Those are our children," Samantha yelled. "You're going to let us through, or you're going to have to shoot me." A Detective gave the okay to let them pass, hoping they could talk some sense into the girls.

While holding the staff, Aminata clutched Sochima's unconscious body, and she wouldn't let him go. She wouldn't let the doctors examine him. She didn't know who to trust. She didn't know if Akhenset would return and whose body he would take over. Amaris stood beside her and fought off whoever tried to take him from Aminata. The police attempted to restrain Amaris, but they couldn't. To their surprise, she was stronger than all of them.

Samantha and Gabrielle ran through the crowd of police and doctors surrounding their children. The girls broke down in tears when they saw their mothers and hugged them tightly. "Mari. What happened? What happened? What happened Mari?" Samantha asked Amaris.

There was so much to say, Amaris couldn't think of where to start. She just held her mother and cried.

"I'm so sorry, Mommy. I'm so sorry," Aminata said to Gabrielle while holding Sochima's body.

Gabrielle saw Sochima with the same blank helpless look in his eyes as he had for two days. It was all too much, and she fell to her knees, broken.

106

Gabrielle and Samantha convinced the girls to let the doctors take Sochima back inside the hospital and evaluate him. The girls felt a bit safer now that their mothers were there, and they agreed to do it—but they would not leave Sochima's side even for a second.

As they had assumed, he was back in a coma, the same as the children had been for two days and as Nana had been for a month. To have the children wake up yesterday, only to have this happen to Sochima again. Gabrielle's heart couldn't take anymore. She didn't understand why this was happening to her family. She needed answers. She looked at Aminata, but Ami felt so lost she didn't know where to start. All she found the energy to say was, "Everything Nana told us is true."

"Everything Nana said is true?" Gabrielle repeated. "What does that mean, Ami?"

"There's just so much to tell you, Mommy, and I know you won't believe me."

Gabrielle exhaled exhaustively. "Try me,"

At that moment, two police officers came to their room door. "Excuse me, Mrs. Gates and Mrs. Garcia, but we need to ask your daughters a few questions," one of the Officers said.

This was the last thing the mothers wanted to deal with. They wanted answers from the girls first, and then they would determine what they should say to the police. "Not now," Samantha replied.

"I'm sorry, ma'am, but it really can't wait."

"Not now," Samantha repeated more forcefully.

Amaris held her mother's hand. She had never seen her this emotional.

"Then may we speak with the both of you outside?" the Officer asked.

Gabrielle and Samantha agreed. "We'll be right back," Gabrielle said to the girls, and both mothers stepped outside, closing the room door behind them. The girls could see their mothers talking to the officers through the glass windows.

Aminata sat next to Sochima and held his hand. She had been trying to find him with her inner eye. All she saw was darkness; all she heard was quiet, and it scared her like nothing else. She held the staff, and she held his hand, and she prayed, "Please Sochi, please, please answer me," and finally she heard, "Ami ... help me."

Hearing Sochima's voice in her mind filled Aminata with hope and life. Her heart jumped; her eyes opened. "Sochi—Sochi? Are you okay?" she said aloud.

"Ami. Help me," he said again.

"Are you hearing him?" Amaris asked excitedly.

"Yes, I can hear him," Ami said.

"Can you see him as well?"

"No, I can't see him. It's all dark. Where are you, Sochi?" she asked. He didn't reply, and Ami feared she lost her connection with him. "Sochi—Sochi," she called.

"Kush," he answered. "I'm in Kush."

"He's in Kush," Aminata said to Amaris.

"Do you know where that is?" Amaris asked.

Aminata closed her eyes and meditated, and she saw stone pillars, a stone temple, and a red sky with many stars. "Not exactly. But I think the eye and the staff can take me there," she said.

"Okay," Mari said.

"Ami, help me," Sochima repeated.

"I'm coming Sochi," she said. She turned to Amaris. "Will you come with me?" she asked her.

"He's my brother, too," Mari replied, taking hold of Sochi's hand. Ami said thank you with her eyes. "But we can't leave our bodies like this without some kind of protection. I don't trust these cops or these doctors," she said.

Aminata remembered something. "When we left the first time. Nana put some kind of protection spell on us. I wonder if it's still working."

"No. It stopped working when we returned to our bodies," Sochima said."

"Do you remember the spell?" Aminata asked him.

"Yes."

"Good," Ami said.

"But now, how do we tell our moms that we're leaving?" Amaris asked.

"We don't," Aminata said.

107

Samantha and Gabrielle reentered the room without the police. They would not budge, and the police relented and agreed to let the girls rest and not question them until tomorrow. It seemed rest was exactly what the girls needed. They found them lying together in Sochima's bed, Ami holding Sochi and Mari holding Ami. They looked very peaceful, but something seemed very wrong to Gabrielle. Aminata did not have Nana's stick, and it was nowhere in the room. Not seeing the stick and the fact Ami held onto it so fiercely outside frightened Gabrielle.

She shook her daughter's shoulder to wake her up. Aminata would not wake up. This frightened Samantha as well, and she shook Amaris, and she would not wake up either. They were in the same state Sochima was in. They were all back in a coma.

"No ... no ... Not again. Please, not again," Gabrielle said, collapsing to the floor.

Samantha fell to her knees as well beside her daughter. It was then she noticed a tablet in Amaris's hand. She picked it up, and it turned on by itself. There was a message on the screen: *Moms, please don't worry. We're okay. We're okay. We know you don't understand. We'll tell you everything when we get back. We've gone to get Sochi.*

ABOUT THE AUTHOR

Heru Ptah is a novelist, poet, playwright and filmmaker. As a poet he has appeared on HBO's Def Poetry Jam and CNN with Anderson Cooper. His first novel a Hip Hop Story was published by MTV Books and given a feature story in the New York Times. Heru was also the book writer for the Broadway Musical Hot Feet based on the music of Earth Wind and Fire and the choreography of Maurice Hines. Children of the Sun is Heru's seventh novel.

ACKNOWLEDGEMENTS

To my mother, Venice, you are the first and most profound relationship in my life. The same love, same respect, and infinite gratitude apply like always. I'm still working on the house with the island in the kitchen.

To Monifa Powell, thanks again for coming into my life. Thank you for being my best friend and my most trusted confidant and reader. Since I met you, you have been my greatest inspiration.

To my inner family: Michelle, Jay, and Shanice. I love and appreciate you all. Special shout out to my two beautiful nieces, Summer and Autumn. To my father, Anthony Richards—Tony Brutus—Rest In Power. Live forever.

To my brother, Tehut-nine, and his family, Marcia, Masai, and Zaniah, love always.

To Mshindo I Kuumba, my brother and mentor, my admiration for you and your talent know no bounds. You transformed the cover into the beautiful work of art I knew you would.

To Sharon Gordon, thank you for your support, your energy and your passion. To Teneise Ellis thank you for being a friend and a great reader. I appreciate you.

To all of the beautiful people who have supported me and my many books throughout these twenty years, from A Hip Hop Story to Children of the Sun, I can not begin to express how much I appreciate you. You saved me.

To the Creator, to Ra, Ausar, Auset, Set and Heru, this book was written for you. It has taken me over twenty years to bring this book to life—and I'm only a third of the way done. I thank you for choosing me as the vessel to tell this story. I am forever striving to live up to the name you gave me.